A Grizzly Death
In Yellowstone

§

A Novel By
Cal Glover

HOMESTEAD PUBLIS
Moose, Wyoming

Library of Congress Catalog Card Number 94-77059
ISBN 0-943972-35-3

Printed in the United States of America
on recycled acid free paper.
Type sent in New Baskerville.

Published by
HOMESTEAD PUBLISHING
Box 193, Moose, Wyoming 83012

First Edition

DEDICATION

For my mother, Ann.

When I was 19 I told her I wanted to hitchhike across the United States, she took me to Interstate 95 and dropped me off; to Carl Schreier, the editor and publisher of this book, who shares my love of Yellowstone Park and whose knowledge, fortunately, vastly exceeds my own; to Ferdinand Hayden, who came to Yellowstone in 1871 and thought, maybe we should save some of this; to President Ulysses Grant, who signed legislation to create Yellowstone in 1872 then immediately went off to have a stiff drink; and to Holly, whose support is as strong as the pillars of the Old Faithful Inn, may it stand forever.

Accuse not Nature; she hath done her part;
Do thou but thine
John Milton, *Paradise Lost*

A Grizzly Death
In Yellowstone

In just three days, the first crews will arrive to nurse Yellowstone National Park's Old Faithful Inn out of its 90th winter. Jim Petersen, the winter caretaker, pauses to sit in one of the large red-leather armchairs. From the middle of the lobby, he looks at the three tiered floors above him. It's nearly dark inside the huge log structure, but he can still make out the wooden stairs leading up to the crow's nest where he first kissed his wife, almost 30 years ago.

He breathes in the silence. He knows that in two weeks, all the electricity will be back on and a new staff will be scuttling about, tidying, straightening, cleaning, preparing for the May 4 opening. He pictures the hoards of tourists that will be swarming inside and around the huge log cabin in just a short time. He relishes the silence for now.

The old 500-ton fireplace disappears through the roof, 85 feet above. He raises his broom and lets it fall, as if the action would dislodge the fallen rocks in two of the four chimneys that have been blocked since the 1959 Hebgen Lake earthquake. The huge rows of furniture covered with white sheets are finishing their winter slumber. And up on the second floor, the piano and the harpsichord are covered as well, and he can almost hear the woodwind quartet, made up of college music majors, playing its soft counterpoint.

Then, suddenly, they are gone, and the caretaker breathes slowly again. There is no noise.

He lifts his flashlight up and shines it at the native knotty lodgepole pine from which the railings and beams have been cut. The flashlight beam barely reaches the top of the Inn, where the dark symmetrical logs taper to a point, and he knows they will have to be dusted in a couple of weeks. Across the lobby is the front desk, a small castle of native rhyolite rock with the four-inch-thick desk top. He can almost visualize the line of people waiting to check in—running amuck in the gift shop or waiting to get into the dining room or ice-cream parlor. He can almost hear George clinking ice cubes in a tall glass at the Bear Pit Bar. But there is only silence.

Past the gift shop, behind him, and down the darkened hall of the west wing, the light diffuses to nothing. No noise comes from the 102 rooms of the main lodge or the 98 rooms of the east wing. The manager's office is still and silent as well.

Once again, it is snowing. The white flakes have covered the window panes on the second floor, and a gray light comes through.

But it is his building now—the emperor inside his palace. For 30 winters, he has guarded the old log cabin, and yes, he is certain, he likes the winters more than the summers. He and his wife, Adele, make a home out of their trailer. They ski a little, and keep an eye on the Inn. It is his only son.

The north wind creates a nearly imperceptible patter on the window pane of the second floor. The wind serves almost as an alarm, reminding Jim that it's time to get home. He stands and stacks his papers and books into a neat pile. Although he has been the only one in the building for two months, he walks to the heavy pine and wrought-iron doors and checks to see that the chainlock is secure. He lays the flat of his palm against the door as if to bid it a good night, then exits out the back, leaving his broom to guard the building. He skis past the east wing, the parking lot, across the road, and to trailer lot 49, where smoke swirling from a chimney brings him warmth even before he enters.

April 23.

Jim Petersen watches from the back door of the Inn. The snow plows must have gotten through from Mammoth because the first of the yellow maintenance trucks is pulling up to the back of the Inn. Jim is ready, though. He has finally swept up his little pile of dust and dirt from the winter, thrown it away, and pushed the gray rubber can behind the bellman's desk, out of the way. He stands with his hands folded over his broom and watches as Gus Kristoff, head of maintenance, gets out of the snow-blown 1953 Chevy pick-up and heads toward him.

"Well," Jim says to himself, "here comes summer."

They are old friends. Jim already has shoveled off the last 30 yards of the walkway in anticipation of Gus' arrival.

"Hello there, stranger!" Jim shouts from the door.

"Hello, you old bear," Gus shoots back, as he removes his big glove and shakes Jim's hand. "They thought I'd better come down here and see if you were out of hibernation yet! How ya doin'?"

Gus stomps the snow off his big rubber Sorel packs and pauses, as if entering an important man's house.

"I'm doing good. Good winter this year. We only had to knock the snow off the roof twice. Snow level's 51 inches, last time I looked."

"How's the wife?"

"Adele's good. How's Lucy?"

"Good. She made some raspberry preserves for you two, if they didn't freeze in that old truck on the drive down." Gus strolls into the lobby where Jim has the emergency lights on. "So how's it lookin' this year?"

"Not bad. All the pipes blew. I accidentally turned on the water and the rooms are all flooded but. . ."

"You old bullshitter," Gus laughs, as he hits Jim across the back with his gloves. "You two have been up here by yourselves too long."

"Well, I suppose it's good to see someone other than those domeheads," Jim half lies, referring to the snowmobilers who tour the park roads in the winter and stay at the Snow Lodge up until the end of March. "This year, one of 'em ran his machine into Emerald Pool."

"That's about par."

In a reverent silence, the two men gaze up at the three floors of the lobby balconies. Jim gives Gus a few moments to see the ghosts, relive some memories, anticipate the future. Gus came here from Minnesota when he was 38, after his two children had married. He works at park headquarters in Mammoth during the winters.

"This your 20th year now?"

"Twentieth summer. Yup," Gus answers. "Twelfth as head."

"Well, let's look at those pipes tomorrow," Jim says. "I think Adele's got something hot on the stove for us."

"Ninety-first year for this old place now. Ain't that right?"

"I never get tired of coming back to this old building," Gus says as they turn to go. "It's a great old place."

May 1.

With the summer opening just a few days off, the atmosphere inside Old Faithful Inn is charged with positive energy. The building itself seems to come alive.

People from all over the world are coming together for the first time. Widowed men and women driving up alone or with a friend, or semi-retired couples coming from Arizona, southern California, and Florida, in their trailers, sharing a community lifestyle with their peers. There will be drives in the park, barbecues, walks at sunset. Then there are the young people who come here to mix work and pleasure. Free, away from home, setting their own rules, experiencing life with a revived exuberance, a charged youthful vibrance. They will work a hard eight hours a day in their new jobs before hiking around the geyser basin at sunset, or going to Observation Point, or maybe visiting Hamilton's for a milkshake or a cold beer.

The gift shop doors are opened and last year's souvenirs are uncovered. Angel ponders a glass moose selling for $235—for the ninth year in a row—and imagines it one day sitting on her bookcase, possibly in a few years, when she retires.

"Hey, Angel. What's this?" asks Mitch, a husky young man from Michigan.

Angel takes off her glasses to focus on his nametag.

"That's the geyser, Mitch. You can also use it as a salt shaker."

"Where should I put it?"

She smiles at the naiveté. "Why don't you stick it up there with the wooden bears."

The floors are buffed, and two returning housemen, suspended by mountaineering gear above the lobby, dust the roof with mops. On the second floor, one of the musicians grimaces as he hits a flat note on the piano.

Seattle, Washington, 1968.

Cecil Dolen, 8, is in the basement of his apartment building, playing with the girl from the second floor, Julie Kelly. Cecil looks at Julie in a different light after what his two playmates from building G told him.

Julie and Cecil are playing hide and seek. The basement is perfect for the game, with its furniture covered in old sheets, tires, chest of drawers, refrigerators and the like scattered about. Cecil has a plan. He knows exactly where he will hide, and now it's his turn.

"You've got to count to 20, Julie."

"I can count to 20."

Cecil stands Julie in the corner and tells her to put the old towel up to her eyes so she can't see. "Start now."

"One. . . two. . . three. . ."

Cecil turns and scrapes his feet in one direction before silently tiptoeing the other way. He wants to make it exciting. He wants to make it like his friends did it yesterday. He crawls under a three-legged kitchen table, propped up precariously. He crawls through three upright tires. Then he opens the door of the old Frigidaire and closes it, glancing back at Julie.

"Twelve. . . thirteen. . ."

Cecil quietly makes his way to his destination. His heart is beating with a strange anticipation, one he has never felt before. There is a new feeling in his chest, down in his little groin. He crawls along the gray basement wall, behind his mother's old stuffed chair and around the old bird cage, careful not to ring the little bell that he knows is still in it.

"Fifteen. . . sixteen. . ."

Quietly, he lifts and crawls under the white sheet covering his favorite hiding place, on the old green sofa.

"Twenty! Ready or not, here I come!"

Cecil's breathing is tight, shallow, and his heart is beating fast. But he remains frozen so as not to make any noise. Now he hears Julie and can picture in his mind's eye where she searches—in the old cabinet, in the old pile of clothes, and in the old refrigerator.

"Where *are* you?"

She looks in the corner in some old boxes, then turns and comes closer. She looks under the old sofa; Cecil's heart is racing wildly. Then she peeks under the white sheet.

"Found you!"

"You found me!" he shouts back. Then he grabs her and pulls her toward him, replacing the sheet over their heads. When their giggles stop, Cecil touches Julie's leg and says, "I'll show you mine if you show me yours," just like Cecil's friends told him they had said. Julie stares back with her innocent blue eyes. She draws her face into a pout but says nothing.

"I'll show you mine if you show me yours," he says again, and there is a strange tingling in his little penis as he pushes down his shorts.

"No."

Cecil is dumbstruck, indignant. He reaches over and tries to put his hand under Julie's dress. His friends said she did it for them and that she had something different. "Come on, Julie, you did it with. . ."

Suddenly, the sheet is jerked back. It's Julie's mother.

"You little heathens! Julie Kelly, you promised me you wouldn't do this! You told me yesterday. . ."

"I didn't mommy. He tried to make me. . ."

In one motion, Julie's mom grabs Cecil up by his arm and shakes him. "You filthy little animal!" She strikes him across the face with the back of her hand. Her ring opens a long line on his cheek that immediately starts to bleed. "Julie, you go upstairs and go to your room!"

Julie's mom hauls a bleeding, kicking, screaming Cecil up to his third-floor apartment, holding the old sheet up to his face, his brown shorts hanging around his ankles. The neighbors open their doors and gawk at the ruckus.

"Betty, Cecil was in the basement playing with Julie. He had his pants off and was trying to make Julie take off hers. I hit him once and he's bleeding."

"Ooohhh! Cecil Dolen! Well, it serves you right, young man." Mrs. Dolen slaps his bottom.

"Thank you, Jean. I'll call you later."

Cecil drops the sheet from his face and runs crying to his room.

At school on Monday, Cecil's entire second-grade class finds out why he has stitches in his face. He is ridiculed, and no one will play with him except to put their hands over their faces where Cecil has a big bandage and shout, "I'll show you mine if you show me yours!"

Despite his tears and vomiting, his mother makes him go to school. Twenty-six years later, there is still a scar.

Tallahassee, Florida, spring.

A young couple sit on a front porch swing outside the pillared, red brick, Tri-Delt sorority house. He is tall, athletic, wearing a pressed, light blue, long-sleeved shirt. His face is clean shaven. She has blond, almost white hair, nearly down to her waist. Her skin is tanned and her eyes are green. Despite her apparent melancholy, she is radiant.

The slightest hint of a southern drawl manifests itself in her speech. "John, let's walk through campus and talk. There are too many people here."

The dew is drying under the cresting sun as they stroll among the pines and red brick buildings of Florida State University.

"I can't believe this day is finally here and I have to leave," Kris says. "It seems like a mistake."

"Yellowstone will be fun. Bears will be chasing you. You'll probably meet a handsome cowboy or forest ranger and get married."

"Oh, John. Stop it. I have no such plan. I'm not even going out!"

"Is that your decision? I mean, is that what you want to do?"

"Well, that's what I'm going to do. You can go out if you'd like. One of the other cheerleaders already asked me if she could borrow you for the summer."

"Really? Which one?"

"Oh, stop it." They laugh and she gives him a slight cuff on his arm—a throwing arm that passed for more than 3,000 yards and 15 touchdowns during the past football season. "She said one cheerleader per quarterback per year."

"Let me guess. Sounds like Dori."

"How'd you guess? Dori's only been after you for three years."

They walk in silence past the music building. Their hands touch and, instinctively, they hold on.

"Well, I'm not going out either."

"John, you should. This is a good chance to meet some other people."

"I'm staying on campus this summer to pick up weights, not women. Besides, I love you, Kris. I don't want to go out with anyone else."

She squeezes his hand and turns into his arms.

"Oh, I wish I didn't have to go, John. Just because mother worked there 24 years ago doesn't mean that I want to."

"Well, Kris, I'll wait for you."

The Inn is waxed and shiny, polished and ready. In the dining room, the lunch settings are in place. In the bar, the glasses are clean and the new bottles are on the shelves, capped with green and red spouts. The souvenirs in the gift shop are displayed, along with the other tourist necessities—postcards, candy bars, film, books and magazines. The rooms all have clean linen and the corresponding keys are in their slots behind the front desk. Imre, the controller, and her auditors have banks counted and locked up in the safe and, in the lobby, the bellmen are standing with pressed uniforms and eager eyes. At exactly 11 o'clock, location manager Faysal Burien walks out of his office in a powder-blue suit with his assistant, Larry Dumbrosky, trailing behind him.

"Eleven o'clock," he announces.

The front-desk clerks take the guest bucket off the thick desk and hand it to the cashier, ready at her station. All eyes follow Faysal, as he steps over the red carpet to the heavy wrought-iron doors. He flips through a key ring before slipping the Schlage into a large padlock and noisily pulling the chain through the black iron locks.

"We're open!" Larry shouts.

Seattle, Washington, spring.

"Hey, Cecil. Did you check out the new cocktail waitress?"

"No. I didn't know he hired one."

"There she is. Look. She ain't bad. You ought to try to get to know her, Cec."

"She's very pretty. . . . Hey, Arnie, help me haul up some beer from the other cooler, will ya? Anyway, I've been happy without dating for awhile. This scar doesn't exactly turn women on, you know."

"Yea, I'll give you a hand. Payday at Boeing today. We'll probably be busier than hell." Arnie pauses. "You haven't been out with a girl since you doubled with Sylvia and me. Why don't you ask her to join us for a drink afterward, or maybe. . ."

"I'll do OK. Don't worry about me."

By 9 p.m., the Puget Sound bar is rocking. Most of the after-work crowd is drinking its dinner. The electric rock-and-rhythm band is into its first set, and the conversation volume picks up accordingly. Cecil Dolen has the new girl on his station, and he is trying to be patient.

"Thank you for helping me," she says, appreciatively. "I'll catch on."

"You're doing fine."

Cecil feels the next question coming, even though he promised himself he wouldn't ask her for at least three nights.

"So you have a boyfriend or husband or something?"

"Nope. Not me. I'm going to live free and easy for awhile."

Although he is thin and only 5'7", Cecil at 34, isn't ugly. In fact, he has an eager, intelligent face that just isn't enhanced by the scar running laterally across his cheek. One thing Cecil has never learned is patience, so by 10 o'clock, he asks the new waitress out for a drink after work.

"I'm sorry. I've kind of made it a rule not to date people I work with."

"That's fine, Laurie," Cecil says.

"Let's just keep it strictly business, OK?"

"Great. Excuse me. Listen, I have to go downstairs to get some olives. See if Arnie knows how to make that daiquiri. It's a new one on me."

At 2:30 a.m., the house lights are up and stale cigarette smoke settles in layers. Arnie reads his co-worker's disquiet.

"Hey, Cec, we're all gonna go up to Jake O'Shaunessey's for a drink afterward. You'll join us, won't you?"

"Don't think so, Arnie. But hell, don't ask the new cocktail waitress because she won't socialize with the hired help."

"Oh, Laurie's going with us."

Arnie takes a step back at the angered flash from Cecil's eyes. Cecil spins back to the bar, slams a six-pack of Lowenbrau into the cold cabinet and curses under his breath.

"Hey, did you two get into it or something?"

"No problem. Hey, listen, I'm gonna count my till and split. I'll finish the restock tomorrow night."

"I'll get it, Cec. No problem."

Cecil pulls out his register drawer and exits into the office.

"Calm down, Cec. Just take it easy."

It's a rainy night. Along the Sea-Tac strip, people are still flowing in and out of the bars that stay open until 4 a.m. Live music booms out of some of the bars, and under canopies and bus stops stand prostitutes. A sleek, royal blue Corvette slowly cruises the right-hand lane. The driver's side window is rolled down a fraction, and Cecil tosses out a plastic bar glass. The steady clicking of the windshield wiper is the only noise inside his car. He is angry. He feels invincible, able to strike or deftly flee. He feels like a hungry animal, and nothing can distract him until that hunger is satisfied. He sees what he wants. She is by herself. He pulls over and flashes his brights twice. He rolls down his passenger-side window, and a young girl with curly hair pops her head in.

"What can I do for you?"

"Get in."

"Are you a police officer?"

"No."

Twenty minutes later, Cecil and Cheryl Lee are inside his house.

"You sure do have a lot of candles."

"Listen, here's $200. I want it to be really good, OK? I want you to do something special for me, OK?"

"One of those, hey? I'm game. What is it? You want me to tie you up? Maybe dress up a little bit? No problem."

"Your name is Laurie, OK? Cute little Laurie. Now Laurie, I want you to play hide and seek with me."

"Hide and seek, huh? Well, that *is* a new one. Do I do this with my clothes on or off?"

"On! Leave them on. You look real sweet just like that. Real cute. Cute little Laurie."

Cecil stands the girl in the corner of his bathroom. "Count to 20 real slow. Do you think you can do that?"

"I think so."

Quietly, so very quietly, Cecil goes into the garage and pulls a brown sheet with white trim from the storage closet. He drapes it over his sofa.

"Five. . . six. . . seven. . ."

He slips off his black uniform pants and stuffs them behind the aquarium. He goes back to the couch. His heart is beating wildly.

This is what man lives for, he thinks. The hunt. The capture. Not some wimpy little bartender who has to take orders from other people and not be able to get what he wants when he wants it. The lousy cigarette smoke. Bad music. Now I can have what I want. I can take.

"Sixteen. . . seventeen. . ."

He reaches into the storage closet for one more prop to complete the scenario. Then, naked from the waist down, he slides onto the sofa and under the sheet. He hears the hooker come out of the bathroom.

"Ready or not, here I come," she says. Cecil hears her twist the door knob, and hears the door squeak where it is warped against the wooden frame.

"Now let's see, you're not in bed are you, you bad little boy. Are you really a pillow? You're not under the bed. No. Hmmm. Are you in the closet? No?

"How 'bout in the refrigerator? Are you in this piece of cheese? Unh umm. That's good cheese. No, that's not you, cause you're a bad little boy. Hmm, you can't have gone outside like a bad little boy because the door's still chained."

She approaches the sofa with the brown and white sheet over it. "You're not in the aquarium are you? You haven't turned into a fish, have you? Uh oh. What do we have here? Are. . . you. . . under. . . here? You are! You bad little boy! You've taken off your pants. And what's that in your hand? What?"

The metal pipe whistles in a blurred arc and explodes into the prostitute's head with a dull thud. There is only a muffled scream as she buckles at the knees and falls. Instantly, catlike, Cecil hops over the couch and descends upon the still figure. He raises the pipe high above him and delivers another blow across the bridge of her nose. A third blow has no effect. She is already dead.

"I'm not through with you yet, you stupid little whore! Cute little Laurie. Yes, strictly business."

Dressed, Cecil retrieves his $200 and carries the woman back out to his Corvette. He drives around. They'll like that, he thinks. It's been too long since I've gone out. Too long without a girl. The newspapers will eat it up. They'll talk about me. I'll never be caught, you assholes. Yea, write it up. Write it good. Little Laurie.

In an isolated area near the Green River, he carries her down by the water and tosses her dead body into the brush.

But in the morning comes the awful dread. His first conscious thought, an image from the night before, comes to him like some horrible dream. But he blinks at the ceiling and realizes it is no dream. Cecil curls up into the fetal position and moans. He crawls under the covers and closes his eyes tightly, trying to ward off the reality.

"My God." It had been four months, he thinks. I thought I was getting well. I thought there would be no more. Somebody knows. Someone must have seen my car, the girl. I hope they see me. I hope they catch me—so they can make me stop.

He starts to shake under the covers. He clenches his jaw so hard his head starts to quiver. Then his arms start to shake, and he bites down hard on a fold of the skin from his forearm. But this does not bring tears to his eyes. It is only when he realizes he can't stop himself, can't control himself, that the sobs and tears start.

"Help me," he whimpers beneath the covers. "Please God, help me."

An hour later, he permits himself a small glimpse of sunlight as he reaches over and brings the telephone under the covers with him. He dials Arnie.

"Arnie, this is Cecil. Listen, I'm having some really bad trouble with my stomach again. Uhh, could you cover for me tonight? Yea, it has been a while since that has acted up. Yea, I should go see a doctor. Thanks, Arnie. I appreciate it."

At 4 o'clock, Cecil enters the University of Washington campus library. He knows where to go; he has been there before. But he can't stop from feeling his face is a beacon, as if any second someone is going to shout, "There he is! That's him!"

From the fifth-floor stacks, he pulls down two new books: *Schizophrenia: Disease or Symptom?* By Abronaust and *Analyzing Murders* by Brickly.

Two hours later, he is exhausted. He has answers and yet no answer. His headache is so bad it seems to him as if someone had cleaved his brain with an axe. The musty smell of old books reminds him of wet, bloodied hair and he feels nauseated. His will to live is nonexistent, but his heart persists in beating. He mechanically stands from the table and walks toward the exit. At the sight of a campus cop, he automatically turns away, facing the big bulletin board. He half gazes at cars for sale, places to rent, roommates wanted. Then something catches his eye. A familiar word—bartender. It is an advertisement half hidden behind newer notices. He uncovers the ad and rips it off the board.

Wanted: Summer Seasonal Help:

> Waiters, waitresses
> Kitchen help
> Front desk
> Housekeeping
> Bartenders
> Others

Contact: Yellowstone Park Concessionaire
Gardiner, Montana 82190

By the light of six candles, with the curtains drawn around him, he fills out the applications. This, he prays, will be a new start.

May 4.

This time of year, on Yellowstone Plateau, it can rain or snow, and on this day, it is raining. The snowbank is at 15 inches and the cold rain will help diminish it. The backcountry and the trails are fit for neither man nor animal now. The elk and buffalo that remained in Yellowstone to winter are in and around the geyser basins and marshes that are clear of snow. The elk are shaggy, their coats rough and matted as they shed their winter hair, and they eat eagerly at the grass where there is a sprinkling of green. The bull elk have just the nubbins of their ivory antlers. Within a month, the cows will calve, but now they wander freely across the nearly deserted Grand Loop Road.

Along Fountain Flats, the buffalo cows are having their calves. An umbilical cord that still partially hangs from both mother and calf means the calf was born that morning, and on shaky legs the calf already scampers along after a small herd as the dominant bull, the herdmaster, massive and black-brown, slowly leads the way towards a new stretch of meadow. From one hundred yards away the orange and gangly buffalo calves resemble golden retrievers that have gotten mixed up in the herd. The young suckle and the adults eat almost constantly now.

At this time of year, grizzly and black bears wake from their long winter sleep, clambering out to meet a new year. They are hungry and will use their keen sense of smell to seek out the elk that have not survived the long, cold winter.

Slowly, Lake Yellowstone starts to break up and invites the return of native waterfowl. Raven and coyote, year-long residents, are active, feeding on carrion.

It rains. A couple from Illinois stands on the boardwalk awaiting Old Faithful's eruption. Since an earthquake the previous fall, the average duration between eruptions has changed from 63 minutes to 74 minutes, and the couple is impatient at the geyser's ponderous playing.

There is no more inhospitable time on the Yellowstone Plateau than the month of May. Sunshine, rain, sleet, snow— any of which could suddenly occur at any time. Not all of the buffalo calves born that spring will survive, for nighttime temperatures can still dip to zero, and the newborns do not have the fat reserves to ward off the cold.

May 5. Cabin 248.

It's just after 2 p.m. and Steve Mathewson, the night auditor, is just waking from four hours of sleep after what he referred to as a "hellacious audit." As he wakens he recounts the previous night's conversation with Yvonne.

"Yvonne?" he asks the overweight assistant controller, whose cigarette smoke has given him a headache. "When did you say we were supposed to be getting that night-audit clerk?"

"We're supposed to get him tomorrow. That's what Mammoth said."

"Does tomorrow mean today because we're doing yesterday's

audit or does tomorrow actually mean tomorrow?" Steve asks, rubbing his eyes.

"Today, I think."

He nods. "Now tell me how I get the average check per cover for the dining room."

Yvonne leaves her cigarette in the back office and comes out to the controller's desk where Steve has 12 different reports surrounding him. He blinks his eyes twice, trying to make the numbers come back into focus.

"OK. You take your food-revenue figure from each of breakfast, lunch, and dinner. It goes here. Then you back out your allowances. . ."

Twenty-five minutes later, Steve blows the last of the eraser marks off the utility rate recovery report. "Thanks, Yvonne. Now what was that report for again?"

A knock on the cabin door brings him back to a conscious level. He realizes that he walked out of the controller's office just four hours and 10 minutes ago. A second knock convinces him he isn't dreaming. He stands, and staggers to the door. It's Earvin, the tall, black resident assistant, standing with a shorter, bearded, raven-haired young man with a suitcase and what Steve believes is a typewriter.

"Did I screw up the audit? Imre send ya'll?" Steve asks in a Virginia drawl.

"What? No. This is your roommate. This is Wilbur Hardisty. What's your name again?"

"Steve. Steve Mathewson."

"Wilbur will be working at night as well, so you should be on similar schedules, which we try to do for you."

"What are you going to be doing?" asks Steve, finally shaking the sleep from his head and reaching for Wilbur's hand.

"I'll be a night-audit clerk."

"Oh! It's you! Well, it's nice to meet you! Come on in!"

After he helps Wilbur unload the back of his truck, Steve leans back on his bed while Wilbur puts things away. In the random pairings of roommates, they are lucky. After just 10 minutes of unforced conversation, the two men know they will get along.

Wilbur is 25, from Palo Alto, California. His beard surrounds a handsome, discerning face, his green eyes sharp with an appraising perception. His black hair, like his beard, is straight and trimmed.

He is quick to laugh as Steve describes the previous night and what lies in store for them in the nights ahead.

"And Imre is the controller. Bad temper with a short fuse."

"I was an auditor at a casino in Reno last winter, but everything was done on computers."

"I've done auditing for two years back in Virginia. It's nothing like this thing. This audit is huge."

"Why'd you come up here?" Wilbur asks.

"I wanted to see the world a little. Make sure Virginia is where I want to settle. I'm also pretty serious about running. I ran in high school and college. I've heard the trails were great here and I'd like to try adding altitude to my training regimen. But if I'm going to be this tired, I'm not going to do much running."

With a small pair of scissors, Wilbur cuts a thread from a tweed jacket. "Yea," he says, "I needed a change of pace. I'd like to do some writing. Maybe we can work something out where I can type when you're not here."

"Don't worry about it. It won't bother me. I sleep heavy. What kind of stuff do you write?"

"Some fiction. Some poetry. I've never sold anything, though. I was an electrical engineering major at Stanford University and realized I hated it. I took one course a year ago in creative writing. Thought maybe the mountains here would inspire me. I'd like to sell some stories this summer. I've got a few ideas."

"I'm hoping the mountains will inspire me too. I want to run in the Pike's Peak marathon in Colorado in August, finish well there, then try to run a sub-2:15 marathon in New York after I leave here."

"Sounds like you're really serious. Maybe it would make good copy for a story."

"Well, if we have many audits like the one last night, the story will be a nightmare."

Wilbur sets a box onto the bed and sits down facing Steve.

"Do you like wine?"

"Yea, sometimes. By the way, is the right side OK for you?"

"The right side is fine," Wilbur answers, dumping the remaining contents of his suitcase, his socks and underwear, onto the mattress. "But where's the room-service phone?" he says, and they both laugh.

May 10.

In the woods, Wilbur Hardisty looks over his just-finished poem. He likes it. He sees where the meter could be better, a line changed, but he decides he will leave it unaltered. Besides, it is a special night. He and his roommate actually have their first night off.

Wilbur looks at the position of the sun in the sky, estimating it to be 5 o'clock, three hours until dark. He knows Steve should be getting back from his run soon. Clear sailing ahead. The thought of a good night's sleep excites him, and he has two bottles of white Mouton Cadet Bordeaux on ice. And Steve said he found the perfect place to drink and watch the sunset.

Wilbur jogs lightly across the road, across the footbridge that spans Zipper Creek, through the cabin area, then slows at the sight of a figure walking toward him—the prettiest girl he has seen since he's been there. His notepad and pencil hit his knee and he drops them.

"Ohh. . . hi. . . hello. I haven't seen you here before." Nice start, Wilbur thinks. Stanford didn't prepare me for this.

"My name's Kitty. I'm the executive housekeeper. Do you work here?"

"My name's Wilbur." He steps toward her and they shake hands. "I'm the night-audit clerk. Except for tonight. It's my night off."

"I sure could use one," Kitty says. "The beginning of the season is the hardest part of the year for me. I've got a staff of 60 new people, and now they want me to open the rec hall tomorrow night so the Chamber of Commerce can have a big dinner."

"You have a little bit of a southern accent—similar to my roommate's," Wilbur says. "Where're you from? "

"I'm from North Carolina, originally. Where's your roommate from?" Kitty asks, as she steps up and unlocks the padlock to her cabin.

"Virginia. He's the night auditor."

"Night auditor. I always think of you people as moles, the way you run around all night long like that. Can you even see at this time of day?"

They laugh together and continue talking for several minutes. Slowly, like the coming of the dawn at the North Pole, the obvious comes to Wilbur.

"Oh, hey, my roommate found a great place to watch the sunset. Perhaps you'd like to come with us. We're going to have some Mouton Cadet—I mean, some wine. . ."

"You have Mout! I love it. It's my favorite! Yes, I'll do it. I could use it after today."

"Great."

"Are you sketching?" she asks, pointing to the notepad.

"No. It's a poem I just wrote. It's a little rough." Wilbur surprises himself by adding, "Would you like to read it?"

"I love poetry. I *would* like to read it."

"You love poetry *and* Mouton Cadet?"

"I should think they would go well together. Let me read it while I'm changing."

Wilbur takes a breath and tries to control his heartbeat and hold her searching gaze. He is instantly taken by her casual, confident manner and glowing good looks. There is something there. Go easy, he tells himself.

"Let me walk back to my cabin—it's only five cabins down—and get my roommate and the Mouton Cadet. Five minutes?"

"Make it four," Kitty smiles.

Inside her cabin, Kitty watches Wilbur walk away as she unzips her dress. She knows she is in control. After nine years in the park, she knows about summer romances. How they start. Where they can end up. But a face like that, with black hair and a neatly trimmed beard and peaceful green eyes. I'm interested, she thinks.

She unfolds the paper and smooths it open on the counter in front of her, hoping the poem will reveal more.

"Hey Wilbur," Steve says, jogging to a stop. "I want you to meet Salina. She was out running on the boardwalk and we jogged back together. She works at the T&I, the Tours and Information desk. Do you mind if she goes with us?"

Salina, a tall, angular girl with a large, thin nose, and just a few freckles, extends her hand to Wilbur.

"No. In fact, I just met Kitty from a few cabins down. She's going to come too."

"I've met Kitty," says Salina. "Nice lady."

"Besides having this beautiful strawberry-blond hair, Salina ran a 17:25 5K last fall in cross country at. . . UCLA?"

"USC!" She laughs and smiles brightly, revealing perfectly set teeth. "Nice to meet you Wilbur; Steve said you went to Stanford?"

"Yes. Only for two years. . . . Hey, I'm going to run into the cabin and get two more bottles of wine. Jump in the back of the camper and get comfortable. I'll be right out."

"Let me get us a couple of jackets," Steve says to Salina.

At Black Sand Basin, the four emerge from the Datsun pick-up. From the parking lot, they walk across the Grand Loop Road onto a dirt path that, 40 years before, was the main road into Old Faithful. Armed with one bottle of Mouton Cadet each, they follow the bend a half mile to the left, past a steel-blue pool of steaming water with a rock overhang.

"I used to come down here to sunbathe," Kitty says. "I'm going to have to start doing that again when it gets warmer."

Wilbur memorizes the spot, and tries to visualize the scene.

Walking behind the others, Salina stops before stepping over a fallen tree. She is wide-eyed, absorbed in her new surroundings, away from the concrete of Los Angeles.

"We're here!" Steve says, standing on the top of a symmetrical, extinct geyser cone about 25 feet high. He holds his hands out in an encompassing gesture and in as deep a voice as the soft-spoken Southerner can muster, says, "Welcome to the domain of Lucifer!"

Salina smiles up at him and decides she likes this fellow a little. He reminds her of the Scarecrow in the Wizard of Oz, as he points and gestures from the little knoll above them.

They find seats on the rocky top of the knoll, facing northwest and looking over the western edge of the Upper Geyser Basin.

"Let's go white white red red," says Wilbur, and while Wilbur opens a bottle, Steve scrambles down the knoll and buries the remaining bottles of the French Bordeaux in a snowbank 20 yards away. Wilbur opens his pack and produces wine glasses wrapped in thick brown towels, and then pours while Salina holds. They sip in silence.

They go unnoticed by strolling sightseers some 300 yards away. They watch a little thermal feature at the bottom of the knoll, and hold a friendly debate as to whether it is a pool or a geyser, as it slowly fills, spouts once to a height of one foot, then repeats the cycle.

They sip wine, talk about their pasts, and their expectations of the summer.

". . . So," Wilbur finishes, "it was not long after that that I signed out of Stanford forever. Then I heard about Yellowstone through a friend of a friend. I thought it would be a good idea to regroup up here and decide if I can make a go of writing."

"I think you write very well, Wilbur," Kitty says. "I loved your poem. Here it is. I copied it. I hope you don't mind."

Kitty hands the folded poem to Wilbur, and their hands touch briefly, warmly, purposely. Their eyes catch one another's and lock for an instant, as if they both held out their hearts, fears, insecurities to one another, leaving themselves vulnerable.

"More grog!" Steve shouts, standing up unevenly. "This is tasty stuff, Wilbur. I'm usually a beer drinker." He weaves back down the knoll.

Salina excuses herself and walks toward the trees while Kitty inspects the conical, frothing pool in front of them. From his day pack, Wilbur produces an odd-looking flute of bamboo, twists together the two halves, and plays. Its soothing sound sails out over the clearing.

"I'm so glad I don't have to work tonight," Steve says, letting out a long sigh.

"How do you guys like working with Imre?" Kitty asks.

Steve turns to her. "You mean the wicked witch of the west wing? It's my goal to try and make her laugh once this summer."

As they sip, a buffalo strays in front of them and lies down, giving the grass a break. He ruminates. Above, blue sky comes in patches and pink starts to show on the clouds of the eastern horizon.

"So you must have an accounting degree," Salina says to Steve.

"No, physical education," Steve says. "Doing night audit gave me days off to train; running is the most important thing in my life right now. I'm still trying to break into teaching. It's tough. Educators now think it's necessary to get back to the basics—math, English, history. They give no importance to education of the body, which I think is just as important as education of the mind. If you don't feel good physically, you're not going to be happy. That's kind of my philosophy."

"What brought you to Yellowstone, Salina?"

"The chance to make minimum wage." She laughs at her own joke. "No, seriously, it's amazing listening to your stories. In March, I graduated with a degree in biology and now I've got to decide what to do with it. Just like you, Wilbur, my parents are trying to influence my decision. My dad would like to see me go to medical school, but yuck, five to seven more years of school! Gives me a headache to think about it. My favorite class as an undergrad was genetics. I had a really great instructor, and I'm leaning toward trying to work in a lab somewhere, probably making square watermelons and stuff like that. That fascinates me."

"A 17:25 is a good 5K time. Are you going to keep up with that?" Steve asks.

"I ran for the scholarship. It's just escapism for me now. No more competition."

"I travel," Kitty says. "That's my escape."

"Yea," Salina says. "I really admire what you're doing, Kitty. I've been wanting to travel for a long time. That's really why I'm here, to get away. It's kind of giving me a chance to think all this through. A career is such a big decision. I may be in med school in the fall, but I really don't want to go back to Los Angeles. The earthquake ruined my last lab class. Right now, I like it here very much. I like the company, and I like this wine."

"We'll form our own society," Wilbur suggests.

"A sunset-watching society," Kitty adds.

"For the drinking of Mouton Cadet," Steve chimes in.

Wilbur swivels to face the other three. In the waning light, with no one around but the buffaloes, and with wine held up to the heavens, he shouts: "The Mouton Cadet Sunset Society!"

"Yea!" Steve yells in response.

"All right!" adds Kitty.

Salina giggles, spilling a little red wine. Steve hurls the wine from his half-filled glass in an arc back toward the treeline. Wilbur grabs the Japanese flute and plays it, standing on the highest part of the knoll, and the three of them stand up and hold their glasses high.

"The Mouton!" shouts Wilbur.

"Cadet!" says Kitty.

"Sunset!" yells Steve.

"Society!" adds Salina.

"Yaayyy!" they all shout in unison.

"Wait," says Steve. "Wait wait wait. We must have a charter."

They help each other sit back down, hemming and hawing in their procrastination. Wilbur pours from the last bottle and Kitty pronounces: "For the enjoyment of life?"

"For the enjoyment of life!" Wilbur and Steve confirm together. They all stand and toast, and the flute playing, dancing and laughing begin again.

After a minute, Steve stops and Salina runs into him. "We must have officers," he says. "We must have a president."

"Highly evolved beings," points Wilbur, "whose moral and intellectual integrity are superior, needs be governed? You do it then. It's your idea."

"No, I don't want to be the president. I think you should be president, Wilbur. Especially since you supplied the Mouton Cadet. All those in favor say 'aye.'"

"Aye," the other three chant in unison.

"That's what I call a fair election," Salina proclaims.

"I want Kitty to be the vice president," says Wilbur. "All those in favor say 'aye.'"

"Aye!" Again, it is unanimous.

"Since I'm the night auditor, can I be the treasurer?"

"Aye!" say the other three.

"That means you have to be the secretary, Salina," Kitty concludes.

"What do I have to do?" the youngest member asks.

They all stop and think. Finally, Wilbur speaks. "You have to write the estate in France and ask how we can get free wine for our wine-tasting seminars. I even have the address. All those in favor?"

"Aye."

Wilbur starts to play again and the other three dance in a circle around him. The dark is descending quickly.

Through Wilbur's inebriated eyes, the geyser takes on a softer appearance. The strolling sightseers have long since disappeared. The wine is a good thing. Pressure, tension are gone. A chance to chase out the demons. Wilbur stops playing and the others sit down. The four of them lean back to back. Moments later, when Kitty excuses herself, the three of them fall over each other. Salina and Wilbur reach down to grab Steve before he rolls down the length of the knoll.

"I was just thinking," says Steve, as they pull him up. "We should have an initiation ceremony. Every good club should have one."

"What will it be?" Salina asks. "No marathons at night through the woods either."

"I don't know. Give me a second to think."

A minute passes. Kitty returns. "I've got it!" Steve announces. "Follow me, Wilbur. Guys first, then girls."

In the near darkness, Wilbur follows Steve down the knoll. "Real ssshhh," whispers Steve, as they head to the woods, approaching the buffalo from behind.

"Are you crazy? What are you going to do?"

"We've got to touch him. Come on. He's asleep."

With muffled whispers of warning from the girls, side by side, they approach the huge black form. From behind, the two men reach out and tentatively touch the huge animal, which makes no movement.

"He's asleep," they guarantee the girls as they climb back up the knoll.

"Let's do it," Kitty says tentatively. "I've never touched a buffalo."

Arm in arm, the girls tiptoe along the same route. In the near-darkness, they reach out together and touch the thick hide. The buffalo bolts upright and charges ahead, and the girls scream and scramble recklessly up the knoll in the other direction. The men come halfway down and embrace the women, turning them away from the snorting and mooing buffalo as it stampedes into the darkness. When the buffalo is out of sight, they all collapse on the top of the knoll, laughing, gasping for breath, rolling across one another.

"God, I think I'm going to have a heart attack," Kitty says.

"It hurts," winces Salina, clutching at her stomach. "I've got to stop laughing. I thought we were going to die."

"I haven't laughed this hard in a long time," Wilbur adds, wiping tears from his eyes.

"I thought you girls said you didn't *feel* like running," Steve bellows.

Finally, it is Wilbur who stands up with the last half of their fourth bottle of Mouton Cadet and shouts as loud as he can: "The Mouton Cadet Sunset Society. . . . For the enjoyment of life!"

Ross Matthias reaches to the log for the lighter and the white marijuana joint. He twirls it in his fingers once and looks up past his campfire at the heavens and traces stars along the Milky Way.

He lights the cigarette and takes a long pull. He holds the smoke-filled breath for as long as he can, expels it in an airy "shoosh," then grabs the bottom half of his cooking pot. He reaches into the upper left pocket of his big green backpack and finds the clove of garlic. When he is satisfied that he has enough cut, he reaches in the main compartment for a carrot and three stalks of green onion, which he cuts up and adds to the garlic. The fire is for warmth and the little Swedish Svea camp stove, with its highly refined white gas fuel, is better for cooking, he tacitly reminds himself.

Then he grabs the flashlight by his right side and his one-liter pot and walks to Hellroaring Creek, huge and swollen from springtime runoff. He steps on a rock and leans out over the river. He only needs to hold his pot under a rock ledge for a second to fill it. Nonetheless, the snow-melted water is cold enough to numb his hand. Ross takes two steps back onto the river's edge, turns his flashlight off and looks at the waxing crescent moon above him. The moon's orangish-yellow barely reflects over the roaring rapids in the inky blackness next to him. The river is at high water. He sits and closes his eyes to listen to nature in stereo. He can hear huge rocks tumbling over in the current, and he considers the never-ending forces of erosion. Glancing back at his gear illuminated in orange from his wavering campfire, he remembers the last time he had camped; it was six months ago in the Sierras.

Too long, he thinks. Makes you crazy to go that long.

He walks back toward the fire, and sautés the carrots, onions and garlic in the pot with butter from a squeeze tube. He adds the cold water and the powdered Newman's Health Food Natural Style Minestrone Soup Mix, stirring it under a medium heat. Then he cuts broccoli and red cabbage into the soup, plus a generous pinch of his own blend of spices and, finally, five dashes of Tabasco. He stirs it slowly, covers it, and then, with a large sigh, sits down on his neoprene pad and rests his back against a fallen gray log. For several moments, he listens to the airy roar of the one-burner stove and watches its pure-blue flame. Then he arches his 26-year-old body against the log, contorting, stretching out the stiffness. The shoulders feel good for the first time out, he thinks.

After taking two more draws on the cannabis cigarette, Ross lifts the Yellowstone topographical map out of the pocket of his pack and unfolds it. It reminds him again how vast the park is—within the 2-million-plus acres are more than 1,000 miles of trail.

Although Ross spent just one summer working in Yosemite the year before, it might take two here in Yellowstone, he thinks to himself. And there are the Tetons just south, another national park, then the Wind River Range south of that—areas he read so much about in *Outside* magazine.

Running his hand over the three-foot-by-three-foot map, he contemplates, relishes what lies ahead.

"What mysteries and secrets do you possess, Yellowstone?" he says aloud. But from his conversations with the locals, he knows the area he is walking through—the north end, with its lower elevation—is the only navigable place in the park this early in the season. It was a 64-mile drive to the trailhead, but he knows from experience that it's better than trudging miles through rotten snow or soggy marshland.

Ross looks at the red line representing his route of travel for the next day, taking him along the Black Canyon of the Yellowstone River. He looks with eager anticipation where there are concentrated degradation lines between the trail and the Yellowstone River—it should mean tall cliffs with awesome views. He wonders about the trail further up, where it goes along the river, and hopes the high water won't wash it out, for he sees there are cliffs on the right. He contemplates his boots drying next to the fire and expects that he will have to walk through some marshes and probably snow. He is prepared, though: Two weeks before he came to Yellowstone, Ross rubbed the boots with mink oil to waterproof them.

He looks on his map at the "X" he has drawn marking his campsite the next night. The width of his little finger's nail is a mile, so he estimates 10 miles the next day, then five more miles the following day to reach the trailhead. Then back to Old Faithful in time for his 5 p.m. work shift to wait tables.

After being immersed in the map, Ross suddenly becomes aware that his soup is bubbling. When he opens the lid, he is hit with a blast of steam and aroma. He stirs the boiling soup and turns the stove key down one-quarter turn, bringing the soup to a simmer. He builds up the fire, and then leans back and gazes into it thoughtfully.

He recalls the past winter, when he worked as a bellman at Harrah's Casino in Lake Tahoe, and remembers how frustrated he would get watching people throw their money away gambling. He could travel for a year on what some of them lost in a weekend. While he unloaded the cars, he would always look to the mountains, wishing he were there.

Thinking further back, he remembers the previous summer, when he was a bellman in Yosemite. It was nice at first, when his girlfriend, Ruth, would come up and they would go camping. But it was when they started having arguments in the backcountry that he started taking his weekends alone. He relished those times, setting off by himself, away from it all.

Here are my friends now, Ross thinks. The trees, the rivers, the earth, the universe. A good book by a warm campfire. Peace and quiet.

He stirs the soup once more. It's nearly ready. He fishes out his squirt bottle of raspberry Kool-Aid and the box of crackers. He lays another branch across the fire, then shuts down the insistent Svea stove. The end of the roar of the one-burner shuts down his thoughts of a mechanical world as well.

"What a meal! Yes, thank you, Pierre. It's so good to be in my favorite restaurant again."

After finishing his meal, Ross washes out his pots in the creek, rebuilds the fire, has two, three, four Mystic Mints for dessert, and settles back against the log with his harmonica.

May 14. Personnel Office of the Yellowstone Park Concessionaire, Gardiner, Montana.

"Look at the red light, please," the photographer tells a young girl, one of the many new park employees at the concessionaire's office to get her ID picture taken.

The light flashes.

"Next."

"Look at the red light, please. No, face forward, please."

"Well, this is my better side, so if I turn this way a little, you know, this scar. . ."

"That's fine."

The white light flashes over the corner of the room.

"Next?"

A few minutes later one of the personnel staff girls calls out, "Cecil Dolen?"

"Yes, here."

"You're all set to go, Mr. Dolen. Here's your ID. If you lose it, it will cost you $25 to replace. You're to report in to Clarence Harps at Old Faithful Inn. Give him this. Then you will report to Penny Baker at the Employee Services Office. She will get you squared away with living quarters. Do you own a car?"

"Yes, I do," says the slight, 5'7" dark-haired man with the curious owl-like expression, blinking as he talks.

"Show this at the entrance station and the ranger will let you in. Then when you get to Old Faithful, you'll need to go to the ranger station there to get a sticker for your windshield so you can get in and out of the park without paying each time. Say, would you have room for a passenger?"

"I could make room."

"Hold on, let me see if I can find her. She is the only other one going to Old Faithful out of this group, so the bus driver wouldn't have to make a special stop. Just a second."

After just a moment, she returns.

"Kris Richards, this is Cecil Dolen. He has offered to give you a ride to Old Faithful."

"Are you all set to go?"

"Yes," says the statuesque young girl with the almost snow-white blond hair. "Kris," she says, extending a hand.

"Cecil Dolen. Nice to meet you."

"Nice car," Kris says, as Cecil unlocks the door to the passenger side. "You're from Washington, huh?"

"Yea, Seattle. Where're you from?"

"Tallahassee, Florida, right now. That's where I'm going to school. It feels so far away now."

With Kris's suitcase strapped to the back of the royal blue Corvette, they drive along the curvy road next to the Gardner River, then up to the plateau.

"So anyway," Kris continues, "John and I started going out before I got the job here and we were pretty serious by the time I was supposed to leave. I almost changed my mind about coming out."

"Why didn't you?"

"Well, my mom worked here as a waitress 24 years ago. She thought it would be a good place to take a break from school. And it will be nice to help my parents out financially during my last year at school. But, well, the last night I was with John, we talked about getting married after we graduate. So we both thought a summer apart would be good. Give us a chance to decide if that's what we both really want."

"Oh, really? I've decided to not ask anyone out for a date either."

"You have a girlfriend in Seattle?"

"No. No, not really. I just needed to get away, that's all. Time for a change, just be alone for a while. I'd like to do some hiking. It looks like you probably like to jog or hike or something, huh?"

"Yea, I do. Every summer, my family goes up to the Smokey Mountains. My sister and mom and I would always hike while my father and brothers fished."

"Maybe we could go on a hike together sometime," Cecil says. "There's got to be some trails here."

"That would be nice. I could use someone to talk to. I mean, a guy who knows my situation and just wants to be friends."

"That sounds good. Be alone and still have friends. I'd like that. Friends?" Cecil asks, offering his hand.

They shake hands, and Cecil gazes deeply into Kris's clear blue eyes.

"Oh! Look out!" says Kris, before Cecil pulls the Corvette away from the path of a honking camper.

Cecil shrugs it off with a smile and a blink. "Damned roads are too narrow up here. I've been on straight roads and interstates too long!"

May 15. Bear Pit Bar, 8 p.m..

Imre, the controller, and Yvonne, the assistant controller, are sitting at the far end of the bar, where employees traditionally sit. Both have cigarettes and mixed drinks in front of them.

"So you must have just started," Imre says.

"I got here yesterday and trained for a couple of hours last night. This is my first shift, really, but Clarence is around in case I foul things up real bad."

"I'm Imre. I'm the controller, and this is Yvonne, my assistant."

"Nice to meet you. I'm Cecil."

"We know that. We can read your name tag," Yvonne chides. "We're depressed because we don't have boyfriends. Are you a happy bartender? Are you going to cheer us up?"

"I'll try."

"Tell us a joke, " Imre says flatly.

This big girl, Cecil wonders, she doesn't have to worry about having a boyfriend. But the other one, why not?

Cecil turns around and sets a polished beer glass upside down on the red plastic screen as he searches through his repertoire of bartender jokes. Just then, Herm, now out of his security outfit and into jeans, big-bellied under a levi jacket, strolls up and sits next to Yvonne.

"Cecil, this is Herm, the head of security. Herm, Cecil."

"Nice to meet you, Cecil."

"Likewise."

Cecil averts his eyes as he leans over the bar to shake Herm's hand. He scoops up a bowl of pretzels and sets them on the bar in front of Herm.

"Watch these two, Cecil. They're the biggest troublemakers in the park."

"We are not, Herm," Imre says with a pout. "We're really good. We give everyone money. Now behave. Cecil was just going to tell us a joke."

Cecil grabs another bar glass and starts to polish it. "Two guys in a bar. One guy says to the other guy, 'I drink to forget.' The other guy says, 'So do I. . . . Why do you?'"

Yvonne laughs loudly, Imre smiles and blows out a puff of smoke, and Herm screws his face in puzzlement. As Cecil makes their order of three Long Island iced teas, he decides he likes being here. The huge, warm, wooden bar brings a feeling of solidity and security.

"Cecil, the Washington on your name tag. Is that D.C. or the state of?" Herm says.

Just then, Slim Grandstrom, the assistant location manager, approaches.

"Got a leaky radiator on the third floor, Herm. I can't figure it out. Could you help me look at it?"

"Sure, Slim," Herm says condescendingly. "Save my drink, will ya, Cec?"

"Sure thing, Herm."

"Ordering," comes a voice from the service bar. Cecil sees that Clarence is gone and responds. He sees Kris leaning over.

"Two bloody marys, please, Cecil."

"Will do. How's it going, Kris?"

"Well, Imre," Yvonne says, "what do you think of him? He's kind of cute, even with the scar."

"I don't think he's my type. Too short. I think I saw him wink at you, though."

"Too small. I'd squish him. I'll keep him in mind, though."

"You keep everybody in mind, Yvonne."

"I'd rather keep him in body. Tied down to do my bidding. Hey, that reminds me. I heard our cute night auditor was going out with that little tramp from the Tour and Information desk. The one with the long legs and strawberry blond hair and the big nose? Does this mean we have to cross him off our list?"

"Oh, well. The story of my life. Next you'll tell me Wilbur is gay."

The big woman shifts in her bar stool, blows out a puff of cigarette smoke and whispers intently. "No, but I heard he's going out with Kitty. I heard they were at the movie the other night and they were wound around each other tighter than the white and red in a candy cane at Christmas time!"

"No no no! Don't tell me that. The bitch! These men are so shallow!"

"I tell you what I think we should do. I think we should have another drink and go up to Faysal's room and seduce him. I'll hold him down first. Then, when he's weakened, you hold him down and I'll maul him to death."

Imre lets out the smoke from a long, cool drag and raises an eyebrow.

"No, huh?"

"OK, you foxy ladies. What's your pleasure now," Cecil asks.

Cabin 414.

"Kitty, that was the best chow mein I've ever had. Just great. And I used to drive up to Chinatown from Palo Alto just to eat. Now tell me, how did you arrange it so you don't have to eat in the Employee Dining Room? I thought everyone had to."

"I just told Tagore that I wanted a cooking cabin. There is another one. A married couple has it. I said I would buy a refrigerator and use my Coleman stove. I told him I wouldn't come back to work if I had to eat EDR gruel. And I was prepared not to come back. But he didn't want to lose a good housekeeper."

"Do you want me to wash dishes now?"

"No. I want you to hold up your end of the bargain."

"You want your massage now?"

"I could really use one."

"Do you have any oil?"

"Hmmm. . . . I think so."

As he pours oil into a small pan, Wilbur wonders if he can hold back his physical desire for Kitty any longer. He wonders if this is the night. We're on such a great wave length, he thinks. But mating courtship must be delicate and each step certain.

Wilbur turns around from the stove and sees Kitty taking off her clothes. With her back to him, he watches her. What a figure, he thinks. How long has it been?

Kitty reaches back to unsnap her bra. Wilbur's hand starts to tremble, and the dish with the hot oil starts to rattle on the plate before he can still it with his other hand. Kitty's pale, round breasts jostle once, then assume a perfect shape, the nipples pointing slightly upward. Her deep brown skin stretches over long, smooth, working muscles, and she lets her skirt fall to the floor. When she slips out of her solid pink underwear, Wilbur automatically floats over to the bed. He sits at the foot of the bed and rubs his hands together, then puts his fingertips in the hot oil and starts to massage her calves. He takes a deep breath and forces his trembling to subside. He then lights a candle next to the bed, turns out the lamp, and directs his concentration to the task. As he rubs oil with both hands onto the backs of her upper legs, she purrs once, then her entire body relaxes, goes limp. Slowly, deliberately, he works his warm, oiled fingers into her soft skin, stretching and contracting her yielding muscles. As he reaches her back, she moans contentedly, turns her head, and then goes silent for 15 minutes. He wonders if she has fallen asleep. Once—finally—he runs his hands the length of her perfectly rounded, glistening body, savoring the contours, and then he moves her sandy blond hair away from the small of her neck and whispers, "Is there anything else?"

"I want you to make love to me."

May 18. The Gift Shop.

It has been snowing almost constantly for 36 hours. Only the heartiest of the early-season tourists still stroll about the geyser basin. Inside the gift shop, it is bright and warm. Several customers move about, looking at the books, magazines, trinkets and stuffed bears. Two elderly ladies are clad in the YP Concessionaire standard uniform—dark brown checked Western-cut shirts and polyester slacks.

"I like chili but it doesn't like me," says Adele Petersen, the 60-year-old wife of Jim Petersen.

"I don't eat the chili here," says Angel Ferguson, the gift shop manager. "They just open a can. I think Barry maybe tries to fix it up a little. I make my own at home with chopped T-bone steak; it's much better."

"I made a big pot of it this winter," Adele said. "I've got a good recipe. Jim likes it. Said it kept him warm inside this old building when he had to be here alone."

"So you had a good winter here then? I think about you two sometimes. I'm down there in southern California and it's warm and sunny, and I can't imagine what it is like up here in the middle of January."

"Lots of snow. And it is cold, there's no doubt about that. But we like it well enough. I'm getting a little old to bounce around on a snowmobile so we sold it last December to a couple of waiters in the Snow Lodge. We still cross-country ski a little."

"There's somebody looking at that glass moose. I swear, if someone doesn't buy it this year, it's going to end up on my dresser at home. I'm tired of looking at it. Excuse me, Adele."

Adele tries to ignore the insistent pain in her chest. As it is 1:30, she looks around the gift shop for something to do that will make her last hour and a half go by more quickly. She sees that there is only one box of the 35 millimeter 100 ASA film left under the glass countertop.

"Mitch," Adele says, reaching for the film-closet keys. "Watch register two. I'll be back in a minute."

She pauses for a moment to look out at the lobby, knowing that, with the coming of Memorial Day, it will get much busier in a couple of weeks. She is weary and inclined to sit by the big stone fireplace and rest for awhile. But Adele believes in setting a good example by always working hard—especially at the beginning of a new season—so she turns and walks down the west-wing corridor to the film closet. She opens the door, and two boxes fall forward at her feet; someone has tried to overstock it again. And the Fuji 200 is not in the right place, she notices. She spends several minutes rearranging the green-packaged film together, to make a place for the Kodak 200 ASA. With her right foot, she slides the 100 ASA film along the wall and takes a mental inventory of what they have. I'll have to tell Angel we need some more of the 24-pack slides, she thinks. And more of the Viewmaster disks.

She bends to lift the case of 200 and, as she gets it above her waist, a sharp pain suddenly shoots across her chest. She gasps loudly and drops the film. She falls forward a little and clutches at her chest. She feels light-headed, faint, and leans against the closet shelves. Her face contorts from a second jolt of pain, but no one is there to notice.

"Oh God," she whispers.

Thirty seconds later, the pain slowly subsides. She puts her hand over her chest as she lowers herself to sit on the case of film that has fallen. She feels empty, weak. Now her heart starts to fluctuate rapidly. Slowly, she takes two deep breaths. A young boy races past her toward the west wing, then stops to look at her with a curious expression. It's a struggle to raise her eyelids and return his gaze, and she is glad he turns and disappears down the corridor. Damned chili, she thinks. No more of that.

The same thing has happened more often over the past year, only this was the worst, she thinks. It was only a month ago when she was carrying that big piece of wood into the trailer that the same pain occurred last. She didn't tell Jim about that. Nor did she tell him about the time they were skiing up to Lone Star Geyser and she had that same sharp pain across her chest.

"Go ahead, Jim," she had said. "I need a hanky."

She rubs an area on her chest near her left shoulder. If it happens again, she decides, maybe she will mention it to Jim and see what he thinks. Just then Angel appears.

"Adele, are you all right?"

"Angel, yes, I'm OK. Just sitting here trying to digest that chili. Look, this box is too heavy for me. Where is that big strong Mitch? Probably chasing the T&I girl again."

"Here, let me help you up. Are you sure you're all right?"

"I'm sure."

On the Grand Loop Road.

About four more minutes until I turn around, Steve thinks, looking up from his watch. Don't want to screw up out here, sprain an ankle or something. Few cars; someone would stop. Sweating now, no problem keeping warm as long as I keep going. Don't have this problem in Virginia in the middle of May. Warm there now. Wonder what kind of miles Donny and those guys are putting in these days. They'll be peaking for that Memorial Day 10k up in Washington. Wish I could have a shot at that one. Wonder what I'll be able to do after a few weeks up here? Altitude's getting a little easier. These long runs help. Speed though! No speed work! Gonna *have* to find somewhere to do the speed work.

Cut left.

Geez, this road is in bad shape. One of these flooded potholes is going to get me yet. Mileage is going good though. May get 180 for the month. Thirty days? Yea. No, 31 in May. If I can get this 15 today, that will be my longest run in a couple of weeks. I better get this 15— I'm almost seven and a half out. Where was that boulder at seven and a half? Hope it isn't covered with snow. No. There was another road going off to the right just past it. Wasn't there a sign?

Easy, slow down. Concentrate. Have got to control my breathing up here—7:15 a mile, no faster. Hell, it's been April 1st since I've done a race. Maybe there will be some in Bozeman. Someone said Jackson. That's closer. Wonder if anyone *runs* races out here. Wonder if it's ever going to stop snowing. Damn trails are going to have to open up soon, before my knees give out. Wonder if my feet are frostbitten. They feel numb. Shoes feel like they weigh 10 pounds each. Wonder if I could outrun a buffalo. Another car. Hey, you splash me and I'll charge a $50 service charge to your folio tonight.

"Hey!"

Asshole. Is that any kind of way to see Yellowstone National Park?

All right. . . the turn-around. That's half way. OK, let's see. . . .
"Fifty-six forty."

OK. Seven minutes a mile for seven and a half miles would be. . . uh. . . 52:30, and eight minutes a mile would be. . . uh. . . 60 minutes. Even so, I'm just a little behind seven thirties. Should get home and take a nap before work tonight.

. . .Imre. She loves to put big red circles around my mistakes on the statistical reports. I think she needs a boyfriend, that's what I think. And Yvonne. Gosh. What a woman. She's two-faced. Watch her. Tells me how she didn't think Imre was doing a good job and how Faysal almost didn't want her hired back. Then she turns around and tells Imre what I said about her being the wicked witch of the west wing. Maybe we should invite her to a Mouton Cadet meeting. I am going to try and make her happy. Everybody else is cool. Just wish Yvonne wouldn't breath so hard. Speaking of breathing hard, I think I'll say a prayer for Salina. And mom and dad.

He crosses himself three times.

She'll have her diaphragm tomorrow. What does she see in me? She says I'm just what she needed. Great. I like this having new friends, a new girlfriend all of a sudden. A diaphragm. I guess I should have asked how one works.

I'm going to have to get Salina to do my easy runs with me. Be nice to have someone on those long trail runs too, so the bears don't chew my ass up. They say there's been a lot spotted this spring. What do I do if I see one? Climb a tree? Run like hell? Trees in here must have burned from those fires in '88. No branches.

Wonder if I can run a 2:15 in New York—5:10, 5:15 a mile?

Good people on that night crew with me. Glad they have a desk clerk on at night. And Herm, the security guy, he's a riot. Have to invite him to a Mouton meeting. And his witty roommate, Shawn, the short guy who works in the warehouse. That was a fun party they threw the other morning. Nocturnal party. I'll be damned. Beer buzz at eight o'clock in the morning. Different stuff for me.

Downhill. Easy on the knees. Coast. I like the mountains and the way I feel strong here. Nine-mile marker by this fallen lodgepole. Nine miles in 67:02. Good enough.

May 24. Bear Pit Bar, 1:30 p.m..

"So now let me get this straight," says Debi Mecy, the petite cocktail waitress. *"You two* are going to go backpacking?"

"Yes, we're going for a wilderness adventure," Clarence answers.

"Have either of you guys ever gone backpacking in your lives?"

"I did when I was in Boy Scouts," Cecil recalls. "About 15 or 16 years ago."

"See, we're veterans," Clarence says, as he and Cecil laugh. "I slept in a sleeping bag in my grandmother's cabin when I was 17. Does that count?"

"How about equipment? Does either of you have any?"

"We're going to go over to Hamilton's Store and buy some in the morning before we leave" Clarence explains. "We're just going out for one night."

"But this could be the start of weekly expeditions. Cleansing of the spirit, the robust life, that sort of thing," says Cecil.

"That's right. We'll be perfect physical specimens."

"You could die in this kind of country in one night if you're not prepared, you guys. Listen, don't go to Hamilton's. For the same price, you can go to West Yellowstone to the Outdoor Shop and get better-quality gear. Will you do that for me? I don't want to lose a good bar manager and a good bartender in the same night. What are you going to eat? Do you guys want to borrow my stove at least?"

"More important, what are we going to drink?" asks Cecil.

"I'm trying to stop," Clarence says meekly.

"I'll just get a pint of rum then."

"No, I've got a fifth of Bacardi Gold Reserve Anejo rum. It's much better. It's my secret stash. I'll bring that."

"I wish I could be there to see this," Debi chuckles.

"My great great grandfather was Davey Crockett," Clarence says.

"And mine was Daniel Boone," Cecil adds.

"Crockett and Boone, huh? More like Crock and Loon, I think."

May 25. Smith and Chandler, West Yellowstone.

"So you both need backpacks and sleeping bags. Then you want one tent and one mess kit between you."

"That should do it," Clarence says.

"Unless you can think of anything else," Cecil adds.

The salesman raises an eyebrow but doesn't say what he thinks. Perhaps he should sell these two to get a couple of flares, or maybe persuade them to rent a cabin instead of camping. The little one with the scar has a wool jacket at least, and a pair of jeans. He looks like he's been camping before. But the big fat one looks like a giant elf, except his red hair is falling out. I wonder if he's hiking in those hush puppies. I should try to talk them into hiking up Mount Holmes.

"OK, let's start with sleeping bags. How tall are you, sir?"

"Six foot three inches and 240 pounds. I was a linebacker with the Santa Monica Repertory Company last fall."

"OK, we'll start with you," he motions to Cecil. "Your height?"

"Five foot seven. And I'm a cold sleeper."

"Now we're getting somewhere."

Cecil buys a fiber-fill bag rated to five degrees above zero for $160. "If I spend a lot of money on one, I know I'll use it more than once," he says as he lays his Visa card on the counter. The salesman

rings up Cecil's other purchases as well: a Jansport frameless pack for
$93, a neoprene pad for $13 and an $8 mess kit.

Clarence buys a $52 cotton sleeping bag, with lions and tigers in
an African setting in the soft interior, plus a $45 Korean backpack
with an American flag on it. Since Cecil has spent more, Clarence
buys the tent—a one-piece "Little Backpacker" with plastic stakes for
$52.

"Now, could I interest you in some mountaineering gear perhaps—some crampons, nylon rope, maybe an ice axe, bivouac sack?"

"Na, pardner," says Clarence, easily slipping into his John Wayne
impersonation. "We're gone up the Yellerstone. Bear country, grizzly bars, I reckon. Let me se yer selection of Winchesters, pilgrim."

"Come on, Clarence. It's getting late. Thanks, sir."

"If we're not out in a year, come lookin' for us. We'll be holed up
in a cave, likely."

Next, they descend upon the food store. Cecil pushes while
Clarence walks ahead and tosses things into the cart. It doesn't take
long to cover all four aisles. They buy two apples, instant oatmeal,
pineapple Kool-Aid (to mix with the rum, Clarence explains), hot
chocolate, a three-quarter-pound bag of M&Ms, a two-and-a-half
pound can of Dinty Moore Beef Stew, a box of Triscuit wafers, a one-
pound block of Cache Valley Swiss Cheese, plus salami, two packages
of Hostess Twinkies, a bag of beer nuts and a novel by Irwin Shaw.

An hour-and-a-half later, at the trailhead, the two spread everything out on the roof of Clarence's 1974 Cadillac Seville, then stuff
it into their new backpacks. It's warm, so Cecil is in a T-shirt, and
Clarence is wearing an Arrow short-sleeved button-down shirt. They
are at the north end of the park, well below snow line, and although
the air is moist, only a few clouds are rolling in from the southwest.

At the suggestion of Ross Matthias, they are heading down to
campsite HG2 by Hellroaring Creek. It's an easy hike down, a 900-
foot elevation drop that's about four miles into the campsite.

"It feels great to get out from behind that bar," Cecil says, as the
parking lot disappears behind them. "Feels really good to get some
fresh air. This is what I came here for. Sixteen years is too long to go
between backpacking trips. How's your pack feel?"

Clarence bursts into song: "Hi ho, hi ho, it's off to work we go.
Do you like musicals?"

"You mean like *The Sound of Music?*"

"Perfect! Edelweiss, Edelweiss, Every morning, I see you. . ."

"You have a very nice voice. You ought to be a performer."

"I am. I told you I was an actor. I was a star in high school. One person said I should go to Hollywood. That's how I came to stop here, to save money to get to Hollywood. The movies didn't want me so I became a singing bartender. My heart's still in the theater."

"I enjoy your singing. Take it away, Clarence Harps."

As Clarence starts to sing, Cecil takes a deep breath. It feels good to be alive for a change. I've got a friend, he thinks. I've got some space, and a chance to forget about the past. The God to whom I've prayed so hard has answered me. My past will slowly dissolve away. I know I will be forgiven. It wasn't really me who did those things. I have a good heart. It's just that other person inside of me. He's not here now; the sky's the limit here.

Clarence and I should get into a routine where we go backpacking every weekend, Cecil thinks to himself. By the end of the summer, we'll be pros. Maybe find some women that like to backpack. Maybe Kris will come with me. I can see her there by a fire, her head on my shoulder. Yes. She'll get caught up in the splendor of the outdoors and fall in love with me.

"Have you done any acting?" Clarence asks.

"Me? No."

"I'm thinking about using the dance floor in the bar as a little stage. Maybe doing some scenes if I can get a couple of people. Some monologues. Dialogues. Small skits. Maybe surround it in a talent night kind of thing. I wonder if Faysal would go for it?"

"He might. Anything is possible here."

Down they go, over the big metal-cabled suspension bridge that spans the Yellowstone River, still brown and swollen with spring runoff, with whitewater cascades as it plunges through the winding, narrow canyon. They enter a stand of large lodgepole pines.

"I wonder what kinds of flowers these are," says Cecil.

"The little white ones with the pink centers are spring beauties and the drooping yellow ones are glacier lilies. I remember that from my first summer here 10 years ago."

Two miles in, they pass through a 40-foot-wide draw, lush and dotted with boulders. The sheer 25-foot wall had been cut by a river that no longer exists.

"Do you think there are bears out here?" Clarence asks.

"I don't know. I was asking Ross, and he said there was one spotted at Cottonwood Creek. And one of the cocktail waitresses said Cottonwood Creek was down in the Tetons. So I don't know."

Somehow there is a natural, pleasant comradeship between these two men. They pass 300 yards from a large herd of elk still waiting for the snow to melt off the Buffalo Plateau before moving up for the summer. They pause at the top of a small rise to look off to the left, admiring the rugged scenery, where the river has cut a canyon carrying the ancient Yellowstone through to the north entrance and on to the Missouri. It's wide open here, affording a huge panorama of yellow-green grass for miles. They walk in silence for awhile; there is no sound but the creak of backpack straps stretching with the rhythm of their footsteps. Their presence at a marshy pond sets three wild geese into a squawking flight before they turn up the trail running along Hellroaring Creek.

"How are your Hush Puppies holding out?" Cecil asks.

"Oh, they're doing just fine," Clarence sings. "A little muddy. It'll come off."

By 6 o'clock, they arrive at their campsite. They lean their packs against the fallen log on the far side of the fire ring, then stretch their backs and shrug away the stiffness. After downing several handfuls of M&Ms each, they walk the 50 yards to the rushing river.

"Do we have a canteen?" Clarence asks.

"No. There's a cup in the mess kit, though."

"I'll just do it pioneer style," Clarence says, lying on his stomach and taking a sip from the rushing stream.

Clarence sets up the tent while Cecil gathers firewood. Just as Cecil marches out of sight, Clarence discovers that the new tent is accompanied with one large coil of string and directions for cutting it into various lengths. Clarence looks over the directions and decides it won't be hard. They've still got two hours before dark, he figures. But then he realizes he has no knife. Or for that matter, a fork or spoon for eating. He grabs Cecil's pack, opens it, and takes out the little bread and butter knife. It will suffice, he thinks, as running his thumb across its slightly serrated edge. As he starts to saw through the nylon cord, he reflects on the walk down. It felt good to sing again. That's what has been bothering me, he decides. I miss singing! I miss the theater!

"I need an audience!" he says to the tent cord. The bar is almost like a stage, he thinks. Perhaps I *can* get a talent night and be the emcee or something. I know where my heart is.

He sings, "New York, New York. . . . It's a wonderful town. . ."

"What do ya say we have a drink?" Clarence suggests, as Cecil returns with an armload of wood.

"Sounds good to me," Cecil says, as he walks off in search of more wood.

Clarence walks back to the creek and half-fills the cooking pot with water. To this, he adds a quarter bottle of rum and half a packet of pineapple Kool-Aid. He stirs it with the butter knife.

Cecil returns dragging a large log and drops it with the other wood.

"Try this," Clarence says, lifting the pot and offering it to Cecil.

"You know, I feel so good being out here that I don't think I will drink."

"Don't think you'll drink! Here I lugged this big bottle all the way down here. I'm the one who's trying to stop drinking and came out here to celebrate our first expedition together. You've got to join me."

"OK. I'll have a few sips."

"Good enough. That's a start."

Cecil takes a sip and then heads out for another load of wood. Clarence intermittently drinks from the pot of liquid and continues the tedious repetition of cutting through the nylon rope with a butter knife; shoulder to wrist for three feet, bottom of foot to crotch for four feet, and almost as wide as he can reach for the five-foot lengths.

An hour later, it's nearly dark. Cecil is so involved with his firewood forays that his accumulated pile looks like a small fort. Clarence has sung songs or recited lines from most of the important plays of the last four centuries, and he has the cords cut and strung out at his feet. Now he starts to tie the cords to the tent.

"Mr. Dolen, sir, would you like to build the fire?"

"I would be honored, Mr. Harps."

"Would you care for another sip of the piña?"

"A sip, sir," Cecil responds. He takes a tiny sip from the pot and knows that liquor is not what he needs. I need clarity of thought for awhile, he thinks. Control. I need to be able to focus. To keep my concentration. To breathe.

Cecil knows the old trick. He's done it before. He pretends to take a sip when it's offered to him and thrusts it back while wiping his mouth with the back of his hand.

"This wood is pretty damp," Cecil says. "Do we have any tissue or paper of any kind?"

"Hmmm. Only the Irwin Shaw novel. Take the middle out and burn it."

"Won't that ruin the story?"

"I've read his stuff before," Clarence says. "It shouldn't make any difference."

It takes 25 minutes and 230 pages, but Cecil eventually has a little blaze going. They rub their hands over the fire, then do a slow 360-degree turn to ward of the settling cold and damp. Clarence slowly weaves his way to the river for another pot of water.

"I think I'll start the beef stew," Cecil calls. "I'm starving."

As Clarence gets back, the darkness is almost complete.

"I think there's something going on in the river. Someone's moving the boulders."

"I need a can opener. Did you bring one by any chance?"

"I didn't. We've got this great butter knife, though. Isn't this great rum?"

"Yes, it is. How 'bout a few cheese and crackers and salami for appetizers while I figure out how to get the can opened?"

"Not for me. That's how you lose a great buzz. "

"Did we bring a flashlight?" Cecil asks.

"I didn't."

"I'll have to find a sharp rock." Cecil puts another log on the fire as he heads off in the darkness toward the river.

"Look out. There's a big river over there," Clarence shouts. "Waist deep in the big muddy. . . ."

Ten minutes later, Clarence has all the cords tied on the tent. Cecil's work with a sharp rock proves fruitless, as does trying to use the knife like a pick axe.

"So do you think I'm doing a good job managing the bar?" Clarence asks.

"I do. I think you're easygoing enough to where the barts and the cocktail waitresses don't feel pressure. I think you should be a little more forceful with George, though."

"But he's been here four years."

"He's too impatient with the cocktail waitresses, and he doesn't like to clean up."

"I haven't had to fire anyone yet. Here, let me practice. You're fired!" Clarence's big voice echoes off the rocks and trees around them.

"That would scare him," Cecil says.

"Scare! Hey, listen to this."

Clarence stands up and leans over the fire so that black shadows cover all but the highpoints of his face. "Mark me. . . . Say 'I will.'"

"I will."

"My hour is almost come, when I to sulfurous and tormenting flames must render up myself. Say 'Alas poor ghost!'"

"Alas poor ghost!"

"Pity me not, but lend thy serious hearing to what I shall enfold. I am thy father's spirit, doomed for a certain term to walk the night."

Clarence steps back from the fire. "How'd you like it?"

"I liked it. I liked the way you did it. I wish I could get this can opened."

"Here, put the can on this flat rock and I'll hold it. Then hit the hell out of it with the sharp end of that rock. Team work, Mr. Dolen. We'll get it."

From his knees, Cecil comes down hard with the rock, denting the can and puncturing it enough to produce a half-inch puddle of stew at the opening.

"We almost got it," says Clarence. "Hit it again."

Cecil raises the rock high above him and brings it down with all his might. With a dull rip, the can explodes, and the beef stew sprays in every direction.

"Damn it!" Cecil scowls.

"Cecil, I think I'm going to give the theater another chance after this summer."

"We just lost half our dinner on the ground."

"That's OK. There's more rum we've got to finish because I'm going to stop drinking after this."

"Damn," says Cecil as he dumps the remaining stew into the mess-kit pan, along with the chunks of potatoes and beef he picks from his clothing. As he nestles it into a corner of the fire, Clarence goes about setting up the tent and, after a few minutes, gets his foot caught in the tangled cords and falls.

"Damn backdrop," he says, spitting out the dirt.

Twenty minutes later, Clarence discards the pineapple Kool-Aid and water and takes a gurgle of the rum straight out of the bottle.

When the stew is finally ready, Clarence only scoops out half of a green cupful. "We spilled my half," he says. "I'll just have a little more of this rum juice here. Please join me?"

Cecil fakes a sip. He thinks he might not drink for awhile. He enjoys the solid feeling of being out in the woods. He feels calm, in control. He sets his dinner aside and rubs his hands firmly together. He takes some dirt and rubs it into his hands, then wipes them off on his jeans. It feels good to him. He likes the underside of the tree branches reflecting the orange flicker of the fire that he made. He wishes he could stay there longer—weeks, maybe months.

"I'm drunk, Cecil. Look, here's my imitation of Dustin Hoffman in *Salesman:* 'I'm scared, Sonny.'"

During the next hour, Clarence manages to get the tent set up but falls down heavily twice in the process. Cecil has built the fire up to three-feet-high flames when Clarence thickly announces, "Lishun, you make a pretty good drink, bartender, but I'm afraid I'm going to have to crawl into bed now. May I have my room key?"

Clarence scoops up the cheese and salami and is numbly chewing off bites of it as he kneels by the edge of the tent. He rolls out his sleeping bag, then sits to take off his Hush Puppies. He stuffs the remaining cheese and salami into his dry shoe, pointing unevenly at it and making a mental note of it in case he wakes up hungry. Within the next 20 seconds, he crawls inside his sleeping bag and is asleep. The bottle, Cecil notices, is empty.

The fire now has extended over the edges of the fire ring and is a huge blaze. Except for its crackle, the air becomes very quiet around Cecil. He stares into the fire and thinks. He opens the doors of his mind, permitting the salient questions in.

Can there be any forgiveness for the things I've done? Can anyone forgive me? Can I have a new start? Could I explain how this happened? It all began when I was so young. I just got a little bit off the track and kept diverging. Can I bring it back to the right track? Then prom night. . . and that first. . . .

He takes a long, deep breath, and pokes at the fire with a stick, pushing the biggest log over the hot part of the flame.

He looks over at the large, still form of Clarence.

Sweating now, Cecil fights a sudden urge to hurl himself into the raging, inky river. Instead, he turns from it and looks in the direction of the hill, dimly flickering now from the large flames. He concentrates on the trees until his thoughts dissolve back to the present. An hour later, the wood is all gone and the flames have receded to glowing coals. He lays out his new sleeping bag in the tent next to Clarence, zips the tent behind him and falls into a dream-filled sleep.

The animal is like a huge mole in that it is a furry mammal, has claws for scratching and digging, and is more active nocturnally than in daylight. It has limited eyesight but an incredibly keen sense of smell. From a mile away, the bear picks up the scent of meat, and it is an easy scent to follow. He also picks up a distasteful sour smell, the scent of man, something his instincts tell him to beware of. He hesitates, but his hunger is stronger than his fear and he trots on, the smell of food looming ever larger in that keen nose. He follows the scent unerringly. Soon the food is very near. The 400-pound black bear raises up on his haunches, and his flared nostrils take in many different aromas.

He works his way to the burnt smell and laps up the delectable chunks of the spilled beef stew. His courage piqued now, he moves closer to the sour smell only a few feet away. He finds a shoe stuffed with meat but reeking of man. He rips the shoe apart and is rewarded with rich tastes he has never before experienced. The sudden sound of a snore coming from the tent startles but does not discourage him. He rummages through the packs, ripping, pulling, biting and chewing at the delicious feast—apples, M&Ms, beer nuts. He falls back into a sitting position and eats at his leisure. Then he makes one final search, lapping up remains before a loud groan from someplace inside a dream awakens instinctual fears in the bear and he bounds away into the night.

Clarence is the first to wake. From in his sleeping bag, he appears to be a huge brown walrus, limbless, preparing to waddle down and slip into the water that is more his element.

"Hey, Cecil, it's raining outside and I'm starting to get wet. . . . Hey, Cec, are you awake?"

"Funny thing. I guess I am."

They both sit up. When they unzip the tent and look out, neither of them says anything. They look out over the carnage that is their campsite, HG2.

Finally, Clarence speaks. "What the hell happened here?" He reaches out and holds up his shredded shoe. "Did you go into a food frenzy or something?"

They look at each other and speak in unison: "Bear." They lean out of the tent and slowly peer around their campsite looking for a sign of the animal.

"I can't believe one of us didn't wake up," Cecil says.

"I'm glad I didn't," Clarence adds, trying to fasten his shredded left shoe to the bottom of his foot. "I had a dream I was doing *Terranova*. I think I'd rather *be* in Antarctica."

Eventually, they get up and walk around the camp, looking at the damage and locating bear prints.

"What do you say we leave everything and make a quick getaway to the car?" Clarence suggests.

"I can't let you do that. You've got almost $200 worth of camping stuff here."

"I've got a headache and I'm really hungry," Clarence moans, locating the one pouch of the instant oatmeal that the bear missed. He walks to the river, dips out a pot of cold water and stirs in the dry cereal from the packet.

"Care for some nice, hot oatmeal?"

"No, thanks."

Cecil throws most of the larger pieces of debris into his pack while Clarence jerks the tent with the stakes still attached straight out of the ground and stuffs it into his pack. Fifteen minutes later, they are ready to hit the trail.

"I'm wet and hungry and cold and miserable," Clarence complains.

"What play is that from?" chides Cecil, cold himself, but still pleased.

Clarence has only a thin jacket on over a sweater and, as they hike, he quickly becomes drenched. His left shoe dangles from his foot and his thin red hair falls into his face. What seems like a hundred years later, they stop and tie Cecil's belt around Clarence's foot to hold on the shoe. A half mile later, he kicks it off into the sagebrush and walks in his sock. Out on the flats, the wind blows the rain in sheets.

Cecil's wool jacket keeps him somewhat dry on top, but his head, pants and tennis shoes are soaked. He makes up his mind to be better prepared in the future. He can't wait to tell Kris about the bear when he gets back.

For a while, the two men walk with only the sound of the raindrops. Blinking the water from his eyes, Clarence conjures visions of hot soup, coffee, chili, and a steamy bath. After the suspension bridge, the return trail becomes a steep incline. Two hours into the hike, Cecil notices that Clarence no longer has his pack.

"Where's your pack?"

"I'll get it on my next day off. Everything's soaking wet so it's really heavy. I'm getting blisters on my left foot and my back is killing me. And I'll never complain about being too hot again as long as I live."

"Well, I'm glad you came. I'm having a good time, if you can believe that. I'm wet but I'm warm. You *are* going to do more backpacking trips with me, aren't you?"

"Not even for the romantic lead role in a long running Broadway musical."

May 30. Old Faithful Inn, lobby.

Slim Grandstrom escorts Lucy and Adele to the controller's office, as is the rule and custom when they turn in their cash and deposits from the early gift-shop shift.

"Our sales were up 8 percent over the last year for the week before Memorial Day, and I think we are busier than we were last year at this time. Look at all these people."

It is sudden, unexpected. There is a cold, piercing yell, and Slim and Lucy turn to see Adele collapse face forward onto the lobby floor.

"Adele!" Lucy screeches, breaking the drone of the crowded lobby.

Slim and Lucy kneel down to see Adele's face contorted in pain. She gasps once and clutches her chest over the left side. Slim slowly turns her over. Her breathing is constricted. There is a loud murmur, then silence, as people crowd around and stare.

"Lucy, go call 1-911. Here's the keys to the office. Get the first-aid kit. Lucy! Here, take the money."

Already Adele's face is ashen white from lack of oxygen. Slim puts his suit coat under her head and undoes several of the snaps of her uniform shirt, hoping that she will be able to breathe.

"Is their a doctor?" he yells. "Brian!" he shouts to the bellman, "go the front desk and see if we have a doctor registered here. Hurry! Folks, please move back."

Within seconds, Faysal is on the scene. He feels no pulse and hears no breathing. He tilts her head back, and he and Slim start CPR. Minutes later, two rangers come charging through the back door with oxygen, a huge medical kit and a stretcher. But Adele Petersen has no use for these things. She is beyond them.

Jim Petersen is in the lodge cabins when someone is able to reach him. He races to the Inn in the old yellow truck. They are just carrying his wife to the green Park Service ambulance when he rushes up and throws himself at the stretcher, refusing to believe what he sees. The rangers stop, feeling lost, out of place, as the woman's husband breaks down in tears, clutching the lifeless figure beneath the blanket.

June 2.

The West Yellowstone air service gives its condolences and offers to drop Adele's ashes over Mount Washburn, where Jim and Adele met 40 years before. There is a quiet ceremony in the Lodge hall, where 152 people gather to offer sympathies. Lucy and Angel, Adele's best friends, and Jim and Adele's two daughters, who had flown in, sob quietly. Later, the urn is taken aboard a Cessna airplane that also carries Jim and his two daughters. They quickly rise above the landscape and head northeast. Fittingly, the day is like it was when Jim and Adele met nearly 40 years ago—a perfect, sunny day. Jim sees the trail and even the exact point on Mount Washburn where she asked him, a perfect stranger, if he knew what kind of flower the tall red one was. And what a flower she was that day! They walked up to the summit of the 10,243-foot mountain together, and she still looked as bright and fresh as one of the radiant lupines growing next to the trail. He could hardly take his eyes off her as they descended the mountain, she collecting her bouquet of mountain wildflowers, and he falling in love before they got back to his car at Dunraven Pass. He knew then that she would be his bride.

Over the roar of the airplane's engines, Jim lets the ashes fall to earth. "She loved the simple things and made a wonderful wife," he says. "May these ashes enrich the soil to grow trees and flowers that are as beautiful and rich in life as was the life of Adele Salmela Petersen."

June 14.

"I liked your new poem," says Kitty. "Very nice, Wilbur." She kisses him on the cheek. "Oh, great, here comes Steve and Salina. Wilbur, did you put the brown sheet over it?"

"Yup."

"You got the sword?"

"Yup."

"Mout?"

"Yup yup yup."

Steve and Salina peer in the shell of Wilbur's Datsun camper at the bulky object covered with a sheet.

"I can't believe we're doing this," Salina says.

"The meeting of the Mouton Cadet Sunset Society now comes to order!" says Wilbur, walking out of Kitty's cabin. "Oh, hey, I brought some bicycle water bottles that just about hold a full bottle of Mout. Here, fill them up and just pull the nipple out like this and squirt.

Here's a bottle for your car. You have a corkscrew, don't you Steve?"

"No, hey, I'm the treasurer."

"I've got one though," Salina sings. "A secretary's got to remember."

Steve and Salina, in Steve's white Toyota truck, follow Wilbur and Kitty out of the Old Faithful area north onto the Grand Loop Road. Five and a half miles later, Kitty spots a landmark. "There it is! Turn left."

They turn down an old service road. A bumpy quarter mile later, Kitty tells Wilbur to stop behind a hill so that they and the vehicles are out of sight. Salina and Steve pull up behind them.

Kitty and Steve hold their water bottles high and take sips of the crisp white wine, then hand them to Wilbur and Salina.

"To Adele," Kitty says. "What we are about to do I dedicate to her. Adele was a very serious practical joker as well." Kitty takes a sip and reminisces. "Once, we planned this out, about five years ago when it was busy in the gift shop I got in line in front of this Yankee woman. When it came my turn at the register, I said, 'Yes, it's my father's birthday tomorrow and I'd like to arrange to have the geyser go off right at midnight. Is that possible?' Adele said, 'Yes, it is. Would you like a long, medium or short eruption?' I said 'Medium. Would there be an extra charge for lights?' Adele said, 'That would be $8 extra.'

"The lady next to me in line was in shock. I could hear her gasping. Adele and I could hardly keep straight faces, even though we had rehearsed. Then I asked, 'And how much would it be to have a bear run behind the geyser at the same time?'

"Then the lady next to me yelled for her husband. 'Henry, Henry, come here!'

"Adele said 'that would be $20 extra to have a bear run through.'

"'That would be a little extravagant to have a bear. I would just the like the eruption.' I said.

"I paid Adele $30, got a receipt, and had to bite down on my cheeks so hard I actually came to tears. I looked back and heard Adele say to the lady who was standing next to me 'Can I help you?' in a complete deadpan expression. God bless, Adele."

"She was right in front of the T&I desk when it happened," Salina says. "Poor thing. I felt so helpless. The next day, I was talking to Angel, and she said if YP Con wasn't so cheap, they would have a doctor here on staff. She said there were many times over the years they needed one."

"I think she feels guilty because about a week before it happened, she found Adele sitting on the floor in the hallway," Kitty says. "She thinks she might have had a slight heart attack then and Angel feels guilty that she didn't tell Jim or make Adele go see a doctor."

"For Adele," says Salina.

"On with it," says Kitty.

They slip the brown sheet off the grizzly bear suit, pull it out and Steve starts to wiggle into it.

"Where did you say you got this?" Salina asks.

"It's been in the Inn attic for years. I've just been waiting for the right moment to try to do this."

"Everyone remember their parts?"

"Yes, Mr. President," Steve says, "Let's do it. It's getting hot in here."

"I'm nervous," says Salina.

"Take a sip of this," says Wilbur, handing Salina one of the squirt bottles. "Anti-nerve juice."

Wilbur and Salina turn the Toyota around and head back to the Grand Loop Road. They wait until there are no cars coming from their left as far as they can see, then they make a right. They get to a point directly opposite Kitty and Steve, then they drive another 50 yards and stop.

"Perfect," Wilbur says. "Look behind us."

The first vehicle coming from behind them is a Winnebago camper. Wilbur and Salina jump out of the truck and start gesturing and pointing excitedly through the woods in the direction of the *bear*. The Winnebago rolls to a stop, and a lady rolls down the window.

"What do you see?"

"Bear. Big grizzly bear. Off in the woods about a hundred yards."

"I see him! Honey, stop! I knew we'd see one."

The husband angles the camper off into the ditch and follows his wife out the side door. The car behind them stops.

A car from the other direction stops. Two cars, three cars, motorcycles, campers, 10, 20, 50 vehicles stop and the people are streaming out. There are vehicles all over the road, stopped in the middle, in the ditches. One by one, the tourists tiptoe through the woods, each trying to get a little closer with their cameras, many with their kids in tow.

The *bear* appears from behind the hill, pawing at the air, half raising on its haunches.

Wilbur and Salina laugh, snap pictures, watch and point.

"Watch out. It may be the man-eater the ranger told us about," a man in lime-green trousers says.

"That was in Glacier Park, daddy."

The *bear* stands up on his haunches and walks forward three steps.

"Let me see the binoculars, honey. There's something funny about that bear."

"Uh oh, Salina. Are you ready for act two?"

"Yea, what the hell," Salina answers. She takes a deep breath and runs toward the bear, screaming in a thick Scandinavian accent, "Oh, look at the little thing. It is so cuddly, so varm and cute. I just vant to squeeze it!"

"Hey lady, no!"

"Hey don't!"

"Look out! Those things are dangerous!"

"Don't get so close!"

Salina runs to the bear, which falls down toward her just as she approaches. She thrusts her padded forearm into the bear's snarling mouth and screams. She clutches the back of its neck and is dragged back, kicking and fighting, over and behind the little hill.

"Don't vorry! I'll save you!" Wilbur shouts, charging toward the hill with a huge sword. "I'm coming, darling!"

Wilbur charges past the wide-eyed tourists, who shrink away in horror.

There are more roars and screams as Wilbur runs and dives over the hill.

"Keep screaming, you guys," Wilbur whispers. "Roooooaaar!"

During the screams, shouts, and animal roars, Steve, soaked in perspiration, wiggles out of the suit and stuffs it into Wilbur's truck while Wilbur grabs a stuffed bear's head from the front seat.

"You forgot to take it off the mount!" Wilbur whispers intensely to Kitty.

"I couldn't get it off the mount. It'll be OK. Hold it in your arms like a football. There. Now, here comes the food coloring. I hope you didn't need this shirt because this red isn't ever going to come out of it."

"Put a little on Salina's arm, Kitty. Good. Some on the sword. Great. Last big yell. One. . . two. . . three."

"Ahhhh!"

"Groooowwwlll! Roooaaarrr!"

"Aaayyyeee!"

"OK, go!" Wilbur yells.

Salina and Wilbur, brandishing a bloody sword, reappear over the hill, sprinting wildly toward the white Toyota.

"Aaahhh! He's got the bear's head in his hands!" one lady screams.

"Ooohhh! Look at the blood!"

"Run like hell!" Wilbur shouts. "There's more coming!"

Some 300 tourists make like scurrying pocket gophers in a frenzied dash back to their cars and campers. In the madness, many of them leave behind their tripods and cameras. They scoop up their children and thrust them into the closest vehicle. Within six seconds, no one remains outside any of the vehicles.

"I thought the girl was a goner," one tourist says to the nine other strangers seeking sanctuary in someone's camper.

"The young man had the bear's head!" says a lady. "I don't feel well, Dan."

Five minutes later, the rangers arrive. With 20 people talking at once, they get various stories. They are suspicious of every version but, nevertheless, six of them go armed with guns and rifles to check out the other side of the hill where they find nothing but tire tracks and a Mouton Cadet label.

Cabin 414.

Just after 9 p.m., Herm, the baby-faced night security guard, knocks on Kitty Karner's cabin door. A party, he thinks. He knocks louder and someone turns the music down.

Kitty opens the door. "Hi, Herm. Come on in. What's up?"

Herm enters the warm cabin and is surprised to find only four people inside.

"I've been getting some complaints about the noise coming from this cabin." He looks about him. "Is this one of those Mouton Cadet meetings I've heard about?"

Wilbur and Steve share the night shift with Herm, and he already knows about the Mouton Cadet Society. In fact, he already has been invited to a special Sunrise Chapter meeting.

"It is," says Wilbur. "Roll call! Kitty Complete!"

"Here Wilbur."

"Steve Mercury!"

"Here!"

"Salina Vanilla?"

"Here!"

"Mr. President?"

"Mr. President?"

Wilbur steps over and answers himself. "Here! I propose that we open more wine!"

Following the sound of a cork popping from a fresh bottle, Kitty pours a glass for Herm.

"I'm afraid I'm on the clock." His face gets that wide, pink grin. "So I'll only have one quick glass."

"To security!" they all toast.

Herm takes a sip, and then straightens himself up. "I see what you are all trying to do. You're trying to make me forget the real reason I came over here. Now, would you folks happen to know anything about an incident about four hours ago that happened up on the Grand Loop Road between here and Midway Geyser Basin? An incident—now don't start shaking your heads no and giving me that wide-eyed innocence. Especially you, Kitty. I've known you too long. An incident, as I was saying, involving a disappearing grizzly bear running around without a head and a Swedish couple with a blood-ied sword and the severed head in question?"

"A grizzly bear?"

"Without a head?"

"That doesn't sound like anything I've seen," said Kitty.

"Not us," Wilbur adds, innocently.

Herm stalks across the cabin like a trial lawyer, then turns and thrusts out a finger. "An incident, had it been a practical joke perpetrated by the owner or owners of one or possibly two small-sized pickup trucks similar if not exactly like the ones that are parked outside?"

"Ahh, hmm. Herm, the MCSS was formed for the enjoyment of life," Steve says. "That doesn't sound like anything we would do."

"Herm," Kitty purrs. "I'm a supervisor. You know I wouldn't do anything like that. It would jeopardize my credibility."

His voice gets thinner and higher, reaching toward soprano. "A bear, had it been a real bear, having approximately the same size paws as the one I saw with my flashlight sticking out from underneath a brown sheet in the back of a small pickup truck parked just outside of the cabin in which I now stand?"

There is a pregnant pause, during which the four Mouton members dart quick glances at each other, hoping someone will take the lead and fall on the live mine.

"Have some more wine, Herm," Wilbur offers.

"No thanks, Wilbur. There's only one way that I can think of to leave this, shall we say, coincidental information, out of my nightly report."

"How?" the four ask in unison.

"Initiate me into the Mouton Cadet Sunset Society."

"Touch a buffalo and you're in," Wilbur says.

"I touched one last summer that I helped the Park Service knock out."

"Close enough. You're in. Any nays?"

"I would also like to nominate Shannon Everitt, Herm's friend from the warehouse." says Steve. "The guy's hysterical and he's small so he can get into and out of a lot of tight squeezes."

"Like the one you just got out of," says Herm. "A toast then!"

"For the enjoyment of life," says Wilbur.

"For the enjoyment of life!" they all shout.

June 8. Cabin 248.

"Hey, you're back!" Wilbur says, laying down his book as his roommate comes through the door. "How was the race? Did you win?"

"No. That's the hardest five-and-a-half mile race in the world."

"It was up the mountain pass, right?"

"Teton Pass is a 10- to 11-percent grade! That's unheard of. It was that steep almost the whole way and we ran up it! I feel all right now, but I'm sure glad I have the night off. I almost passed out up there. I was weaving. I could feel my eyeballs rolling back in my head. I didn't know where I was. I feel as weak as a little kitten now. Can I still stay in the Society if I drink a beer?"

"I think so. Tell me about the race."

Steve pulls a six-pack out of a brown paper bag, pops the tab on one, then collapses backward on his bed.

"We started out and some guy with the longest legs I've ever seen took off in front, so I decided to keep up with him. Lasted for about a mile then the road got really steep and I lost him. I don't think he even slowed down. But I stayed in second. I wanted to run fast, but I was barely moving. My legs started getting really heavy."

"So you finished second?"

"Some other guy caught me in the last hundred yards. Some local."

"How'd Salina do?"

"Fifth woman. I don't think she enjoyed it very much. She

sneered at me when she crossed the finish line. We're both sore. But it sure did feel good to race again."

June 21.

Steve and Wilbur are in Wilbur's truck driving down to Jackson, Wyoming, in search of a track.

"Wilbur, I'm going to go crazy if I don't find a track," Steve had said. "I've got to run fast against a measured distance. I want to know where I'm at for that Fourth of July 10k."

So when the girls planned a night for themselves, Steve lured Wilbur by offering to buy dinner if he drove to Jackson with him and yelled out splits as he ran around the track.

Wilbur already misses being away from Kitty, for their relationship has been passionate and intense. It is a love shared equally, openly, without jealousy or fear of losing. She makes every day new and different for him.

Wilbur rolls down the window and takes a deep breath. He feels strong, balanced.

Although Steve's relationship with Salina has not been as intense as Wilbur's with Kitty, it is full of much happiness and laughter, the best moments occurring on their runs through the backcountry.

Though both men are on their own tonight, they cannot help thinking of their women.

Steve is in the passenger seat, bending forward from the waist, trying to stretch his tight hamstrings.

"Now tell me, who is going to be there for this women's-night-out dinner?"

"Kitty, Salina, Imre, Yvonne, and Kris, a waitress in the dining room. Do you know her?"

"Well, yea, that's Salina's roommate. You know her. That's the real pretty girl with the real blond hair?"

"Oh, yea. She *is* pretty. You know Herm's got a crush on her? He's been flirting with her, and he told me he's going to ask her out," Wilbur says.

"He probably won't have much luck. Her boyfriend is a hot quarterback. Passed for something like 3,000 yards last year. His picture is all over her side of the room. She's even got a picture of him from *Sports Illustrated* on the wall. She told Salina they were going to be faithful to one another this summer and maybe be married next year."

"Well, I'd give anything to be invisible and sit next to that table and hear the conversation tonight. Kitty promised to tell me if Imre laughs or smiles."

Dude Restaurant, West Yellowstone.

"What should we talk about?" Kitty asks, sitting at the head of the table.

"Men!" Imre and Yvonne respond in unison.

The waitress comes to take their order. 'Spare no expense' is their motto for the evening. They decide to order different dishes and share. Kitty orders a T-bone steak, Yvonne a prime rib, Imre king crab, Kris the salmon, and Salina, undecided, finally settles on surf and turf—lobster and steak.

"Listen," Yvonne says, "Imre and I think Kitty and Salina should pick up the tab tonight. Wilbur and Steve are in our department and we had them first. You guys stole them away from us."

"At least you control them at night!" laughs Kitty.

While eating her salad Kitty's thoughts drift away. "Anyway, now I've got to make up my mind again whether I want to live alone or with someone. And if I want to live with someone, why not Wilbur?" was how I was going to finish that statement, ladies.

With Wilbur, Kitty has felt a rebirth of sexuality that now, at 28, still is not yet at its peak. She feels her 30s will be her best decade: She will be more confident of herself and more able to meet big challenges. She thinks that this will be her last summer working in the park and that she will take an executive housekeeper's position somewhere else and establish a career, perhaps getting into upper-level management. Could Wilbur fit into that plan?

Kitty thinks of how, at 16 years old, she made a promise to herself not to get trapped in a life like her mother's, where she was constantly occupied with the business of raising six children. No, I don't want a life like mom's, she thinks. Yet I feel this craving to bear children now. Will it be too late when I decide that children are what I want? What if I play around until it's too late? But maybe I like this freedom. Maybe I do want to live life alone. If I had a career, Wilbur and children, would I be happy? I've always craved my independence. Demanded it, in fact. But the Petersens, they were in love right up to the end. And the Kristoffs too. And since my brother moved to Atlanta to play in a band my parents are alone, but at least they have each other. I just want someone to look at all the pictures of things of a life gone by and know their significance. Someone to help believe it was all worth it.

Kitty suddenly becomes aware of the silence at the table. She wants this to be a happy night. "What do you want out of this summer, Yvonne?"

"Hell, I just want to get laid."

They all laugh. But, inside, Yvonne knows that probably will not happen this summer, or next. She forces her gaze away from the dessert tray and hopes she will not let herself order two of them.

The waitress refills her water.

Yet I could do so much for a man, so much, she thinks. A little affection, and I would dedicate every inch of my being to him, make him feel like a king. What is sex like?. . . . If I could isolate myself from the rest of the world, then I could lose weight, have a chance. But then that's why I'm here in Yellowstone. To get away from Pittsburgh where a good day was being able to snack all day, then have a hot sandwich during Dave Letterman. Then why did you buy a box of Devil's Food Cookies today? Yes. Why? So I could come to dinner with these pretty women, try to eat less than any of them so they would all think that I'm trying. Right. Eat daintily. And spend the rest of the night unfulfilled, thinking about those cookies so hard no one can even talk to me. I'll devour the cookies, a couple of sodas, and feel sick in the morning. Then it gets back to suicide. No, not tonight.

"I'm going to buy myself a pair of pink tights and take that aerobics class in the rec hall."

"Good for you," says Kitty. The encouragement surprises Yvonne, though. She was going for a laugh.

The busboy takes the salad plates away.

"I need to start doing some stretching or exercising," Kris adds. "But I'm always so tired from waiting tables I just don't have the energy."

Imre sees an opening, a chance to satisfy her curiosity.

"So we understand you have a boyfriend back in Florida, Kris."

Kris starts to answer, but the waitress sets the first plates of food down. Then Kitty asks the waitress to open the two bottles of wine she and Salina brought with them.

"Yes," Salina answers for her. "You should see this guy. She's got pictures of him in our room. Kris, I'm sorry. I'm not embarrassing you, am I?"

Kris shakes her wispy blond head. "No, it's OK. I like hearing about him."

Kittly leans forward to Kris. "Kris, if the busboy doesn't stop staring at you, you have my permission to stab him with your fork."

"I keep telling her to get him to come out here," Salina continues. "I mean, this guy is centerfold material, girls, and the quarterback of the team—the whole nine yards. Besides that, he's got a nice smile. When Kris first moved in, she told me she wasn't going to date, and I thought that was nuts. But when I saw her boyfriend, I realized it was worth it."

"At least he could come here for my days off," Kris smiles. She takes a bite of the tender salmon. It's good, but perhaps not what she wanted after all. Just like she is not sure what she wants out of this summer. She feels empty, detached from the other four women.

She wishes she could tell the others the truth—that even though she is sure she is in love with John he is the only guy she has ever gone to bed with and she is just not sure if she wants *not* to see anybody else.

What am I doing, she thinks. I'm just 21. Am I ready to be a bride and a wife? Kris Richards, you'd better be sure about this. Is John a good lover? I am so programmed to saying no all the time. Cecil wants me to go camping with him. It would be nice if he could be just a friend. I could use that. He's pretty easygoing. Or that security guy, Herm. He's pretty nice, and he's older. Maybe he would make love to me once or twice without any commitment. I could ask him outright.

She giggles aloud and puts her hand over her face.

"What's so funny, Kris?" Salina asks.

"I was thinking about Herm. The security guy."

"Herm," Imre groans. "Watch for him. He'll try a hundred different ways to charm you. He's so cheap, though, that he'll never ask anyone out on a real date. He loses his money playing poker instead."

"Hey, this is good wine," says Yvonne. "What kind is it?"

"It's a white wine, Yvonne."

"I know that, Imre. I can see that. I only had two or three cocktails."

"It's Mouton Cadet," says Salina. "French."

"Speaking of French, are we all going over to the Stagecoach after this?" Yvonne asks.

"I'm up for it," Kitty says.

"Sure," Salina seconds.

"What does that have to do with French?" Imre asks.

"Nothing. But you do want to go, don't you?" say Yvonne.

"I'm ready to dance," says Kitty.

Yes, why not, Imre says to herself. I know what it will be like. I've known Kitty for what, five summers now? Kitty will dance every dance, even if she has to dance by herself or ask a man. She'll get the others to dance too. She doesn't have to deal with the kind of assholes I get. Always coming at me with some phony line. Always trying to give me that 'you've got beautiful hair' line. Kitty has everything. Me? Nothing.

So I've put five of the best years of my life into this company and what have I got to show for it? Money? Sure, $7,500. All this money and nowhere to go. I'll probably stay winter season again. Probably get old and die here like Adele.

"Yvonne, lighter."

And I've got this great tobacco habit that I didn't have my first summer. So I drink a little too much, and so what that I get angry at my staff. But look at the imbeciles they send me year after year. These people don't even know how to count! Steve and Wilbur are getting better, but to make Mammoth happy, we've got to be perfect! Yes, sure Kitty. I'll go to the Stagecoach. I'll even have a drink. But I'm not going to dance and act like a fool. I'm not going to pretend. Not with the kind of men that go to places like that.

"Aren't you going to finish your crab, Imre?"

"No, Yvonne. You want it?"

Yvonne pulls the giant leg apart and forks out the meat. She takes a bite and passes it around, each of them taking a bite of the succulent orange-white meat, dipping it in the hot, drawn butter, melted from the little flame of a candle.

"None for me, thanks," says Kitty. "I'm full."

"Salina, what's Steve up to tonight?" Imre asks.

"He's going down to Jackson with Wilbur. He said if he didn't find a track to run on, he would die."

"I didn't know this running stuff was so important to him. I thought he was going to have a fit when I almost didn't give him weekends off. Did you know he went to Faysal?"

"Well, it is important to him. He thinks he may be able to win money racing if he has a good summer training. Maybe even get a sponsor."

"He told me he averages eight to nine miles a day," Yvonne says. "Does he have any energy left at the end of the day for. . . you know what?"

"Yes, Yvonne. He's so sweet. He told me I was the first real woman

he'd ever been with. I got my new diaphragm. He asked me which
one of us is supposed to wear it."

They giggle, drink their wine and talk. Imre and Yvonne puff on
cigarettes.

The table is cleared by the waitress and the busboy. The process
is interrupted momentarily by a crash, as Kris knocks over her glass
of wine onto the busboy's white shirt.

"Excuse me, I'm so sorry," Kris apologizes.

"Don't worry. It's OK," says the busboy.

"Anyone for dessert or coffee?" the waitress asks.

Kitty furtively watches Yvonne involved with an obvious inner
struggle, so when Kris and Salina decide to share a piece of chocolate
cake, Kitty volunteers to share one with Yvonne.

"And a Grand Marnier, please," Kitty says.

"Oh, yes. B and B for me," adds Salina.

"And Kahlua and vanilla ice cream—without the vanilla ice
cream, just the Kahlua," says Yvonne.

Imre orders coffee, no cream or sugar.

When the cake arrives, Salina stares at it, playing with a bite,
thinking. She had hoped this evening would bring about a different
perspective, different insight on her dilemma. She knows she must
soon make up her mind about whether to go to school fall term.

Do I go to medical school like my father wants, or do I go for a
masters in genetics like I'd prefer, or do I just go off to travel which,
after meeting Kitty, is what I'd really like to do, she thinks. What a
decision. Damn it, I just got away from all that. Kitty never went to
college and look at her—she has poise and confidence, she is
intelligent and has a good, well-paying job. Look at all the places
she's been and things she's seen. I know what doctors go through.
They have to start practicing right after medical school to pay off the
loans. They get married and start having these little tailor-made
vacations like mom and dad—two weeks in Acapulco or Hawaii or
wherever. Dad's put me through four years of college already,
although a track scholarship helped, so I still owe him. Mom's right.
The money I'm making this summer is supposed to help with the
first year of medical school. But I'd give anything to take some time
off and give myself a chance to think this through. Back to Los
Angeles? I can't, I don't think. The Stagecoach? Can't we just go out
into the woods where I don't feel fear when I'm walking alone?

"Great cake," says Yvonne.

"Salina, I'm about to eat your half. Try this." says Kris.

"Ummm, yes. It's good cake. I love it. Just don't want these freckles to turn into zits."

After Yvonne figures out everyone's bill on a pocket calculator, the girls, with full stomachs, proceed from the Dude Restaurant to the Stagecoach Bar. Despite having to coax, almost beg, Imre to dance, they finally all get up and dance to the country-rock band. They dance with the local cowboys, with other employees from the park, with themselves. They dance as hard as they can—wishing their wishes, hoping their hopes, dancing, sweating.

July 4.

Wilbur is sitting by a bend in the Firehole River, naked. He is above the geyser basin, away from the old road that now is a foot and bicycle path. Steve has gone to Jackson for a 10k Independence Day race, so it's a good day to spend alone. He threw his notebook and his shakuhachi in his backpack and peddled his bike away from the hysteria.

He intermittently reworks his poems, plays the flute, and does yoga. From contorted positions, he lets the sun reach parts of his body that usually don't see the light of day.

He reads the poem again.

So this can't be one poem, he thinks. I change the meter, change the accent, even change the rhyme scheme here. My creative-writing instructor would go nuts. Can't you just communicate? Writing is only the heart in conflict with itself, like Faulkner said. Does this work then? Do rules matter? Do I still need to *learn* how to write?

He stretches, plays, and writes.

There. That will show them, he thinks, looking over his work.

Kitty will like the first one. I express what I'm trying to express. Is there anything more important?

He remembers something from the half term of creative writing he sat through before dropping out. His instructor told of a Thomas Pynchon novel, written in the 1970s, that came loose leaf in a box. When you got it home, you threw the entire thing up in the air and whatever order it landed in was the order in which it was read. But he also remembers the instructor likening writing to making cabinets. That learning it was a craft, and no matter how much talent you have inside, you have to have a teacher, a director to guide you, take you along the way, be the writer's mirror, make the cabinet work.

He lies back on his elbows and reads the poems again. What kind of cabinets are these? Would they stand up? Would they open or would they jam?

He watches a blue bird land on a branch over the river, crook its head once, and take off.

From his back, he throws his legs over until his toes touch the earth. Just as a mosquito bites him on the back of his leg, an idea for a story takes seed in his mind. He can see it. The day he went with Steve to Jackson to watch him do a track workout. That lady in the old house behind the track, the lady in the wheelchair who was watching. I haven't been able to get her out of my mind. There's something there. Yes. What's it about?

He sits up and puts one leg over the other, stretching his torso in one direction, then the other. Two things, he remembers his old writing instructor used to say: One, what is the story about? And two, what am I trying to say?

Well, the story is about an old lady in a wheelchair who builds her life around watching a runner. And the piece is about. . . going for it. Trying against adversity, which is what I'll have to do as a writer— strive against. . . .

He jumps up. It comes to him. He remembers reading a short story in one of the running magazines Steve subscribes to. There is a market!

He offers his nakedness to the sun with outstretched arms. He sees the path before him. "I will not be denied!" he shouts to the river.

Cabin 248. 6 p.m..

Steve storms into the cabin, while Wilbur is pounding on the typewriter.

"How'd the race go?"

"I lost."

"What do you mean you lost? You finished last?"

"Just as well."

"To the same guys who beat you in the hill climb?"

"No, I left them behind. I would have won except Paul Pilkington of Athletic's West showed up and ran a 29:46. Beat me by 10 seconds."

Steve opens a bottle of red Mouton Cadet with aggravated, deliberate movements. The jagged outline of salt stains are still crusted on Steve's black shorts, a sign of a determined effort.

"Damn it! I was right with him until the last mile. Then he said,

'Let's go for it,' and just ran away from me. My legs turned to putty. He won a $70 pair of Nikes. I won a stinking T-shirt."

With that, he tosses the yellow T-shirt with the fireworks graphics on the floor and pours red Mouton Cadet over it before Wilbur can object. He takes a huge swallow, then kicks the sopping mass against the trash can, knocking it over and sending apple cores, yogurt containers and other trash all over the floor.

"The hell with it!" he shouts, taking another sip and slamming the bottle down, then spitting the wine into the sink.

He opens the door, grabs the dripping T-shirt and flings it against cabin 249, where it clings momentarily and falls heavily to the pine needles and gravel. He slams the door, flops down face-first on his bed, then leans on his elbows, addressing Wilbur and his pillow: "I'm going to win Pike's Peak," he says with resolute conviction. "I don't care if I die doing it. I will not be an also-ran. Second place is no place!"

"You ran a 29:56. Didn't you say your best time previously at that distance was 30-something?"

"Yea. Nine lousy seconds. I've worked this hard for nine lousy seconds. The world record is under 27 minutes now. The course today and the conditions were perfect. No excuse."

Steve starts to help Wilbur pick up the garbage.

"I've started a story I'm pretty excited about," Wilbur says. "It's about a runner running on a track and an old lady watching him."

"Well, if it's about me, make it about a loser. No! Not a loser, I hate losing, damn it."

July 6. Gift Shop.

Angel is dusting the shelves in the gift shop when she stops to ponder the glass moose. She recently marked it up to $245. Well, my friend, she thinks, we are both feeling a little brittle these days, aren't we? Wish me happy birthday, won't you?

Being in the park hasn't been the same for her this summer, not since her friend Adele died right before her eyes. Angel feels the years and she is unsure whether the pains she feels in her chest are psychological or physiological. She feels the weight of her 64, no 65 years today, and neither Billie, her trailer mate, or the youngsters on her staff make her laugh as they have for the past eight years. This summer, she does not kid or laugh with the children as they reach up to the counter to pay for a miniature bear or a postcard. Now, when the tourists look at her name tag and ask her what part of

California she is from, she knows she can just say 'southern California' with the right tone, and not be considered rude. But she will not avail herself to frivolous conversation.

The stuffed bears and elk that had for so many years brightened her day with their painted smiles now seem cheap, mere litter to end up locked away in a child's toy box, torn and forgotten. The calendars, the Viewmaster pictures and the placemat photographs are mostly from the 50s and 60s, and sarcastically mock her, reminding her of a time when she cared about every little detail of her life, when she had energy, a husband, and children under her wing.

She walks with her duster to the side door, shakes it outside, peers into the beauty shop and thinks, today even Billie has forgotten it's my birthday.

She looks at her hands. They are speckled with age spots. Where did the years go? When will they end? She contemplates pulling down the shelf full of the irritating knickknacks, thinking that it would take all her strength and it would be a last heroic act, etching her place in history. Instead, she just brushes her duster superficially along the edge. She looks at herself in the mirror framed with embroidered scenes of the park. She puts a hand up to a face that seems so much more wrinkled and sad than it did the night she and Billie went out on the town in Reno three short months ago. She starts to reach down for a bear, a runaway that has fallen from the den, but her back, which has acted up of late, shortens the movement. She kicks the bear under the counter.

She looks outside at the geyser basin and wishes that once, just once, for one whole day, that Old Faithful would refuse to go off, and that all the springs would dry up and the Firehole would be barren of water, and that the tourists would leave. She wishes her husband was still alive, and that Adele was alive and standing behind register one.

She looks at the chubby girl who came from Canyon Village to take Adele's place. She watches as the girl hunts for the price tag on a sweatshirt that she must have sold 200 of by now. She notices that the brown polyester pants and brown, checked, Western-cut shirt are too tight on the girl, and she wonders how they look on her. She looks at the people shopping and hopes that the things they buy bring at least some brief happiness or meaning to them, and that they have meaningful lives with happy endings. Happy endings, happy birthday, Angel Ferguson.

Like clockwork, just like any other day, Mildred Blount shows up with her till at 3 o'clock sharp. She looks at the glass moose, noticing that someone had actually picked it up and then placed it precariously close to the edge. She ignores it, forces a smile to the evening crew, and z's out her register.

"How are you today, Angel?"

"Just fine, Mildred. Another busy morning."

In the accounting office, she finds she is $8.38 short, and remembers she had a void, but is indifferent and does not go back to the register to search for it.

"How's business today?" Imre asks. "I heard you guys sold a turquoise necklace for $800."

"Really? No, not me, it must have been in the Indian Shop."

Angel says hello to Faysal on the way out, and looks forward to the 20-minute walk back to her trailer, via Hamilton's Store. Tall, soft clouds roll overhead and the parking lot is typically full and busy. As she passes the east wing, she sees Old Faithful just going off and the hordes of people surrounding it, so she can take her time and still beat the geyser rush to the general store.

At Hamilton's, she buys a large bag of marshmallows to put in her hot chocolate. What the hell, she thinks, it is my birthday.

She eats one while waiting in line, then exchanges greetings with Douglas, the store's grocery manager, who lives with his wife, just three trailer slots down from her and Billie. She passes between the post office and the Snow Lodge and out through the employee cabins where she sees Moe Gelado and Valerie from the Pub, who invite her to play a round of frisbee golf with them.

"I don't think I'd do very well today, Moe."

"Can't play worse than I'm playing today," Moe laughs. "My putting is terrible. Fore!"

She passes the cabin where Ursela, her second-year employee, lives and, on a whim, knocks on her door, thinking she might invite her over for some hot chocolate and maybe some gin rummy, but there is no answer. She walks on, over the little foot bridge that spans Zipper Creek and across the Grand Loop Road so as to take a short section of the Howard Eaton Trail back to her trailer, delaying being alone in the trailer on this day. The trail opens up into a big gravel softball field, then goes between the Kristoffs' trailer and the Olsons' trailer to her own. She stops, looks to the forest and sighs.

I feel old today, she thinks. If I didn't feel 65, I might walk up to Fern Cascades. But I think I'll just drink my hot chocolate, put on a record and take a nap instead. She opens the door.

"Happy birthday!"

"Surprise!"

"Happy birthday!"

Angel is dumbfounded, floored, breathless. Wide-eyed, she gapes around at the shining faces of Billie, Faysal, Mildred, Jim Petersen, Herm, the Kristoffs, a good portion of her staff, Kitty, Imre, and several more of her trailer neighbors. They sing heartily: "Happy birthday to you. . . Happy birthday to you. . . Happy birthday dear Angel—the best gift-shop manager in the whole world. . . Happy birthday to you!"

She can find nothing better to wipe the tears that stream down her face than one of the big, puffy marshmallows, which brings shouts and squeals of laughter. Angel cannot yet force words out to express the sudden wave of love she feels.

Her friends lead her to the center of the crowded living room.

"I. . . you guys. . . How'd you all get here so fast? I just saw everyone back in the Inn. Drat you Billie Mackey, I bet this was your idea. I thought you were in Bozeman getting yourself fixed up."

Faysal is the first in a long line to give Angel a hug and a kiss on the cheek, and Herm, eyes as bright as Christmas lights, walks out with a huge white cake. Someone turns off the overhead light, and 65 candles light Angel's beaming, wet face.

"It's going to take me 10 minutes to get enough breath back to blow that hard," she says.

Herm raises a hand and asks for silence.

"If you get them all in one breath, you get your life-long wish—a date with me."

"Does that mean we have to play poker in the boiler room?" Angel asks, still wavering between tears and laughter.

Then she rears back and blows with all her might, leaving just one candle lit.

"That's OK, Angel," Faysal says. "That was the extra one to grow on."

"But you can't have any now," says Billie. "I went all the way to Germany on my last day off to pick up some bratwurst, and Jim's going to start his grill. We have potato salad and corn on the cob."

"And this," says Jim Petersen, now clean-shaven and looking happier than anyone has seen him since Adele died. Beaming, he comes out of the back bedroom with a huge card and a large, gift-wrapped box.

"I'm going to get even with every one of you for this," Angel says.

"Imre, I just saw you. You could have warned me. I'm going to throw all the detail tapes away and make my deposits in pennies and nickels. Kitty Karner, give me a hug. I'll never save another *Billings Gazette* for you again."

"Open the present, Angel," says Kitty.

She unties the ribbon, then slowly unravels layer upon layer of the blue wrapping paper. With the box on the table and all her friends gathered around, she slowly lifts the lid off the 12-by-12-by-six-inch box, and the tears once again start flooding down her cheeks.

Slowly, her hands shaking, she carefully, delicately, lifts out the translucent glass moose. She holds it aloft, then sets it down on the table and looks at it with clasped hands. Then, strongly and firmly, she hugs all her summertime friends.

July 10.

Cecil Dolen is pleased with the new accessories to his camping regalia and has learned more about packing them. In his cabin, with things spread out on the beds, he systematically fills his pack. On the bottom goes the brand new Camp IV tent with separate attachable waterproof rain fly. Then goes his little Svea one-burner stove—complete with pots, fork, knife, spoon and eyedropper for priming the stove. Next are the polypropylene underwear around the stove so it won't press against his back. Then he puts in his food with an extra pair of socks, plus T-shirts and briefs surrounding it. On top of that, he places his blue chamois shirt and Woolrich jacket and finally a poncho, because it looks like it might rain. In the side pocket, he puts a flashlight with its two new size D Duracell batteries. Then he pulls it back out and checks to make sure it is working properly. He passes the beam across his eyes, and when he blinks he can only see the little bulb and the reddened image of the flashlight beam.

In another side pocket, he puts the plastic bag containing a Johnson and Johnson first-aid kit and a half roll of toilet paper.

From the countertop by the sink, he takes a Yellowstone topographical map, a compass, matches, a lighter for backup, an unopened letter from his mother, and a deck of cards, hoping Clarence will want to play some poker for matchsticks, or maybe pinecones. He puts these last items into the smaller front compartment. With his stretch cord, he now fastens his neoprene pad and his sleeping bag to his pack. As he ties his boots, he looks once around the room to see if he has forgotten anything. Satisfied that he hasn't, he hoists the pack on his back and walks out the door toward Clarence's cabin.

"Come in," Clarence answers to Cecil's knock.

Cecil looks around Clarence's cabin and sees his backpack is empty. His unrolled sleeping bag lays haphazardly over his unmade bed. Books, magazines, and clothes are scattered throughout the room, which is lit only by the light coming through curtained windows. On the wall, the top right corner of a poster depicting a young Orson Welles has come unglued and droops over. Cecil surveys the items on the table: two cans of sardines, a pound of Swiss cheese, a mostly full package of Oreo cookies and a half bottle of bourbon.

"Cec! Have yourself a liddle drink while I ged everything ready," Clarence says, wavering in his seat at the table. "I'll manage to pour. Get it? I manage?"

"You're drunk," Cecil scowls.

"No, I'm not. Shust had a couple of drinks to scare away the bears when they come after us this time. Remember last time? Well, thish time I'm ready."

Cecil's scar turns a dark crimson as his face flushes in anger.

"Damn it, Clarence. It's 4 o'clock already. Let's go. Throw everything in your pack. Maybe some hiking will sober you up."

"I'll be ready. I *am* ready." Clarence leans back, smiles, and turns to Cecil. "He takes his rouse, keeps wassail, and the swaggering upspring reels, and as he drains his draughts of Rhenish down. . . ."

"Let's go if you're going."

"OK," Clarence says, wobbling into an upright position. "All I've got to do is find this other boot. . ." He takes a step on unsteady legs and falls heavily onto his bed. "Earth tremor."

Clarence rolls up on his elbows and almost throws up into his backpack before he checks himself. "The boot! There's the other boot, Captain."

His motor coordination nearly spent, he reaches to adjust his glasses where there are none. Wavering back and forth, he tries several times to grab the glasses from the bed, finally managing to surround them as someone would a fish in a shallow pond. He guides them back over his nose. "Whaddya say we take a liddle bit of bourbon for the trip?"

Cecil sets the bottle up. "That's really great, Clarence. You're disgusting, you know that?"

Clarence gropes, trying to find something to help him up.

"I'm out of here," Cecil says, disgusted. "I'm going to take the

cheese and the sardines. Thanks for screwing up my weekend. You
can have a good time by yourself. Good luck, you drunk."

"Why Estragon, it's obvious what we're doing here. We're waiting
for Godot! Estragon? Cec? I'm ready to go camping."

Clarence manages to sit upright with his legs out in front of him.
His head swings loosely in circles.

He laughs, then pauses.

"My hour is almost come, when I to sulfrous and tormenting
flames must render up myself."

He takes a breath then yells as loudly as he can. "I'll be your foil,
Laertes!"

Clarence waits for applause but there is none. He realizes Cecil
is there, waiting for him to go camping, but looks around the cabin
and sees no one.

"'Tis gone!"

Now he is alone, and it is still. It is, he decides, time for a drink.
"I haven't had much to drink yet, and it is my Saturday."

On his third attempt, he manages to seat himself back at the
table. He raises his eyebrows and squints through his right eye, trying
to force one bottle to materialize where he sees two. He reaches for
the bottle and knocks it over, causing a loud clink that seems to echo
from somewhere else. The bottle slowly rolls toward him and he reels
backward in his seat.

"What magic is this? The bottle beckons to my command!"

He unscrews the top and, with one hand, leans the bottle while
with the other he guides the wavering tip into the clear water glass,
filling it two thirds. In that dimly lit cabin, he takes a sip of the
straight bourbon and thinks maybe someone watered it down. Was
it Cecil? Wasn't he just here? Aren't we going camping?

"It is Saturday," he says to the backpack. "Tuesday, you say?
Betcha a buck. Whatever."

He looks at the drooping Orson Welles poster and at the lions
and tigers that line the interior of his sleeping bag.

"Why can't you guys lie down and stay still?" he says.

He laughs, hiccups. The room starts to waver out of focus and he
thinks he should have something to eat. He reaches across the table
for the package of Oreos, but his depth perception misleads him,
and he pushes the package onto the floor. Half of the cookies roll
off in different directions around the room.

"Horse potuty."

He reaches for the backpack for support but it slowly falls away from him under the sink. He bends over, closes one eye, and looks on the floor. "Gravity is behaving strangely tonight."

He stands up and immediately falls down, missing the bed this time. The middle of his back hits the metal bed frame and he gasps. It is a dull, numb pain he feels as he lands in a sitting position on the dusty floor.

I bought sardines! And cheese! I know it. "You can't fool me, Laertes!"

He pushes himself up to look on the table. He determines that they must have taken the same fate as the cookies and returns to the floor.

"Oh, Captain Ahab. It is a great fish you seek. There are none like it in the sheven sheas."

He crawls on his stomach, searching under the bed and his dresser for the sardines. He imagines the cookies are plankton and scoops several into his mouth as he comes across them.

Several moments later, a wild, repulsive feeling wells up from the pit of his stomach. It is coming up and he cannot stop it. He starts to shake. Just in time, he reaches for the Oreo package and vomits into it, heaving again and again. He reaches up to open his cabin door and is hanging outside as he throws the infested bag out and heaves on his doorstep. His body convulses. He slithers back inside his cabin. He needs something to drink, something to clear out the taste. He reaches for his glass of bourbon but knocks it over, spilling it onto the floor.

"Water. Please."

He knows the sink on the other side of the cabin is out of reach but tries to crawl to it anyway.

In his effort, he crushes several of the cookies and, as he gets to the sink, consciousness no longer can sustain him: He falls face down under the sink.

Several moments lapse before he can open his eyes. He can't move but now he is standing in the opposite corner of the cabin. He looks around the cabin and sees his still form lying beneath the sink. He wants to shout but can't. Which one am I?

He moves to sit on the bed, still looking at his own form lying on the floor. If that is not me, why can't I get up and look on the bed? Turn around and look!

He tries. Things swirl. The cabin turns completely around two, three times, and now he is looking in the backpack for the sardines.

"Yes!" he says, "in the backpack! I left them in the backpack! Camping. I'm going camping. Got to get ready. . . ."

But there is no noise to accompany the words and he looks over again at his form beneath the sink.

"Get up! Get up!" he urges himself.

But he can't. Sweat rolls into his eyes. He sees a crushed cookie underneath the sink. He must look on the bed, see if he's there, but the room swirls wildly and he can't. He throws up again, and the figure on the bed becomes Captain Ahab, then Orson Welles, then Laertes. In turn, they watch him and laugh.

Then the figure is him again. The figure sitting on the bed stands, moves to the table and reaches for the bourbon. No! No! Don't do it! Please, no.

Then there is darkness.

Cecil Dolen is angrier than he has been for a long time but he is determined to go camping with or without a partner. He throws his backpack onto the passenger seat of his sleek blue Corvette and charges forward out of the driveway, spewing gravel behind him. He takes a left turn out of the cabin area and guns the 400-horsepower engine. In the next quarter mile, the powerful sports car reaches 60 miles per hour and Cecil races through the stop sign at the fire lane, past Ranger Howard Minden, who is driving the patrol car down the lane perpendicular to Cecil. Minden quickly manages to fix his radar gun on the passing car, then pursues it. Just before the overpass, Minden turns his siren on and off, and the blue Corvette pulls over. Minden recognizes Cecil as he steps out of his car. Cecil has served the gray-haired ranger and his wife drinks on several occasions.

Cecil explains the cause for his anger and subsequent speeding, but it is of no use. The ranger is writing a citation even while Cecil is talking. He is cited for speeding and running a stop sign.

The citation comes complete with a lecture about the importance of following rules of the road.

Cecil displays his anger with just a bit of sarcasm. "I'm sorry. I shouldn't have been speeding." He puts his license back in his brown leather wallet. "This won't go on my record back in Washington, will it? I mean, since this is a national park?"

"You bet, Cecil. It's all Internet now."

"Can't you give me a break? I won't do it again."

"Drive slowly and you won't." .

Ranger Minden gazes at Cecil as he turns to leave and then scuffs at the gravel next to his car door. He wonders about his question and writes a note on the three-by-five pad next to the radio: Check Dolen, Cecil, Sea Wash. He responds to his name over the radio. There is another moose jam up by Kepler Cascades.

Cecil blames the citation on Clarence but refrains from further taking it out on the accelerator. He follows the cloverleaf around and heads south toward the trailhead for his reserved campsite. When he passes the road that leads to Bitterroot and Lupine dorms, he remembers that Kris has the night off. He pulls over and lets Ranger Minden pass him and drive out of his vision before turning around and venturing up the service road to Lupine dorm.

"Hey Cecil," Debi says as he enters the lobby. "No work tonight?"

"Hi Debi," Cecil calls back as he heads to room 115. Kris answers the door in a white T-shirt and garnet shorts.

"Hi Cecil. What's up?"

"Listen, Clarence and I were supposed to go backpacking together, but when I showed up at his cabin, he was so drunk he couldn't even stand up. Now I don't have anyone to go with. I remember you said it was your night off, and I was wondering if you might like to go."

"Well, Cecil, I'd like to but I've already made plans."

"Oh really? What sort of plans?"

She pauses. Her first impulse, somehow, is to lie. But, she thinks, why should I? "I've got a dinner date with Herm."

"A date! Wait a minute, I thought you weren't dating."

"Well, we're friends. It's not really a date like that. He knows about John and everything."

"You've gone out with him before?"

"Once to West Yellowstone with some other people. Come on, Cecil, you sound like my father."

"Well, damn it, I would like a date like that. Are you sure you won't change your mind? I really don't want to go by myself. I've already got the campsite reserved. I've got food. And remember, we're friends too."

"I can't do that, Cecil. Herm is going to be here in 20 minutes. In fact, I have to hurry to get ready. Listen, I remember Keith and Vanessa were going backpacking. I bet you could go with them. I just saw Vanessa. . . ."

"I don't want to go with another couple. Come on, Kris."

"Well, Cecil, you have to let me know ahead of time," she says. "I'm not going now."

"Friends, right? We're friends? So I'll give you four or five day's notice and you'll go backpacking with me?"

Kris steps back slightly, pulling back her hair behind her ear. "Didn't I say I would?"

Cecil can't get the little one-burner flame to light. He doesn't know that he was supposed to attach the wick to the stem himself; the wick is back with the box and the instructions, in his wastebasket at his cabin. Holding the flashlight in his teeth, he unscrews the lid to the fuel tank for the third time. He peers inside the tank and takes out an eyedropper full of the white gas and squirts it on the priming dish. He takes three extra drops and squirts it on the generator, on the control valve and the holding tank. When he gets the flame of his Bic lighter three inches from the holding tank, he sets off a small explosion that causes him to flinch. A pure, blue flame encompasses the little Svea. With his extra T-shirt, Cecil grasps the key and tries any setting he can, but the cooking flame doesn't materialize. Quietly, the little blue flame circles once around the priming dish of the Svea and then disappears. Cecil looks into the campfire, then stands up and kicks the unit, sending it clanging off into the night.

I wanted so much for this to be a good night, he thinks.

He looks at his fire and, with a surge of willpower, reels his anger back in. He points his flashlight beam at his scattered cooking gear and walks over to retrieve it.

Don't get mad. Patience. Control. It's time to grow up a little.

After nicking his thumb slightly, he manages to cut the tape holding together the two cans that will make chow mein. He dumps the contents into a pot and adds the extra can of mushrooms that he brought along as a surprise for Clarence, and three slices of the Swiss cheese.

He gets two two-inch-thick, symmetrical logs from his pile of firewood and lays them parallel over the fire ring. He sets his shiny new pot with his dinner on top of the two logs, so that the flames reach up just to the bottom of the pan. He puts his neoprene pad between him and the big log and leans back. He remembers the letter he received that day from his mother. He finds it in the backpack, swats at a mosquito on his neck, and opens it:

Cecil,   July 3rd

Hope you had a nice Independence Day as this will reach you after that. Do they have fireworks in Yellowstone, since it is a national park? I was there once when I was young, with grandma and grandpa, can only remember Old Faithful and Mount Rushmore.

Hope you like it there. Do you think you might go to Chicago and drop in on your father in the fall? Make sure you write him first and let him know you're coming.

Your Aunt Flossie drove up from Portland last weekend and we had a real nice time. I took her over to the rainforest and we stayed a night in that wonderful Lake Quinault Lodge. She's still having problems with her foot, so we didn't do too much walking around. I am fine except for the headaches, but well, you know about that.

Got your last check from the Porting Place and deposited it in your savings. Don't worry. I didn't check on your balance. Do you have an account there in Wyoming?

Nothing new here. The weather's been nice for two weeks but I expect it will rain pretty soon. Your baseball team isn't doing so well. The mayor was in a car accident but is OK now.

Nothing else new. Hope you are enjoying yourself out there, Cecil. Must be a nice change from the big city. Are you eating OK? Not bar snacks, I hope. Have you met any nice girls? How about some grandchildren?

Write when you get time,
Mom

Cecil wads up the letter and the envelope and tosses it into the fire. He looks back at his new tent and shines his flashlight inside it; then he shines it out into the night and thinks he might eat and take a walk over to Lone Star Geyser and see if he can catch it erupting. He looks around his camp and it gives him satisfaction. He takes a sip of water from the wide-mouthed plastic bottle and looks into the night sky. He pushes back the images of another life, another place, so far away, but always attempting to creep into his thoughts. He thinks maybe he will get Clarence's job by telling Faysal that Clarence drinks on the job. Then I'd be bar manager and Kris would respect me.

He pictures Kris in the bar wearing that yellow sweater, waiting for him at one o'clock to lock everything up before they go to his own, private cabin with no roommate. Other guys would have tried to put the moves on her at the bar, but she would always go home with me. Maybe we'll take up chess or something. I'll let her beat me every once in a while. Then she'll giggle and poke me for being so smart and wrestle me into bed. The candles will be lit, making her skin glow orange and warm. We'll make love. . . .

Cecil has his arms wrapped around his drawn-up knees. He is lost, mesmerized in these images, when one of the logs holding the pot burns through. The pot tips over, spilling most of its contents, and the fire hisses. Cecil reaches in and grabs the pot with his right hand and there is yet another hiss—this one of flesh burning.

"Ahhhooowww! Damn it!" he yells and looks in the fire to see his dinner completely lost. He looks for something to grab the pot with but can find nothing before all the chow mein drips out.

"Damn hell damn bitch!" he screams, clutching his burned hand, now throbbing with pain. The outer layer of skin is instantly white and shriveled. But it is the look in his eyes that reveals the sudden, total transformation of a man. It is a demoniacal, maniacal look— as if someone threw a switch in his mind and alternated the current. He stands, holding his hand, and his rage is total; it froths over, out of control. He kicks his backpack once, a second time, harder and more savagely than the time before. He kicks at the fire, sending flaming logs away from the fire ring. One of these, he grabs by the unburned end and hurls it into the night. He cusses through gritted teeth and kicks at the neoprene pad resting against the big log.

"Bastard!"

He picks up the flashlight recklessly and charges 50 yards through the darkness to the Firehole River. Possibly only the brief early evening rain prevents the thrown log from setting fire to the fallen pine needles and dry grasses.

Cecil immerses his hand in the cool water and the physical relief is instant.

"No dinner," he snarls. "You stupid idiot, you get no dinner tonight. . . Stupid asshole."

He looks into the heavens. The stars and a last quarter moon mock him. The trees and the river mock him, and with his burnt hand, he punches at the water.

The other side takes over.

"Fire? I'll show you fire."

Leaning on it and grabbing it with his good hand, Cecil uproots the trail sign that stood before the footbridge. He thinks about Kris. He knows he must go out again soon. I am a man now and I will kill, he thinks. I live for that only. No more cute Cecil, always unconfident, unsure. I waste so much time, being less than myself. I am here now, and this time nothing's going to stop me. I am free. I am strong. They will respect me.

He drags the trail sign back to his camp and drops it in the fire. Over a never-ending stream of vile curses, he stacks the rest of his firewood on top of the trail sign.

It is dark, still, quiet in the cabin when Clarence wakes from dreams that were too frightening, too real. The smell of vomit is the first thing to reach his consciousness, and he retches from it. The last of his stomach's contents is exorcised from him. He spits onto the wooden floor. Now he is aware of an incredible pain in his head, and he recalls the last visions he had—then the final image of himself reaching for the bottle.

"No," he moans aloud. His clothes are wet from perspiration, and he pushes himself away from the corner. In the dimmest of light, he is relieved to see that he is in his own cabin. His head pounds more as he starts to rise, but the need for water galvanizes him. That's it, he thinks. No more booze. No more. Please.

He shakes from the memory of earlier and starts to panic, wondering if he is even himself, and not there in the cabin, somewhere in the dark watching himself. He shivers. He looks under the sink where the images appeared and gasps when he notices a dark shape huddled, moving? It is an effort of courage to walk across and flick the light switch, and he is relieved to see that the dark shape is his backpack. The artifacts in his room, of his life, are strangely calm and peaceful, despite the nakedness of two bare, overhead bulbs. He looks down at the puddle of vomit by the table, not remembering it, and he looks at Oreos scattered here and there. When he looks at the nearly empty bottle of bourbon, pain shoots through his head. He reels at the sight of it. He grabs the bottle and drops it into the garbage. From his dresser, he takes open bottles of brandy, liquor, and vodka and throws them in with the bourbon bottle. He opens the lower drawer of the dresser, reaches under his T-shirts, hesitates briefly, then pulls out a bottle of the Special Reserve Rum, full and unopened in its cloth pouch, and sets it with the others.

He walks out of his cabin into the cool of the night, opens the green garbage can and dumps the bottles inside; as the bottles break, he feels a little satisfaction and a great relief, like someone has released him from a tightly drawn shoulder harness.

His sweat-stained shirt chills him, and he shivers in the cool night. It is quiet, most of the cabin lights are out, and he realizes it must be quite late. He looks up at the stars.

"Well, Clarence Harps, this is it. What are you going to do now?"

He turns around and gazes back into the shambles of his lighted cabin. "Try starting over, I guess."

For two hours, he cleans his cabin, picking up, sweeping, scrubbing, wiping. He pins up the Orson Welles poster and does his laundry. He finds a sack lunch that is two days old but downs it ravenously, along with almost half a gallon of water. Then, with his room in order, he pulls out a box from far underneath his bed. He thumbs past old scripts, programs of his shows, reviews, past *Actors on Acting* until, with a smile, he finds the book he is looking for: *An Actor Prepares* by Constantine Stanislavski. He opens it to a passage he has underlined: "Our aim is not only to create the life of a human spirit, but also to express it in a beautiful, artistic form."

He takes a deep breath, runs his hand over the page, and turns back to the first chapter.

July 17. Old Faithful accounting office, 2:49 a.m..

Wilbur walks in from the back of the controller's office with a long calculator tape. "You look a little bummed out, Herm. What's the matter?"

"Ahhh. I've got to punch out. I'm supposed to come back and work on Saturday afternoon, my day off. The Secretary of the Interior is coming on Saturday to make a speech, and the rangers want me to be in his entourage for security reasons."

"The Secretary of the Interior of the United States?" Wilbur asks.

"Yea. Why?"

"That man would pat himself on the back for extinguishing a species. His attitude toward national parks and forests is that they should be money-makers. Be accountable."

"He's coming here to make a speech? Sounds like a publicity gimmick to me," says Steve, leaning over the desk as he cross-checks the room revenue report.

"I think it might be," Herm says. "He's going to make his speech in front of Old Faithful and we're even supposed to time it so it erupts while he's speaking. There's supposed to be reporters from *Newsweek* and *Time* and everything."

"No kidding," says Wilbur, pulling at his beard. But it is the gravity of the way he says it that makes Steve and Herm turn to him.

"I don't like the vicious way he's tugging at his beard," Herm says.

"He's trying to pull his brains into his head. It's called thinking. Try it sometime, Herm. It might hurt at first. Then I think you might like it."

"Very funny."

"Why do they want you there, Herm?" asks Wilbur.

"They think that once the employees hear about it, they may try to harass him. They think I'll be able to recognize possible hecklers."

"Look at the wheels turn," Steve chortles. "The man's brain is turning into a calculator, he's been running tapes so long. Get back in there and get me a credit-card figure before you hurt yourself."

"I hereby call a Mouton Cadet meeting for tonight at Kitty's," Wilbur announces. "Mandatory attendance."

"You aren't going to get us all arrested by the Secret Service are you?" Herm asks. "This guy will have security everywhere."

"I won't have to dress up as a bear again, will I?"

But Wilbur hardly seems to hear them. He thumps at the end of his nose with a yellow pencil as he floats past them out to the front desk. As Herm passes the desk on his way out, Wilbur is peering out the window at the geyser basin.

"Six o'clock exactly, Herm," he says without looking. "Make sure you tell Shannon."

"Yes, Mr. President. Is this an official meeting?"

"The wine will be chilled."

July 20.

"This is crazier than the last thing we did," says Salina, wearing a backpack that has "Sunset" stenciled over the chest strap and "The enjoyment" on the waist strap. All members of the Mouton Cadet Sunset Society, except Herm, are in a secluded clump of trees near Old Faithful Geyser.

"This is going to be great. The Society makes a political statement," Kitty says, as she slips off a backpack that says "Cadet" over the chest strap and "Conservation" over the waist strap.

Steve zips up his pack and leans it against a tree. "Society" is lettered over his chest strap and "of life" is lettered over the waist. "I wonder if they let you run in the federal penitentiary?"

Wilbur's pack says "Mouton" over the chest strap and "Supports" over the waist strap.

"This plan is so tight," he says, proudly. "I've covered every possible contingency. I've given this a lot of thought over the last three days. We've all gone over it five times. We all agreed we'd do it. What can they do to us?"

"What am I supposed to do again?" asks Shannon, the newest member of the Society. His worried, narrow face is capped with thinning hair. He is wearing khaki pants, a white shirt and has two black leather camera bags at his side.

"Good grief. Let's go over it one last time. You did put the valve in the ground right where I showed you last night?"

"Yes, it's still there. I checked this morning."

"And you've got film in your camera?"

"Really, this one is for the history books," says Kitty.

"I've only got four shots left," says Shannon. "Let's go over this and then I'll run to the gift shop and get more film."

"OK," says Wilbur. "One last time."

Boardwalk in front of Old Faithful Geyser, 2:02 p.m..

Through local newspapers, radio, and word of mouth, the message is out that the Secretary of the Interior will be speaking in front of Old Faithful Geyser. A larger than normal crowd gathers on the boardwalk waiting for an eruption and the Secretary to speak. On the podium is the official seal of the Secretary of the Interior. Red, white, and blue semi-circular drapes hang from the bottom of the platform. It is a sunny day for the crowd that has gathered to await both the Secretary and the eruption.

Inside Faysal's office in the Inn, an entourage of eight is gathered around the Secretary.

"Mr. Secretary, the eruption is expected for 2:15," says one of his aides. "They give it 10 minutes either way, so if you went out right now, you should be safe."

"I'm ready," says the spectacled, fading gray-haired man, now looking into a mirror and straightening his olive green tie.

"You have your speech?" asks a woman in a blue suit dress.

"Yes, Ophelia."

Herm, Ranger Minden, and three Secret Service guards lead the Secretary through the lobby and out the huge red and wrought-iron doors.

On the boardwalk, Herm purposely stops and keeps Ranger Minden to the left side of the podium as the Secretary steps to the microphone before a quiet Old-Faithful-at-steam phase. There is a perfunctory applause and a murmur through the crowd as uniformed people discover exactly who it is that is making the speech.

Shutters click and movie cameras whirl. The tourists and photographers take pictures of the Secretary and of the geyser quietly steaming in the background.

At first, only a few people to the far right of the podium notice the two guys and girl dressed in white frock coats and white tennis caps as they roll a huge wagon wheel up from the back side of the geyser to an area behind three lodgepole pines. They watch as the girl comes up and fits a four-foot tall pipe over a valve that is sticking up from the earth near the base of the trees, some 50 yards from the geyser.

As the Secretary continues speaking, a few more people turn their attention to the right side of the geyser, where one guy holds the pipe in place while the guy and the girl fit the wagon wheel over the end of the pipe. They watch as the girl studies her watch and points to the two men who give the wheel a slight turn, just as the geyser plays.

The geyser plays higher. Behind the trees, Kitty nods her head, speaks, and Steve and Wilbur turn the wheel slightly. A few tourists start to wander from the speech and crane their necks to see the curiosity 70 yards away.

"Hey dad, what are they doing over there? They don't have to turn Old Faithful on, do they?"

"Son, Old Faithful is a natural phenomena. . . I think."

"I think it's some prank. Maybe some protesters," says a lady. "They should be arrested."

The geyser plays to a height of 12 feet. Kitty motions in a counterclockwise circle, and Steve and Wilbur turn the wheel that way with seeming great effort.

On the podium, the Secretary's attention is distracted, as several of his listeners are drifting away.

Two Secret Service men gaze out at the audience as yet more eyes drift to the right. One of them takes a casual step back and looks but cannot see over Geyser Hill.

"What's going on?"

"I don't know." With an almost-imperceptible hand sign, the Secret Service man directs an agent up to the podium.

Kitty feels the tremor; she can hear the rumble. She points her finger at Steve and Wilbur, who slowly force the big wheel counterclockwise just as the geyser erupts.

"Mr. Secretary," says the woman in the blue dress suit, pointing to the eruption.

The Secretary turns his head to see the geyser in full eruption. He faces the audience and smiles broadly. "What great timing Mother Nature has! Let us all pause to appreciate this magnificent display. Isn't it beautiful?"

He turns with his aides to face the geyser, and whispers out the side of his mouth, "Where the hell's everybody going?"

Ranger Minden's radio crackles. It's Ranger Mortensen from up on Observation Point with a Secret Service man. Herm, fidgeting nervously behind him, inches closer to Minden to listen.

"Howard, I can't believe it. It looks like someone is pulling that old wagon-wheel bit under a clump of trees toward the Lodge side of Old Faithful. Stop them, will ya? The Secretary's losing his audience."

"Ten-four. Hell! Herm, stay here. I'll be damned. What a time for someone to pull something like that."

"Sure, Howard." As Howard steps away, he joins the Secret Service agent, and Herm pulls his own radio from his hip strap. "OK. Minden and one of the agents are coming now. Get out of there, pronto."

"Roger. That's a copy," says Wilbur, as he slips the radio back into the deep pocket. Wilbur turns and addresses the man standing closest to him. "Sir, excuse me. We're having some real trouble with Riverside Geyser. They've blown a main valve down there and they're going to need some help at once. Could you help us out?"

"Uh, sure, I guess so."

"As soon as you see the water running out in Old Faithful—you'll know it because the eruptions will start to lower—turn this wheel clockwise. Just keep turning until there is no more water coming out of the geyser."

"You mean these aren't natural?"

"Understand we had to be accurate for the Secretary's visit. Helluva time for virus to get into the mainframe and have to go manual, huh?

"Old Faithful stopped working only about three years ago," Wilbur whispers. "We give it some help so that it may appear to be its natural self. Would you like to see an American Institution die?"

"I think he should have a white coat just in case the main valve doesn't seal tight and the geyserite sprays him," Kitty adds.

"Yes, you should! Here we go. Thank you, sir. You are a credit to America. What's your name, sir?"

"Bert Naumann."

"Wilbur," Kitty whispers. "Let's get out of here. I think there's someone coming."

Kitty, Steve and Wilbur start to leave through the trees. "You're doing a great job, Bert," Kitty says. "Just remember now, when it goes off, just keep screwing the crank. Just like the Interior Department."

Kitty, Steve and Wilbur scamper back into the woods, where Salina is waiting. "OK," Wilbur says quickly. "You guys stuff the frocks into the backpacks. Hats green side out. Yellow shades on! Make sure you have the right packs on. Make sure you stand where you're supposed to stand. This is going *so* good! Quickly."

As the eruptions subside, Ranger Minden and the Secret Service agent approach Bert Naumann, the Interior Secretary starts his speech up again, and Kitty, Steve, Wilbur and Salina emerge as four backpackers from the woods on the far side of the boardwalk. As the Secretary regains half of his concerned audience and some of his composure, a small girl near the front asks him, "Isn't it hard to breathe in a costume like that?"

There is a collective chuckle from the onlookers and the Secretary pauses, shuffles his papers, and smiles at the child's mom. "May I?" he says and holds the child aloft. "In closing, may I say that this is our heritage that I hold in my arms. The administration appreciates your unending support for our programs, guaranteeing a future for the next generation. I thank you."

Two of the photographers click pictures as the young girl in the arms of the Secretary looks dolefully at him, puts her hand on his face and squeezes his nose and cheek together.

The Secretary steps from the podium to applause and chuckles. He laughs with the crowd as he hands the child back to her mother, then waves as his entourage gathers around him and starts back to the Inn. At the west end of the boardwalk they approach Kitty, Salina, Wilbur, and Steve walking toward them.

Shannon steps alongside the procession with his camera held aloft. "Shurime Muir, *Outside Magazine.* How 'bout a picture with the backpackers, Mr. Secretary? Would look good for our cover."

"All right. Quickly please." He shakes the backpacker's hands as they all smile and back up for the cameras.

"Hayduke Libbs," Wilbur says enthusiastically, shaking the Secretary's hand.

"Secretary Roesser. Nice to meet you. Mountain supports?" he asks, pointing to Wilbur's backpack straps. "Is that a rescue group?"

"We're trying. Are you the Interior Secretary for the whole United States?" Wilbur asks. "You must be a very fast typist."

"Mouton Cadet Sunset Society Vice President," says Kitty, reaching for his hand. "Mona Estrus."

Shannon, along with photographers of *Time, Newsweek* and *USA*

Today, snap pictures of Wilbur, Kitty, the Secretary of the Interior, Salina, and Steve. From left to right across their chests and waists, the logo reads: "Mouton Cadet: Sunset Society: Supports Conservation: and the Enjoyment of Life."

Mount Washburn, same afternoon.

Imre and Yvonne are in Yvonne's Subaru, driving up Chittenden Road, the dirt road that takes them two thirds of the way up Mt. Washburn. They park and start to walk up the trail that leads to the fire lookout looming on the summit.

"I'm feeling really lonely today, Yvonne."

"So what's new? No, I don't mean for you. I mean for me. That's how I feel all the time. It doesn't matter."

"I haven't had a boyfriend this whole summer. The only dates I've had are with Gilbert, and he's just a friend."

"Oh, Imre, you want to get drunk or something? I've got a bottle under the seat in the car."

"I don't want to drink anymore! That's not what I want. It's not like a warm man. A body. *Some*body."

They walk in silence up the flower-laden hill. Mountain lilies, blue mountain forget-me-nots, Indian paintbrush, purple lupine, harebells, asters, monkey flowers—white, pink, yellow, blue, red, purple flowers are everywhere. In the wind, gazing down the mountain slope, the entire hillside appears to be a huge, multi-colored carpet swimming in graceful, waving motion.

A quarter mile up, Yvonne stops. "That's far enough for me," she says, panting.

"You're never going to lose weight if you don't get some exercise."

"That *was* exercise! Besides, I think I'll just sit here and let the mosquitoes suck all the blood out of me. I'll lose weight that way."

"Suit yourself."

"You want to drive down to the Tower store and get a six pack of chocolate milk after this?"

Yvonne sits herself down on a rock on the leeward side of the ridge. "Guess not, huh?"

She looks after Imre. I hate to see her like this, she thinks. I try to make the best of it. I wish she would too.

Imre picks several of the blue forget-me-nots and twists them in her fingers as she walks up. The wind blows her raven-black hair across her face and she *feels* attractive. But she remembers the dreadful, completely isolated feeling she had two mornings ago while she was doing the balance sheet. It felt as if she was detached physically from her body. Her will to live deserted her. It took a conscious effort to breathe.

She sits down, facing the wind. She looks below to Yvonne, who is waving an insect away.

I shouldn't hang around her anymore, Imre thinks. I've even managed to bring her down. I should leave Yellowstone, but then where would I go? Back to Chicago? No way. All my friends are married. Families. My mom. . . God, two days in that city would drive me crazy now. But where else is there? This is it.

She lights a cigarette, and the gusts of wind blow the smoke away behind her. Ranger Rick, why did you leave?

From her pocket, she takes out a small notepad and pen. She writes the first line:

Here we dream. . . .

She looked out over the unpopulated mountains, and the rest comes in a torrent:

Following the footsteps
        of so many shadows.
Who tried and didn't make it
Who wore a saddened face
The dance of singers
        who cringe from the moon
        and hide from the daylight
        and the shifting sand dune. . . .

She takes a puff of the cigarette. She closes her eyes, and her feelings ignite the words that she scribbles across the page.

Here we dream
        of lovers never seen
        of efforts never final
We wonder about
        the famous rich ones
        and travels never ventured.

Here we wonder

of what we've never learned
how much we've never said
how it could be different
to do it all over
and forget this mental stutter.

Here we sit
   with head down, dejected
   the scorn won't flee
   the bright day's loss
   of ungiven summer flowers
   despairingly braving the wind.

So there, Wilbur Hardisty. You are the writer. What do you think about this?

She reads her poem again and puts the small notepad back in her pocket. She feels around and fishes out an orange prescription bottle. "Halcion, .25 mg," it says, "Take one capsule at bedtime or as needed for sleep." She contemplates the little capsules that have rendered her into a softer world these past three years. She knows why she has always kept an extra bottle, full, on hand at all times, and why she renews her prescription with this one in reserve. She dumps them into her hand and counts them, putting two at a time back in the bottle. Thirty. If a half dose makes me sleep, 30 should do the trick. Yes, I can see it. Faysal and Slim and maybe Herm could come into the room with the master key. I'd leave Beethoven's Seventh Symphony on the CD, just playing over and over. No notes. Maybe a poem. They'd talk about it.

She holds up the little orange bottle and sees both sadness and release. No balance sheets, no telephones, no numbers, no loneliness. She lays her arms across her drawn-up knees and rests her head. The flowers do not make her glad. The wind does not dry her tears.

July 22. The Inn lobby, 2:15 a.m..

Herm is leaning over the counter of the front desk, recounting with Steve and Wilbur for the fifth time the events of the Saturday two days before.

Herm laughs. "I heard that even when they released that guy you got to turn the wheel, he still believed Old Faithful was run manually and that he was going to 'expose the whole shoddy operation.'"

"Shannon took the film into West Yellowstone today," Steve says. "He said he thinks he got some great shots."

Wilbur is cocky. "See, I told you that everything would work out OK. Everything went flawlessly. The guy we got to turn the wheel couldn't give them a description of us. If one of the magazines or *USA Today* prints the shot with us and the Secretary, the whole world will see our picture and no one will be able to recognize us with the dark shades and hats. There's no way anyone can catch the notorious Mouton Cadet. . . ."

"Good morning Ranger Minden!" Steve says loudly.

Herm nods his head. "Funny, Steve. Now don't be. . . Ranger Minden!"

"Good morning, fellas. Herm, could I have a word with you?"

"Sure, Howard. Let's sit down over here. I didn't think you worked nights."

"I usually don't. Ranger Morris is at a law-enforcement seminar in Denver. I'll be filling in on night patrol for a couple of nights."

As Herm and Howard Minden head to the big leather chairs, Herm turns and rolls his eyes dramatically at Steve and Wilbur. Disconcerted, they look helplessly after him.

"Uhh, Brenda, do we have any more check-ins?" Steve asks, as he sidles over to the room rack and realizes he is not within hearing distance.

"No, Steve. Sold out again."

"Howard, can I get you some hot chocolate or something?"

"No thanks."

"All right. So what can I do for you?"

Howard Minden takes off his flat-brimmed hat and holds it in his lap. "What do you know about Cecil Dolen?"

"Cecil Dolen? Not much. I don't think he had anything to do with that thing Saturday, though."

"I didn't say he did. What do you know about him?"

"Nice guy. Quiet. I've never even seen him drink. Does his job well, I've heard. Every once in a while, he'll stay in the lobby and chat after a late shift. Talks sports. Drives a sports car."

"I know that. I gave him a ticket a couple of weeks ago for doing 60 miles per hour right through the fire lane. What else do you know about him?"

"That's about it. I think he's got a crush on one of the waitresses here. . . Why're you so curious? Is he in trouble?"

"No, not really. He was just real curious when I gave him the ticket as to whether it would go on his record back in Washington. That's where he's from. So I ran a check on him."

"And?"

"Well, nothing, really. But seven years ago, he was charged with assault on a girl. Girl was a prostitute and later dropped the charges. Looks like the prosecutor never pursued it since he had a clean record. Probably nothing, but I just wanted to see if he'd ever caused any trouble around here."

"Gosh, Howard, I've never even seen him in the Pub. He hangs around with Clarence, the bar manager."

"OK. Good enough."

Ranger Minden and Herm turn to talk about the tribulations of their jobs.

"God, what a summer it's been," Minden says. "Did you hear about the guy at Norris today?"

"No, what happened?"

"Everyone in the whole country will hear about it, so I might as well tell you. Right about sunset, some guy was walking his dog. . . ."

"Killed an elk?"

"No, Herm, damn you. Listen to the story. Had his dog on a leash but the dog got away. Dog jumped into Echinus Geyser, 198 degrees Fahrenheit. Guy jumped in after him right in front of 30 people."

"Holy mackerel! Dead?"

Ranger Minden nods his head. "I heard they managed to get the guy out in only 20 seconds. But 198 degree water? Huh uh."

"You're right. That one will make headlines. Hey, that reminds me. Did you see the story in the Casper paper a couple of days ago about the Park Service rangers and biologists tranquilizing the bears with PCP?"

"Haven't read it yet but there's been a copy of it laying around the station."

"It was a reprint from a *Cleveland Plain Dealer* story. That bear that killed that guy over by Hebgen Lake had been immobilized with PCP. They wonder now if it may cause some pretty violent after-effects. Says bears keep it stored in their fat tissues. The article said PCP is the same stuff as Angel Dust. Do you remember that kid that freaked out on the stuff, what, a couple of years ago?"

"I remember the incident. It's no secret they've been administering PCP to bears. Hell, we're law enforcement. I don't even know what PCP is. When that kid took it is the only time I've heard about it being associated with Angel Dust. I know it's classified as a very dangerous drug for human consumption."

"What do you think it does to the bears?"

"I don't know, Herm. There's so few up here. I just wish they'd leave them alone. We've got a bear that's been hanging around Mallard Lake now that's been getting a little bit too brave. Looks like we might have to bait him."

"Mallard Lake. That's only two or three miles away. Think I better start doing my rounds in the station wagon again. Too much happening here this summer."

"Oh, yea. That's the other thing. Did you get anything at all on the people who pulled the wagon-wheel gag while the Secretary was speaking? The superintendent was part of his entourage, you know. He was mad as hell."

"Gosh no. I thought maybe the Secret Service would be able to figure that one out. They're the pros."

"Well, the only thing we can figure is that it might have been a group from down in Jackson that calls itself Earth First. That's Earth First! with an exclamation point to show their conviction. They've been known to pull stuff like that. Also something about some backpackers wearing a sign or something?"

"I saw the backpackers. They had their picture taken with the Secretary. Don't remember a sign."

Howard rises. "Well, nice talking to you Herm. Hey, maybe I'll take you up on that hot chocolate now, if the offer's still good."

"Sure, come on back to the kitchen."

July 24. Pelican Valley, 10:14 a.m..

Ross Matthias sets his pack down on the wooden bridge spanning Pelican Creek and stretches his shoulders under a brilliant blue mountain sky.

"I can't believe this weather!" he shouts. Under a rising late-morning sun, he does a slow 360-degree turn. He can't see Lake Yellowstone any more, and it appears he now is at the center of the two-mile-wide valley. He looks upstream. He can follow the slow, meandering creek for a quarter or half mile before it blends with the lush deep green of midsummer grasses frosted over with wildflowers. He looks northeast, where the trail, after crossing the rust-colored creek, shoots toward a tall round peak. Ross can see where the '88 fire "spiked out" and made a run along its flank. Ross pulls out his topo map and determines the peak to be Pelican Cone, but the thin red lines that denote trails tell him he will turn north before he reaches it.

He continues his reconnaissance. Across from him, he sees four large dark shapes, and as he squints and shields his eyes, one of them move slightly. Buffalo.

He sits down on the old wooden bridge, dangles his legs over the edge, and takes a plastic sandwich bag from his pack. He leans over to focus on a wiggling shape in the water. A cutthroat trout darts upstream under the bridge. He can feel the sun warming his back, his shirt moist where the 50-pound pack rested. He slips off his chamois shirt and spreads it over his pack, exposing it directly to the drying forces of the burning yellow sphere.

He takes a deep breath and is glad now; he has enough distance between him and the road—between him and civilization. He shivers once in the glow of the thought, in the warmth of the sun, in the anticipation of taking the psychedelic psilocybin mushrooms that he now carefully removes from the aluminum foil inside the sandwich bag. He fishes in the side pocket for the tubular roll of chewy Dutch mints, for the dried mushrooms are pungent and foul tasting, and these ones, he notes, are loaded with purple. The poison. The stuff that gets you high.

He pulls out the two three-inch stems and two of the brown, orange and purple mushroom caps and sets the four pieces in a line on the bridge. Methodically, he wraps the remaining stem and cap back in the foil, places them back into the plastic bag, then pushes the bag down deep in the pack. He takes a pull at the first stem, tearing it off in his teeth like jerked beef, then quickly pops two mints into his mouth. With his molars, away from his taste buds, he rapidly chews the repulsive, rough mass and swallows it down, chasing it with a large gulp of water from one of his plastic water bottles.

"Yesss!"

With an expression of disdain, he repeats the process. He expects that in just five or 10 minutes, he will be getting off like a bandit, for he has taken no food for the day, and the four-mile hike in has burned up anything he might have had in his stomach from the night before.

Four minutes later, he swallows the last of the mushrooms and all but two of the mints. Now, for a moment, he leans back against his pack, closes his eyes and listens to the occasional gurgle of the stream and his own calm, even breathing. Three minutes later, his own laughter galvanizes him: He heard a sunspot flare up 93 million miles away.

He realizes he should get moving again, lest he spend the entire day on that little wooden bridge in the center of the valley. That wouldn't be bad, he thinks, but then again there are treats in store for me up ahead.

He slings the pack back on and it feels snug, balanced, solid. He crosses the bridge and makes a right turn. With the pack on, he must turn his entire torso back around to take one final look at the bridge behind him.

"Good-bye."

The trail is in two parallel tracks, and Ross thinks that maybe it was an old wagon route. He walks, finding a rhythm and letting the creak of the swaying pack lull him.

Now for some time alone, he thinks.

He gives his thoughts free reign, and they are bordered only by the long, wide valley. He lets his mind flash over individual faces among the thousands of people he has waited on. He sees the people he has served—tired, hungry, happy, impatient. Yes, he thinks, impatient. So many of them are impatient. They've got to eat in a hurry so they can see the whole lower loop in one day, or get out to see Old Faithful while it is still light, or they've got to make it all the way to Salt Lake City that day, or they've got to catch their tour bus and God help them if they're late—the tour director will be upset, for he has schedules to meet. Why do people rush through their lives like that? But then again, they don't have a place to come to that's like this, a place to be by themselves.

Ross laughs, and inserts his index fingers behind the muscles in his jaw, relieving a familiar tension, a side effect of the drug. Infinite strength surges over him in a flood. He shivers.

My God, what a beautiful place. What a beautiful day.

"Hello!"

Who are you talking to?

That bird over there. "Hello, bird."

Boy, it feels good out here. The backpack even feels good.

And hell, that's another thing. That's right. The other waitri. Some of them are all right. Janis is great, but some of them are so tight, their butts squeak when they walk. Cheap. I mean they are tipping the bus people with pennies, nickels and dimes. We're making more than most of the supervisors, and that's a fact. And there is so much backbiting and slander. Why can't they leave it alone? Feel sorry for Erbine, the dining-room manager. What did he tell me, three-fourths of his problems are dealing with employees, trying to keep them happy, listening to the gripes.

Why can't the people at work treat one another with a little more respect and dignity? Talk to each other. I don't know. Life's so short. . . .

Wait a minute. I'm walking too fast. That's it. No more work. I'm going to start having a bummer or something.

He stops and gazes at a little pool some 20 feet across and 15 yards off the trail. He walks over to it. It is bubbling, it is possibly a good place for a warm soak, but he is inclined to push onward. He tries to bend forward with his pack on to check its temperature, but the weight above him shifts forward, nearly sending him face first into the pool.

There I go. I should learn to live by my own words. Take my time.

He lays his pack in the grass, and again approaches the bubbling pool. Though it is not warm, it is not cold, but the bottom looks to be too soft for standing or sitting in to soak. Looking back, he can see the orange trail marker by the bridge, and he finds himself glancing at his watch.

"Forget it," he says, pulling the velcro strap off his wrist and zipping the watch into his pack.

There is no time out here, he thinks. Nature takes time. There is no future, no past on this day. There is only the present, and it is a perfect present.

A shock of energy shakes his body.

He looks in the direction of the lake through contracting and dilating pupils and watches clouds roll and waver in opposite flow of the grasses and flowers. He takes a deep breath, slings his pack back on his shoulders and hikes on.

His pace is slow but steady as the valley narrows and the trail works its way to the treeline. He comes over a small rise and startles a huge bull buffalo directly on the trail below him, just 15 yards away. Both man and beast start backward in a rush. The buffalo charges off 20 yards in the opposite direction, turns, and huffs his displeasure, and Ross gives him a wide berth in passing.

"You're bigger than me, Mister Buffalo, so I'll just do a little slide slip. Sorry to disturb you." The buffalo eyes him warily and returns to eating.

Now he is at the trail junction where he must turn north. He is at the confluence of Raven and Pelican creeks, so the width of the valley is halved again as he splits off. As the valley has decreased from more than two miles across to just 200 yards, Ross senses the intimacy in his surroundings.

Now the trail cuts off through the woods. His mind wanders.

I'm saving so much money I can do whatever I want to come fall. Should have $4,000 in the bank by the end of the summer. Maybe get my car tuned up, get some new tires on it and just go. Or how about Europe? Maybe. Possible. Like to take some time to learn— about the world, about myself.

He bends down to a little creek passing in front of him, scoops a handful of water and drinks it.

God, what a beautiful trail. What was I thinking about?

So we have this most pristine of lands that we have to baby-sit for the rest of eternity and regulate the hell out of. All this land and now I break the law if I don't camp in campsite PC4?

He chuckles. The trees hear him. They wave their branches in salute as he passes. He veers off the path and, for 10 steps, he parallels the trail from 10 feet away.

"Felon."

And yet we want more people to drive more cars to pollute the air with more smoke, to graze the land with more animals to create less topsoil and more deserts and therefore wipe out more species of animals and clear more land for more people, he thinks. What is our goal?

There are skyscrapers on the planet! Why? Better to put them vertically than horizontally, I guess. At this very instant in Los Angeles, that piece of land known as Interstate 5 is crawling with cars and trucks, six lanes of them, endless. Back and forth, up and down. Right at this moment. Television. Crime. Some earth. Before I get to that hill up there, someone will be born somewhere on the earth and someone will be murdered. We're the most intelligent species, yet we're the only one that kills its own kind for no reason.

"And here I am in heaven."

He walks for 15 minutes, not really thinking, just feeling himself as a living, moving thing. He lets his perceptions broaden to his surroundings. He hears a squirrel scamper down a log and chirp at him. He can see it without looking. He raises his head to the sun through the trees, taking in the warmth of a soft, summer day, feeling the sanctity of being alone in the woods, and the pleasant, floating, endless organic strength of the psychedelic mushrooms at their height.

He comes out of the trees and sees the first point of interest that the topographical map had promised him. On his left is what appears to be a large clay hill with tiny craters and volcanoes and steam billowing lazily up. His map calls it the Mudkettles and Mushpots.

He heads up to a lodgepole at the base of the mudpot area and takes off his pack. He walks a few steps to experience the falling-forward feeling, but he feels stronger than he did when he left, or when he was at the bridge.

He yells out as loud as he can and is surprised to see part of the opposite hillside move, as an elk bounds away into the trees.

He slips out his neoprene pad from under the stretch cord and sits on it with his back against the tree. From this vantage point, he can see Pelican Creek wind snake-like up the tapering valley to his left. In here, the grasses are taller than in the broad part of the valley. Across from him is the bald summit of Pelican Cone.

He takes a deep breath and relaxes completely for a moment, letting the hallucinogenic drugs take over. He bends forward at the waist, stretching out his hamstrings and rubbing his lower back. He wonders why mushrooms always give him lower back spasms.

After several minutes of stretching and bending, he rolls and lights a marijuana cigarette and becomes aware of the hisses and gurgles of the thermal area next to him. He watches occasional explosions lift small bits of mud into the air 10 feet away. He stands up and twists his torso, then takes another deep puff, watching the day brighten and crystallize. Upon exhaling, he retrieves his 35-mm camera from inside his pack. He stretches his body toward the sun and, as soon as the inspiration comes to him, he undresses completely. There is no one around.

Wearing only a camera, he walks over to the first little mud volcano, a one-foot-high, pale-blue cone. Just as he snaps a picture, it throws up a little mud that lands in his hair.

"You little devil," he admonishes, as he pulls out the warm mud.

He walks over to another bubbling pot, this one a wide pool of blue-gray mud, more watery, and the little bubbles hold their form at the surface momentarily before bursting into puffs of steam. He takes a picture at one-five-hundredths of a second and starts to move up to another thermal feature.

"Wait a minute." May never see this place again. Must look at it—really look at it. Remember this until you're 80, for you might never come here again.

He takes off his camera and gets down on his hands and knees. Careful not to leave sign of his presence, he leans over and touches the inside of the mud pot with his finger. He looks closely at the thick, slippery, clay and silica liquid.

Look closer.

He gets it five inches away from his eyes and notices fine, multicolored fragments as he spreads it between his fingers like fingerpaint. He wipes it off on his arm, then crawls around on his hands and knees.

Must experience this with every cell in my body, because it is right now!

He crawls to another little volcano and puts his ear to the hard rock. He can hear it well up from down in the earth and emit a splash of the silica. "Sounds like a cowboy spitting." He looks from ground level at the rock and now sees there is orange lichen on it; the rock is alive.

He walks now, only a few steps away, and bends back down to smell the pink and blue and yellow flowers. He crushes a bit of sage between his fingers, and swoons. He looks closer and sees insect life—the local residents—on the plants, and the flowers, and on the ground.

How removed are we from the earth, he thinks, watching an ant carry a twig. How far have we come mentally and socially and how far have we come as animals? We have put a gap between ourselves and the earth and, as we get older and more complacent, we want our comfort and we don't really want to hear what it cost us and sure, the earth will always provide for us, won't it? There will always be the good things from it and vegetables come from the grocery store at least until the population doubles again in forty or fifty years. But I am so lucky to be up here where there is no television or radio, no media to remind me of the constant problems of the planet. . . .

He draws his hand over the side of the clay mud pot.

Now how many of us would know how to live off the land if we had to? I wouldn't know how to raise a garden, wouldn't know where to begin. We've become specialists. The Shoshoni Indians used to live up here, but once I ran out of salami and cheese, I'd start to get pretty hungry. Who am I fooling? I am modern man.

He stalks his way uphill, feels textures with his bare feet, smells the chemical vapors, listens to the symphony of bubbles and gurgles, feels the sun warm his body. He does 25 push-ups, finishing with a roar. Then he lays down on his back and tilts his face to the sun before moving on.

He is at the top of the geyser area now. He turns and takes in the entire panorama, the length of Pelican Creek before it disappears into the trees a mile and a half to his left, the green, flower-frosted valley that awaits him, and the terraces of mud puts, mud kettles, and the mud volcanoes beneath him.

It almost looks like an artist's palette below me, so many different shades and hues. It's like a Stravinsky symphony in motion. Each feature, each bubble has its own tone. There are the tubas, the flutes, a French horn.

With that thought, he turns, calling to the thing tugging at the back of his mind, whether or not to go as far as the next puff of steam billowing up from a half mile behind him up in the woods.

"Do it," he decides.

He takes off at a trot, naked and barefoot, and he feels light, elastic. Places are opening up for his feet at each step. He plows uphill, his huge thighs glistening, bulging in their exposure to sunlight.

"Wait—slow down," he says aloud, relaxing to a walk. "Then again, it feels good to run." He bounds up again for a hundred yards before an abrupt incline slows him to a walk.

"I love you, Mother Nature!" he yells out. He picks up a pine cone and presses its sharpness into his palms.

He comes out of the trees at a 50-foot-wide pool with small bubbles rising here and there and with just the slightest bit of steam swirling around the top. He knows the water will be in the vicinity of 105 degrees Fahrenheit.

It's so much easier to bend over and move without clothes! "Warm, feels good."

But, he thinks, the center looks deep. There's not another person around and the area bordering the perimeter is soft with algae and mud, like maybe I could get stuck, and the harder I work to get out, the further I sink. And the further I sink, the hotter it gets.

He moves around the pool, checking for possible places to enter. At the runout on the other side, there is a small grass land bar and, with a stick, he stabs at the soft bottom. He sees he couldn't step in. He would have to dive.

But it might be a real problem getting out.

He checks it once more for temperature and, whether by choice or by accident, he lets his momentum carry him forward. He does a flat dive out into the center of the pool, then comes up and voices his exhilaration at being immersed in the soft, warm mineral water.

"Ahhh, praise Neptune!"

He wades about for several minutes before he dog paddles back to where he got in. All it takes to beach himself is a stroke forward then a simple side-straddle move and he is sitting on the grassy shore, dripping. Twice more he dives in, paddles the circumference of the pool and vaults himself out before he realizes he left his clothes spread out over his pack and his $500 camera lying by the mud pots.

"They're OK."

He brushes his thin blond hair back and wipes the water from his face. But he knows there is more to see that day, so he takes off in a trot back down the hill to the mudpots.

Nothing has changed, so once more he walks over to consider the strange thermal features, so incongruous to the surrounding area, a lush little valley dotted with burned-out areas. He gnaws on half of one more stem of the psychedelic mushrooms, chasing it with water and his last mints.

Though his stomach is tightening as a side effect of the mushrooms, he eats a slice of cheese, three crackers, a bit of salami and a handful of gorp as he puts his clothes on over his still-moist body. He spins himself into his pack and returns to the trail.

So what is society going to do with me? I feel like the man who knows too much. Should I enjoy being alone this much? I wish I had someone to share these revelations. . . .

It is the first time he finds himself wanting for company. He suppresses the whim.

The experience at the mud volcanoes will be a memorable one to him. The mudpots and mushpots, the sky, the swimming hole, the valley, the clarity of the revelations, the feeling of omnipotence, the moment of nirvana.

After half an hour of hiking, he comes to another confluence in the creek and there, next to it, is the mutilated carcass of an elk, only its legs and head have not been eaten away. Ross feels the hair bristle on the back of his head, for he sees the elk has been killed recently; the scraped earth reveals signs of a struggle, and bear tracks are well defined in the soft soil.

He breathes in the rotting smell and finds himself walking very quietly around it, his senses alert. He circumvents the elk far to the left. Then there is something else to occupy his thoughts, a creek crossing. He thinks it over and chooses his second option, taking off his boots, socks and jeans and wading across.

After crossing the creek, he leaves the last semblance of wide open spaces for the trees. Again the trail is laden with pine needles as it works its way uphill. He hikes for an hour in silence and his thoughts are balanced, solid, linear. But occasionally something he can't release in the back of his mind bothers him. His thoughts turn to what he might like to do in the fall, and somehow Europe doesn't feel right to him. Is that it? So many people have been to Europe and it's going to be winter, and I want a new horizon.

The important thing is that I take my time and enjoy all this, he reminds himself.

Another half hour on the trail and still something, some problem will not surface. He has always used mushrooms as a cleanser, a rinse for his mind, purging all his unwanted demons, a chance to look at life from the other side.

Dig it out. Unblock.

When the trail comes out of the woods again, he stops to take a break. Studying his topo map, he sees that the trail goes north to a junction, then doubles back.

Why doesn't the trail just go across this meadow in front of me?

"That's it; that's bothering me. It's the trail. The trail is still too focused, a final link with the world. "I'm going this way," he says, drawing a hypotenuse with his finger to his destination.

No more civilization. No more trail.

Despite three creek crossings and submarining his boots several times in the swamps, he manages to cut a mile off his hike.

Free walking, free thinking, unstructured. "Make my own trail."

When he sees one of the orange trail markers reuniting him with the trail, he feels that he has finally broken some new ground for the day, for his life, a new horizon. Something different.

But now the sun tells him it is getting on evening, and he wants to get to his campsite. A half hour later he decides campsite WS1 is fine. It is right on the edge of Fern Lake and there is a bit of flat ground. There's a fire ring, and someone has left a good pile of wood.

During the next four hours, Ross sets up his camp, gathers more wood, explores the area, builds a fire, cooks and hungrily eats a huge pot of stew. After several handfuls of gorp, he gets up to walk 200 yards and clean his pot in the lake outlet. Afterward, he sits back to watch the stars through the trees above. Only the crackle of the fire and the soft sounds of his Hohner Special 20 key of G harmonica break the silence. He plays an old cowboy song. His soft, wide-set brown eyes reveal weariness as he reflects upon the 14 miles he hiked that day.

He switches his thoughts to his other problem—where he wants to go in the fall. He closes his eyes and scans the globe in the living room of his parent's house and suddenly lights upon a location. He remembers, as a child, pondering the long island so far away.

"New Zealand!"

He stands, claps his hands and struts to the lake, charged with inspiration once again. "I'm going to New Zealand," he shouts into the inky blackness. It echoes, "Zealand. . . Zealand. . . Zealand. . . ."

By myself?

He turns from the blackness of the lake and walks back to the fire. He fortifies himself. Yes, by myself, he answers. Take the road not taken and see what there is to see. "I'm going to New Zealand," he tells the fire.

July 27. Cache Creek Road, Jackson, Wyoming.

The girl with the electronic stopwatch shouts times to the second runner as he flashes by her. Then she turns her head to see the third-place runner approaching quickly from 30 yards away.

"6:03, 6:04, 6:05, 6:06," she says, as the tall, lanky, curly-headed figure passes. She watches him go and sees a fourth runner 50 yards down the road, then more in the distance.

6:05 for the first mile, strong uphill. I guess that's OK. Not far behind Riev. Just pace off him. Wish I knew who that guy was running in first. Wasn't Pilkington. Nobody I've seen in any of the other races. Just pace off Riev. Feel great today. It's beautiful up this drainage. No wonder these Jackson runners are tough, they have all these great trails to run. Riev and Shawn are going to do Pike's Peak. Less than one month away.

Breathing. Control the breathing. Two steps in breath, two steps out breath. There you go. Good. Now pick out a line. Cut the corners. Control your center of gravity. That's it. Not too much up and down. Same smooth effort as the flats. Crest the tops of the hills without slowing down. One step just like the other. Glad I didn't wear my long-sleeved shirt. Warm now for sure. Hey, no surge. Just stay on pace. Surge if you think you can take him for keeps. Eleven-mile race. Just cruise for awhile here. Feel like I've got an awful lot left, but they talked about a saddle before we run down the other drainage. Save. Conserve. Get those lines off your face. Arms relaxed. Let them hang for a couple of strides. That's it. Everything relaxed. Get Zen. That's it. Relax and run faster.

Half-way marker. I hope this is the top of the saddle. OK. Now this is where they said to look out for the overgrowth covering the trail and covering the logs across the trail. Where's that first guy? Gone. Fourth gear. There goes Riev. Downhill for sure. Weight back. There you go. Gonna have to change your vision. Only a few steps ahead. OK. Now to increase speed, increase leg speed by swinging the arms faster. Small steps. Control. "Whoa!" Up! That was a branch. Hit that thing and I'm on my face. Riev's moving away from me. Here comes Shawn. No way am I going to let you pass me, man. No way. Damn weeds are waist deep in here. Wish I could see where my feet are going.

Riev's still gaining on me. How do you run this stuff? Where's Shawn? Don't look. Yes, look. He's right there. Me in fourth? No way. I killed these guys in a 10K. What do they know about running in the mountains that I don't?

"Comin' roun'."

The hell you are! Reckless abandon. Hell with form. Branch! Up! Ahhh. . . Ohhh. . . Falling! Arms out!!!

"Unnnhhh!"

"You OK?"

"Yea." Get up. More runners behind? God, somebody could break his shin on that thing. Go. Stay with Shawn at least. Spit the dirt out.

This is war now. Go. Something bleeding down there. Stomach a little. Leg, too. Nothing broken. Couldn't run this fast.

At the seven-mile marker a support crew member holds out a cup of water.

"Water?"

"Yea."

OK. Four more miles. See if those long runs helped out. Where's their footprints? Where's the trail? There's Shawn. This is the creek crossing I heard them talking about. There's Riev and the other guy, closer than I thought. Hell with the log. Jump it.

Made it.

Fell in the creek, tripped over a log and almost got beat to death by flowering weeds but feel good. Time to regroup.

Let's move up.

Now legs, lengthen it out. Flat now. Slightly downhill. Pick a good line. Beautiful dirt road. Like Virginia. Home turf. There's Riev, maybe 60 yards. Catch Shawn first.

Pass Randy at the nine-mile marker.

"Hey Steve, run together?"

"Let's go." Good-bye. OK, where's the lead guy? Go get him.

10-mile marker.

Person.

"One more mile to go!"

Sharp corner. Go for him now. Pick up distance. Long sweeping bend, he'll never know I'm gaining on the lead guy. Side trail. He didn't take it. There's his footprint. Run a sharper line than his, close to the ditch. Last mile. Go! More. Push it. Respond! There is your prey.

Quarter mile to go. Damn, his dust isn't even settling before. . . there he is! Fifteen yards. . . . Two runners! Three runners? Shawn! Riev! Came down from that side trail. Said it was a free-for-all. There's the finish!

"Come on Steve!"

Beautiful Salina.

"Go Randy!"

"Shawn!"

"Marty!"

Sprint! On the right. Track speed in your faces, suckers. Get 'em. "Ohhh!" Watch the elbow, pal. Don't look back; just go! Someone trying to win my race, go pump those legs now, who's that in the corner of my eye? Fifty-meter kick in your face sucker 'cause I've got *this* much more hell with this pain. Stop running pull over quit everything go stop go go go pump pump faster faster faster faster faster I've won!!!

"Yea!!!"

Sugarfoot Cafe, Jackson. Noon.

Steve leans back and takes another sip of the cool strawberry daiquiri. Stiffly, he raises his feet with his brand new Birkenstock leather sandals onto the white wicker chair across from him. "These things are really comfortable. I wonder if Imre'd mind if I wore these to work?"

"Steve, right after lunch we're going to get that cut cleaned up. That dried blood looks terrible."

"I kind of like it. A badge of honor from the battle. I feel like a gladiator. Tell me again about the ending."

‌‌‌‌‌‌

"It was great. We could see Randy and Shawn coming down the trail from one way and you and that other guy coming from around the left. When everybody saw you guys so close, it was like a charge of electricity went through the air. But it looked like you were running a little faster, and you were. You were great. You went right past everyone with maybe 85 yards to go. That's when they all started chugging like freight trains to keep up with you. That little guy. . . who was he?"

"Said his name was Marty something. He was just passing through from Texas. Houston, I think. Said he'd ran a 2:14 marathon before."

"Yea? Well he was really going for it. They were back there throwing elbows like in a basketball game or something. Finally, at the end, that guy just dove for the line."

"I saw him out the corner of my eye."

"Well, you beat him, that's for sure. I think Shawn and Randy were dead even for third. It was exciting. Blood, dust, sweat, everything."

"Excuse me. Who gets the ham panini and who gets the antipasta plate?"

"We're gonna share. It doesn't matter. Thank you so much."

"Anything else right now?"

"Uhh, two more strawberry daiquiris, please."

"Sure."

"Steve, such lavishness."

"Salina, I love to win, I've got to admit it. I love to race and I like going as fast as I can. I would never go too fast. I'd always want to be faster until I was the fastest distance runner on the face of the earth."

She reaches over and takes his hand. "Steve, somebody's got to finish second."

"It doesn't have to be me. I'm going to win Pike's Peak now. Riev was third last year. Shawn was fifth. We're talking about a one-two-three sweep."

"I think it's this way," says Kitty. "It's been so long since I've been back here."

"We're lost for sure," says Wilbur. "Ten minutes away from the car and we're lost forever."

He follows Kitty through the lodgepole, thin here, dotted with occasional hot springs. He watches her walk, the way she holds her head up, the way she seems to walk with dignity, almost royalty—with poise, yet with an adolescent sexuality. Wilbur notices that she's lost weight and looks just great. She has the body of a 16-year-old girl. He wonders if he could just let his passion fly here, grab her in his arms, make love to her on that patch of moss.

But his instincts tell him to remain cautious; his impetuosity may underscore the three-year age difference that worries him sometimes. She seems to him to be so much more calm and controlled than he. So much more experienced.

He feels that somehow he needs to get a story published, accomplish something important before he can truly gain her respect, and his own self-respect. Make her see that she truly does belong with him. I'm halfway finished with that runner story. I should get on that. Why can't I finish it? What *is* the ending?

I love this woman so much. But something lately hasn't been right. Not like in spring. Sometimes it's just not the same Kitty. Just by vibrations, I can feel she doesn't want me there. I'm intruding on some personal privacy; she makes me a stranger. That old boyfriend, Byron, is still in Mammoth. But she's got me over the edge now. I would fight for her. I need to see her. It's almost like a physical addiction. God, what an empty summer it would be without her now.

"We're almost there."

"We're lost for eternity, I'm sure. Have to live like wolves. I'll beat the bears back with sticks while you make bread from hand-ground pine needles. In five years, they'll discover us. *National Geographic* will do a story."

"Wilbur, we're less than a mile from the highway."

"You saw that *Twilight Zone* too?"

"I'm going to bring you a typewriter and leave you out here. Chain you up. Let your imagination go wild. Bring you stir-fried vegetables once a week."

"And Mout." She *is* a great cook. I don't think I've eaten in the EDR but twice in the last two weeks. What can I do to repay her for that? Marry her. But aren't I too young to get married? No, not to Kitty, not to this woman.

"We're here! I've found it."

Wilbur pushes aside a tree branch and they both look over the 12-foot-wide warm water creek. Kitty sticks a hand in it.

"Perfect," she says, and sits down to start undressing. "It's the same as I remember it."

"It's deep enough right here?"

"You'll see. *I'm* going in. This place is so nice."

Wilbur looks over the rust-colored stream bottom. He walks 15
yards upstream and puts his hand in the water. "It looks like people
have been getting in up here too," he says. He walks back to the bank
next to Kitty, sits, undresses, and slides next to her into the bubbling,
warm cascades.

"Ahhh. Kitty, this is great. Thanks for showing it to me."

"It is nice. I used to ride my bike up here a lot. I'm going to have
to start doing that again."

"I'd like to do that too."

"I'm not spending enough time out of doors this summer. I feel
so relaxed," she says.

Wilbur looks at her leaning back with her eyes closed. Droplets
of water and steam on her high cheekbones make her face seem so
youthful and fresh, so inviting. The tumbling hot water moves and
massages her pliant breasts, and her nipples are erect. He reaches
over and brushes away little bits of obsidian sediment that have
settled in her belly button, on her flat stomach. He thinks somehow
that he shouldn't try to make love to her now, that she is absorbed
within herself, but he starts to massage her thighs, slippery smooth
in the hot mineral water. He reaches the inside of her thigh, and a
moan of delight comes from her parted lips. She lowers herself into
the warm eddy and rests her head against an exposed rock. Wilbur
rolls over to kiss her. He draws her face to his, and she does not resist.
He raises his dripping body above her.

August 1. Lupine Dormitory, Room 115.

So you're going out with Herm again?" Salina asks. "Sounds like
this is getting pretty serious."

"I hope he doesn't think so," says Kris. "I've never kissed him or
anything. I like his company. He's funny. Don't you think he's cute?"

"I think he looks like the Pillsbury Dough Boy."

They both laugh as Kris straightens the petite black bow tie on
her white satin long-sleeved shirt.

"Well, he's a lot different from John, that's for sure."

"Did you get a letter from him today?"

"No. It's been two weeks. He's probably forgotten all about me
by now."

"I doubt that. The mail takes a while to get here. You know that."

Kris slips on her matching black vest. "Do you think Herm should
have to pay? I mean, he asked me to go, but it's not a real date or
anything."

"God, I knew I should have kept up my subscription to *Cosmo*. How are we going to know how to deal with a crisis like this? Where do we turn?"

"Oh stop, Salina. Come on. You California girls are supposed to be way ahead of us Southerners in these matters. Should I pay? What is protocol?"

Salina gets up off the bed and steps into her purple running sweats. "Who paid the last time?"

"Herm did."

"The whole thing?"

"Yea."

"That's a miracle." Salina rolls her torso and grasps her calf. "Then you should pay for dinner tonight. Insist on it. But tell him to pick up a half case of the white Mouton Cadet. Tell him I said it's his turn."

"Can I go to a meeting sometime without committing a felony?"

"Sure. If you can get Herm to pay for a half case of wine, I'll see that you get a medal of honor."

"Hey, how are you and Steve getting along? I haven't seen him for a few days."

"Great. This summer has been perfect for me. It's better we're on opposite schedules. He's not around too much, which gives me time to myself. I didn't realize how much I needed that. I'm finally catching my breath from school." She rotates and grabs her right calf. "Steve's consistent, you know what I mean? Well-mannered. At least as long as his training's going well."

"Herm's very well-mannered too."

"He is?" Salina asks, reaching up to the ceiling.

"Yea. He opens the door of his Jeep for me."

They both laugh as there comes a knock on the door. Salina bounces onto the bed next to the door and puts a finger to her lips. "Ssshhh."

Kris opens the door. "Hi Herm."

"Hello, my dear. Ahhh. . . you look lovely tonight as usual. But you are dating the handsomest man in the park, so that is not surprising."

"I'm all ready, Prince Charming!" says Kris, grabbing her purse and jacket as she silently forms the words to Salina with a wink and a smile, "Pillsbury Dough Boy!"

Stagecoach dining room, West Yellowstone.

Kris watches Herm peer over the large menu, his head bobbing slowly up and down. "Well, I don't know," he says. "After buying those four bottles of wine, I'm a little short. Maybe I'll have the chopped steak. That sounds good. Topped with an onion ring and *your choice* of potato. Hmmm."

Kris puts her hand on Herm's forearm. "Herm, I'm buying tonight. Have whatever you'd like."

"No, that's OK, Kris. We should be OK." He chuckles, "Just won't be able to pay the tax or tip the waitress, that's all."

"Herm, I insist."

Kris watches Herm's eyes shift to the right side of the menu. "Really? I did have the chopped steak the last time I ate here. I've never had the Cordon Bleu. Sounds good. What is this? Pate?"

"That's *paté!*"

"*Paté.* Made with port wine, served on a bib of romaine lettuce with Melba toast. Sounds good. Now what's this? Vichysoysa?"

"Vichyssoise, Herm. It's cold potato and leek soup."

"How do you know so much about international cuisine?"

"I'm a waitress, Herm. We used to serve vichyssoise back at the place I worked at in Florida. Let's try one of each of those appetizers."

"I'll buy some wine then."

"OK. That's a deal. I'll have the shrimp, Herm."

"Shrimp. I see. Deep fried or sauteed?"

"Sauteed, please."

"My my. OK. That sounds good."

With folded hands, Kris lets Herm garble the order to the waitress and finds herself again putting her hand on top of his. "You did great, Herm."

"Thank you, Kris. I'll get the hang of being a classy aristocrat yet."

Kris is self-conscious about the hairy hand that has returned her gesture by grasping her hand. She squeezes back. "Herm, excuse me. I have to powder my nose."

Herm watches Kris seemingly glide out of the room and thinks, this could be the night. A few more glasses of wine would make us both more relaxed. Yes, this could be my lucky night. A tall, beautiful blond. She looks *so* good. And how about the way she's been grabbing my hand. Real natural. She's mine. The moon is full. Subtly mention that we must go hot potting after dinner. Even cleaned up my cabin just in case she wants to spend the night. The charisma is flowing tonight. Impress her.

"Kris, what are you doing?" she asks the mirror. Stop leading him on like that. Come on, girl. Have a good time tonight. You know he's going to want you to go hotpotting after dinner. He even has two towels in the back of his jeep. And I want to go. But not if I let this get out of control. John, why haven't I gotten a letter from you?

Over appetizers, they laugh at each other's work stories: Herm's pine marten scampering around the lobby and Kris's attempting French and accidently asking if the party would care to order something from the book store. Herm spreads a cracker with paté and dips it in the vichyssoise.

"Herm, what are you doing?"

"Well, I've always been a *pate* and potatoes kind of guy, Kris. Ordinary, yet fascinating and exotic at the same time."

They laugh. Kris's face reflects the luminosity of the wine, and her eyes reflect the bright yellow points of the candles in the room.

"So what else has been happening at night lately?"

"Oh, not much. I caught a couple of your co-workers trying to pee in Old Faithful the other night. Caught them with their pants down, so to speak. Which reminds me, will you be ready to do a little hotpotting after dinner?"

Kris takes a sip of wine and pulls a strand of blond hair behind her ear. "Yes, I'd like to try it. But wait. We can't. I didn't bring a towel."

"Funny coincidence. I just happen to have two towels in the Jeep."

"It will be dark. Did you bring a flashlight too?"

"Full moon, we won't need one."

"Herm, you think of everything, don't you?"

"Yes, but let me I.D. that fingerprint. I don't go hotpotting with just anyone, you know. Name please."

"Galadriel, Queen of the Elves. Now could you let me have a little more wine?"

"Certainly."

"Herm, did you see those guys playing poker in the next room? Didn't you tell me you were the world's greatest poker player?"

"I may sit in for a couple of hands after dinner just to win enough to cover the evening. If you stand behind me, you shall bring me good luck."

"I heard one of the guys in the EDR call you aces and eights. What does that mean?"

"Uhh humm. It means I'm lucky. Evidenced by the fact that you are with me tonight."

Forty minutes and another bottle of wine later, Kris and Herm leave the dining room. Herm is fortified with a $20 bill to enter the no-limit poker game and try his luck against the local gamblers.

With Kris's arm in his, he walks down the corridor to the poker room. "Poker is 10 percent luck and 90 percent bluff, my dear. I have the advantage, since none of these poker players have ever seen me play before. They will have no idea where I'm coming from."

"Yes, they will, Herm. You still have cordon bleu sauce on your cheek. They'll know you're coming from the dining room."

"Very funny," he says, wiping his cheek with the back of his hand.

Herm leads Kris through the swinging gate into the dimly lit room, bright only around the table, where serious, unrevealing faces watch the betting action through layers of thick tobacco smoke. The dealer, a thin, wiry man with a heavily wrinkled face and an unfiltered cigarette hanging from the left corner of his mouth, peers up at them from under the bright light. "Seat number six open, sir."

Herm and Kris meet the gaze of the player in the first seat on the dealer's left—a heavily bearded, cigar-smoking man with a fringed mountain-man jacket and a wide-brimmed leather hat. He blows out a puff of blue smoke and scrutinizes them before returning his attention to the table.

"Go get 'em, Herm."

"Come stand behind me for good luck." She lets him give her a kiss on the cheek.

For his $20, Herm gets three red $5 chips and five $1 yellows. Kris sees that around the table the player with the next least amount of chips has three times that many, and most have substantial stacks of each color. The mountain man has the most, three five-inch-high stacks of reds. He squints at her and puffs before she stands in closer to Herm.

The dealer pushes a pile of chips to a man in a cowboy hat, then slides a four-inch-wide disk to a lady on the opposite side of the table.

"Low ball," she says, sliding a yellow chip toward the center of the table.

Herm turns around to Kris. "Low ball."

"What's that?"

"Make the worst hand possible."

"Good luck, Herm. The way I heard you play cards, you should have no trouble winning this one."

Herm looks at his five cards and shows them to Kris: Ace, two, five, six, nine. The betting goes around the table. Herm matches the $2 opening and raises $5. There are five calls, two of the players grunting at the newcomer's abrupt raise, a change in the pattern. The dealer goes around and gives cards to the remaining five players in the hand. Herm takes one. He shows Kris and she sees he has thrown the nine away and drawn a seven. She gives him a blank, 'Is-that-good?' expression.

The betting comes around to Herm. "Call three, raise 10," he says, pushing all his chips to the center. The mountain man folds and the man with the cowboy hat stays. "You're called, sir," says the dealer, and Herm and the man with the cowboy hat lay down their cards.

"Seven, six, five, three to seven, six five, two—you win, sir," the dealer says, and pushes the pile of red and yellow chips to Herm. Kris thrusts her fist forward and squeals, breaking the reverent silence. She pats him on the back. "Way to go, Herm."

"Nothing to it, my dear." Herm turns to the dealer. "Will they accept chips at the bar?"

"Yes, sir."

"Thank you," Herm says, as he tosses a $1 chip to the dealer. It rolls across the green-felt table into one of the red stacks of chips in front of the mountain man before the dealer can surround it.

"Thank you," says the dealer, twice tapping the gratuity on the metal chip rack before depositing it into his shirt pocket.

Herm turns to Kris. "Kris, would you be a sweetheart and get us a couple of cocktails. Get whatever you'd like. I'd like a Jack Daniels and coke," and he hands her a red and two yellows.

By the time Kris returns with the drinks, Herm is involved with the next hand and his pile of chips is nearly spent again.

In the center of the table are five cards spread out face up: A four, two jacks, a nine and a five. Herm takes a strong sip of the cocktail and shows Kris the two cards he has in his hand—two fours. "Hold 'em," he whispers. She doesn't understand but watches Herm push the last of his chips into the center. The next two players drop out and it is Herm and the lady opposite him remaining.

"All bets are called. Show your cards, please."

"Full house," Herm beams with a snap of the cards. "Fours over jacks."

"Jacks over nines," the lady quips back.

Herm leans over to look at her hand. "Two pair?"

"Full house. Jacks *over* nines."

The dealer pushes the pile of chips to the lady and Herm looks down at the patch of green between his hands. He turns to Kris, forces a smile, then looks back across the table to the mountain man, who squints at him and blows a puff of smoke under the overhead lamp.

"Tough luck," he says.

"Thank you," says Herm, as he stands up. His hand slips into his pocket and surrounds the piece of paper he knows to be his last $5.

"Would you like to watch more, Kris, or would you rather leave?"

"I'd rather go hotpotting," she says.

Herm shrugs to the gazing faces of the poker players. "Next time."

The full moon has come up over National Park Mountain behind Herm and Kris, illuminating the hillside opposite them and the meadow where the two-foot-deep hot stream runs next to the Madison River.

"This is so great," Kris says. "I can't believe this is the first time I've done this. This feels wonderful."

"I'm surprised there's no one else down here. Usually on a full-moon night, there are a lot of employees around."

"Are you sure this one is legal?"

"Yup. The definition of a legal hotpot in Yellowstone Park is that you can go anywhere after warm water mixes in with cold water. They know the Madison River is 15 yards away and that it's mixing with the warm water coming out of the ground right over there."

"Oooh, what was that?"

"Bubbles? There are gas bubbles coming up from the ground. Perfectly harmless."

"They tickle."

"The best way to enjoy this hotpot is to lean back and put your head against the bank; just lie back and observe the universe. I've seen up to 20 shooting stars from here in one night."

"OK. Like this? Oh, look at that moon. I've never seen it that bright. I can't even focus on it. This is beautiful."

"So are you, Kris. You look so beautiful tonight. The moonlight shining off your skin. I'd really. . . ." He leans over to kiss her. His lips just touch hers for a moment, but the softness of their mouths meeting lasts for just a second before she turns her head away.

"Herm, I want to. I really want to, but I can't. You have to understand."

"Why can't you?"

"Because John and I made a promise to each other that we wouldn't. Herm, it's not that I don't like you."

"I feel that you are attracted to me."

"I am, Herm. I can't explain it. You're older. You're so different from John. I feel comfortable being around you. It's like you bring out a part of me that even I don't know about yet."

Kris leans her head back on the shore and Herm sits next to her. "Would you like a leg massage? Prevents those varicose veins."

"That would be nice. Sure."

"John. Somehow it hurts me to hear you say that name. I know he's a star football player and all. He must be a wonderful lover. The jocks always get the pretty girls. I wrestled a little in high school, you know."

"Herman?"

"Yes, Kris."

"I don't know if he's a wonderful lover or not. He's the only lover I've ever had."

"He is? The only one? And you're talking about getting married? Do you want to live your whole life with only having one lover?"

She closes her eyes, bringing shadows of grimace to her fair, even face. "I don't know that. I really don't. That question has been driving me crazy all summer long. I'm only 21 years old!"

"Well, how are you going to find out if you never have another lover?"

She touches him on the arm for a moment, then moves to splash water over her exposed breasts. He has come to the end of her logic. "I don't know. I guess maybe I'm a little unsure about having made that promise to him. Maybe he feels the same way. It's been over two weeks since I've gotten a letter from him."

Herm kneads her smooth-as-silk calves with his pudgy hands. "Well, I guess I have a confession to make too. I haven't been with a girl this whole summer. I haven't wanted to since. . . I met you, Kris."

She touches his face, brushing away a drop of water from his brow. "Herm, you must have lots of girlfriends. You're good looking and you're witty. You're always making people laugh."

"You think I'm good looking? I didn't even think you'd even go out with me because I was fat."

"I think you're very handsome."

Herm raises out of the water onto his knees, bends over Kris and hugs her. He runs his hand up the side of her smooth, sleek body from her ankle to her shoulders. She squeezes his body to her and rubs her cheek against his before he sits back down and continues massaging her, working his way up to her thighs. "You have no idea what saying that does for the confidence of an ordinary guy like me coming from a beautiful girl like you."

"Herm, you're not ordinary."

"That's all I need. Someone to care for me a little. Someone to share with. Someone to say nice things like that every once in a while. I could conquer the world, Kris."

"I have many nice things to say about you. You're sensitive and affectionate."

"See Kris, a guy like me has maybe one chance in a lifetime to be with a really beautiful girl. A classy girl. I'll probably be married to some dark-haired hag who chain smokes and wears stretch pants."

Under water, Herm's forearm brushes lightly over her silky pubic hairs.

"Herm, don't say that. Blond hair doesn't last forever. It will be gone and it will just be me. So don't set me up like a goddess. Don't you like me because we get along together and have fun? Because we talk?"

"Of course. You know that. We get along really well."

She pauses, then lets out a sigh. "Look at this." She rolls over away from him and reveals a round, discolored patchy scar on her right hip.

"How'd it happen?"

"When I was 10 years old, I fell off my bicycle. I cried for days. I didn't ever want to leave the house. I thought it would spread and I'd look like that all over."

"It doesn't matter. I would still care for you if we looked the same. Even if you were my exact female counterpart. That's why being with you is so special to me. But I'm 28 now, and how many. . . ."

"Herm, don't touch me there! That's too far up to massage."

"Sorry. Even if you weren't the most beautiful girl in the park, I would still have to say this: I love you, Kris."

She reaches up to hug him. "Oh, Herm. Don't say that."

"It's true. We have a great time together. We laugh so much. I think about you all the time. I really *love* you."

She looks into his round face, blue-white in the reflection of the full moon. Timid, vulnerable in his sincerity. "Herm, kiss me once, please."

He bends over her again, smoothing the silvery blond hair back, slowly moving his head toward hers, then kissing her fully, totally on her moist, parted lips. Their rhythmic passion grows wildly into squeezing, caressing, holding, touching. Soft moans build steadily from inside Kris. Herm lets his hand slide up her side and surround her breast. Then he rolls over, supports himself above her, and as he starts to lower himself on top of her, she moves to receive him. With her thrashing beneath him, he starts to enter her.

"No! Please, help me! No, Herm, I just can't," she cries. "I'm so stupid! This is my fault. I'm really confused. I shouldn't have asked you to kiss me just then." She slides away from him. "I don't. . . I made a promise. I'm sorry."

Herm sits down and there is a long pause. He lets out a short sigh. "I'm sorry too. I wanted to make love to you. More than I've ever wanted anything. But I must learn to do the right thing. I wanted to seduce you tonight, like you were the ultimate prize in the universe or something. I mean, I meant everything I said. I just don't have a lot of self-respect right now. I need to find the way to build that inside myself. If I had that, do you think you would be mine for a while?"

"That's just it. I don't know if I want to be anybody's right now. I still need to learn about what I want and don't want. I need to find out about myself. There are so many questions I'm just starting to ask myself. When I first met you, I was attracted to you somehow. . . sexually. I was going to ask you if we could just have sex." She pauses. "I saw you for the first time. You were wearing your badge and uniform and you were talking to Faysal and some other people and you were so in control and confident, just. . . so manly."

"We could try just having casual sex too," says Herm. He drops an arm in the water. "God, now I'm confused."

She sits up and faces him. With her head resting on her forearms, she looks up at him, thinking, "No, I still promised."

Just then, the noise from a large group of people comes into focus. The laughter gets louder as they approach the spring. Herm and Kris look into each other's eyes.

"Right now, could we just lie against the bank and hold hands for a few minutes before we get out?" Herm says.

"That would be nice. I would like that."

August 4. Mallard Lake.

Tina helps Jorge gather their remaining food supplies and put them into the black tent stuff sack. Then they sit back down facing the fire.

"It was a very good dinner," says Jorge, the bus boy from San Blas, Mexico. "What do you call it again?"

"Chow mein. Or just call it stir-fried vegetables, except we put chicken in it."

"I shall open a Chinese restaurant in San Blas, I think."

"Hey," says the petite Tina, poking Jorge, her round face pouting under her even-cropped brown bangs. "You promised me you were coming back to the park next summer, remember?"

Jorge sets the cheese in the sack and walks over to embrace Tina. "Yes I am, Tina. And you will be coming back, and I'm going to be waitri and send money back home so my parents can come see the Yellowstone Park and meet you."

"Promise you won't drown in your father's fishing boat this winter?"

"I promise. I shall bring you the biggest *camarones* you've ever seen."

"What are *camarones*?"

"Shrimp. Like you."

"Jorge!" She slaps him lightly on the arm. He grabs her and tickles her ribs, and they lapse into a giddy laughter.

"Stop!" she giggles.

As Jorge lays another log across the fire, Tina looks into his smooth, brown face and bright, honest eyes. He is so beautiful, she thinks. So considerate and proper. She tries to imagine her father and mother's reaction when she tells them she has a Mexican boyfriend. What would they say if they did get married at the end of next summer, like they had talked about?

"I think we've got everything," says Jorge. "How many doughnuts do you want for dessert?"

"I'm full. I don't want one now, Jorge. But go ahead."

"I will take one out. Maybe in an hour," he says, placing it on the log by the fire.

They walk 50 feet away. With Tina holding the flashlight, Jorge cleans off the dishes in the lake and puts them into the tent stuff sack with their food. Then he tosses the sack over a tree limb and hoists it up with a rope.

"Is that good enough for you, Miss Picky?"

Albany County Public Library
www.albanycountylibrary.org
307-721-2580

User name: DIRIENZO, SARA M.

Current time: 08/29/2010,14:29
Title: Sushi lo : a novel about modern Iran
Date charged: 8/29/2010,14:29
Date due: 9/19/2010,23:59
Item ID: 39092051210666

Current time: 08/29/2010,14:29
Title: The beckoning silence
Date charged: 8/29/2010,14:29
Date due: 9/19/2010,23:59
Item ID: 39092066727116

Current time: 08/29/2010,14:29
Title: A grizzly death in Yellowstone : a novel
Date charged: 8/29/2010,14:29
Date due: 9/19/2010,23:59
Item ID: 39092060798267

"I think so. Are you sure that bear hasn't been around here?"

"The ranger tell me no one. . . has report it in this area for almost three weeks."

"The ranger *told* me."

"The ranger told you too?"

"No, Jorge. . ." He smiles at her.

"The ranger *told* me. *Comprende.*"

Back by the campfire, Jorge builds up the fire, sits, then puts his arm around Tina, drawing her closer to him.

"So have you decided if you like America yet, Jorge? Do you like it better than Mexico?"

"I learn a new word this week. Hypocrite. Did I say it right?"

"It means saying one thing when the truth is something else."

"I think maybe Americans are hypocrite. I think a Mexican, that you can always tell what he is feeling like. They are more simple. They say what they think easier. I think it is because there is more family that stay together. No secrets. I think Americans are not so much family. I see the young ones get done with their meals and want to run around by themselves here. The older people always be by themselves here. They come on buses by themselves. Teenagers by themselves. In this country, there is supposed to be much love, but I don't see it too much. I think Americans don't let people know their feelings. When they are mad or even when they are happy, Mexicans can never tell a lie with their eyes."

"I want to be more Mexican. So I won't hold back when I tell you that I still care for you very much."

He looks at her profile, her chin set in earnest as she gazes into the fire. He softly takes her chin and brings it toward his face. "Tina botina, *bonita senorita.* I like you too. I love you. I am lucky."

They kiss long and passionately. They let their heads fall against one another's and nestle closer. The fire crackles and Jorge lays another log on it.

"Tell me more about Massachusetts. Do they play soccer?"

"They play more ice hockey. It's like soccer only on ice. They use skates and sticks and a flat thing called a puck. About the size of that doughnut."

"What does Massachusetts look like?"

"There are some mountains, but not like these. The fall is the— what was that?"

"I did not hear anything. It's. . . ."

"There it is again. Jorge. . . ."

He pauses to listen. "Get up," whispers Jorge. "Get behind me. *Donde. . .* where is the flashlight?"

"Here it is." She grasps his arm tightly. "Jorge, what is it?"

"Get in the tent, Tina! No, wait. It is something wants our food. Get back. . . Maybe a squirrel. The sound is the cook pot."

The light from the flashlight shows nothing through the darkness. Slowly, instinctively, Jorge backs away from the fire, keeping Tina behind his outstretched arm. At the sound of another shuffle, the hairs on Jorge's head stand on end. Every nerve and muscle is taut as he peers intently into the blackness beyond the fire. He can hear something scraping the thick nylon of the stuff sack, then a "huff" sound, then scratching on a tree trunk.

"What should we do?" Tina whispers.

Jorge backs her up to a lodgepole pine. He sticks the flashlight in his mouth, and interlocks his hands, making a foothold. "Go up the tree and hang on to the branches. Fast!"

Jorge nearly throws her up to the lower branches.

"It's coming! Jorge!"

He turns to see the form materialize out of the darkness, running toward them from the other side of the fire. It is a huge bear, a grizzly. The last of Tina's weight disappears from his palms; she is in the tree, just beyond his outstretched hands. He instinctively steps behind the tree and, from 15 yards away, hurls the flashlight at the bear, hitting it with a glancing blow off its side. It snaps its wide jaws in that direction. The blow momentarily deters the rampaging animal. But then the bear charges wide around the fire, partially raising up to its back feet as it runs just beyond the light of the fire.

Tina winces, then whispers a scream. "Run, Jorge!"

Jorge dashes to the fire and grabs the unburned end of one of the flaming logs and throws it at the animal. The log roars as it spirals toward the bear, landing short and lighting its larger-than-real features—its rippling muscles under silver-tipped fur and its head, the head of a demon gone mad. It rears back on its hind legs and walks forward, revealing its eight-foot-tall form before it drops down and instantly charges at the moving form of Jorge. Jorge races to a pine tree as the bear covers the 20 yards with three powerful strides.

"Jorge!"

He catches a lower limb and spins himself around the side away from the animal.

"Jorge!!"

With his adrenaline-spurred strength, Jorge lifts himself into the tree as the bear runs up and swipes forward, ripping off tree bark. Jorge reaches to another branch as the bear plows to a halt, then stands up on his hind legs and takes a blind swipe that catches Jorge's leg. Jorge cries out. The blow loosens the grip of his left hand. But his left foot lands on the branch below. Jorge regrasps the branch above, then pulls himself higher up the tree, avoiding another powerful strike that snaps a two-inch-thick branch. Again, the bear lunges at him, but now he is beyond its reach.

"Go higher, Jorge!"

Jorge hears a loud snap of a branch and, to his greatest horror, looks over to see Tina fall out of the lodgepole on the other side of the fire, 20 feet away. He looks down as the bear's tiny, almost useless eyes turn away from him, blink, and look to the other noise. The bear focuses on the movement. The instant the bear moves to the new noise, Jorge drops down to the ground behind it, not feeling a severed branch cut into his stomach.

"Hey!"

The bear halts its charge toward a motionless, horrified Tina and wheels, facing Jorge, who waves frantically from 15 feet away. Jorge runs to another tree and jumps to the lower branch, pulling himself up and away as the grizzly charges past him. The bear turns and lunges after Jorge, and a sharp claw catches his right shoe, knocking it off his foot. Jorge hoists himself up and looks at Tina; she is shocked, panicked, staring blankly.

"The lake, Tina! Run to the lake!"

His voice awakens her, galvanizes her, and she disappears beyond the light of the campfire. Now the bear growls for the first time, and at the blood-curdling sound, Jorge involuntarily pulls himself further out of danger. The grizzly tries to shimmy up the tree after him, but its mass is greater than its strength; after getting only a foot off the ground, it slips heavily back to earth, and Jorge hears the splash of Tina in the lake. The bear flashes its huge, yellow canines at Jorge and growls a hideous mad bark as it turns toward the lake.

"Hey hey! *Oso!*" shouts Jorge, and the bear leaps at the tree. Now Jorge is five feet above the bear's greatest effort, and after two attempts to leap after its prey and one more attempt to climb after him, it turns its attention to the ground.

"Stay in the water and have no noise," Jorge shouts.

The bear barks once again in Jorge's direction. Its putrid odor reaches Jorge's nostrils now before the bear leaves and starts prowling around the camp, its silver-tipped hair reflecting the orange of the fire. The bear sniffs at their packs and swats them as if they were the weight of Styrofoam. His head disappears inside Tina's pack and pulls out a jacket, which he bites once and leaves. He sniffs about the tent and sets a paw on it, collapsing it. The bear reacts by pouncing on the fabric, ripping it. Then it turns back to the tree where Jorge is perched. Jorge's heart races wildly. He moves in closer to the tree's trunk and hugs it. He forces his breathing to a noiseless panting as the bear tries once more to climb, getting a little farther than it did the last time before falling. It sniffs Jorge's pack once more before going off in the direction of the food sack. After several minutes, there is a loud crash. Jorge cannot see but he knows the bear got the food at last. For 15 minutes—that seem like 15 hours—he listens as the bear tears, chews, crunches. Only now does Jorge become aware that the warm spot under his shirt is blood; he can feel the cut. His hands and the insides of his legs also are scraped and bleeding. He wonders why he feels no pain there. He shields his eyes and squints past the dying fire into the blackness but cannot see or hear Tina. He thinks calling to her may bring the bear back, so he remains silent, looking vainly through the blackness. He hears the bear move off through the night and waits, listening. He counts to 50 in English, praying silently, then shouts, "Tina?"

A crying voice comes back. "Jorge? My God! Are you all right?"

"Wait there and do not move. The bear might be close."

"I'm cold, Jorge. I'm scared!"

The tenor of her voice nearly sends him running after her, but he holds back. "Come to the edge of the water and hear. I will shout when you can come out. Stay with no noise."

At half-minute intervals, he shouts into the night and listens, hearing nothing. Two minutes later, Jorge drops to the ground. He reaches into his wood pile and takes two long branches with dead, brown pine needles and ignites them in the dwindling fire. With a huge torch, he walks several steps toward where the food sack was. He picks up the flashlight and drops it as the broken glass falls out of it. He holds the branches high above him and can see the remnants of their food pack, some 40 feet in front of him. In the darkness ahead, he hears nothing, sees nothing. Just as the torch fire starts to recede, he backs up to the fire. Then he drops the branches into the fire and hurries to the edge of the lake. As he runs up to Tina, she is standing in knee-deep water, her arms held tightly to her chest. Jorge wraps his arms around her; she is soaking wet and shaking so hard even his tight grasp cannot still her. "Stay here for one more minute," he says.

She clings to him with animal strength. "No! I'm not staying here alone!"

"I have to make more fire, Tina. The *oso* is gone. I see where it ate all of our food. It's OK now. We are all right. It's gone."

"Jorge," she clings to him still, shutting her eyes tightly against the nightmarish images. "I was so scared. I thought I was going to die. I thought you were going to die."

Now the tears come to her without restraint, and he lets her hold on for several moments before he turns his head and sees the flame of the fire flicker.

"We are all right now. It is gone."

Within 15 minutes, they have a huge fire burning. With Tina looking out, Jorge leans a backpack against a tree to make a foothold in case they have to climb again. And over a thick limb he ties a length of rope so it may be easier to pull themselves up. They spend the long night awake, cleaning their cuts and scrapes, listening and gaping into the night, anxiously awaiting the first light of dawn. Tina crouches in her sleeping bag next to Jorge, wide-eyed and ready to bolt any second, for the sound of a tree creaking sends her into a panic. Every once in a while, when Jorge thinks she is asleep, Tina shivers violently, and only his strong embrace can neutralize her trembling.

August 4. Old Faithful Ranger Station.

As Rangers Robert Mortenson and Susan Lynwood clean the wounds and scrapes, Jorge and Tina continue to tell Ranger Minden of the events of the night before.

"It seems so unreal now," Tina says. "Like it never happened. Like it was some terrible nightmare."

"And you're sure you had no odorous food lying around the campfire?" Ranger Minden asks. "Or you didn't spill anything."

"I tell you, we did not," Jorge insists.

"We kept a very clean camp," says Tina. "I was scared of. . . bears."

"You give me the permit from you. You explain everything and I understand. The food was hang up. I even read about grizzly bears."

"And you say it was a grizzly bear. How do you know this?"

"It was huge," says Tina. She winces from the antiseptic.

"It had the round face. I read this. It had the hump over its back. In the night, its hair shines."

"Did you notice if it had a tag on its ear or a collar around its neck?"

"I did not see a tag," says Jorge.

"No," says Tina. "I don't think so."

Minden and Mortenson exchange glances. The description is correct. Ten minutes later, the Lake Hospital ambulance pulls up outside and the attendant walks in.

"OK," says Minden. "We're going to take you two down to Lake and look you over at the hospital there. You'll probably only have to stay one night. The cut on your leg isn't too bad. And I don't believe that cut on your abdomen will require stitches, Jorge, but we'll want a doctor to look at it anyway. He may run some tests." He touches Jorge on the shoulder. "You acted very courageously. Both of you. I'm very sorry this had to happen. We'll pick up your backpacks and equipment today. We'll tell your supervisors what happened. Just relax for a couple of days."

After Jorge and Tina leave in the ambulance, Minden takes off his hat, smooths his gray hair back and sighs. "OK. First thing, close that trail, both trailheads. Bob, Sue, you've been up there recently. Can you recall if there's any place to land a chopper?"

"Mallard? No. Nothing but trees, right down to the lake."

"How about the cage? Is there any way we can land it up there?"

"I think you'd be able to drop it in the shallow water if nothing else."

"Susan, call in Gary and Steve from backcountry. Ask them their exact 10-20 and how long it will take them to get back."

Susan goes to the back room and Minden waits for Ranger Mortenson to turn from the picture of the grizzly on the wall and face him. The two men hold each other's gaze for a long pause. Finally, it is Minden who speaks. "That's so unlike a bear to charge into a campsite like that," he says. "Even a grizz. No food and two people sitting by a campfire. God." He shakes his head. "And not even three miles from Old Faithful."

August 7. Kitty's Cabin.

The word of the bear attack has spread rapidly throughout the park and the Rocky Mountain states via the newspapers and radio. The *Helena Daily Herald*, the *Jackson Hole Guide* and the *Jackson Hole News*, the *Billings Gazette*, *Casper Star-Tribune*, and the *Denver Post* all run articles based on the Park Service news release.

Kitty, Wilbur, Salina and Steve are sitting around Kitty's table.

The end results of a spaghetti dinner are lying about the cooking end of the cabin—empty plates, salad bowls and wine bottles. Salina and Steve are dressed in sweat clothes. Steve is bending over as he sits, stretching his tight hamstrings. Kitty and Wilbur are dressed in jeans and T-shirts.

"It's nothing unusual," says Kitty. "Every year, there's something happening like that. Last year, in Hayden Valley, a buffalo killed a guy that got too close."

"I heard they got the bear this morning," Salina says.

"Great," says Steve. "Nothing like a good bear scare to clear out the backcountry trails. I ran up to Fairy Falls yesterday and there was *nobody* on the trail."

"How did they catch it?" Salina asks.

"They landed a culvert trap up at Mallard," Wilbur says. "The bear goes in the culvert trap to get the meat, the door shuts behind him. Herm told me the rangers said the meat was laced with Sernalyn to knock it out. But when they rode up to Mallard Lake this morning, the bear was still conscious and the meat was gone. They had to shoot it up again."

"What did they do with it?" Salina asks.

Wilbur picks up a piece of lettuce from the salad bowl and eats it. "They stuck it in a harness and relocated it by helicopter up north of the park, just over the park boundary on ranch land. Sernalyn is the trade name for PCP. You might have heard of it as an illegal drug referred to as Angel Dust. They're using this drug now to tranquilize the bears. Has anyone heard of it?"

"I've heard of it," says Kitty. "I think one of my brothers took some once."

"I've read about it somewhere," Salina says.

"I took some once, about three years ago," says Wilbur. "Didn't know it was PCP. I thought it was cocaine, which I had never tried before. It made me less aggressive all right. It induced psychosis. It almost made me commit suicide. I was totally outside and detached from my mind and my body. It was terrible. I actually went into a convenience store, bought a pack of razor blades, and was sitting on the beach, contemplating how worthless all of life was and how clearly I saw that it was the destined night of my death, when all of a sudden, I just came to. It was scary. I threw the razor blades into the ocean immediately. Angel Dust is the strongest hallucinogen in the world."

"Why are they using it on bears then?" asks Salina.

"The University of Minnesota used it in a laboratory with bears and other animals as a tranquilizer. But they still aren't certain about the residual effects. There has even been post anesthetic violence in bears, sows chasing their cubs, that kind of thing. I meant to bring over that copy of the *Jackson Hole News* where I read this stuff. It said the researchers think the drug is stored in the fatty tissues of bears and is metabolized as they come out of hibernation. It might contribute to the recent abnormal behavior of several of the bears here in the park, and maybe the one that attacked Jorge and Tina."

"I was in the EDR today at lunch when Jorge and Tina got back from Lake Hospital," Salina says. "It was like they were heroes; everyone crowded around them, applauding. It must have been an unbelievable experience. I could still see the fear in their eyes. Like they weren't over it yet. I don't care how far away they relocated that bear. I'm not going camping."

"I've been reluctant to run trails," Steve admits. "But Pike's Peak is only two and a half weeks away. I'm not going to do all my long runs in loops around the boardwalk or on the road."

"Come on, you guys," Wilbur says. "How about a little courage? What do you say tomorrow night we walk along the northern park boundary with honey and bacon grease smeared over us and confront our deepest fears?"

"I will if you will," says Steve.

"I can't," says Kitty. "I'm going to a wedding tomorrow night. Steve, how's our treasury funds? I was going to pick up a case of Mout. It looks like we're about out."

Wilbur touches Kitty on her shoulder and rubs her neck. "Kitty, you'll get up there too late to go to the state liquor store. They close at five, remember? Who's getting married, anyway?"

"A couple of old friends of Byron's and mine. No, Wilbur, I'm going to pick up the Mout the next morning."

"You're going to spend the night up there?" he asks, turning his shoulders toward Kitty.

"Well, yes, Wilbur. Do you think I'm going to come back tomorrow night, then drive back up there the next morning?"

"Where are you going to spend the night?"

"Probably at Byron's."

Wilbur pushes the wine glass across the table, knocking it into the glass salad bowl. His voice rises in pitch and volume. "At Byron's? What do you mean you're going to spend the night at Byron's?"

"We're still friends, Wilbur. I mean, I went out with him for four years. We'll have a lot of mutual friends there. I'm looking forward to seeing him, actually."

Steve catches Salina's eye and grasps her hand. "I think we were just going," Salina says. "Massage therapy time. The dinner was great again, Kitty. Thanks."

"You guys don't have to leave," says Wilbur, turning back to Kitty. "You're looking forward to seeing him *and* you're spending the night? Are you going to have sex with him too?"

"Wilbur, I didn't say that. We've been through a lot together. I'd like to see him again."

Wilbur turns his back to Steve and Salina, who are putting on their jackets. "Now I'm sure we're going. Good night, Kitty. See you at work, Wilbur."

The door shuts. Wilbur grabs Kitty's arm and says, "Well, what are you saying, Kitty?"

"I'm saying I'm going to a wedding with an old friend. I didn't say I was going to make love to him. You and I aren't married, you know."

"But you didn't say you weren't."

"He's been calling me at work. Dick and Kim are old friends of ours." She tries to take his hand, but he jerks it away, folding his hands under his arms. "It's just something I need to do. My relationship with Byron is over. I don't think. . . ."

"You don't think! What do you mean you don't think! I thought you loved me."

"I do love you, Wilbur." She turns away from him, taking the wine glass, trying to bring the conversation back down to a rational level by lowering her voice. "Wilbur, I do love you. I didn't know how you'd react. We haven't known each other for that long. I didn't want to get real involved right away. There's just something I need. . . ."

"The hell with your needs!" he says. "You want everything, don't you, freedom and security! You've tried something different and now you realize you didn't have it so bad after all, is that it?" He stands and backhands the salad bowl, causing several glasses and plates to fall and shatter. "You're still in love with him, aren't you?"

"No. I don't think so. Not like that. It's all. . . ."

"Well, that's just great, Kitty." He goes to the bed and grabs his jacket. He is vehement in his anger now. He kicks one of the wicker chairs and sends it bouncing into Kitty's chest of drawers. "Hell of a summer. Play adolescent games with me until you decide you're bored and it's time to go back to your Mammoth lover. Summer's coming to an end, time to get back to reality, the fling is over. Is that it, Kitty? Why don't you just go to hell!"

"Wilbur, let me explain. Can't we talk?"

The door slams so hard the entire cabin shakes. She watches the little basket of soap and shampoo next to the door swing back and forth, and realizes that it just had to happen. She knows it might cost her the relationship with Wilbur, whom she doesn't have as much in common with as she does with Byron, but who she loves more, somehow. But she knows she will make love to Byron the next night. It's something she wants to do, needs to do, and can't explain. It is something she feels has to happen if she is ever to move on, to stop holding back her feelings for Wilbur, or whoever is after Wilbur. Or, just maybe, she'll find out that Byron is the one she loves after all.

She takes another sip of the red French wine, but it tastes heavy. She feels bloated, restless. She wonders why she didn't wait until they were alone. But she knows that once they were in bed together, she would not have told him, then would have slept with Byron anyway, and lied to Wilbur about it. She knows it had to be this way, but for some reason she cannot rationalize it in her mind.

"I love you; I must let myself love you," she says aloud, not knowing to whom she speaks.

She kneels down by the mess on the floor, putting the unbroken pieces by the sink and the debris into the garbage.

Wilbur sits at the desk in the back room of the accounting office. He tosses the love poem to the back of the desk. It flutters and turns upside down, covering the accounts-receivable vouchers. He stares at the unaudited statistical reports in front of him but does not see them. He has yet to run a tape on the stacks of credit-card vouchers at the right side of the desk. Z tapes and detail tapes are scattered about the desk in front of him. He is not conscious of them either. Where the previous night he saw only anger, tonight, in his mind's eye, he sees the girl he loves 50 miles away in the arms of another man. He clenches his jaw against the image of them making love. Again he considers getting into his car and driving the 50 miles to Mammoth Hot Springs. The residential area is not large. He sees himself pulling up where Kitty's car is parked and bursting in on them, catching them just before Byron starts to make love to her.

Wilbur had walked past her cabin on the way to the showers. In spite of telling himself he wouldn't, he glanced to see that her car was indeed not there.

After a while, the sound of Steve running a calculator in the front office comes into focus. It annoys Wilbur, like a wind blowing a squeaky door back and forth and never shutting it.

"Can't you stop that damned noise?"

"I can't put it off print, Wilbur. I'm in the middle of the advance deposits."

"That's pretty important, isn't it?" says Wilbur. Then, angry at himself for getting short with his roommate, he gets up and walks out of the office. "Sorry, Steve."

"Don't worry about it, Wilbur. I'm done posting room charges already. Why don't you. . . ."

The wrought-iron latch clanks shut. Wilbur walks out through the lobby past Brenda, past the night porters as they buff the lobby floor. He walks outside toward the geyser.

What a fool you are, he thinks. How easily I let myself be sucked in. I am so in love with her. More than I ever thought I would let myself be with another woman. It hurts.

He lies back on a bench in front of Old Faithful and looks up at the stars. He considers quitting in the morning, leaving, finally being able to get on the road and just go.

Again, he shuts his eyes to the image of Kitty making love to Byron. He wishes the night wind would simply carry him away. He does not pay attention to a sound in the distance. He does not care if a bear pounces upon him right where he lies. It makes no difference at this moment.

He thinks about his productivity as a writer for the summer—I haven't even finished the one lousy short story. So here I am, 25 years old, making $5.15 an hour, have a total of $300 saved, no college degree, no future. I have done nothing with my life. Have alienated myself from my parents, can't write and can't even keep a girlfriend.

"What a man. What a credit to mankind."

Oh, but hey. I did write five poems to Kitty.

I will get them back. Those dearest of gifts, part of my heart and soul. No, she will not keep them. She will not have them to look back on and laugh at. Was I just an interim affair? Right in front of Steve and Salina, too. Sunset Society, right! Rename it Blind Faith Society. I can be the president and only member.

Maybe I'll go back East and write. Make enough money until I am impervious to pain, to people. Where I can simply buy women when I want them, then dispatch with them as I please. Treat them like they need to be treated, led by the nose. Money. . . that's it. Byron has money.

Enough. That's enough.

He gets up and heads back to the Inn, taking one last glance at the steaming cone.

"So Steve," Wilbur says, as he comes back into the accounting office. "My girlfriend's spending the night with another man tonight. What do you think I should do?"

"Well, Wilbur, you don't know that she's sleeping with him. I think you should talk to her. I know other couples that have been friends after they've dated and broken up."

Wilbur sits down behind Steve. "I don't feel much like being here anymore. I'm thinking about leaving."

"You can't."

"Why not?"

"I balanced the credit cards for you. You owe me a favor and I don't want you to leave."

"I'll get some Mout and we'll get hammered in the morning. It sure couldn't hurt."

"I can't tomorrow. As soon as I wake up, Salina and I are driving to Jackson for that half-marathon on Saturday. Why don't you come with us? Run the race. That way you'd be too tired to think about. . . women."

"No, I think I'll drive into West Yellowstone tonight and drink until I fall down."

"That's another way to do it. I betcha everything will be all right."

August 9. Death Canyon, Grand Teton National Park.

Kris Richards leans to the right, away from the smoke, and watches Cecil put his head down to the ground and blow on the fire, coercing it into flames.

"Cec, I don't know. The ranger said we weren't supposed to build a fire."

"Everyone does it. I saw two fire rings on the way up here, right next to the creek. Besides, I like fires. And how else are we supposed to see to open our wine?"

"But you can tell other people have used this spot for a campsite, and there's no fire ring here."

"There is now, isn't there? I'll clean it up in the morning. You'll never know we were here. It's going now." He rises and walks to his pack. "Look at all the wood here. No one will miss it.

"Now," he proclaims, lifting the bottle up, "for a little fun and relaxation."

"I probably won't have much, Cec. I'm pretty tired. Remember, I worked a breakfast-lunch today."

"The wine will make you feel better. Listen to your bartender. Bartenders know what's good for you. Hey, I also bought some of this cheese spread. I had this the last time I went camping. It's good. And here are some Saltines."

He sets the cheese spread and crackers on her lap, then squeezes the outside of her leg. "This will pep you up. Do you want me to fix you one?" he asks, reaching back toward her.

"No, Cec. I think I can do it. Jalapeno?"

"I think it's even better than the garlic."

"Cecil, are you sure there are no bears around here?"

"You heard what the ranger said. He said there are a few black bears somewhere, but they haven't seen a grizzly this far south of Yellowstone in 28 years."

"But can't black bears be dangerous too?"

"Nonaggressive species, dear. We'll go for a walk later and hang our food anyway."

"Go for a walk at night?"

"Yea. I've got the whole evening planned. On the other side of the creek, I saw some big boulders. I thought we'd go up there and watch the stars for a while."

Cecil pours wine into two Sierra cups and hands one to Kris. As he puts the bottle behind a log, he watches Kris take a sip, then starts to look in his pack for the dinner ingredients. Good, he thinks. Plan A. We'll get drunk. Loosen up. Relax. She's in the tent. No changing that.

Cecil lifts out the can of Dinty Moore Beef Stew from his pack and goes about the business of making dinner.

"So, Cecil, who have you been going out with all summer?"

"No one else, Kris. You know that."

To the stew, he adds two fresh carrots and half of a yellow onion. Kris takes another sip of wine out of the Sierra cup. "I haven't gotten a letter from John in over three weeks."

"That's because he knows you and I were meant for each other, Kris."

She laughs under her breath. "Cecil!" She looks into the fire. "Never leave a quarterback alone on a campus. He's probably like an insect in a spider's web, trapped by another wily woman. I'll never see him again."

Cecil stands to pour more wine.

"Not too much, Cecil. If I drink much more, I'm going to fall asleep. How far did we hike in?"

"About four miles. There's no one between us and the trailhead."

Cecil adds a generous squirt of the cheese spread to the stew. "Are you having a good time?"

"Sure."

He looks into her eyes. Those beautiful blue eyes. He knows he could be in love with her forever.

"Really, Cec. How have you liked working here? Being a bartender in Yellowstone?"

He touches her on the knee, then kneels down to adjust the flame to a simmer. "Just a sec." Then he sits next to her, taking his wine cup. "It's been the best summer of my life," he says, looking at her. "Being free out here in the wilderness. Getting away from the chaos of Seattle. Getting to know you."

"I'm glad we got to be friends, Cecil. You always have something nice or funny to say when you're working the service bar. I guess I've been a grouch lately. But I've had a good summer. I'm glad I came out here."

Cecil laughs. "I'm glad you did too. When you're working with me, it's always a lot of fun."

"How has Clarence been to work for? He seems really happy lately."

"He's been really good. He stopped drinking, you know. Partly thanks to me. He sings in the bar, tells jokes. The other night, he got up on stage and did some monologues from different plays. He was really good. I was surprised. I think everyone was impressed."

During the next hour and a half, they eat, wash the pots and cups, and hang the food. Afterward, Cecil leads Kris to a huge boulder, the top of which is flat enough to lie on in the sleeping bags and gaze up at the heavens.

"I've never seen so many stars," says Kris. "This is just beautiful."

"May I hold your hand?"

She turns from the stars and looks at him. "I guess that would be OK, Cecil."

He squeezes her right hand tightly in his.

It's working. Her hand feels so good, so soft. It is such a beautiful hand. Kris Richard's hand. If I twiddle her thumb. . . .

"Now my head's at a funny angle."

"Here, lift your head. I'll put one of my shoes underneath your head. You can use that. Is that OK?"

"Yea, that's OK."

"Now where was that hand?" He takes it, squeezing the softness and gazing at the night sky.

"So Kris," Cecil says after a few moments of silence. "You really haven't been sleeping with that fat security guy, have you?"

"No, Cecil. I told you before I wasn't."

"Kris, I haven't slept with anyone either. Don't you think it's amazing neither of us has?"

"Yes, it is amazing."

"Oh! Did you see that shooting star?"

"Wow, that was a bright one!"

They are silent for a few minutes. Cecil wiggles closer to Kris, ignoring the protruding piece of rock beneath his shoulder blade.

Yes, he thinks, try it. The massage technique.

"You know, my back's pretty sore from the backpack." He squirms a little closer but does not get the desired response. "How's yours?"

"Kinda stiff. But mine's always stiff from having to lift those trays and all."

"Maybe we can give each other back rubs."

"Not tonight, Cec. In fact, I think I'll crawl into the tent. It feels really late."

"It's about that time, isn't it?"

As they get inside their sleeping bags, Cecil catches a glimpse of the long, tan legs before the flashlight rolls off his lap, sending the tent into darkness. The last thing he sees as he turns the flashlight off is her face turned toward his. He wonders if it is a subconscious message, that she is still receptive to his kiss. He rolls on his left side, facing her, taking her hand in his left hand and rubbing her shoulders with his right hand.

"That does feel good, Cecil. I guess my shoulders are a little sore. It's been a long day."

He rubs from her shoulders toward her waist, under the down sleeping bag that is already reflecting her warmth. He slips his hand under her white T-shirt, touching her silky underwear with his little finger, and the blood pulsates through his entire body. I've got to control myself now, keep it together.

Eventually, he hears her breathing become even, slow. He is afraid she might fall asleep from his soothing massage, that he better take advantage of the mood and the night. He scoots down, moves his face slowly toward hers, and plants a wet kiss on her half-opened lips.

"Cecil! Oh, what are you doing?"

"I'm kissing you."

"I don't *want* to be kissed."

"Kris, I love you."

"Oh God, Cecil. Not you too."

"Me too! Who else?"

Kris rolls on her back.

"Herm?"

Cecil rises on his elbows. "Well, I really love you, Kris. I want you to be happy. You should give me a chance to make you happy. It's very important to me."

"Cecil, remember at the beginning of the summer? You drove me down to Old Faithful from Mammoth. We decided we were going to be friends. We shook on it. I have a boyfriend back in Florida. You know that. It would mean a lot to me if I could have a man for a friend."

"But he's stopped writing you."

"Well, I haven't given up on him. Come on, you must have a girl back in Seattle, don't you?"

He rolls on his back and stares up at the tent. "Kris, can I tell you something that I've never told anyone else?"

From the tenor of his voice, she senses his fear, his reluctance. She wishes she could just sleep, but says "Sure, Cec."

He forces the words out slowly. "I did have a girlfriend in high school once. In my senior year. We went together for about five weeks, leading up to the senior prom. I took her, corsage, tux, a gown for her, rented car, the whole thing. The prom was in this hotel resort down in Tacoma. I had even rented a motel room. I was hoping we would make love. I went from the ballroom where they were having the dance back to the room to refill the flask. We had bought some gin. When I got back to the dance, she wasn't there. I looked for her for awhile, then went back downstairs, thinking maybe she'd gone back to the room. When I came out of the room, I saw a couple of guys from the football team. I asked them if they'd seen her. They said yea, room 319. They kind of laughed and threw me a key. I walked into 319 and she was in there. . . with some guy from the football team. They were naked. . . they were. . ." He pauses, drawing in a deep breath and letting it out slowly. "That's as close as I've come to having a girlfriend. All my life I've been just missing out, it seems."

"Cecil, I'm sorry. That's a terrible thing to have happen."

He pauses. "Well, you're very different, that's all. We could have a really good time together. I'd be happy. You know, I make good money as a bartender. I could help you through school."

"Cecil, I'm so sorry you haven't had any girlfriends. That seems so sad. You're a nice person."

He turns his head toward her and can make out her face in the starlight filtering through the netting. He reaches over to smooth her fine, blond hair behind her ear and lowers to kiss her. His lips barely touch hers, and she turns away.

"Cecil, stop! I can't love somebody out of sympathy. You can only be my friend, and not even that if you can't act like. . . ."

"Well, just forget it!" he shouts, jerking into a sitting posture and kicking the sleeping bag away from him. "You're no kind of friend!" She puts her hand on his back and he pushes it away. He grabs his pants, a jacket and shoes in one arm and jerks down the zipper of the tent with the other, then crawls recklessly through the opening. "The hell with it! The hell with it all! You'll learn!"

"Cecil, come on. You're acting like a child."

"Just don't talk to me!" And he is out in the night, grumbling to himself as he rolls up several brown bags from the groceries to rekindle the fire. He grabs the unfinished bottle of wine and takes two gulps from it. Inside the tent, he can see Kris's blond head turn away from him, and she gives out a long sigh. He takes another sip from the bottle and puts more logs on the fire. It is building inside of him, that anger and frustration that has been so long repressed. Something fights the anger, but it is weak, overwhelmed. He finishes the wine and grabs the tequila from the bottom of the pack; he knows exactly where it is. He walks away from the fire and looks out over the broad plain of Jackson Hole. With no moon, it is merely a black sea beneath him.

Be a man, he says to himself. Have a little strength.

A shooting star crosses the sky above him. The hell with you, he thinks. I have no time for petty wishes. A man takes what he wants when he wants it. Yea, a great summer. So I've been this cute and funny little guy behind the service bar. A nice guy. That's what she thinks of me, huh? A clown, a joker? Acting like a child, huh? Show a little macho, Dolen. Show a little courage. What kind of thing is that, thinking you have to get a woman drunk to seduce her? Or trying to be romantic, weak. A joker, huh? Only a friend, huh?

He takes another shot of the tequila, then another, but spits it out. "The hell with this stuff," he says to the night, hurling the bottle against the rocks and shattering it before turning around and facing the glowing campfire. Hell with it. And she's here. Right here. Time for plan T—Take.

He walks over and hoists up a pillow-sized boulder and drops it. With a dull thud, it breaks into two. Yes, we will be lovers.

He stops in his tracks. Some minute seed of rationale, a tiny bit of cultivated civilization, calling him not to give up what he has tried all summer to achieve. He looks into the night, at the huge walls of the canyon above him, at the tent and through the mosquito netting at the flickering orange shape of the girl's head.

"There's nobody else here."

He relinquishes his hold on the last, fleeting rational thought. His breathing quickens. He gives into something stronger, welling up inside his breast. It brings him instant relief, a burden lifted from his conscious being. His blood flow, his adrenaline, his strength all increase. The familiar feeling of perverse omnipotence returns to him. He clenches his fist into his palms, digging his nails deeply into his flesh.

But no, he thinks, this is just man, just normal and natural, just how we are supposed to be. She'll love it. That's the way it always happens. She will love me after this. I will have what I want. The conquered knows its master.

Looking at the still blond head, Cecil walks to the pile of wood and takes out a three-foot branch, three inches thick. He clenches his fist around the branch and feels his biceps beneath his shirt. He ponders how light the log feels, how much physical dominance he feels.

Rainy time. Two more bloody marys, Cec. Re-order. I told you he didn't want salt on his margarita, Cecil. Another round, bartender. Your turn to stock, Cec. Another joke, bartender. How do you like living here in Yellowstone, Cec?

In his mind's eye, he can see what he wants, what he will get, just how it will look. She will learn passion.

He takes a step toward the still figure of his prey, a pretty cheerleader. So much cleaner than the whores. No chance of disease. How 'bout a cheer for old Cecil? Lay yourself down, naked underneath me.

He takes another step toward her. He steps quietly, turning the stick in his hands. Fire. More fire to see her by.

He lays another branch on top of the flames.

The image of her under him burns in his mind. He sees how she will be dependent on him from that point on. She will be worthless without him.

Take her now.

"Cecil?"

The sound of her voice startles him, awakens him. He takes two deep breaths and halts his shaking body. He shivers from some sudden cold. But he steels himself, raises the branch and takes a step closer to the right of the tent, out of her sight.

"Cecil, I want to talk to you."

"What? What do you want?"

"Hey, I'll give you a massage if you'd like. I've been really selfish. I do want you to be my friend, and I'm not trying very hard to do my part." She pauses. "I'm sorry. Why don't you come on back and lie down on your bag."

He stays where he is for several long moments, feeling his breathing, his strength, recalling the images. Instantly, he has a headache. He tries to charge himself back up. He contemplates the branch in his hand, but the savageness is leaving; it becomes heavier, coarser. The images won't come into focus. He takes one more deep breath and flips the branch into the fire.

"It better be a really good one."

August 10.

Wilbur glides on his bicycle down the asphalt trail in front of the Old Faithful Inn, weaving past strolling tourists. The early evening is still and quiet under a gray sky that casts no shadows. It has been three days since he stormed out of Kitty's. He did drive to West Yellowstone the night before, but the cathartic drunk he intended ended up being spent in the theatre watching a dull Western. Afterward, he drove home and spent the night alone in his cabin. He sporadically worked on his story until 3 a.m., when he sank into his bed fully clothed.

With his day pack strapped to his back, containing what he now surmises to be his closest and most trustworthy friends—his writing tablet and his Japanese flute—he coasts up to Castle Geyser. He leans the 10-speed against a garbage can and sits down across from the 17-foot-high cone, the oldest geyser in the basin. He takes out his flute and plays, running up and down the pentonic scale, not thinking, just fingering, twisting the notes, stretching and compressing the rhythm.

As two parents are watching the steaming cone, he looks up to see a young girl staring at him; it breaks his concentration. He puts the flute back in the pack and takes out the pen and writing pad. He inspects his thoughts. Where the first night he felt anger and the second night jealousy, this evening he feels sullen, bored, deserted and old. He stands and looks out over the wooden railing. He flips through his notepad to a clean page and writes the first stanza to a poem.

Fate has put me here, he thinks. It is trying to tell me something I need desperately to understand. Why here? So many changes. What is it I must learn?

A puzzle. He thinks that if he rides and forces open his writer's powers of perception the answer will come to him. He peddles farther down the asphalt walkway. The tourists look tired to him, their children cranky, now at the end of their day. He stops himself from imbibing their weariness, for he senses something to be revealed here, something especially for him.

He parks his bicycle under a clump of trees. He sits, plays, thinks. Over the next 10 minutes, two more stanzas come to him.

It is Saturday, his second night off, so he has no place to hurry to. He waits patiently until Spasmodic completely subsides before riding to the end of the boardwalk at Morning Glory Pool. There is no one nearby. He plays the flute next to the calm, steaming pool. Then he writes some more.

Satisfied with his creation, he moves on.

He takes the little spur that leads to Riverside Geyser. The sign tells him it could go off any time in the next half hour to three and a half hours.

They say it is supposed to be the prettiest geyser. Perhaps I will come back and see it sometime, if I stay.

He peddles toward the sound of water being forced upward through an opening. The next stanza comes to him before he gets off his bike.

After 15 minutes, Grotto Geyser shows no hint of subsiding. Back at the intersection, he looks down and sees only two groups of people meandering about the boardwalk. He rides past the sign that says, "No bicycles beyond this point." The boards rumble beneath his tires and, at his approach, the marmots dart to their sanctuaries beneath the boardwalk. I'm back to square one, he thinks. What do I do?

Grand Geyser, the biggest geyser, is the hardest to predict. How true, he thinks, how true, and peddles on. Past Vent, Triplet, Economic geysers. Past the silent invitation of Beauty and Chromatic pools. He wonders if Steve could be back from the race, hopefully full of cheer and energy.

He stops at the end of the boardwalk. He knows Old Faithful must have gone off recently—people walk past him without noticing him.

It uplifts his spirits to see Steve's car in the driveway; it draws his attention away from Kitty's car, which he can see out the corner of his eye, five cabins down. He skids his bike to a stop in the obsidian gravel, jumps off and opens the door to his cabin.

"Hello, Steven. How did your contest go?"

Steve and Salina are lying on the bed dressed in their sweat clothes.

"Great! I finished second! 1:07:22!"

"I never knew you to be so self-absorbed at finishing second. If I remember the quote, you said 'finishing second is like dying.'"

"But guess what?" Steve jumps up. "Guess who beat me? Jimmy Sandlin. Beat me by only 20 seconds. The man has run a 2:13 in New York! He's sponsored by Reebok! I beat Randy Riev by almost a minute and Shawn by two minutes!"

He strides over to the door and points to his running log and draws a line under the day's entry with his finger. "I'm ready for Pike's Peak."

"I'm happy for you. Congratulations. But, more important, did you bring back any Mout?"

"One bottle," says Salina. "After the Shah of Old Faithful did so well in the race, we spent all our money on seafood salads and piña coladas at the Alpenhof."

"And a new pair of running shoes."

As Salina opens and pours the wine, Steve is exuberant in telling Wilbur every detail of the 13-mile race. He shows Wilbur his trophy—and Salina's for finishing third in the three-mile race. Like a child at Christmas, he holds out his new shoes to Wilbur. "Less than eight ounces each."

"Have you and Kitty made up yet?" Salina asks abruptly.

Wilbur shoots a glance at her and takes a breath. "It's all over, Salina."

"I talked to her, Wilbur. She misses you a lot. She wants to talk to you."

Wilbur swirls the wine in his Sierra cup and rises to flip over the cassette he's listened to so many times during the past three days: Cole Porter. Just before he punches in the tape, he changes his mind and replaces it with Big Head Todd, Sister Sweetly, Bittersweet side up.

"Does anyone want to go to the Bear Pit for a drink?" Wilbur asks. "I'll buy."

"Sure," Salina says.

"I'll go," Steve adds. "One night of celebrating before I get down and fine tune for Pike's Peak."

"Imre wants to see me in her room at 11 o'clock," he announces.

"What on earth for?" asks Steve, stretching out on his neoprene pad.

"She was going out to eat and said she would be back and she wanted to see me. I don't know. But if I'm not back by 10 o'clock tomorrow morning, call in the rangers."

An hour later, when Salina takes too long to go to the bathroom, Wilbur suspects her of stopping by Kitty's. Salina averts her eyes when Wilbur casts a suspicious glance at her. "I'm ready to go," she says.

It's an incongruous group that heads over to the Bear Pit. They leave behind the empty bottle of white wine and even Steve's bottle of red that he had been saving until he wins Pike's Peak. Steve is still full of race talk, leaping, running ahead 30 yards and running back. Salina walks quietly and catlike, and Wilbur is building on an artificial high, the reaction to three days of physical and mental depression.

"Hey, Cecil. How ya doin'? Three Wild Turkeys with a splash of water," Wilbur says, as they slide onto the bar stools.

Despite protests, Salina and Steve join Wilbur in sipping the 101-proof bourbon. For a $10 tab, he leaves a dollar tip, and slides a second $10 under his cocktail napkin. Salina leans back from between the two men. "Both you guys are too full of energy. Relax. One subject at a time, please."

"Salina, I've almost finished my short story. Do you think I can be a millionaire off of one short story? OK. You've forced it out of me. I wrote a poem this evening while riding my bike around the geyser basin. I haven't even read it yet."

"Kitty showed me one of your poems. It was beautiful, Wilbur."

"She did? She showed you one?" No, he thinks, it's over. Forget it. Break it now. "This one's better. Let's read it together."

"Last race before Pike's Peak. Do speed work on Tuesday, power run on Thursday, long trail on Sunday, then taper. Carbo load. We're going with Shawn and Randy, Wilbur. Shawn's going to run the up and back. All of us will run in the top five, at least. I think we can run. . . ."

"Can't you talk about *anything* but running?" says Salina in exasperation. "You're beginning to sound like a junkie."

His chest falls like a sail without wind, and there is a sudden silence among the three. "I'm sorry. I had a good race today. It's something that's important to me."

"Is it more important than everything else?"

"No. Not everything," he says softly, touching his hand to her knee.

"I'm trying to read Wilbur's poem. He may even be another Barry Manilow or something, Steve." She smiles and pinches his nose. "I'm sorry. Didn't mean to jump on you."

Shannon sits down next to Steve. "Hey, Steve. How'd the race go today? Hey, Cec. The usual."

By 9:30, they are joined by enough co-workers to have commandeered several of the tables. Clarence has set up a sound system for CDs and tapes. With his collection of hats, disguises and noisemakers by his side, he does impersonations of AM, FM, country Western, Motown and mellow disc jockeys.

"This is the sound of K-ELK radio coming to you from Old Faithful, Wyoming. There will be a free concert next Friday by the Ravens. The concert will be held in Hayden Valley and will be sponsored by Carrion Pizza Parlors, the pizza with guts. Now back to more music with. . . Yellowstone's own. . . Yogi's Bad Boo-Boo."

Erbine and Faysal, both in suits and ties, join the table. Off-duty waitri join them by pushing together tables to form one long one. A German couple sits next to Wilbur. Wilbur congratulates Erbine on finally settling on a good crew of dining-room cashiers and buys him a drink.

They talk about the scam they discovered two weeks before that cost two waiters their jobs.

"He might have gotten away with it if he didn't misspell 'void,'" Wilbur laughs.

Yvonne comes in, and Wilbur dances with her. He dances to chase the demons out. He spins and turns, bends down to the floor and jumps up into the air howling. He slaps the backs of the other men; he sweats and sings with the songs.

In uniform, Herm comes in and whispers into Faysal's ear, and Wilbur attacks him verbally and with gestures from the other end of the table. Wilbur stands on his chair and introduces Steve as the next winner of Pike's Peak—"the local hero, right here from our very own Old Faithful." A bus girl he doesn't know buys him a Wild Turkey, and he kisses her hand in appreciation. He laughs at his own jokes, and at Shannon's. He laughs so hard his stomach cramps. Leaning over Erbine, talking to a front desk cashier, he hears behind him, "Excuse me, can I have this dance?"

It's Kitty.

He is completely surprised, dumbfounded. His jaw drops and his lips start to move but words do not come out. He looks to Salina, only to see her turn her eyes away from his and drag Steve onto the dance floor. He looks back into Kitty's clear, gray eyes. He thinks no, damn no, then yes, then no again. He starts to turn away, to ask the German girl to dance, when Faysal leans over him and says, "Kitty, you look wonderful tonight. Will you dance with me?"

"Well. . . ."

"I'm dancing with her," Wilbur says, leading her toward the crowded dance floor. Her soft, warm hand in his melts some of his anger. It makes such a good fit, he thinks, then he drops the hand as he turns to dance. The air between him and Kitty is charged with electricity as they dance to a Motown medley. But he remembers the pain, as the crowd forces him to dance closer to her.

"Now," screams Clarence, dressed in a tuxedo T-shirt, white gloves and a top hat, "the sounds of the Temptations!"

"I've got sunshine. . . on a cloudy day. . ."

As the couples come together for the ballad, Wilbur and Kitty face one another.

"Do you still want to dance with me?" Kitty asks, as the lights dim.

Wilbur focuses his uncertain stare past Kitty to Salina, who is peering back at him as she slides into a booth.

"Why don't we talk?" Wilbur says.

"Do you want to come over?"

"No, not your place. How about the third-floor lobby?"

They sit on one of the long, red-leathered bench-style sofas overlooking the fireplace.

"I've missed you, Wilbur."

"Did you sleep with him?"

"Yes."

Wilbur slides lower in the seat, putting his feet up on the railing and turning his head away from her. "Well, then what the hell's the use of this conversation? I don't understand what you're trying to do. One more Wild Turkey and I would have been completely over you."

"I love you, that's the use." She holds his gaze. "Wilbur, I don't know if I can explain what I did. Byron and I spent four years together. I've grown up with him. We've learned a lot from the places we've shared, the things we've seen. I've been asking myself a lot of questions this summer, and you were in most of them. I haven't been giving you my all. I didn't know if either of us were ready for that. I wasn't sure if the love between Byron and me was gone or not. We never had a clean break, you know. Somehow, for me to make love to him once more was to take one more look at those last embers of a fire that glowed brightly and beautifully for a long time. The lovemaking, well, there was nothing there really; we both had to admit that afterward. It's over. It's been over. But what we had, we'll both remember. I don't even know if we can be friends now, though. We still managed to squeeze in an argument. He's going to Baltimore at the end of the season. We didn't even exchange addresses.

"My heart is open for you now," Kitty continues. "All of it. I believe I'm taking another step forward in my life this summer. But before I went to Byron's, I knew that what I was going to do may cost me our relationship. It was something I tried to prepare for, but I didn't realize it would hurt this much. I had to make sure it was over. I just don't feel I have that many chances left."

Wilbur looks at her. He stops his hand from touching the tears that well up in her eyes and overflow down her cheek.

"Through your outlook of life and your poems, you've given me a new direction in life. Something, now, I probably don't deserve to have. You're completely honest with the world. Byron and I loved and hated each other. The timing was always off or something.

"With you and me, it's just better," she continues. "I don't know. I guess I screwed up." She reaches in her jacket pocket. "Here are your poems. They are more dear to me than anything. You can have them if you'd like. Then, after a period of time—five months, five years, 100 years—we'll be gone from each other's memories. But if you want to give us another chance, I'll be waiting."

Wilbur takes the poems. "I've got a date with Imre in two minutes."

He walks down the lobby toward the west wing.

"So what's up, Imre? You've called me in to give me a raise?"

"Not quite, Wilbur. Here."

Wilbur looks at the white, rectangular piece of paper.

"Disciplinary Action Report? A DAR? Me? What did I do?"

Imre sits down in a hard-backed chair and lights a cigarette. "Well, for starters, you cussed out Tricia in the Pub the other night."

Wilbur pauses. The muscles in his jaw jut out as he takes a breath.

"I've told them to keep extra detail tape back there. It means I have to make two trips to the Pub in the middle of the night when I'm busy."

"Well, you couldn't have been too busy, because I know you were gone for at least 45 minutes that night. You weren't even in the office."

A rash of cuss words form in his mind. Instead of letting them out, he furrows his brow and says, "Who told you this?"

"It doesn't matter, Wilbur. What does matter is that this DAR could have just as easily been a discharge."

"I was having some personal problems that night."

"That wasn't the only night. Your work from both Wednesday and Thursday's audits look like you hadn't even checked anything. And I could tell by Steve's handwriting that he balanced the credit cards. Mammoth found four mistakes on your Food Check Variance Report from Thursday night."

"OK. Two nights. I'm not a computer. I have off nights, Imre. I'm only making $5 an hour."

"You're making more than a lot of people who would like your job. I've got two good dining-room cashiers wanting to work in accounting. . . ."

Wilbur reads the typed report.

"So what does this mean?"

"It means that since I think you're capable of doing good work, I'm rescuing you this time by not firing you. I thought that by my asking you this in private, it might save some embarrassment. Do you want to work here or not?"

"Imre, I was born to be a writer, not an auditor. Everything seems to be going crazy at once. Can I let you know tomorrow? Will you at least give me one day?"

"All right."

He folds the white sheet up and puts it in his pocket. "And here I thought you were going to try to seduce me."

"Not on your life," Imre says, blowing her cigarette smoke toward the ceiling above him. "Here, you have to sign this one at the bottom, acknowledging that you have received the DAR."

He signs it, noticing Faysal's signature next to Imre's.

Imre watches the door shut and smiles. A night for Mussorsky, she thinks, slipping a record on her turntable.

Wilbur walks past the third-floor lobby again. Kitty isn't there. He stops back by the Bear Pit. Where 20 minutes earlier, he was not only a part of the Saturday night madness but even leading it and feeding it, he now interprets the noise as intrusive chaos. He wants to unplug the music, grab the microphone from Clarence, and describe his life to that point and ask for suggestions, but he turns away. He is on his own.

He walks through the bar toward the rollicking table of employees.

"Do you want to dance some more?" Yvonne asks.

"No thanks." He slides in next to Steve and Salina. "Hey, are you guys going to be spending the night in the cabin tonight?"

"From the tone of the question, I would say you'd rather we didn't," Steve answers.

"Does this mean you two straightened everything out? I don't mean to pry, Wilbur, but remember, I am the secretary of the Society. I'm *supposed* to take notes. And besides, you two belong together."

"No, Salina. I need some time alone."

As Yvonne pulls Salina aside, Steve whispers over the music to Wilbur, "After a half marathon, two bottles of wine and two Wild Turkeys, I'm too tired to even pucker, Wilbur. I'll spend the night at Salina's and let you two have the cabin."

"No," says Wilbur. "It's not that. I need to do some writing."

It's the only thing concrete he has to turn to, a place to start and put back the pieces, try to make them fit into some kind of pattern. He can create order only in his own world. In his cabin, with the bare overhead light illuminating the clean white page in his typewriter, he searches for an end to his short story. He thinks, the lady, the track, the runner. What has to happen here? What has to happen to me?

By five o'clock he has completed the story, rewritten it into a legible draft, written a cover letter addressed to the editor of *Runner's World,* and stuck the story into an envelope—it is ready to be mailed.

He sits back in his chair and stretches. His enthusiasm for finishing the story overcomes his weariness, he becomes aware his heart is pounding heavily. He sobers to the fact that it is time to face the decision as to whether to stay or go. He sees the answer in front of him. He picks up the envelope with his story in it. The return address says, Old Faithful Station, Yellowstone National Park, Wyoming 82190.

"I have to stay, don't I?" His own voice startles him in the before-dawn stillness. He looks over his original. Around and around. That's what the runner does. That's what the lady does who watches him from her wheelchair. That's life. Then this must be a beginning here. Pick a point, a place chosen of my own volition. Mr. Hardisty, let's start over right here. Now.

"Kitty!" He leans the envelope with the finished manuscript against the typewriter, where it will be the first thing he sees when he comes back. He puts on his jacket and turns off the switch to the naked bulb that had been burning above him for five hours. Outside, the first purple rays of dawn are creeping over the mountains. He slowly walks the 50 yards to Kitty's cabin, taking deep breaths of the chilled air. He taps, then pushes the heavy door open.

"Wilbur?"

"Yea. It's me."

"Tell me quickly if you're here to say hello or good-bye."

"It will take a while, Kitty. But I'd like to start over right here. Right now."

She runs naked from the bed and throws her arms around him. He hugs her and then holds her at arm's length. "But Kitty, before we know it, the summer will be over. What then?"

"You're going to Mexico with me!"

His jaw drops as he stares into her face, bright even in the darkness of the cabin. He has more evidence, he thinks, that women are omniscient. Only then does he realize her nakedness. "Well, don't you think you're a little overdressed?"

He reaches out a hand and puts her hair behind her ear. "Can we sleep for a while now?"

Ranger Bob Mortenson takes his customary early-morning patrol of the geyser basin on Gilda, the 7-year-old chestnut mare. One hundred yards out in the meadow he sees Wayno the buffalo, the resident dominant bull, grazing in the tall grasses. Mortenson stops the mare and squints. What he thinks he sees, he hopes is not true. But when he focuses his binoculars on Winfred, he sees it is true; there is an arrow lodged through the buffalo's hump.

"I can't believe it."

Later in the day, the wildlife biologist concludes that the straight point went through the fatty part of the hump and is causing the animal no discomfort.

"How would we get close enough to pull it out, anyway? We knock the animal out, it rolls onto the arrow and tears tissue. We'll just have to leave it."

August 19. The Bear Pit Bar, later that evening.

It's the end of a Sunday night. Except for Yvonne sitting at the bar nibbling on pretzels, all the customers have left. Debi is bringing the last of the glasses to the bar for Cecil to wash. Cecil puts the swizzle stick in his last drink of the night—a Long Island Iced Tea for Yvonne.

She lights a cigarette and drains the last of her second drink before pulling the new one closer to her. "You guys want to do something after you get off? I have the next two days off and don't feel like driving up to Bozeman again."

"I'd like to have a drink," says Debi. "I'm tired but could use something to wind me down."

"How 'bout you, Cec?" Yvonne asks.

"Yea, I'll have a drink. But where can we go? My roommate's asleep."

"So is mine," says Yvonne.

"Mine too," says Debi. "We could sit in the lobby."

"I really don't want to listen to Herm's gibberish," says Cecil. "Misinformation at your service."

Just as the momentum is about to die, Yvonne gets an idea. "Let's go hotpotting. What do you say, Cec?"

"Everybody keeps talking about hotpotting. I've never been." He shuts off the sink and turns around to dry his hands. "Hell, I'll go if Debi goes."

Debi is reticent. "I don't know if I have that much energy."

"You don't have to work in the morning, do you?"

"No, I'm on 6 till closing again."

"I have a three-liter bottle of burgundy at home, unopened."

Debi empties the last of the pretzels into the plastic garbage can. "OK, I'll go. This is my last summer to goof off before I get a real job. I promised myself to take every advantage. But listen, I'm done. How long will it take you to close up and make your deposit, Cecil?"

"About a half an hour."

"We'll make it in 15," says Yvonne, slipping off the bar stool. "I'll Z out your register for you and make the deposit."

"All right," Debi says. "I'm game. Pick me up at my cabin?"

"Fifteen minutes."

It is 27 minutes later when they knock on the door of Debi's cabin. They knock a second time and Yvonne notices the lights are out. They knock a third time, louder, and hear a rumbling inside before Debi comes to the door, bleary-eyed and dressed in a striped T-shirt that comes down to her knees.

"You guys, I passed right out. I'm really tired. I woke up and thought you guys just blew it off so I went to bed. I can't make it tonight. No way. Maybe some other time."

"You do look tired," says Yvonne. "We'll forgive you."

"Thanks. Sorry, you guys. See you at work tomorrow, Cec."

The door shuts and they walk back toward Yvonne's car. "You still want to go, don't you Cecil?"

"I don't know, Yvonne. Entice me."

"I have the wine."

"That would be pretty good. I need to relax."

"I've got some of these." She holds up a small orange pill bottle, and shakes the capsules inside.

"What are they?"

"Downs. Sleeping pills. Imre gave me some. If you drink and take one of these, you can catch a really great buzz."

He inspects the little red and white pills and abruptly swallows two of them. Then he grabs the wine from the front seat and takes two sips. "Can't stand on one leg," he says, handing the bottle back to Yvonne.

They arrive at H loop of the Madison Campground with not quite half the bottle of wine left. Since Yvonne has only taken one of the pills, she is able to hold the flashlight with one hand and guide Cecil on a slightly meandering line as they head toward the hot stream that runs next to the Madison River.

"We're here," she says, pointing the flashlight through the steam at the eight-foot-wide, 40-yard-long stream. "Cecil? Where are you?"

Cecil is lying on the ground where he has fallen. He holds onto the bottle of wine while Yvonne pulls him up and points him toward the steaming spring. Wow! Yvonne thinks, that Halcion is really kicking in. First timer. He shouldn't have taken two. I wish he wasn't so short and skinny.

"It's time to get undressed, Cecil."

"Is this the hotpot?" Yvonne pulls him backward before he walks straight into the hot water.

"Take your clothes off first, Cecil. And make sure you remember where you put everything, because it's cold when you get out, and it's dark."

"Is this the hot spring?"

"Yes, Cecil. Strip!"

The big woman sits on her towel. When she is nearly undressed, she pulls the bottle away from Cecil, who has managed to get one shoe knotted. She shines the light in his eyes and watches him vainly try to pull back his focus from infinity. As he reaches again for his shoes, he falls backward, landing on his elbows. He faces the light again and smiles.

"I see you now."

"Can you still manage to undress yourself?"

"No problem."

Yvonne takes a sip of wine, pulls off her stretch pants, and watches Cecil wrestle out of his clothes.

"It's a good thing I'm wearing snaps," he says.

"You're not, Cecil. Those were buttons."

With his pants slid down just over his buttocks, Cecil says, "I'm not wearing my sweat pants, am I? Where's that bottle of wine?"

"Not until you get your clothes off. Those are your jeans, Cec. You've got to take off your belt first. Then undo the snap, then unzip them."

He falls over on his side and squirms out of his jeans, pulling them inside out over his shoes.

"I love this hotpotting," says Cecil. "Look at all those shooting stars."

"We're not in the water yet, Cecil."

"I *know* that." He looks around. "Which way is it?"

"It's eight feet in front of you, Cecil. It's where all the steam is coming from."

Cecil fights his way out of his T-shirt, stands up, falls, then crawls toward the water.

"Cecil, take off your shoes and. . . ."

With a splash, he disappears from Yvonne's vision into the steam and water, and Yvonne gathers herself up. She hopes the hot water will sober him up a little. She raises from the ground and follows him into the two-foot-deep stream.

"Thish is great!" Cecil bellows. "Now can I have a ship of wine?"

"Here. But just a little one, Cecil."

He turns over and clutches the bottle.

"It goes in your mouth, Cecil. The big aperture, just to the left. That's it. Whoa, cowboy. Not too much. Got to keep a watch out for submarines and alligators and stuff like that."

When she takes back the bottle, Cecil's hand proceeds forward, grabbing one of her huge, drooping breasts. She leans forward, closing her eyes.

"Madam, you are hereby excommunicated from the liddle biddy tiddy committee," Cecil says, giggling.

When he starts to take his hand away, Yvonne reaches and replaces it on the other breast. He fondles it momentarily, lifts the massive breast and drops it, letting it splash heavily in the hot water.

"Volleyball," he says, "bump and set, bump and set," lifting her breasts in both of his hands, letting them drop.

"I'm a woman, Cecil. Be gentle with me."

They sit for awhile, talking and drinking. Cecil touches Yvonne's breasts from time to time, and Yvonne massages Cecil's legs. Then Yvonne hands the wine back to Cecil, and as he raises it, she puts her hand underwater, goes up from the knee, and touches his penis.

She gasps and gazes into his half-closed eyes. Cecil moans contentedly and leans back against the shore, opening his legs.

"Do you have any more of those sleeping pills?" he asks. "They're very relaxing."

"No, honey, you don't need any more. Does that feel good?"

Cecil blinks at her heavily. "Yes, it does. But you just can't hold it. You've got to do something with it." He raises his torso out of the water. "Do it soft. Light. That feels good." He lays back. "You know, you look a lot better underwater in the dark."

"I'll take that as a compliment. Do you want another drink?"

"I thought that was my line."

"You are a beautiful man, Cecil. You know, I've always liked you, ever since that first day you made drinks for Imre and me. Do you remember that? I do. I remember every detail. We drank Long Island iced teas that day. No one else can make them as good as you do, either."

He chuckles. "They'll never catch me in here."

"Who?"

"Nobody."

"You know, I always thought that you and I might get together

like this. Just the way you looked at me that day, I could tell you liked
me. You always put extra booze in my drinks, too, don't you? That
was a sure sign."

"Not so hard."

"Sorry. I don't have a lot of experience in these things, but I'll
learn. I could make someone very happy. I'm losing weight too,
Cecil. I walk to work now. Next Saturday, Imre's going to go with me;
I'm going to try to make it up to Observation Point.

"You know what?"

"What? What is it, Cecil?"

"I'm going to take off my shoes."

She releases him and gives him a boost from behind as he crawls
back onto land. Two squishy steps later, he falls down. Yvonne takes
another sip of the wine and discards the second-date notion—
tonight is the night. She bites her lower lip in determination and
caresses her hardened nipples. Cecil crawls back to the hotpot and
Yvonne turns on her back and lays her head against the shore. Cecil
falls over her into the water and she gently pulls him toward her,
guiding him over her. She clutches the back of his head and guides
his mouth over hers. She is surprised and aroused when he responds
and returns her wet, passionate kiss. Now, she thinks, now is the
moment we've all been waiting for, folks. This is so romantic, the
stars, the water, the night, the man. A man! My body is so hot. I want
to be touched all over.

She spreads her legs. With one hand, she cups his small buttocks
and, with the other hand, she guides him slowly into her.

"Oh baby," Cecil murmurs. "Oh yea. This is great."

Oh baby! He called me oh baby. Oh, God that feels incredible.
He's inside me. There it goes! This is what I've lived for, kept hope
for. It's better than I imagined.

"This is incredible! My God!" she yells.

"Oh baby."

She raises her huge thighs against his, lifting him totally out of
the water, and then drops, losing him.

"Ohhh."

"Oh, baby. I want some more," moans Cecil. "You got what it
takes."

She guides him back into her and uses small, intense movements.

For two minutes, their rhythm works to an almost-violent climax.

"Oh! My God! I'm. . . ."

"Kris. . . ."

"Yvonne. Yvonne, baby, your lover girl. It's happening! I'm going to have an orgasm!"

"Me too, Kris."

"Yvonne!"

"Ahhh!"

"Ooohhh!"

Through a chorus of moans and groans, Yvonne hurls Cecil once, twice, three times completely out of the water. She holds him fast with her right hand and makes sure she doesn't lose him from her explosive heaves. She folds her legs around his and embraces him tightly. Cecil gasps.

"What did you say, my darling?" she asks, releasing him slightly, looking into his face.

"I can't breathe."

She hugs him once then lets him go, and he slides back down into the water, spent, unconscious. Yvonne lifts him back up by his armpits, checks his breathing, and lets his wet head lie on one of her still-tingling breasts. She slides down a little further into the water and luxuriates in the new sensations she is experiencing.

"I'm a woman now," she says to the stars, smoothing back the wet hair of her lover. "Thank you, God."

"Huh?"

"That's OK, baby. You just sleep now, take it easy for awhile."

I could be pregnant, she thinks, and she pulls back his head and looks into this face, trying to imagine a child from the two of them. She runs her hand along his scar. Still curious, she reaches down to feel him become flaccid.

She lets him lie there for 20 minutes as she pets and massages him.

"Cecil, we should go now. Although I want to cherish this moment forever."

After 10 minutes of intermittently splashing and poking him, he does not reawaken, so she carries him ashore and softly lays him down on the ground. After she dresses herself, she kicks away a buffalo pile from under his arm and dresses him as best she can. She stuffs his underwear and wet socks inside his shirt.

"Can you walk, dear?"

Still she cannot wake him, so she puts her shoulder to his midsection, an arm on his back and lifts him up, carrying him the 300 yards through the darkness to the car. Minutes later, Yvonne lunges and lurches his 400-horsepower Corvette out of the Madison Campground, and back home to Old Faithful.

August 19. 5:36 p.m..

Clarence knocks on Cecil's door a second time. After no response, he lets himself in. It takes several seconds for his eyes to adjust to the darkened interior, then he makes out the cocoon-like form of Cecil lying under his sheets.

"Cecil!"

Clarence takes another step inside, kicking over a shoe, and a little rivulet of water empties across the floor ahead of him.

He shakes Cecil and calls again, "Cecil!"

Cecil moans and Clarence shakes him by the shoulder. "What do you want?"

"You were supposed to be at work half an hour ago. Are you coming?"

Cecil opens one eye and fights back the twisted sheet.

"What time is it?"

"Five-thirty."

"In the morning?"

"No, Cecil. You're supposed to be at work. It's Monday, Cecil."

Cecil sits up in the bed, poking the pillows and the mattress as if verifying their reality. He squints his eyes, trying to evoke a concrete image out of a long void in time. "Monday at 5:30?"

"Yes, Cecil. Get dressed."

"How did I get here?"

"Get dressed and I'll fill you in."

As he rubs his eyes, the last thing he can remember is being at Debi's. "No wait. I took some pills. . . was driving my car up to Madison to go hotpotting." He rubs his eyes but visions of the remainder of the evening do not materialize. "Why do I have these wet clothes on?"

"I'm glad I quit drinking," Clarence says. "Come on, lover. Rise and shine. While you're getting dressed, I'll fill in the blanks. Everyone else knows, so you might as well."

"Water," says Cecil. "Please."

Clarence gets him a glass of water. "Yvonne is flitting about the lobby like a newlywed. She's got a lily in her hair and she's looking at everyone like she's just married Tom Cruise and she can't be more pleased."

"I think we went hotpotting."

"I'll say you did. The story circulating is that you got to the hotpots after you had some wine—she didn't mention pills. Her face just lights up; she says that the sky was full of stars, it was just the two of you there and that she achieved her goal for the summer, to be a real woman. Did you make her a real woman, Cecil?"

"What the hell happened? You're not trying to tell me I had sex with Yvonne, are you?"

"She's telling everyone to ask you what happened next. But from the glow on her face, we can guess what happened Cecil, you devil."

"Why the hell do I still have these wet clothes on?"

He pulls back the sheets to reveal his shirt inside out, his pants wrinkled and twisted. He blinks drowsily at Clarence, who smiles and hands him a scented envelope with 'Cecil' scrawled in flowery letters.

Cecil is busy as soon as he gets to work. Debi, waitri, and off-duty employees sitting at the bar all have something to say.

"Hey, Cecil, heard you had a wild night in the hotpots last night," someone chorts.

"I passed out; I don't remember anything," Cecil shoots back.

He is still too numb to get angry, and he hopes that, as soon as his shift is over, he will be able to get in a quiet place and piece together the events of the previous evening. Occasionally, while making a drink or ringing up a sale, an image will come to him, then leave before he can grasp it. When he goes to the liquor storeroom in the back of the kitchen, he passes Kris.

She takes him by the elbow, "Are you all right, Cecil?"

"Yea, I'm all right. Whatever you heard can't be true."

"It's OK. It probably released a lot of tension."

"Kris!" He drops a second case of beer on the hand cart. "Kris, can I stop by and talk to you after I get off?"

"If it's not too late."

At 10:30, the inevitable happens. By trying to keep busy, he pretended it wouldn't happen but he tried to brace himself for it just in case. He turns to deliver a beer and staring at him, dressed in a white satin shirt, a lily behind her ear, with make-up and red lipstick, is Yvonne.

"Hi, Cecil," she says provocatively. "Imre and I will have the usual. You remember, don't you?"

He looks around to see Clarence turn away with a repressed smile and a group of employees staring at him from the other end of the bar.

"I'll be right back," Imre says, sliding off the bar stool.

In an anxious whisper, he shouts, "What the hell happened last night?"

"Don't you remember?"

"Cecil, ordering," says Debi. "Two gin and tonics, one Rob Roy, a glass of Chablis and a Coke."

By 1 a.m., Cecil can no longer work around the situation, for once again it is Debi, Yvonne and him alone in the bar. When Debi leaves for the women's room, he walks down to the end of the bar to a beaming Yvonne.

"I'll tell you the truth. As hard as I try, I can't remember anything about last night. Be honest. Did we or didn't we?"

To answer him, she puts down her Marlboro and picks up a furry small white toy rabbit Imre bought her in the gift shop. "I'm waiting to see if it lives or dies," says Yvonne, with wide-eyed innocence. She senses his sudden stern demeanor. "Do you want to get together after work? Maybe just play some cards or something? Talk?"

"No, Yvonne. You might have ended whatever chance I had for my relationship with Kris. I'm going to have to talk to her after work."

"You don't like me anymore."

"No. I was so high I didn't know what I was doing."

"Well, you sure enjoyed it at the time."

"Cecil, it's almost 2 o'clock in the morning. What do you want?"

"I came to talk."

"Maybe tomorrow. I'm sleeping, Cecil. Good night."

As Kris starts to close the door, he jams his foot down, blocking it. "You haven't got a letter from John yet, have you?"

"No!" She takes an angry breath, and pushes the door closed in front of his face.

Cecil knocks again. "Kris!"

"Keep it down out there!" comes a male voice from inside another dorm room.

Cecil knocks once more on the door, louder. Kris opens it and glares at him. "Cecil, I want you to stay away from me."

Cecil sneers at her and slaps the door hard, with the flat of his palm. She shuts the door firmly, then locks it. Cecil turns and walks off, pounding his fist on the walls and doors along the way, cursing a vile revenge.

After the initial jockeying for position on the asphalt road approaching Pike's Peak, Steve runs easily up the winding, crushed gravel trail. Now he takes a breath and focuses on his favorite image when running uphill—a machine grinding away steadily uphill in low gear.

Keep your pace, he reminds himself. Relax now.

He runs on, yet soon it is hard to call it running. Surviving is more the word. Like the runner half a switchback in front of him, he can only take short staccato steps looking for good footholds, avoiding sharp rocks or talus. He climbs higher. It is an effort to keep his eyes open. He hears music now; it seems surreal, here high on the mountain. Then he glimpses a blur of color near the summit. The finish? He looks at his watch to see the ascent record of 2:05 come and go. It is an incomprehensible feat to him that someone could be finishing now, propel a body that high up in that short a time. He rounds another steep switchback with a high step and instantly, unconsciously, he is walking.

Keep standing. Breathe. Oxygen. Light-headed. Must walk for a while. Don't close your eyes. The clouds below, so far away, so white. Dizzy. White. Swirling. Easy! Sit down! No, I'm OK. A few more steps. Focus on the trail. Color of my shoes. That's better. What is happening? Don't look at the cloud bank. Too white.

He walks two switchbacks and the trail levels out a little. When he is sure the dizziness has passed, he trots in a light jog.

God, no one passed me. Those guys below me are walking too. No wonder. This is hell up here. War. Too long. Too far. Too steep. Big ass mountain. Must be 13,000 feet by now.

"Water?"

"Thanks."

Feel better now. Almost went down. Start again. Keep going. Take that guy up there. There's the finish. 2:10 now. How far is it? OK. Flat part. Take him.

"On your left."

But the runner in the dark green T-shirt reacts to Steve's words by spurting ahead. Steve regains his composure and pursues. They scramble, walk, run up the next three long switchbacks. It is anger Steve uses to press forward. "On your left."

Still he won't get over, he won't even look around.

Which one of us will pass out first? Let's do it.

A right turn and the slow-motion race at 13,500 feet continues. Steve's thighs burn. Suddenly, weirdly, looking so out of place, the runner in the green T-shirt silently drops to the trail, crumpling, as if the skeleton that supported his muscles was removed. His head grazes a rock and Steve jogs to the inside to get around him.

"War. . . pal. . . I tol' ya. . . Move o'er."

Now Steve can hear shouts coming from the finish line. He can hear the music and see the large crowd sitting among the boulders above him and even the finish-line banner.

He rounds the switchback and watches a bearded runner below him step around the still figure in the green shirt. Then the runner in the green shirt crawls to his feet, only to have his legs wobble, and he falls again among the rocks. In the middle of the switchback, Steve stops. He looks at the finish line. He looks back at the supine runner in the trail below him, crawling, struggling to regain his feet, dangerously nearing the edge of a 80-foot dropoff. Steve sees the bearded runner turn the switchback and run toward him. Steve looks at his watch and sees 2:30 approaching. He looks up at the finish, then down at the fallen runner.

I've got to go back down there.

The runner gathers himself again and takes another step toward the edge of the dropoff, then collapses again.

"Send someone down for this guy," Steve says to the bearded runner as he passes Steve with a look of panicked exhaustion.

As he turns, the immediate pain in his thighs is gone and the feeling of suddenly changing his momentum to downhill nearly propels him too fast; he barely has the strength to brake himself. His knees buckle, his thighs burn. Steve kneels next to the runner who, despite a faraway, frantic look in his eye, is conscious.

"Got to finish. Top 10. Help me up," he mutters, saliva frothing around his mouth.

"You're OK. Just relax."

The runner's leg starts twitching, cutting his knee into a sharp piece of rock. Blood starts to trickle out. A tall, blond-headed runner appears on the trail and stops. He and Steve move the runner over to a flat stretch of trail. Bending his legs to carry the man nearly drains Steve's waning strength. His legs buckle. Then he looks up to see two medics charging down the hill with a black bag and a folded stretcher. Steve and the other runner wait for several moments, and one of the medics has to restrain the flailing runner when he tries to stand up.

"He'll be OK. Just some altitude sickness," the older medic says. "You two go on, you've still got a great time going. Thanks for staying and keeping your poise."

Steve and the blond runner look at each other. "Staying was easy," says Steve. "Keeping going is the hard part."

They laugh and shake hands. "After you," says the thin, blond-headed runner.

Steve pauses. He takes a deep breath and looks out over what he thinks must be most of Colorado stretching beneath him. "What a great run," he says, and they turn and start jogging just as two other runners turn the switchback below them.

"Beautiful!" says the blond runner.

"Magnificent!" says Steve, and now the top of the mountain and the music and the cheering people all come into focus. The green forests, and blue lakes below come into focus, the clouds in the distance, the taper of the horizon.

Three more switchbacks, Steve thinks. So winning is not the only thing in life after all. Not if I can feel this good just accomplishing the task. Hell, I can start to enjoy it now.

The crowds are thick now, sitting and standing amid the boulders around the trail. The shouts and applause well up like a wave. Steve takes the turn and catches the eye of the tall blond two steps behind him.

"Finish. . . together?"

"Yea."

"Go Steve!" He hears but cannot see Salina. He smiles and waves. I'll get a big hug and buy her dinner tonight. Crab legs!

The music is loud, the applause is loud. In the wide part of the last switchback, Steve and the blond take hands and hold them up, to a rising chorus of cheers.

Over the loudspeaker comes a voice: "Steve Mathewson of Yellowstone National Park and Rob Greenwood of Breckenridge, Colorado! A tie for 15th place. Let's hear it for Steve and Rob!"

Steve looks up amid the screams to see 2:37:58 flash over the digital clock.

"Good run!"

"All right!"

"Way to go, 837!"

Support volunteers escort the two embraced runners through the chutes. The pain in Steve's legs give way to an unsteady weakness. Then, after four giddy steps, the tired is replaced by a shiver of effervescent joy. Salina comes and hugs Steve, and he hugs her back with all his feeble but inspired strength.

"Are you OK?" she asks, putting an arm around his back and smiling up at him.

"I feel great. I just learned poise."

Randy embraces him, muttering something about finishing third. He looks in his hand only to find someone has placed a Pike's Peak T-shirt in it, for finishers only.

He turns to the east, looking down the mountain. "What a great race!"

August 25. Old Faithful Inn, T&I Desk.

"The reason we celebrate Christmas in August," says Tina to an elderly couple, "was that in 1937 snow fell constantly for three days. Early even for this altitude. The tourists that had planned on leaving Old Faithful simply could not: The roads were impassable. After three anxious days of pacing, and waiting for the storm to lift, a tourist from San Francisco suggested a 'Christmas in August' celebration. They sang carols and exchanged gifts instead of pacing the lobby, waiting for the storm to end."

The lobby of the Inn is decorated festively; an ornamented tree stands near the fireplace, and Christmas carols ring out from a cassette player behind the bellmen's desk. Next to the cassette player is a smaller tree with gifts beneath it.

On the second floor, Kitty oversees the mixing of two punches—one alcoholic and one not—as maids, inspectresses and porters snatch chips with dip, crackers, cheeses and Christmas cookies. Aaron, a black man in Kitty's department, is nominated to be Santa Claus. He beams and ho-hos as he hands out gifts from a laundry bag.

In the Bear Pit Bar, Clarence tries vainly to mix green food coloring to a tequila sunrise to produce a Christmas drink.

The front desk is decorated and the clerks, beaming with holiday smiles, are wearing red and green flowers on their shirts. Even the accounting office has been decorated, despite Imre's voiced apathy.

"Christmas is in December," she had said.

She turns to see Sandy, bright-eyed, gazing at her, holding the finished lunch report. "OK," Imre sighs. "You can go upstairs to housekeeping's party. But come back soon. I may need you."

"Merry Christmas, Imre," Sandy says as she departs, leaving Imre alone again.

The employee dining room is decked out with actual cloth tablecloths and napkins. There are cheers from the long line of employees as Barry brings out the first turkey to go along with the ham, stuffing, sweet potatoes, mashed potatoes, cranberry salad, homemade breads, pumpkin pie, tossed salad, ice cream and eggnog.

Nearly two miles away, on Kitty's Knoll, Wilbur, sitting by himself, tries to think of a name for his poem before he leaves to meet Kitty for dinner in the EDR.

At the T&I desk, Jorge waits until Tina opens his gift to her—a Spanish-American dictionary. He hugs her. He knows she has only one more week on her contract before she goes back home. But he is grateful for that week—her father had wanted her to come back right after the bear incident.

At 6 o'clock, some employees head over to the softball field for the park championship game—Old Faithful Maintenance against Canyon Village Dining Room.

In the bottom of the seventh inning, with the sun near setting and close to 200 spectators on the sidelines, it is 13 to 11, Old Faithful leading. Someone that the Canyon Village team refers to as "Bruiser" hits his third home run of the game with two runners on.

"I'm going to see if that guy would like to work in housekeeping next year," Kitty says. "We've got to win at least one game."

"Well, it is sure a mental blow to all of Old Faithful," says Wilbur. "Psychological traumatizing of a demographic population. Losers." He stands and dusts off the seat of his pants. "Kitty, we are out of Mout. We'll have to stop by my cabin and get another bottle for the talent show."

"And the winner of the park-wide talent competition for this year is. . . Clarence and the K-OFI Radio Broadcast of a Day in the Life of a Typical Touron Family! Congratulations! Come get your check for $100!"

Kitty and Wilbur are invited to attend the celebration party in Clarence's cabin. Clarence makes a huge bowl of his famous Perfect Punch, with the Special Reserve Bacardi "Anejo" Rum.

"I propose a toast," says Slim.

"A toast," the others shout in unison.

"To Clarence Harps, for bringing culture to Yellowstone National Park, even if it is, shall we say, low brow."

After everyone's cup is filled, all hold up a hand except Clarence. Rhonda, noticing this, hands him a cup of the punch. Clarence hesitates; he hasn't touched a drop of liquor for almost seven weeks. But the night brings back visions of cast parties and happy times, and it is his favorite drink created with his own hands. Besides, it is a celebration, and they did win the talent contest—and it is Christmas.

"To the director," says the waiter who played the radio broad-
caster.

"Salud!"

"Cheers!"

Kitty drinks. Wilbur drinks. The cast drinks. Clarence drinks.

An hour later, Clarence holds his third drink in his hand. His cast
talks him into doing impersonations—Ed Wynn, Jack Benny, John
Wayne. At 1:30 a.m., Kitty and Wilbur are the last to leave.

"Good night, Clarence," Wilbur says.

"Are you sure you don't want us to help you clean up?"

"No, thanks, I can do it. Merry Christmas!"

He turns back to his empty cabin. I had liquor, he thinks. And I
told myself I never would again. I think I can do it, though. I can
never let it get like it was, but every once in a while. . . .

He starts to straighten up his cabin, carefully rinsing and drying
the borrowed glass punch bowl, throwing away the paper napkins,
plates and cups.

Where did summer go? When did nature turn the corner?

The high mountain sedges in the meadows are golden, swaying
in that slightly cool breeze that portents of winter. The nights get
colder. The wild berries—gooseberries, strawberries, huckleberries,
raspberries, thimbleberries, buffalo berries—make their appearance. The fall mushrooms force their way up through the pine-
needle forests, prompted skyward by the cool rains. The plant life
subtly changes. There is aster, groundsel, elk thistle and Canadian
thistle, knapweed.

The rivers get lazy; they are pure and majestic. This will be their
lowest level until winter leaves the precipitation frozen on the shore.
In the north end of the park, the aspen leaves start to turn a
luxurious gold as the trees withdraw their moisture into their trunks.
Places that were swampy or marshy finally yield to the hiker and
backpacker.

The mountain tops are clear from snow if they ever are. The
occasional dusting they may get during a night is gone by late
morning.

In the early morning sky, just before sunrise, Orion makes his
appearance, flexing his muscles, preparing to face another fierce
winter.

The animals sense the sun lowering in its daily zenith. Elk are
tannish brown with a dark brown neck; their coats glisten as they

bulk up for the winter. The bull's rack of antlers that have grown up to an inch a day stop growing. Now they will shed the blood-filled velvet by rubbing their antlers against the trees.

Bears have also rapidly increased their weight—the largest grizzly can weigh 1,000 pounds. The buffalo eat constantly to gain bulk for the coming winter. The males huff and snort, physically enforcing order, voicing their dominance during the August rutting season and then drifting from the cows to live an isolated winter life.

Bicyclists peddle around and enjoy the less-congested roads.

It is good weather to backpack, the days crisp and sunny, an 8 o'clock sunset, and the nights are cozy and comfortable around a campfire or in a good sleeping bag.

September 3. Kitty's cabin, 3:04 p.m..
"Are you sure this is going to work?" Salina asks.

"No," says Wilbur.

"How in plantation do you come up with these things?" asks Steve. "That's what I want to know."

"The assistant manager of the lower gas station is a friend of mine. We bicycle together sometimes. About a week ago, I was waiting for him to get off before we went on a ride up to Midway. I was watching them dig this ditch in front of the gas station. That's when the idea first came to me. Herm, you're sure the rangers are in a meeting?"

"All but two of them are at that big district ranger meeting. Supposed to be over by 5 o'clock, and they are coming for dinner at the Inn at 5 sharp, right past the gas station."

"Shannon, did you get that gated Y?"

"Yup. Here it is."

"Kitty, film?"

"I've got 32 pictures left in the camera," Kitty says. "Just in case *Newsweek* doesn't show up this time."

Wilbur, Kitty, Steve, Salina and Herm stand around a dirt mound at the edge of the lower gas station. On cue—Wilbur touching his right ear—a small burst of water and air rises four feet above the little dirt mound.

"It's working!" Salina says.

"Of course it's working," says Wilbur. "Herm, you'd better rope off the area. We should have more visitors to see the nation's newest geyser pretty soon. Steve, let's get in uniform. You all know the plan."

After 20 seconds, the "geyser" subsides. By the time Wilbur gets back, dressed in a ranger's uniform, a crowd of about 20 has gathered. "OK, ladies and gentlemen, please stand back. We've called the park geologist from Mammoth, and he should be here shortly."

"Ranger Lee," says Herm, "I've been monitoring the geyser and it's been going off regularly every 10 minutes, right to the second. In fact, it should be going off again in about 10 seconds if it behaves like it has been."

Inside the gas station, Curtis Kesey waits for a sign from Wilbur. When he sees it, he turns the water and air compressors on. He can hear the roar of approval from the crowd. A smile crosses his face, and he laughs under his breath. Exactly 20 seconds later, he turns off the valves and strolls out to watch the crowd react.

"You should call it 10-Minute Geyser," says a tourist.

"Sir, that will be up to the park geologist," Wilbur says. "But it is a good suggestion, and I'll see that he gets your name and home state. Write it down on this pad, please."

Thirty minutes and three eruptions later, a crowd of about 100 people watch "10-Minute Geyser" erupt with pinpoint accuracy. So accurate, in fact, that with 20 seconds to go, Wilbur leans his ear to the earth and nods, while Herm initiates a countdown with the crowd.

"Three. . . two. . . one. . . ."

The new geyser erupts to applause, shouts, and whistles, and the sounds of shutters clicking and camera motors whirling.

At 4:27, the "park geologist" arrives. Steve is dressed in baggy African-style khakis and a safari cap. Wilbur the ranger explains the situation to him and the "geologist" observes as 200 people chant "Three. . . two. . . one. . . geyser!" Right on schedule as the crowd applauses.

"Phenomenal," Steve says. "This is geologic history, Ranger Lee. Pass around the notebook. I want everyone's name and home address. We may call on you as witnesses to this great event."

He looks into Wilbur's eyes, then toward Old Faithful. "I'm afraid Old Faithful may no longer be the most famous or the most accurate geyser in Yellowstone."

But at 4:55, the crowd of 200-plus counts down and nothing happens. No eruption. Steve puts an ear to the asphalt and looks troubled. The crowd opens as he walks to his running-gear bag, pulls out part of an old wishbone-shaped antenna with Wilbur's Avocet bicycle computer duct-taped at the connection. Walking back across the street, he holds the two ends over the pavement and the aluminum tip starts quivering up and down.

"He's using a divining rod!"

"A computerized version, the Monkey Wrench Corporation," Steve says. "Still one of the most reliable methods of locating water underground."

Steve taps on the ground in several places with the end of the divining rod, making slight adjustments on the bike computer and causing the "divining rod" to fluctuate.

At 5 p.m., Shannon comes through the crowd and motions Wilbur to the side.

"OK," he whispers. "The rangers just got out of the meeting and they're on their way over here. Four cars; the superintendent is in the first car."

"Perfect."

Wilbur winks almost imperceptibly at Steve and nods.

"Just as I thought!" Steve exclaims. "There is a sinter or geyserite buildup beneath the road here. Listen to this." He taps the road with the blunt end of the divining rod. "The ground water is trapped. If we don't get it to erupt, we will lose this little geyser. If this powerful little spouter makes a run to the north, Old Faithful could be dormant before the fall. It's up to us! Please! Everyone form a circle. Everyone has got to walk in tiny steps toward the center to force the water to erupt through this geyser. Back up. Everyone, please, a big circle. That's it. Now, tiny steps, press down hard. Force that asphalt to squeeze down. Did you call the superintendent, Ranger Lee?"

"He should be here *any second.*"

"OK. Sir, you had the idea for naming the geyser, so you should get the credit when the superintendent gets here. Here's the notebook with everyone's name in it. Give him this. Ranger Lee and I are going to get the backhoe and the excavator. And keep inching ahead, everyone! Pressure! The Park Service appreciates your support."

Steve and Wilbur duck into the gas station, leaving the crowd circling around the little mud mound.

"Give them just a little water pressure, Curtis. Here comes the superintendent's car! See you back at Kitty's cabin."

They rush out the back door, passing the station manager, who is just arriving at work.

"What's the big commotion, Curtis?"

"They've discovered a new geyser right out in front of the station."

"No kidding. Look at all those ranger cars. This must be big."

"It is, but not big enough for me. It's my last day. I've already processed out, and my car's already packed. Looks like I'll be heading out. I should be back in Denver by 3 a.m."

"Well, good luck to you." They shake hands. "I'd better see what's happening to my gas station."

"Now just wait one minute!" the superintendent shouts. "One person at a time, please! You, with the notebook, what's going on here?"

Ten-Minute Geyser erupts again, to a height of eight feet, spraying the superintendent, his staff, and some of the onlookers, and to the cheers of the crowd and incredulity of the superintendent's staff—one of whom reaches down and digs around the base of the erupting geyser, exposing the metal Y.

Just then, the station manager passes through the crowd. "Whoever belongs to that Park Service rig is gonna have to move it right now. You're blocking traffic."

The Bechler Region.

In the dark, Ross Matthias dog paddles around the center of Three Rivers hot spring, through the swirls of cold to hot to warm water. A finger of cold water assails his midsection and he turns back to the center of the pool. He completely submerges his 6-foot-4-inch frame near the bubbles. With his right foot, he tumbles over a rock and the escaping water nearly burns him. He moves to sit on the underwater ledge where the water blends to just the right temperature. He can reach behind him to the little grassy shore and stir his simmering soup by the flickering candlelight; a candle nestled under a cliff, sheltered by rocks.

Looking to the other side of the steamy pool, he brushes back his blond hair from his forehead. He can deny the feeling no longer. "I need a broad," he says to the night. Now the image of his old girlfriend comes in the form of wanting. He can almost see her in the water across from him, materializing through the steam, swimming toward him, then lowering himself back into the water, taking her in his arms, kissing her fully, passionately, caressing her smooth, wet skin, then floating with her in his arms out past the center of the pool to the other shore, then climbing onto the shore to the grassy spot. . . .

He shakes his head and wipes the steam droplets from his brow, repressing the visions.

He sighs and turns to his steaming soup. Turning off the stove brings back the stereo effect of the three water sources, the enveloping darkness.

He takes the pot off the stove and discovers it floats in the hot water in front of him. He takes a mouthful and thinks, I've hiked more than 250 miles this summer—alone, peaceful. It's made me strong.

As a wind comes up, he stacks more rocks around his wavering candle. He checks to make sure his flashlight and lighter are handy on the shore. Despite having hiked a rugged 10 miles to the spring, he has the appetite to eat just half the pot of soup; the gorp—the mixture of M&Ms, raisins, cashews, and sunflower seeds—tastes better. After five handfuls, he puts a rock on the lid of the soup and stashes it under the shore bank. Then he puts the rest of his food into a stuff sack, jumps out of the spring and dashes to the trees. He hangs the sack over a branch 20 yards from the pool.

Back at the hot spring, he deftly rolls a marijuana cigarette on the bank. He lights it with the candle, then shields the flame with his right hand as he scans his topo map. He puts his finger on the point where he will disembark from the trail and bushwhack along the divide tomorrow.

He looks at the cigarette burning in his hand and once again contemplates its magic, the ability to make loneliness fade. He takes another deep pull on the cigarette.

Then he turns his attention back to the map, planning tomorrow's walk up to the divide, leaving the trail and bushwhacking to Summit Lake. No problem.

He takes another large draw on the cigarette and lays it by the candle. After he replaces the map in his pack, he turns to the hot spring and closes his eyes. Now he consciously regulates his breathing, slowing it and his pulse.

After about four minutes, he enters a trance-like state, focusing on the soothing trickles and gurgles of the hot water surrounding him. He very slowly lowers his body further into the water. He imagines his body dissolving, spreading out the length and width of the hot spring, his very molecules dispersing, subject to the eddying currents of hot and cold.

His skin becomes a permeable layer, permitting the cleansing, swirling current to pass through him.

Without letting his heart rate increase, he lowers himself into the water and floats toward the bubbling center.

When Ross crawls out of his tent the next morning, the low, threatening gray clouds seem out of place. The clear, sunny skies of the previous day seem like another time. It is a fall day now—windy, with just the hint of a biting nip, coercing him back into the hot spring before he eats or breaks camp.

Three hours later, after hiking steadily uphill, he is relatively certain of standing on the divide. He strikes out away from the trail onto a westerly ridge. In the first few steps, a sprinkling of rain falls on him. But he reminds himself that he has the gear to survive whatever weather nature hurls at him. He takes a last glance at the trail and turns away.

He is able to stay on the ridge, meandering around fallen trees. The area is heavily timbered with ever-present lodgepoles that bend and creak in the gusting winds. The high, raspy sound of the wind through the treetops unnerves him.

Something else is bothering him. Diverging from the Bechler Trail for eleven miles to Summit Lake through grizzly and black-bear country. They'll be starting to locate and prepare their denning sites. And should something happen to me here, no one is going to find me.

Maybe I should take those mushrooms.

He feels for his Old Timer, the knife of tempered steel ready at his waist. He unsnaps the buckle, goes over in his mind for the thousandth time the act of unbuckling and dropping his backpack and sprinting for a tree, the *right* tree, or having no alternative but pulling out the six-inch blade and going for the bear's jugular vein just behind the ear.

The rain gusts and the sky grows darker by a shade, bringing him back to reality. The wind howls through the treetops and a second gust of rain prompts him to step under a lodgepole, take off his pack, and put on his dark blue Gore-tex jacket. He looks down to his left wrist where there is no watch; the last, symbolic gesture was to leave it in the car. He looks back, and the thought of turning around crosses his mind but he decides it is, after all, only a little rain. The clouds are moving quickly; it could clear up and be sunny.

He pulls out his map and compass and hovers over them. His reading tells him he must travel west for another half an hour, then northwest.

He slides back into his pack and looks behind him. It looks just like where he is going. He settles into a stride.

He reaches a clearing on the ridge where he takes another

reading, using Shoshone Lake in the distance as a reference point. Satisfied, he hikes on.

This is as rich as a man in the late twentieth century can be, he thinks. I'm lucky. I've got freedom and no responsibilities. I'm able to come to a place and really question my worth, goals. To see how I react when my basic needs aren't at my fingertips, not taken for granted. I want the edge. I want the challenge, an inner challenge. If I make a new path, so be it. If I return the same route, that's OK, too. But it must be adventure! It must be interesting.

The skies continue to darken. Ross breaks out of the trees and the cold wind and rain from the southwest cut across him, stinging the left side of his face. It is the effort of carrying the 51-pound pack over rugged terrain that keeps him warm. The ridge is easier to follow but he is increasingly exposed to the deteriorating weather. In the distance, he hears thunder. Lowering gray clouds hide the mountainous horizon, as he slowly weaves his way north. In the crux of a saddle, he looks up at a long, rocky incline ahead of him. The treeless ridge above him looks to be taking the full force of the storm, and Ross decides to keep to the leeward side, in the forest,in the security of the trees.

Over the next hour and a half, the gusting rain turns into a steady drizzle. Walking with his compass in his right hand, he drops down into a meadow. A cow elk that had been watching him suddenly bounds away up the opposite hill. Ross follows a northerly ridge that should slant farther west, if he is where he thinks he is. Under the Gore-tex rain jacket, he starts to perspire. Breaking out of the trees, he comes upon a lake, some 90 feet wide. He takes off his pack, takes out the bag of gorp and the map. But the lake and the map do not make sense to him. Of the only two lakes within 50 miles, one is on the west side of the divide, which he is sure he did not cross again, and the other is five miles away, near the trail he turned from. To double-check himself, he makes a guess of the direction of due north, then looks through his compass. He is 30 degrees off.

With the weather worsening, he decides to strike out due north toward Old Faithful so he is sure to get back in time for work the next evening.

He keeps his compass in his shirt pocket as he determines to keep going north. Six hours into the hike, he grows weary. His shoulders strain against the weight of the heavy pack. The straps cut and pull at him, and it feels as if his shoulders might wrap around and touch him. His lower back and legs stiffen. From head to toe, he is moist—

either from the seeping rain or his own perspiration. He wants to stop and set up camp, but it is still early in the afternoon. He knows if he stops now, there will be nothing to do but sit in his tent and read. Besides, he had hoped to make it to a group of hot springs on the divide—two miles from Summit Lake and the trail out—before stopping for the day.

A half hour later, he comes to a 15-foot-wide stream in his path. Fatigue overtakes him; he gets out his map and can only guess at which of three different drainages he may be in.

But it can't be any of these, he thinks. The divide has got to be over that way, within a half a mile.

"Damn it."

He wipes the wet hair away from his forehead.

He looks at the stream and follows it down to where it disappears to the right and the southwest. The rain comes down harder.

How could I have dropped low enough off the divide to come upon a stream this large? Where in the hell am I? This can't be the Firehole. Ouzel Creek?

He double-checks his compass reading to confirm that he must cross the creek. He walks 100 yards up and down to find the narrowest crossing, then takes off his boots, socks, rain pants and blue jeans, and straps them under the bungee cord at the top of his pack. He steps into the cold stream; it feels good on his reddened, weary feet. The bottom by the stream edge is soft and sandy. Another step and he is surprised to sink to his knees. It didn't look that deep.

No turning back now. That's the way I have to go. Then I'm going to take the first campsite I can find.

Another step and he sinks deeper, up to his crotch. Then suddenly, on the next step, his foot slips on unstable rocks. He tries to throw himself forward, letting his momentum carry him to the other side of the stream. He spreads his arms out for balance. Another step and he starts to panic as he is suddenly up to his waist, still two steps from the center of the stream. He stalls there briefly, unable to move forward or back. The creek water laps at the bottom of his pack, where he stuffed his sleeping bag. Now he becomes more buoyant in the water, and the downward motion of the current is working across his body, shifting his weight over his right foot.

Back up. Get out of here.

He manages a step backward but the sudden transfer of weight pulls him back faster. With a quick reflex, he gets his right leg behind him, saving himself from falling. But when he goes to replant his left leg, his bare foot finds only a slick rock. His momentum is thrown forward, the foot slips off the rocks and, with a snap, twists grotesquely inward. His ankle slams hard into another sharp rock, just above his ankle bone. His entire weight is over the outside of his twisted ankle. He screams out in pain, reaching for the ankle. It buckles under, and he falls on his left side into the water, his pack crashing over him. The pack is buoyant above him as he thrashes underwater, under the weight of the pack. As he starts to float downstream, the pack keeps him from turning in the water or coming up for air. Ross grasps underwater with his arms and legs but can touch nothing. He opens his eyes but can only see the blur of the dark creek bottom. He desperately reaches out for the shore, for anything, but the pack on his back refuses to let him break the surface. He feels the pack bump into something but cannot grab onto it. He wriggles out of the pack to his elbows, but it is quickly taking him farther under water. Then the pack flips over like a sinking hull, pulling him down to the bottom, face up. He opens his eyes and can see the surface of the water disappear above him.

God. . . please. . . air. . . up!

He tears at his unrelenting shoulder straps, now kicking at the creek bottom in a futile attempt to reach oxygen.

His pack roughly hits the bottom of the creek and the current starts to lift his legs over his head. He knows that would mean his death, and he kicks with all his might to help the current turn his legs so he remains face up. In two quick movements, he squirms out of his shoulder straps and lunges toward the surface. Something holds him to the bottom.

God help. . . . Let me go!

Panicking, with his eyes wide open—frantic with the death of water closing in on his near-bursting lungs—Ross tries again to lunge away from his pack. But again something pins him down, holding him strong to the creek bottom.

The waist strap is still buckled!

His lungs burst in exhalation, just as he reaches down to release the buckle. Then he shoots up, crashing the surface of the stream, sucking in air and water with a huge "uuuaaahhh!"

He takes another short breath and coughs out the creek water he breathed into his lungs. He strokes once to stay afloat, refusing to let his head go underwater again. With a second stroke, he is at the shore, clinging tightly to the tall grasses, choking, panting, gasping for air. For a full minute, he clings to the shore, spitting up water and sucking air.

He looks upstream and guesses where he got out of his pack. Then he hoists himself up on the shore, vomiting water again. He shivers violently. Panting, he relives the terrifying feeling of being trapped at the bottom, as if the devil himself had his hands around his waist. Shivering from fright and cold, he becomes aware that it is raining harder again. The reality of his predicament sets in. He looks back at the stream as if it were his murderer, pulls himself out of the water and lies on the ground, afraid that somehow the stream may grab him and pull him back in.

I've got to go back in and get the pack or I can start digging my grave out here.

On his first attempt at stepping fully on his sprained left ankle, he falls to the ground. The pain and frustration overwhelm him, nearly bringing him to tears, but he steels himself. He has to.

He starts over.

He turns the pockets of his Gore-tex jacket upside down and lets the water rush out of them. He looks at his left ankle, already swelling, and puts a finger where the contact with the sharp rock bruised him and slightly broke his skin. He sighs and looks upstream.

I've got to get the pack. If the current carries it downstream. . . I'd be without warm clothes or boots, or fire, or sleeping bag, tent. . . .

I've got to go in there and get it.

He crawls on his hands and knees back up along the creek, dragging his lame ankle behind him. He peers from different angles for a sign of the dark green pack beneath the surface. Then he catches sight of the dull gray top of the frame, and lets out a sigh of relief. It isn't moving.

He knows he can't take it out piece by piece or his boots or clothing might float off. The whole pack must come out at once.

From a sitting position, he slides into the stream again. The cold does not register until he is in up to his thighs. He backs out, trying to force his mind to come up with an alternative to going under the water. He looks around, as if someone might be there.

"There's no other way."

He takes a deep breath of air and plows in. In the near-freezing water, he reaches for the distorted shape of the backpack frame and, on the second try, his fingers blindly grasp it. But the weight of the pack holds him to the bottom of the stream. He must retain his grip on the pack or the current will carry him downstream. He grabs the underside of it and, using his strong right foot, is able to lift it part of the way up the opposite bank. Ignoring the cold and his need for air, he positions himself again and jerks it up. It gets heavier closer to the surface, and he moves it up less than a foot. But he is able to hold onto the frame with his left hand while he raises his head out of the water for air. The cold chills him to the bone, and he manages to swallow the next wave of panic.

On the next attempt, the sand gives way under his step and his hand slips from the frame. But he again grasps the pack quickly and, in three heaves, inches it up to where he can grab the base of the tall grasses on the shore and pull himself and the pack ashore. He collapses next to the pack. His legs throb from the cold. He is exhausted, spent, but it is some relief to see both of his boots still under the bungy cord, and all the contents still inside. He puts an arm around the sopping pack as if it had rescued him from death.

On hands and knees, Ross drags the pack 30 yards to a flat piece of earth under a tall pine. He recognizes the signs of hypothermia— a numbing, drunken desire to sleep. He knows his only chance is to keep moving.

What first? he asks himself. Fire. Hope to God the lighter works. What the hell *happened* back there? If I can't dry out the sleeping bag. . . fire, then tent. Dear God, at least make it stop raining.

He fishes out the lighter. Lying on the pine needles, he flicks it 50 times with only weak sparks. The matches are soaked.

"Give me a break!" he shouts.

Under the Gore-tex, the clinging wet T-shirt and chamois shirt seem to make him colder, so he takes them off. He pulls out the things from his pack: Everything is soaked. The rolled-up polypropylene long underwear is as wet as everything else, but he puts them on with his rain suit over them. He knows if he can move around to generate body warmth, the synthetic silk will return some warmth. But he cannot stand on the swollen ankle. He downs five handfuls of gorp, soggy and tinted from the discolored M&Ms.

Then he pulls out his tent. As darkness approaches, he sets it up, with cold, stiff fingers—sometimes crawling, sometimes hopping on one foot. It is, at the very least, a psychological relief to have a place to get inside. He cannot stop shivering, partly from fear, partly from cold. He sits inside the tent for several minutes, and draws himself into a tight ball. He gets sleepy, heavy. He half-opens one eye to watch the rain fall in the settling darkness. The meager warmth of his body is gratifying. He wonders what defense system is holding off the hypothermia and how long he could last if he slept for a bit. He is so tired. But he shakes off the fatigue and, with much effort, pushes himself up.

He pulls out his water-logged sleeping bag and spreads it in front of his tent. Then he rolls it tightly, kneeling on top of it, forcing as much water out as possible. He knows the fiber fill will dry quicker than a down filling would.

He takes the sleeping bag inside the tent and lays it out, supporting it on the pots and the wind screens from his cooking kit so that air will circulate around it.

Next, he finds his flashlight. He can hear the water inside it; it's useless. Nevertheless, he disassembles it and lays it in the corner of his tent, hoping to fix it later.

The cold creeps further in on him. He rubs his hands over his body, creating friction to dry him—and to warm him, at least temporarily. As the nightmare refuses to end, Ross looks outside to see wet, heavy snowflakes now mixing with the rain in the near-night grayness. He refuses to think about it.

What I'd give to be back in that hot spring, he thinks. Or in my warm cabin or on a beach somewhere with the sun beating down on me. Just let me stop shivering. I want to live. Let the lighter work, God. Cold is death now.

The next thing he pulls out of his pack is his toilet paper, rolled up in a plastic bag. Part of it is soaked, but part of it is dry. He pulls away the wet part in clumps and piles layers of the dry sheets on the ground in front of the tent, shielding the fragile paper from the rain and snow with his body. Then he opens his cannister of white gas, fastens the spout to it and pours some over the tissue. He says a silent prayer as he flicks the lighter. On the fourth try, there is a small explosion and a blue flame. He can't help himself from laughing aloud at its welcome presence.

"Thank you," he whispers.

Carefully, tenderly, he piles more sheets of tissue over the soft, tenuous flame. He grabs his paperback and tears sheets out of the middle, holding them over the flame until they smolder, then laying them carefully to the fire. From under the pine tree, he grabs the driest twigs and needles he can find and lays them, teepee-style over the flame. In a couple of minutes, he has a tiny fire, crackling and smoking from the wet. He crawls around and picks up twigs and small branches. The smoke rolls up into his face but it is warm and he relishes it. He knows he must get more wood before the darkness completely envelops him. As he feeds the fire sheets of paper and small twigs, he puts his wet hiking boots back on, wincing every time he moves his left ankle. The pain pounds with his heartbeat as he stands up. As he puts his foot down, he finds that it is least painful pointed a few degrees inward. He bends once more to resurrect his little fire before he limps off to gather firewood. The first long branch, he uses as a cane. Then, with an armload of wet wood, he gets too much weight on his left foot and falls to the ground, dropping the wood in front of him.

After three ventures of less than 40 yards each, he has a small pile of wet branches. Over the next hours, when he is not satisfying a voracious hunger or nursing the fire, he is holding his sleeping bag above the flame, turning it, drying it, section by section.

Now the rain is gone and it is snowing harder. He tries to ignore this, concentrating on the fire and his task—survival.

As the third wave of fatigue comes over him, Ross cannot stave off sleep any longer. Although the outside of the bag is warm and dry, it is still wet inside. As the snow starts to settle on the ground around him, he pulls his stiff, exhausted body back into the tent. He lies with his head toward the fire. He hopes that he can keep the fire going.

His left ankle is stiff, tender. He has to guide it slowly into the sleeping bag. Once inside, he zips up the tent, shutting out what he determines to be the single worst day of his life. He curls into a fetal position, deep inside his sleeping bag and pulls the bag over his head, leaving only a small aperture to breathe through. Within seconds, he is fast asleep.

In the night, his body temperature drops dangerously low. His metabolism is already slowed from fatigue, and the damp sleeping bag whisks away the little warmth he produces. It is his youth and strength that carry him through that night. After 14 and a half hours of sleep, he wakes up in the same fetal position. The first thing he notices is his throbbing ankle, which quickly reminds him of his situation. At once, he is ravenously hungry but, as he turns his foot, he knows he cannot hike out and therefore must divide one day's food into at least two. While still in his bag, he slowly stretches out his rigid muscles and wonders about the new pain in his left knee.

Then he looks up at his tent and realizes it is drooping. He takes a deep breath and hits the tent roof with the back of his hand. The snow slides noisily down the nylon. He turns and opens the zipper to look out at three inches of new snow covering the ground.

"Great." He closes his eyes and slides back into his bag.

It is neither snowing nor raining but the still-gray sky adds to his despair. From the texture of the snow, he knows the temperature is around freezing. As he sees the sun through the gray clouds, he guesses it is about noon. He expects they will come looking for him when he does not report for work at 5 p.m. They will go to campsite SG2. But they won't find him there.

He zips the tent back up, takes a sip of water, rolls on his side and gives in to sleep, hoping somehow he will wake up in a better place.

An hour later, Ross wakes again with an unrelenting need to urinate. After guiding his disfigured left ankle into a nearly frozen hiking boot, he ties the laces tightly and stands outside the tent. The blood rushing to his extremities causes his ankle to throb so severely that he must sit back down and rest his foot. When the pain subsides, he stands up again and slowly adds more weight to the ankle.

He limps in ever-widening circles around his tent, picking the driest pieces of wood out of the white mantle of snow. After half an hour, he drops the fourth pile of branches next to his tent.

Over the rest of the day and night, it does not snow or rain and, with a larger fire, Ross is able to dry out more of his sleeping bag. He sneezes, then laughs off the threat of a cold as insignificant compared to his needs for food, shelter and warmth. He divides the remainder of his food into equal amounts. His dinner—half an apple, a half-inch slice of cheese, a wet section of crackers and a handful of gorp—leaves him hungry, but he rolls the food inside his stuff sack where it will be out of sight. He scratches at his three-day-old beard. That night by the fire, he packs snow in the plastic toilet-paper bag and holds it to his ankle. The swelling recedes, the range of motion increases, and he determines that the next morning he must strike a course due north.

His hopes rise the next morning when he unzips the tent to a clear blue sky and finds his ankle feeling much better. Using a branch for a crutch, he is able to walk straight ahead. Forty minutes later, with his pack ready to go, he walks over to fill his water bottle at the stream.

I *will* get out of here alive, he thinks, looking into the water that was nearly his death. I'm not down yet. Not Ross Matthias.

He firmly plants his walking stick and heads out. He meanders slowly, constantly checking the compass he holds in his hand. His feet become cold, then numb, walking through the icy melting snow. The ground is spongy beneath his boots, and he must be conscious of each step with his left foot. He can only try to ignore the dull, pulsating pain, gritting his teeth with each stride. After two hours, he hears the rush of something passing and shouts out. But what he thinks is the sound of cars is only the wind in the treetops. In the woods, the snow in the trees is melting and the cold snow and water that fall on his neck and down his back piques his frustration, but he plods on.

I've *got* to come across a road or trail soon if I keep heading north, he reasons. The divide is no good, too much snow up there and there's a chance I wouldn't be able to see the road anyway. Best to go north, no matter what, one direction.

Bear tracks!

The hair stands up on the back of his head and he freezes where he stands. In the sudden quiet, he looks at the fresh tracks crossing his path and heading to his right. He looks to where they disappear up a hill and, standing still, hears nothing but the breeze through the treetops.

Those tracks are really fresh. Look for climbing trees. Undo that damned waist strap!

He looks down at a perfect print of a big pad and the five thumb-like prints above it. What worries him is the claw marks three inches in front of the pad prints—they tell him it was a grizzly bear that crossed his path. It is an eight-inch print from pad to claw.

Just keep moving. Just listen and watch and keep moving.

An hour later, he takes a break and again divides his food. The little surge of energy from the small nourishment is almost instant. His stomach rumbles and asks for more. He tires steadily.

Late in the afternoon, it is his ankle that forces him to give up the quest for the day. His right calf is tight and knotted from favoring his left ankle, and his left Achilles tendon aches from walking with his foot at an acute angle. His vertebrae seems out of balance and twisted.

On a flat piece of ground, he sets up the tent and spreads his sleeping bag out. He does not bother with a fire. After the evening's meal, he has just one bit of apple, three M&Ms, two raisins, one cashew and no white gas left. His stomach is knotted and hard; he looks around at the grasses and shrubs, wondering if any of it might be edible. He tastes the bulb of a sedge growing by a creek, but it is bitter and he spits it out. He slides into his sleeping bag and surrenders to a deep, encompassing slumber.

Eleven hours later he is dreaming he is back in California. He dreams he is twelve years old again. He is mowing the lawn. His mother is waving for him to come in for lunch, she is wearing her polka dot dress but he looks at her quizzically: it is too cold outside for that, and he is in a T-shirt. He signals to her that he wants to finish mowing the yard. She is shouting to him but he cannot hear her over the roar of the lawnmover. She shouts again. He looks down and the lawnmower gets louder. . .

Lawnmower?

Ross bolts up in his sleeping bag. The sound of a helicopter grows stronger and fades as he recklessly throws himself out of his sleeping bag and falls out of his tent. He stands up, grimacing as he puts weight on his sore ankle, then yells and waves his arms in the direction of the whirling motor. But it soon fades into silence.

He lets the adrenaline motivate him to pack up. Before he slings the pack on his back, he finishes the last of his food, savoring each morsel. Though the ankle feels better in the first few steps, he can tell his muscle strength is dwindling. He wonders if he should find a clearing and set up his orange tent in the hopes that the helicopter returns.

But the helicopter sounded pretty far away. What if I'm just outside the search area and they don't bother to fly over my camp? I'm not where I was supposed to be. No. One more day. I can make it one more day. Go north. There's got to be a road soon.

Weakly, wearily, he hikes on. The woods, the grasses and creeks, the rocks that had been his best friends become his enemies. Once more that day, while in the woods, he hears the helicopter. He runs limping with the pack on, looking frantically for a clearing. He finds only a small gap in the trees and can't tell how close the chopper comes. The effort nearly drains him. He leans against a pine tree and lets himself slide down its trunk, as the sounds of the chopper disappear far in the distance. Tears well up in his eyes. He allows two minutes to feel sorry for himself, punches the ground, and pulls himself back to his feet.

A song. I must know a song.

"Ninety-eight bottles of beer on the wall. . . ."

When he gets to 38 bottles on the third time around, he trips over a partly exposed root and falls to the ground. He tries to raise himself up but has no strength. Panting, he lets his face lie in the snow for several moments, drawing in the frozen moisture with his tongue. Just as he starts to lose consciousness, he crawls to his knees, looks ahead and blinks once, twice, three times before he is certain of what he sees 10 yards away.

A trail! That's a trail.

He crawls to it on his hands and knees, then smooths away the layer of wet snow to reveal a boot print in the mud. He looks both ways to where the trail winds through the forest, then, far to his left, sees the most reassuring proof—an orange trail marker high up on a pine tree.

A trail.

He lets his head down and kisses the ground, then pulls himself up by his walking stick. The compass tells him the trail runs northwest and southeast from where he stands. He looks over the map, clearing his mind to make a decision.

If I'm over here on the Madison Plateau somewhere and this is the Bechler trail and I go left, it's 40 miles to West Yellowstone. But if I'm here somewhere and the river I fell in was the Firehole and I go right, it's 50 miles to the Grand Loop Road. The correct choice and I could be at a highway in a mile or two.

He dwells on it, staring into the melting snow. It's difficult to rationalize. He wonders if his decision-making may be dulled by fatigue, and he bends over and touches the trail again to verify its reality. He considers getting in his bag and just sleeping, hoping someone will come along on the trail. But he decides to follow the instinct telling him to go left.

Twenty minutes later, exhaustion has almost completely taken over his conscious will. He is hiking completely by reflex. His store of carbohydrates has long since been depleted and his body is breaking down muscle for energy. His head is down and he is staggering. Sometimes he plants the branch in his left hand. Sometimes he simply drags it. When he opens his eyes fully, he sees a Dairy Queen for a brief moment. Mindlessly, he breaks into a run before he blinks the image away. He looks through the woods but cannot find it again. Ten minutes later, he is asleep on his feet when he veers off the trail and trips, falling face forward and just missing a rock with his head. Almost automatically, like a punch-drunk boxer, he gets to his feet and walks on. A short distance down the trail, his own laughter startles him for a brief moment. He stumbles on. He runs into a tree and reaches out for it. Turning away, he starts walking the way he came. When he opens his eyes and sees his own tracks, he knows it must be a good sign and walks faster. He falls. He is confused but knows he must keep hiking. Now, perhaps only by luck, he rises and heads northwest again. He drops his walking stick behind him but, after several moments, his left arm goes up and plants as if it is still in his hand. Looking into the distance, the trees double and triple through criss-crossed eyes.

"Ninety. . . twelve bottles. . . ."

He wonders what happened to the pain in his ankle. He is not aware he is still limping, but now favoring the right ankle.

Three minutes later, he focuses hazily on a pile of elk droppings. He interprets them as food, the darling Swedish meatballs his mother made on Sundays. He drops to his knees and puts one, two, three of the droppings into his mouth and chews. The foul, pungent taste is repulsive even now in his delirium, and he spits them out.

Death is close now, but somehow it brings a warm, snug feeling. A calm inner peace comes over him: He will be able to sleep undisturbed.

Two minutes later, he raises his head and looks through his blurred vision down a long stretch of trail ahead of him. He blinks at what he sees—not believing it, yet welcoming it. He blinks again. The image won't go away, but he knows it isn't real. He knows he must keep hiking. One foot in front of the other. Eight bottles. . . . He blinks again but still the image won't go away. Instead it is getting larger.

"Ross!"

He hears it as an echo from somewhere far away. He uses the final bit of his willpower to focus. He reaches out and falls forward, reaching for the mirage, the orange- and yellow-clad man from the accounting department running toward him.

"Ross! Is that you?"

He falls forward and sees the surface of the water disappearing above him.

September 11. Old Faithful Inn lobby, 3:08 p.m..

"There you are, Howard," says Herm. "Sorry I'm late. I didn't get to bed until after 9 this morning. We had a propane leak in the kitchen last night. I just woke up."

"It looks like you haven't quite yet, Herm," says the white-haired ranger. "Where can we talk?"

"It looks like Faysal is in a meeting so we can't use his office. Dining room's closed. We could sit in the bar."

"How about if we walk around the boardwalk?"

"Sounds good. Can I buy you an ice-cream cone?"

"OK. If you're buying, this is an opportunity not to be missed."

Outside on the boardwalk, the uniformed ranger and Herm stroll behind the crowd headed to the geyser.

"Every year, I'm amazed at how quickly things drop off after Labor Day," Herm says. "Two weeks ago, I bet there were three times this many people waiting for an eruption at this time of day."

"Visitation was still up 1.6 percent from last year over the Labor Day weekend."

"I love this blueberry ice cream. What did you want to see me about anyway?"

Minden wipes his mouth with a napkin. "How about this Ross Matthias? What do you know about him?"

"Hey, how is he anyway?"

"OK. He's still at Lake Hospital. They moved him up to fair condition. When we got him to the hospital, his body temperature was 94.7. Good thing for Matthias, he was only a mile from Lone Star Geyser and we were able to drive most of the way in to get him. There was no place to land the chopper where he was. If that runner didn't happen to be jogging up there, he probably wouldn't have made it either. He's lucky to be alive."

"It's been a strange summer."

"You say that every year, Herm. What is this kid like?"

"I don't know him very well. He's quiet. Everyone likes him, though. All the waitri were real worried when he was missing. I heard Erbine say he could use more waiters like him. He said he does his job, gives good service, and is dependable. He likes to backpack."

"I doubt he'll be doing much more of that for awhile. He was suffering from hypothermia, malnourishment and he had a badly sprained ankle. He was in shock when we got to him. He's supposed to be released tomorrow but the doctor doesn't even want him working for at least four more days."

"He picked the wrong time of the year to get lost."

"You know he was hiking off trail. Well, he's liable for the rescue costs. Could cost him more than $4,000. The final decision is up to the superintendent. I don't know. He seemed like a good sort of fellow to me. I think we issued him a backcountry permit almost every week this summer. He always went alone."

Minden pauses and looks into Chinaman's Spring, musing over the fact that they took the sign away after someone in the Park Service complained it was not 'politically correct.' "He reminds me of me when I first came here. He said he doesn't have any insurance, and his medical bills alone are going to be pretty high. I've got to fill out the report and send it up today. I think I might just say he lost the trail in the snow."

"It's about time you started getting softer in your old age, Howard."

"And you're getting fatter, Herm. You'd better apply for backcountry ranger next year so we can get you back in shape."

"I exercise a little. I hiked up Mallard Lake about a week ago."

"That's great, Herm. Now what else was there? Oh yea. Do you remember me asking you about Cecil Dolen back in July?"

"Sure. You had given him a ticket for speeding. Then you found out he had been arrested for beating up a hooker."

"He was acquitted of that charge. Do you know anything else about him since the last time I talked to you?"

"Well, the story is he got real loaded one night and had sex in the Madison hotpot with one of the girls from the accounting department. He also went camping with the waitress I've dated a few times. She didn't say anything about it, though. Have you got something else on him?"

"This morning, I got a call from a *Ms.* Robaidek in Seattle, Washington. This lady is a volunteer on the task force investigating what she called the Green River murders."

Herm stops and turns to him. "What?"

"Don't get excited, Herm. Your ice cream will melt. It seems this investigation has been going on a long time and, about five months ago, they installed a new computer to help them solve it."

"Since when do computers solve murders?"

"I've read about this computer system. It's a Digital VAX. It's the same system that helped the Seattle Police Department catch Ted Bundy, if you remember him."

"I thought that was Florida."

"Florida, and Utah before that, and Seattle before that. Hey there! Don't you be throwing things at that geyser, son!"

"Yes, sir."

"Anyway, they can feed any kind of information they want into this computer. It processes thousands of pieces of evidence—license numbers, past records, even fingerprints and hair follicles. With this computer, they ran 18 lists. Twenty-five names appeared on five of those lists. Bundy was one of the 25."

"So Cecil's name appeared on one of these lists?"

"This Ms. Robaidek said his name appeared on four lists with 988 other people. One in a thousand chance. In fact, the killer may not be on any of the lists. I guess that prostitute thing put him on one list and that careless driving charge put him on another one."

"What are the other two lists?"

"I don't know. I didn't ask."

"So what are you telling me this for? This sounds like law-enforcement kind of stuff."

"She wants his fingerprints or a strand of hair or both. I thought you might be able to help me out. Keep it among ourselves."

Herm pops the last of his ice-cream cone into his mouth and wipes his fingers with the napkin. "Fingerprints wouldn't be any problem. He washes the glasses in the bar and I go back there when I'm on duty sometimes and get a Coke. Hair, I don't know. I just can't sneak up behind him and cut some off."

"Can you get the master key to his dorm?"

"No. He lives in the cabins. They supply their own padlocks."

"I suppose I could authorize a fire check. Be subtle about it."

"I know someone who could get in there. He likes Kris a lot, the waitress friend of mine. She and Cecil are good friends. I bet she could do it. But Howard, I've watched Cecil all summer. He's just about the most timid guy up here. Just plain awkward sometimes. In my wildest imagination, I can't picture him as a criminal. It's almost absurd." He shakes his head. "Computers."

"Well, be careful. If we don't get it, we'll just send them the print. Now what are you going to have the girl do?"

"Let me work on that. Cecil's on tonight, I think. I'll give Kris a ride to work tonight; I know she's on. I've got some ideas."

"Great. I'm in the station all day tomorrow. Come by there. And by the way, what do you know about that geyser that mysteriously sprung up in the gas station last week?"

"Me? Nothing. Well, I mean I heard about it."

"What puzzles me is they timed it just as the superintendent, the assistant superintendent and district rangers were just getting there."

"A lot of people knew you were having dinner at five in the dining room, Howard. I mean if they were employees like I think you're inferring."

"The assistant manager of the gas station was in on it, that's for sure. He had checked out and had left the area by the time we dug up the hoses. Sounds like maybe he was part of the group that did the wagon wheel trick when the Secretary of the Interior was here and the bear trick at the beginning of the summer. When we dug up the gated Y, we found the same wine label on it. Mountain Cadet?"

"Mouton Cadet," he corrects him.

Ranger Minden turns and faces Herm who looks away and says "Howard. So, besides all this, how are you doing?"

The ranger swallows the rest of his ice cream and wipes off his fingers and mouth with the paper napkin. "Pretty good, Herm. Looked out my window last night at sunset and there were a couple of guys setting up camp in back of my house. Had a fire going and everything. They had a permit for Mallard Lake and couldn't find the trailhead. By the way, what were you doing up at Mallard Lake a week ago? We just opened the trail back up five days ago."

"I drove up to the water-treatment plant and walked in from the service road. I would have missed the sign. Why was it closed?"

"The grizzly that attacked Jorge Riez and Tina Noakes."

"That was more than a month ago. There hasn't been any more trouble up there, has there?"

"Standard operating procedure. Once a bear has been evacuated from an area, we close that area for a month. Bears, especially grizzlies, tend to come back to where they find food."

"I thought you dropped him way the hell north. Like 80 miles away."

"Yea, we did. This is off the record, Herm. But the bear that attacked Jorge and Tina *did* have an ear tag, number 397. It's one of the bears tranquilized with Sernalyn."

"We talked about that earlier this summer," Herm recalls. "Sernalyn, Angle Dust, PCP, all the same thing. The park biologist was testing it as a tranquilizer on nuisance bears, right?"

"Right. It's been used on 397 quite a few times." He pauses. "And 397 is the grandson of a bear we used to call Old Scarface. Now Old Scarface was the dominant male in all of Hayden Valley from about 20 until about 15 years ago. Old Scarface weighed more than 1,000 pounds and you can imagine why we called him Scarface. He was a battler. In his prime, he broke into the Mary Mountain cabin one night with a ranger inside. That door had been bolted with a three-inch-thick beam. Old Scarface broke through it and killed the ranger inside. That ranger was a friend of mine, Carl Mann. Well, we didn't kill Old Scarface. We helicoptered him 100 air miles away into the Shoshone National Forest. But I'll be damned if he didn't show up two weeks later. I watched him open a camper out in the parking lot here like you or I might pull open a bag of pretzels. Went right inside. When he came out, we killed him."

"So you think 397 could come back here?"

"I doubt it now. With that snowstorm we just had, the grizzlies tend to start moving to their denning sites; 397 spent last winter up in Hayden Valley, 10 miles from Mallard Lake. But he'll probably find a new denning site where we dropped him off."

"In a cave somewhere far away, I hope."

"No, Herm. Black bears tend to find caves and natural dens. Grizzly bears dig their dens out."

Herm knocks on the door of Kris's room and Salina answers, dressed in her running gear.

"Herm, I thought you were Steve. What's up?"

"I need to talk to Kris. Is she still here?"

"I'm in the bathroom, Herm! I'll be right out. I'm running late for work. Think you could run me over in your Jeep?"

"Sure, 'cause I need to ask you a small favor, too. I'll be out in the hall talking to Miss Physical Fitness. I'll meet you in the lobby."

"What's up, Squirmin'?" Salina asks, as they walk down the corridor.

"Don't call me that! Listen, tell Steve and Wilbur no more with the Park Service pranks. Minden is starting to get suspicious."

"Why do you think so?"

"He asked me about 10-Minute Geyser. I think he took a lot of heat from the superintendent."

"Maybe because I told him the whole story, Herm."

"You what?"

"Only kidding." She reaches up, kisses him on the cheek, and pats him on the belly. "There's Steve. We're on our way to Mallard Lake. Want to come with us, Herm?"

"Nah, I ran up Mount Washburn this morning. I'll probably take it easy tonight. Four thousand sit-ups and then maybe a little full-court basketball."

Steve jogs up to the dorm. "Hey, Herm, how ya doin'?"

Kris crashes out of the door, pulling on her jacket. "Let's go, Herm, or I'll miss dinner."

"See, Salina, I can't go with you. I have to take Kris to work."

"Next time, Herm. Let's go, Salina."

"See you guys later," says Herm. "Tell Steve what I told you."

In the Jeep, Kris ties her hair into a ponytail behind her. "So what was the favor you wanted to ask me, Herman?"

"Well, now that I think about this, it's pretty stupid," he says, laughing under his breath. "There's a small chance that our little Cecil may be in trouble. Some computer. . . . Well, to vindicate him, we need to get a strand of his hair."

"What kind of trouble?"

"Well, I didn't tell you this before because I didn't want to start any rumors over things that didn't happen. But four years ago, Cecil was charged with beating up a prostitute."

"Cecil Dolen? The guy I went camping with?"

"Yea. Cecil. Don't tell anyone about this. Well, the charges were dropped but some computer spit out his name on a list of possible suspects in a homicide case. The rangers got a call and they need a fingerprint and a strand of his hair. I think I can get the finger-prints."

"And you want me to get a strand of his hair. How am I supposed to do that?"

"You two are good friends. I thought maybe you could ask him if you could borrow a tape from him. He's at work, so maybe you could get the key to his cabin."

"We have exchanged tapes before. But Cecil and I had words about three weeks ago and the only time we see each other now is at work. He still tries to talk to me but I've been doing my best to avoid him."

"Words about what?"

"Nothing really. He woke me up early in the morning and wanted to talk. Yea, I guess I could do it. But Cecil beating up a prostitute? The night we went camping, he got mad because I wouldn't have sex with him, but I never felt threatened."

One mile later, Herm swings the Jeep into the back entrance of the dining room. "So what time do you think you'll be getting off?"

"Ten-thirty or 11 lately."

"I'll just be coming on. I'll be in the back parking lot in the station wagon. Look for me. I'll drive you over there."

"All right."

"Don't tell anyone about this. OK?"

She nods.

"You look a little down. Still no letter from Ralph?"

"*John*, Herm. No!" She looks away. "It's been five weeks. I've written him three times."

"Why don't you call him?"

"Then I'd have to tell him about you and me, Herm," she teases, kissing him on the cheek as she slides out of the Jeep. "Got to run. I'll look for you in the parking lot."

From the driver's seat of the company station wagon, Herm recognizes Kris's stride from a hundred yards away as she leaves the Inn at 10:58 p.m.

"Kris, over here."

"Herman, gosh, I feel like I'm in a James Bond movie or something."

"Did you get his keys?"

She slides in the passenger seat of the station wagon and Herm backs out. "Yes, I got them. He really wants me to wait there until he gets off. He said he really wanted to talk to me."

"What about?"

"He didn't say. He just told me that we hadn't spent enough time together."

"What did you tell him?"

"I told him I was really tired and I probably wouldn't wait for him, and that I would bring back his keys."

"Good girl. Where's his roommate?"

"Cecil said he has gone to West Yellowstone and wouldn't be back till tomorrow."

Herm eases the yellow station wagon in the near-pitch-dark cabin area.

"Herm, can you go in with me? I'm not used to doing things like this."

"I can't. In fact, I'm going to park in the dark here. If someone sees me in there, or his roommate comes in and mentions it to Cecil, he might get a little suspicious. Plus the fact that it's illegal. Go on. Here's an envelope. Put the hair in here. He must have a brush or comb or something. And don't forget to take the tapes you were supposed to borrow."

As Herm watches from the shadows, Kris walks across the road and fumbles with the lock.

She goes in, turns on the light and looks around at the scattered clothes, books, magazines, beer cans and the like. As she closes the door behind her, she looks down to see a tube of cheese spread that someone has evidently stepped on and ruptured. She moves to the left side of the room, Cecil's side, and steps up to his dresser. Looking among the letters from home, the *Playboy* and *Penthouse* magazines and various pieces of paper, she can't find a brush or comb. She slides open the top drawer of his dresser and finds his crumpled undershorts and T-shirts. In the second drawer, she sees a brown, faded copy of the *Seattle Times*, socks, a *Guide for Bartending*, and more *Playboys* but no comb. She pulls her hair back, bends down to the third drawer and opens it, finding opened and unopened cans of beer and pop, a half-finished bag of potato chips and discarded cookie and cupcake wrappers. On the top of the dresser, she rummages through his tapes. She finds one of the tapes she asked for, and puts two more in her waitress pouch with the dinner checks she realizes she forgot to turn in. She turns to his unmade bed and guesses that the linen hasn't been washed in five weeks. She turns the yellow-stained pillow over but cannot find any of Cecil's hair. She glances around the room and catches the object of her search on a shelf by the sink—a brush with a comb in it. As she moves across the room to it, she sees she will have no problem getting hair from the brush. As she opens the envelope and puts a clump of hair inside, she realizes that his roommate has the same color hair and that it may be his brush and comb. Kris folds the envelope and puts it in her apron pocket, then holds the hairbrush up closely to her eyes with her back to the light, mentally comparing Cecil's head to his roommate's to the brush. Just as she is stretching out a strand of hair, the door flies open.

"Cecil!"

Cecil pauses in the doorway, his expression twisted from the light of the naked bulb in his eye and curious suspicion. "What are you doing?"

"I. . . was brushing my hair. My. . . hair gets so tangled at work." She pulls the greasy brush through her fine blond hair. "Why aren't you at work, Cecil?"

"I got Clarence to cover for me for a few minutes. I remember that Chili Peppers tape you wanted to borrow was locked up in my car. You look really stressed, Kris. You'd better lie down on the bed and get one of Cecil's soothing massages." He closes the cabin door behind him.

"No, it's OK."

"Come on. Relax. You look scared."

"You frightened me."

He takes the brush out of her hand, then pulls a gob of the black hair out of the brush, rinses the brush once in the sink and says, "Kris, sit down. Let me brush your hair for you."

"That's OK, Cecil. I can brush my own hair."

"Come on, Kris. We're supposed to be friends, remember? I gave you the keys to my cabin so you could borrow some tapes. Now sit down. You owe me more than one favor, especially after the way you've been ignoring me lately. Why is that?"

Reluctantly, nervously, she sits down and closes her eyes as Cecil takes her hair in his hands behind her and starts brushing it out. She can smell the bar odors—cigarettes, beer and booze, along with Cecil's perspiration. "Kris, did you get a letter from John yet?"

"No, Cecil."

"It just seems like you've been avoiding me lately. I told you that you and he were through. I could see that. I tried to tell you. We're supposed to be friends and comfort each other through these kinds of things, remember?"

Kris flinches away from his strong brush strokes and stands. "Cecil, I have to get home and you have to get back to work."

"It's not busy. Clarence can cover for awhile. I'd like to comfort you, Kris."

"I'm tired and dirty and need to get back to my dorm room and take a shower."

"Come on, Kris. Stay for awhile. Now that I think about it, it *is* my turn to give you a massage. Come here to Cecil." He throws his arms around her and falls on the bed, pulling her with him. "Whoooa!" he shouts as he reaches around and grabs her breast.

"Cecil!"

"Come on, Kris. Both of us are hungry for a little affection. How 'bout it?"

As she pulls his hand away from her breast, he quickly reaches down and runs his hand up her dress to her crotch.

"Cecil! Stop! Cecil!" she screams.

As she spins away from him, the door bursts open. It's Herm.

"What the hell is going on in here?"

Kris stands up and glares at Cecil contemptuously. "Cecil, how could you?" As the tears come to her eyes, she storms past Herm, stops and thrusts the envelope into his hand and storms out the door.

"OK, Cecil, what happened?"

Cecil rises from the bed and smooths his rumpled clothes. "We were just starting to get a little intimate, that's all," he says, with a sneer. "What are you doing walking into my cabin anyway?"

"I was. . . just on my rounds and heard a scream from inside here. I was checking. . . ."

"Yea, well, why don't you just leave Kris and me alone. We can get along fine without you. She's mine now, so just stay out of my way. I have to get back to work, so you can get out of my cabin."

Herm jabs his index finger into Cecil's sternum repeatedly as he utters a warning: "If you ever try to hurt Kris again, I'll break both your hands so bad you won't ever be able to hold a drink, much less make one."

"Don't hassle me, campus cop."

September 14. Mallard Lake, 11:04 p.m..

Gro Hege Vestol of Vaasa, Finland, wiggles into her goose-down sleeping bag. It gives her security from the cold, moonless night. To take her mind off the night sounds, she vents more of her anger at her two traveling companions for deciding to stay in the hotel instead of camping out. Didn't they agree, back in Finland, that they would only stay in hotels once a week at the most? And hadn't they stayed in hotels five times in the last two weeks? Perhaps Gustav and Lisen *are* lovers now.

She relives the trip in her mind. How happy and close they were in New York. How they had found a Volvo that was the same year as Gustav's back home, and how new and exciting everything was to them in this country. Then driving to all the new and interesting places.

Still, she wishes she had some company. She wasn't worried about bears. But the ranger that issued the permit questioned her for camping alone. Sure, there had been a bear here, but that was over a month ago, and he said they moved that bear 80 miles, that's 128 kilometers away.

Her ears bend to the sounds of the night again; a branch creaking, a duck calling from the lake. In the distance, an elk bugles, a sound that startled her the night before until the young man from North Dakota explained what it was.

Were they going there next? No. California next. San Francisco and the park with the big trees.

She thinks she will just stay camped there for one night and not two as she planned. She is anxious to see the coast and swim in the ocean.

Frozen into position by the sound of branches cracking, she holds her breath for a moment. When she hears nothing else, she breathes slowly through her nose. She wishes she could force herself to sleep but her heart is beating so strong she can feel the blood course through her chest, rustling the nylon sleeping bag. She pulls the bag higher around her.

Whether her eyes are opened or closed makes no difference because it is a new moon and there is no light in the tent. But she closes her eyes anyway, listening, reaching for the sound in the night yet not wanting to hear again what she thought she heard.

There are lapses of silence but then she is sure she hears something walking through the woods and she opens her eyes wide. She hears a slight *huff* in the woods—or was that a duck flying overhead?

Then comes the unmistakable sound of the pots and pans rattling inside her stuff sack. She recalls shining the flashlight on the orange sack. She remembers that she hung the sack at least three meters up, and that she couldn't even reach it by jumping.

Now she sits up in her sleeping bag. She gropes for the flashlight, flicks it on, and points it through the unzipped top of the rain fly. She can barely make out the rolling smoke coming from her extinguished fire 15 feet away. She can see nothing beyond the fire. She cannot see the number imprinted on the ear tag, number 397.

The large male grizzly drops down onto all four paws, ignoring the swinging food that it cannot catch. He sees a blurred light coming from the direction of the man smell, which he can associate with his madness. At 800 pounds, he has yet to lose a fight as an adult, and his fear is overwhelmed, buried. It moves toward the light.

Gro Hege Vestol hears it moving closer. Her body pumps with adrenaline and blood but fear freezes her in place. When her flashlight beam crosses two orange beads in the night, she squeezes it so hard her nails dig into her palms. The hair bristles on the back of her neck. The steps grow louder, and now she hears breathing. She wheels around in her tent and gropes wildly for the zipper but can't find it. Starting from the bottom, she madly traces her hand around the seam and finally finds the zipper. She hears the emphatic *huff. . . huff* only feet away and, as she pulls the zipper up, she can feel the animal charging toward her. As she gets the zipper around and is halfway out of her sleeping bag, the bear's tremendous force bowls her over, toppling her inside the tent.

Everything becomes slow and vivid. The sound of the metal tent poles clanging comes into focus clearly as her face hits the ground through the tent opening. Then the animal is upon her. Instinctively, she screams and huddles into a fetal position, swinging blindly to ward off the attack. She hears the fabric tear right next to her and suddenly both the tent and she are being dragged across the ground. She screams again. The huge bear bites into the fabric, barely missing its prey. Growling, he shakes the tent back and forth in its tremendous jaws.

The sour smell permeates its nostrils now and its fear is absorbed by its ferocity. It goes berserk. It strikes with its huge front paws once, twice and, on the third time, slashes its sharp claws through her back, raking the sharp points over her rib cage. The blow pushes her through the opening and rolls her over. Now the smell of hot blood fills the bear's nostrils. Crying out weakly, frantically, Gro Hege tries to scramble away on all fours. She runs into a log next to the fire ring. She regains her balance and rises to her feet just as the bear pounces on her. She disappears under its weight before it lashes out, sinking its teeth into her shoulder and flinging her several yards through the air. A desperate shriek and the smell of blood alerts the grizzly to the direction of the prey. It swallows a bit of the sweet flesh and wants more.

Through reflex, Gro Hege grovels in the dirt, trying to crawl away, toward the lake, but the carnivore is upon her instantly. It swats her back the other way. Nearly sightless in the starlight, it pounces upon the still form, biting through her leg, severing her left foot. Gro Hege does not feel the jaws clamp on her left arm and fling her over. When the massive grizzly sinks his teeth into her back, she is already dead.

September 15. Old Faithful Inn, dining room, 8:08 p.m..
"I can't believe we still have almost a month to go," Imre says, lighting a cigarette and unfolding the menu.

"I think it's gone by *fast*," says Yvonne. "So much has happened this summer."

"To you maybe. Not to me."

"Oh, hi Ross! How are you feeling?"

"Good. Better. I'm just about over my cold. My ankle's better. Everyone has been really nice. It's something I won't forget."

"We won't either, Ross," Imre says. "You had everybody worried. I didn't know whether to send your check to California or just drop it out of a helicopter somewhere over the Madison Plateau."

"Imre, Ross almost died out there."

"He looks OK now. Let's see how fast he can get us a couple of drinks. I'd like a bloody mary."

"I'd like a screwdriver, Ross. Please."

"I suppose you'd like that bloody mary with a shot of Tabasco on the side, huh Imre?"

"Funny, Ross. Just a stick of celery you can use to put in your ear. Or wherever."

"Will do."

They watch Ross walk, with only the slightest limp, to the service bar, then Imre turns to Yvonne. "So, are you pregnant?"

"No. I got my period a couple of days ago. It's just as well. I didn't really want to be a mother. Besides, Cecil and I haven't even spoken since the day after we hotpotted. He's been acting really weird lately. I don't think I'd want him for a husband, Corvette or no Corvette."

"See, Yvonne. I told you men weren't worth the trouble."

"Oh it was worth it all right. I had an orgasm! Did I tell you?"

"Yes, Yvonne. You said it made you quiver."

"All over. I want some more of them. Next time I want love, too. Cecil kept screaming 'Kris!' I've lost fifteen pounds this summer and on my last day off I hiked all the way to Lone Star Geyser and back and only had one scoop of ice cream that night for dessert."

"A regular tower of willpower. That's what you are."

"You watch. I'm going to lose so much weight I'll start having regular dates."

"Fat chance."

"Imre! Give me a break, huh? I'm trying. At least I haven't given up like you have."

"I haven't given up. I'm perfecting the art of apathy."

"Well, that's not what I need right now, OK? I'm on a roll." Yvonne pauses and she and Imre look at each other over their menus. "Come on, Imre. We've helped each other through some tough times this summer. Let's be nice for tonight, for the last month even."

Imre softens her voice. "What would you like to eat, Yvonne?"

"I don't know. Do you want to get two things and share?"

They look over the menus until Ross comes back with their drinks.

"So," says Imre, reaching for her bloody mary, "you sprained your ankle and fell in a creek."

"Yea. Something like that."

"That was pretty stupid. Why didn't you stay on the trail?"

"I thought it would be much more fun to be lost for four days so I could come back here and you could ridicule me. Can I take your order?"

"I'll have the Cornish game hen and onion rings, Ross," says Yvonne.

"Imre?"

"Since I'm in my prime tonight I think I'll have the prime rib."

"End cut, center cut, or perhaps a nice, thick verbal cut?"

"Funny, Ross. I think the dip in the creek did wonders for your personality."

"Thank you, ladies."

"He's cute, Imre. I think you should ask him out."

"I don't think he's my type."

"Why not?"

"He's normal. Besides, it's more fun to torture him."

"Well, he's more your type than Wilbur would have been."

"I suppose you heard he and Kitty are going to Mexico this winter."

"Yes! And she's four years older than he is. What a scandal! He writes her poetry. Now that's love. That's what I want. Can you just picture being some place romantic with a man like that, having him recite poetry to you on the beach with a couple of Piña Coladas and then he'd have to protect you from the killer bees. . ."

"Listen, Yvonne," Imre says. "Let's talk about something other than men tonight, OK?" She takes a long sip of her drink. "I want your opinion on who I should name employee of the year in the accounting office."

"Steve and Wilbur did the best job."

"Forget it. Not them."

"Why not?"

"They're too arrogant. And they work the night shift so I never have time to beat them down like they deserve."

"You're a hard woman, Imre Nendza."

"I'm a supervisor. That's what they pay me to be."

"Then Helen was the next best."

"Good. That's who I thought. Now, we're also supposed to come up with something funny that happened over the course of the summer for the survivor's party."

"How about the night you left the safe unlocked and, when you came in the next morning, Steve and Wilbur had their dinner trays in the safe with those $100 tips all over?"

"No, that wasn't funny. I almost fired both of them."

"That picture of you glaring at them was funny."

"No, it wasn't. How about the time I forgot to tell Steve I Z'ed out the Micros accidently, then he couldn't balance until 10:30 the next morning?"

"Or the time Erbine put that new cashier on by himself and he worked half the lunch shift before someone realized he was running the credit cards face down through the imprinter and there was no one's name or number on $796.32 worth of vouchers?"

When Ross brings out the salads, Imre says, "Hey Paul Bunyan, how about a couple more drinks?"

"You bet."

"So, Imre," Yvonne says, "have you decided what you're going to do for the winter yet?"

"I guess I'll be the Snow Lodge controller. The controller at Mammoth wants the job. Tagore said I've got three weeks to decide. What are you going to do?"

"I guess I'll go back to Pittsburgh and help mom out in the bakery. I told her only through Christmas though. After that, I'm going to get my own job and live by myself somewhere. Live my own life."

Two drinks and one hour later, Imre and Yvonne push their plates away.

"The Cornish game hen was good," Yvonne says. "Didn't you like your prime rib?"

"It was OK. I'm getting drunk and it feels better. Do you want the rest?"

"No thanks. I had a bite. Take it up to your room with you."

As they light cigarettes, Ross comes by with a tray and takes Yvonne's plate.

"Hey Ross," says Imre. "I'd like a piece of cheesecake for dessert. You don't think you'll get lost between here and the pantry, do you?"

"No, Imre. I think I'll make it. Would you like me to put the rest of your prime rib in a doggy bag?"

"No, Ross. Why don't you keep it for the next time you go backpacking. If it gets dried out, you can always jump in the creek to rehydrate it."

"Why don't you go to hell."

"Well, well. What kind of way is this for a waiter to talk to a customer? He hasn't even got his tip yet."

"Come on, you guys. Be nice," Yvonne says.

"I don't care if you're a tourist or a supervisor or the Queen of England. I don't have to listen to sarcasm like that from anyone."

Imre looks stonily ahead. "Shut up, Ross."

"Your love life, or lack of it, is no secret around here, Imre. You aren't ever going to find anyone who will be able to put up with you, because you can't even live with yourself! You're despicable!"

Imre pushes her chair back and charges out of the dining room. Ross now notices waitri, busboys, and guests at the nearby tables staring. He casts an angered yet apologetic glance at the surrounding tables, then turns to Yvonne. "Sorry. I shouldn't have lost my temper." As he turns to go, Faysal comes rushing in from the Bear Pit.

"Ross, give someone else your tables and go into my office. I'll be there in a moment."

"Sure, Faysal."

As Ross heads toward Faysal's office, he sees Yvonne get up and follow Faysal into the kitchen.

When Ross opens the door to Faysal's office, he sees Imre there, in Faysal's chair, crying. He pauses just inside the door. "I'm sorry. I shouldn't have lost my temper."

"It's *my* fault," Imre says.

The self pity in her voice catches Ross off guard.

"You're right," she continues. "I do have a lot of spite. I know you almost died out there."

"Why are you always so bitter? People. . . ."

She looks ahead to the wall and pulls back her tears. "Maybe it's because the last time I opened myself up to man, I got hurt. Bad."

"I'm sorry. Don't cry. Here." He hands her a Kleenex from Faysal's desk.

"So I figure if I'm always rude as I can be, no one will ever try to break the shell. I just don't ever want to feel that hurt again. So I try to hurt others, I guess. I won't let anyone close to me ever again. It isn't worth it."

"Come on, Imre. No one can live alone."

"You do it. I've heard that you hike by yourself all the time. I have a lot of respect for you. You do something, at least. I just sulk in my room and feel sorry for myself."

"Imre. . ." He sits in the wooden chair next to her, putting his hand over hers.

"When you were lost I was really worried," she says. "It was like it was me out there all alone. I stayed awake each of those nights and wondered where you were. I had this picture that you were really cold and miserable out there. It had snowed. I was really pulling for them to find you. You came back and everyone was so glad and they applauded you and gave you gifts, but nothing changed with me. No one saw that I was lost and cold and lonely too. See how mixed up I am? I worried about you, but then I was mean to you the first chance I had."

After five beats of silence, Ross speaks. "I. . . I thought the trees and rocks and mountains would be all I ever needed, would be my companions, keep me out of trouble—that I belonged in the mountains and was such a part of it I could never get hurt. . . ."

"See, that's what I mean. You have something. You want to be alone and can make it work for you."

"What I was going to say was. . . well, the last few times I went hiking, especially the last time, I wished there was someone there with me. I mean, what good are all those fantastic things and places I've seen without someone to share them with?"

They face each other for the first time. Ross lifts his hand from on top of Imre's and wipes a tear from her eye.

"I'm sorry I yelled at you," Ross says.

"I'm sorry I was such a bitch."

They both laugh in their sudden embarrassment.

"We're both alone," Ross says, touching her cheek again. "You know, I think you're the first person I've touched this summer. A very pretty person too."

Imre looks into his brown eyes. "Do you think you could take me hiking? I meant to go at least once this summer—when you're all better?"

"I'm better now. I'd feel better if I had some company, just in case we had to cross a creek or something."

Imre laughs through her tears. "I feel like such a jerk telling you those things. I've had a couple of drinks. It just needed to come out."

"It's good that it did. Being alone is a good thing sometimes. But I need someone to tell about the things I've seen, the things I've thought, to talk about those days I was lost." He stops and gazes into Imre's large, sapphire-blue eyes. "Could I hug you?"

From their sitting positions, they reach out and embrace each other, both laughing through their tears. At that moment, the door to Faysal's office opens. Faysal, Erbine, Yvonne and Leigh, a waitress, stop and gape as Imre and Ross untangle and turn to them.

"Wow," says Yvonne. "Maybe I should have ordered the prime rib."

"It was my fault, Faysal," Ross says. "I flew off the handle."

"Right in front of your customers!" Faysal chides.

"No, it was my fault, Faysal," says Imre. "I goaded him the whole time we were in there."

"That's right; she did," Yvonne says.

"Well, it looks like you've ironed out your differences."

Faysal wonders about the sudden glow he sees in Imre's eyes.

Something needs to stop the complaints about her coming from her own staff. Maybe Ross is what she needs.

"Ross, are you sure you were ready to come back to work? Do you need another few days?"

"Yes, I'm fine, Faysal. But not tomorrow. It's my day off."

"Mine too," says Imre.

"OK you two. Any more outbursts like that and it's a week each in the EDR. Leigh will finish your tables tonight, Ross. Now go on. My dinner's melting."

Ross walks Imre to her door on the third floor of the west wing. He wonders how he has never before noticed the glow, almost a sheen, of her raven-black hair and the deep blue eyes.

"Would you like to come in?" she asks.

"Sure."

She takes off the Beethoven's Seventh that had seemingly been her theme music for the summer and replaces it with Haydn's Surprise Symphony.

"It reminds me of the Banana Splits theme song," says Ross. "Did you ever see that when you were little?"

"Yea. I used to watch it all the time."

"How old are you? We must be about the same."

"Twenty-six," Imre says.

"What month?"

"February, the eighth."

"Mine's the fifth of January," Ross adds. "We're only a month apart. Same year."

They talk late into the night and, just before the sun comes up, they fall asleep in each other's arms, without physically loving or even kissing, but holding warmly, closely.

September 16.

On their hike up to Mallard Lake, Ross and Imre discover they have more in common. He is surprised to hear she likes backpacking and the outdoors. And they listen to the same musical artists.

"I actually have an accordion back in Appleton," Imre tells Ross. "I haven't played it for years though. My father played viola in the Milwaukee Symphony."

"I play harmonica. We can jam as long as you play in G."

"You've got a nice rear end. You know that?"

"Well thank you. You get to walk first on the way down. Imre, I just realized you haven't smoked any cigarettes."

"I thought it might bother you."

"You'd stop if it bothered me?"

"Yea. My first boyfriend, when I was sixteen, he smoked and I didn't. It was so terrible to kiss him. I'll always remember that. It's not very enjoyable for someone who doesn't smoke to kiss someone who does. That was a dumb thing to say. It's like I'm inferring. . . you and I haven't even. . . I mean just because we slept together. . . no, I mean we really didn't sleep together. Oh boy. . . ."

Ross turns around on the trail and lifts her up in his long arms and sets her down next to him. He looks steadily into her eyes and smiles at her, drawing her raven hair behind her ears. He kisses her then. Long, totally, with mounting passion.

They break with a gasp. "There were some nights I sure would have liked you in a tent with me. Last night was so good for me."

"If you kiss me like that again, I won't have enough breath to make it to the lake."

A mile later, approaching the lake, Ross asks Imre the question that has been on his mind since the night before.

"Are you. . . sure you have to stay and work the Snow Lodge this winter?"

"Why, Ross?"

"Why don't you come to New Zealand with me?"

"New *Zealand*? I don't know. Isn't that up by Iceland somewhere? Why New Zealand?"

Ross sees it before she does. He can't believe it but it's there, 15 yards in front of him. He stops and his face quivers and twists and he blinks his eyes at the horror—it's the mutilated body of a person. The torn shreds of a tent. Blood everywhere. The hair on the back of his head stands up as he pulls Imre to him and covers her eyes.

"Ross, what. . . ."

"Don't look. My God, start backing up, Imre."

She starts to pull away from him and he turns her, shoving her brusquely in the other direction. It scares her, suddenly reminding her how her last boyfriend would change so quickly. And now it's happening again. She turns but focuses past him to the grisly, bloody figure. She puts her hands to her face and screams. Ross rushes back to her and puts his arms around her, shielding her face, laying her head against his chest.

"Stay right here. What in God happened?"

Then he realizes it was a bear and that it still could be close by. "Back up slowly. Don't look. My God!"

He boosts her up a pine tree with low branches, then climbs another tree 10 feet away. He yells once, twice, three times but hears nothing in the eerie late-morning silence. He tries to avert his eyes but cannot help catching the sight of an arm lying away from the torso of the bloody figure—he cannot guess its sex. A knot wells up in his throat. Imre wretches and vomits. Her face is contorted in panic. Ross yells out once more before they descend the tree and scramble as quickly as they can the three miles back to Old Faithful, hand in hand when the trail makes it possible, shouting ahead in case the bear is still in the vicinity.

Frightened and exhausted, they do not stop until they see another couple walking toward them at the trailhead.

Between breaths, Ross blurts, "Don't go up there. There's been a terrible accident."

"What kind of accident?" says the short, dark-haired girl with a thick Scandinavian accent. "Our friend was camping there. A girl a little shorter than me? Long blond hair? What happened!"

Ross and Imre shoot each other a horrified glance that immediately tells the Finnish couple it was indeed their friend. "Gro Hege!" shouts the girl, and starts to run up the trail. As the tall, thin man catches her in five quick strides, Ross takes Imre's hand in his, tacitly communicating what they know. Ross's lips move but no words come out; he shakes his head at the man in disbelief.

"What sort of accident?" the girl begs.

"You'd better come with us to the ranger station," Ross says. "I. . . I can't be sure it was your friend. What color tent did she have?"

"Orange. It was orange," says the man.

In the ranger's office, Ross asks to talk to Ranger Susan Lynwood or Ranger Minden, but the Finnish girl is near panic. She pulls at Ross's sleeve.

"Why don't you tell me what happened? Where is Gro? Tell me!"

The dark-haired man puts his arm around her. "You can say it."

"It looks like there was a bear attack," says Ross. "We didn't get close enough to. . . determine an identity."

"We have a Gro Hege Vestol registered for last evening," Minden says, after flipping open a large, heavy-bound book. "Is that your friend?"

The Finnish girl now turns and cries wildly in her friend's arms. With a look of terror, her friend catches his breath and whispers, "She is still alive! She must be. Let's go now!"

Again, the girl starts for the door in a rush.

"Lisen!" the man shouts sharply. "Wait!"

Imre can only go to the young Finnish girl and put her arms around her. She grabs Imre's arm and holds tightly. She buries her head in her hands and starts to shake, and the sobs become louder.

"Are you positive?" Minden asks quietly. Ross and Imre answer with silent nods.

Minden has Ranger Lynwood stay with the two couples while he gets on the phone to the superintendent. Then he calls Ross into the back and talks with him alone for several minutes.

A half hour later, the Park Service has two culvert traps in the air, heading toward Mallard Lake, suspended from helicopters—one will be baited that night and one will have an armed ranger locked inside. Two armed rangers already have been dispatched to the lake on horseback and Minden, following instructions from the superintendent, arranges to have Imre, Ross, and the Finnish couple transported to Mammoth, where they will report to the superintendent.

"The superintendent doesn't want this to get out until after tonight," Minden tells the four of them. "Perhaps it was a bear attack, perhaps not. If it was a bear attack we hope to catch the animal tonight. He wants you to understand that this can cause unnecessary panic if it gets out. Imre, Ross, I'll cover for you with Faysal."

"We're both off today," Ross says.

"Yvonne is off tomorrow. I'll need to be back or let her know," Imre says.

"OK. Ranger Lynwood will take you to Mammoth. Take 15 minutes to get whatever you need for one night. Remember, don't talk to anyone about this. We'd like 24 hours."

Another ranger opens the screen door and leans in. "We're ready for you, sir."

"I'm terribly sorry this had to happen to all of you. I'm on my way up to Mallard, and I'll get any information about what happened to your friend up to Mammoth as soon as I can."

Minden looks to Sue Lynwood, who nods and bends to put her hand on the Finnish couple's shoulders and lead them out the door.

Imre puts her head under Ross' neck and whispers, "Will you still take me to New Zealand?"

He pulls her closer to him.

Old Faithful Inn, kitchen, 8:29 p.m..

Erbine strolls up to two waiters and two waitresses leaning against the counters talking.

"OK," says Erbine. "It's eight-thirty. Someone can go home. We're not going to get any busier."

One of the waiters says, "Kris worked lunch, Erbine. She should probably have first choice."

"Do you have any tables, Kris?"

"Just one. I just brought their desserts."

"OK, Kris, you go next, and you three flip a coin to see who goes after that. Seven should be enough. Kris, straighten up the walk-in a little for your side duty."

"Thanks, Erbine."

"It's too slow to keep two bartenders out here, you guys," says Clarence. "Cecil, I want you to go in the back and work on the inventory."

"Why do I have to do it?"

"I did it last night," George says.

Clarence watches Cecil fling the bar rag down, turn and start undoing his tie. Clarence wonders what is troubling Cecil; it seems to be more than the usual September burnout.

"Are you OK, Cecil?"

"Yea, sure. I'm just tired of being told what to do, that's all."

Cecil stalks through the kitchen and down the corridor to the liquor storage room. He kicks a stack of boxes and sits down, fuming, on another short stack. He looks on Clarence's desk at the white sheets waiting the tally marks and sneers at it. "The hell with this job." He sits there for five full minutes. Just as his anger wanes, as he is about to get up, he sees the object of his frustration walk by.

"Kris!"

He walks out of the liquor storage room and crosses the corridor where she is reaching for her time card.

"Kris, didn't you hear me?"

"What do you want, Cecil?"

"What are you doing? Why are you leaving now?"

"I'm going home." She slides her time card in until it punches, replaces it on the rack, and faces him, glaring contemptuously.

"So I guess you told everyone about our little disagreement the other night," Cecil says quietly.

"No, Cecil. But if you don't leave me alone, I sure will. I want you to stay away from me, Cecil."

"You didn't spend the night at home last night, did you?"

Hatred flashes in her eyes, but she walks by him, heading for the florescent light of the kitchen. He steps in front of her quickly. "I went to your dorm room last night after I got off work. One-thirty in the morning, and no one was there, Kris. I walked by Herm's cabin and I could hear your voice. Are you making love to Herm, Kris? What if I told everyone *that*? You're having sex with the head of security!"

"It's none of your damned business, Cecil! Now get out of my way!"

She pushes past him. Cecil runs up and grabs her arm. Kris angrily jerks it away and wheels at him.

"Don't touch me! Just stay away from me!"

"You little bitch!" Cecil shouts.

Just as he is about to strike her with the back of his hand, Barry Aardel steps from around the ovens. "What the hell is going on back here?"

As he approaches them, Kris turns and rushes away through the kitchen. Barry turns to Cecil with a quizzical look, not believing that he caught him about to hit her. "What the hell was that all about?"

"None of your business." Cecil turns and walks back down the corridor, steps into the liquor storage room and slams the door behind him.

By the time Kris makes the 10-minute walk back to her dorm room, she has cooled down.

She is to leave for Tallahassee in three days and, a week from now, she will be in her room at the Tri-Delt sorority looking over her notes from the first day of class. It seems far away to her, like another world.

She opens the door to her room. "Hi, Salina."

"Hi, Kris. What are you doing home now? It's not even 9 o'clock yet."

"Erbine sent me home early. It's real slow."

Kris's hopes rise as she sees the letter on the bed.

"Yea, you got a letter."

A quick glimpse at the handwriting tells her it is not from John. Her hope turns to curiosity. "It's from Dori"

"Who's Dori?"

"One of the varsity cheerleaders. We're kind of friends, I guess."

Kris changes into her jeans and the dark blue sweatshirt with the three deltas, then sits down on the bed to read:

Dear Kris,   September 10.

I just saw your roommate a couple of days ago and she said you would be coming back at the end of next week, so I thought I should tell you all that has happened since you left. You might want to prepare yourself for your return.

John broke his leg in practice about five weeks ago; it was his tibia. He was pretty depressed. He was worried about it hurting his chance for the pros and, since you weren't here, I started to look after him. He needed someone.

It started off slow. After the hospital, he went right back into his dorm. Since he lives on the fourth floor, I would go over to take him up his meals. I tried to cheer him up a little. When he was able to get around on his crutches, I would drive him to class, then drive him to the gym. He has such strong willpower, he still insisted on doing whatever he could with the weights, and it was torture for him not to be able to work out with the team. He could only watch from the sidelines.

Kris, John and I got to be very close during all of this, and on one Saturday night. . . . Well, we're more than just friends now, Kris.

He talked about you at first. He didn't even want to write you and worry you. Later, though, he confessed that he always knew you and he were just not right for each other.

We're very much in love now, John and I. His attitude has been much better lately. He should be able to get around without a brace pretty soon and, in a few weeks, should be able to scrimmage with the team again. He might even be ready to play by the Alabama game.

We both decided that it would be the right thing for you to hear this from us instead of getting back and hearing it from someone else. Kris, he did say you were right for him at the time and he'll always remember you, but it's time he started thinking ahead. He said that with my support he could still get drafted in the first round next year.

He said it would be better if he didn't see you at all when you got back. It would be easier for everyone involved.

I hope this doesn't come as too much of a shock, Kris, and I hope you and I can still be friends. Sonya from the drill team has taken your place on the squad. She works well with Robbie. Marjorie said you could still be an alternate if you are interested.

Sincerely,
Dori

Kris drops her hands to her lap, takes two deep breaths, then wipes away the tears welling up in her eyes. Her sniffling draws Salina's attention away from the letter she is writing.

"Kris, what is it?"

She turns her head away from Salina and reaches for a Kleenex. She sniffs again, then blows her nose as Salina crosses from her bed, sits down next to Kris and puts her arm around her.

"John is seeing another girl. He broke his leg and I wasn't there, so someone else stepped in and took my place."

"Dori?"

"Yea. I guess I really blew it, huh?"

"Kris, all this time you've been loyal to him and now this happens. It's not fair." Salina looks at the pictures of John that have stood next to Kris's bed over the four months they have lived together.

Kris rises slowly from the bed and walks over to her closet, takes out a jacket, and puts her flashlight in the pocket. "Listen, Salina, I'm going to go for a walk around the boardwalk."

"Do you want me to go with you?"

"No, I feel like being alone now." Kris turns to Salina and forces a smile. "Thanks, anyway."

9:03 p.m..

Salina finds it hard to get back to her letter; she feels so sorry for her friend. She wonders if she should take the pictures of John away, if it would help Kris forget about him.

Outside, toward the lobby, Salina hears shouts and hoots, which she interprets as yet another dorm party.

The noise grows louder. There is more shouting, but she can't quite make out what anyone is saying. She ignores it.

But when the third wave of racket emanates from the hall, Salina gets up to see what's happening. Down the corridor, people are shouting excitedly in the lobby. She walks toward the noise.

"What's going on, Walt?"

"Alex and I were walking down the road and, like 30 feet in front of us, was this big-ass bear coming toward us. Look. He's still out there, messing with the garbage can. He's huge!"

Salina's sudden terror cuts through the excitement and chattering voices. "Kris is out there!"

She pushes her way through the crowd to the front porch.

"Whoa!" comes a voice. "Don't push my ass out there!" For, sure enough, 50 yards away is the huge dark form of a grizzly. The crowd of 15 or so employees oohs and ahhs as it easily lifts the "bear proof" top off the garbage can.

"Did anyone see Kris?" Salina shouts.

"I saw her as we were coming out of the Inn," says Alex. "She was heading down toward the boardwalk."

"Has anyone called the rangers?"

"No."

"Don't call the rangers. They'll probably shoot it or something. This is the first bear I've seen all summer. Five days before my contract ends!"

"Who's got change?" Salina pleads.

She frantically dials the ranger station on the lobby phone. "Yes, there's a big bear out in front of Lupine dorm and my roommate is out walking around the geyser basin. You've got to send someone to get her."

At that moment, 40 yards to the right of the dorm entrance, Jorge appears, leisurely walking with a fellow busboy.

"Jorge! Allen!"

"There's a bear!"

"Run like hell!"

Jorge and Allen cut between the cars and make a break for the door. The huge grizzly makes a feint in their direction, rises partway up on his hind legs to sniff the air, then turns back to the garbage can. Panting, Jorge and Allen race to the door and into the arms of the other employees. Jorge turns and peers out into the night.

"Let me see your binoculars," Jorge says. He focuses on the animal. "This is the same bear that attacks Tina and me."

"How can you tell?" Alex asks. "They said that bear was relocated north of the park."

"That, amigo, is one face I shall never forget in my lifetime."

They watch as the 800-pound grizzly locates the object of its search and pulls it out of the garbage.

Someone steps through the crowd and hurls a white frisbee at the bear, striking it broadside. The bear bites at it. As Salina gets off the phone and steps to the back of the crowd to try to see over, she hears someone say, "It's heading toward the boardwalk."

"Come back here, you coward," shouts a voice, and the others laugh.

"Wow, look at him run."

Old Faithful Inn, dining room, 9:09 p.m..

Ranger Howard Minden heads directly to the table where Faysal, Slim Grandstrom, Herm, and two of Faysal's dinner guests are just finishing their meals.

"Herm, I need to talk to you right away," Minden says.

Herm rises, sensing the urgency in Minden's voice. "I was just getting ready to punch in. Come on back to the time clock. Excuse me, everyone."

Ranger Minden follows Herm into the kitchen, moving swiftly past the waiters and waitresses and down the long corridor to the time clock.

"What is it, Howard? It smells like you've been riding a horse."

"I just got back from Mallard Lake," he says. "Listen. . . ."

Cecil Dolen stops in the middle of wiping the bourbon from his lips with the back of his hand. On the other side of the liquor-room door, he hears the murmur of two voices. As he quietly moves toward the door and puts his ear against it, he matches the two voices with names and faces.

". . .and a Finnish girl was mauled to death up there by a grizzly."

"Holy Jesus. That's only three miles away. This happened last night?"

"Probably the night before. Listen, Herm. I got back to the station 15 minutes ago and just got a call from Seattle. They made a positive identification with Dolen's hair. Herm, they believe Cecil has murdered eleven women!"

Herm stares in disbelief at Minden, and a million thoughts race through his mind. First, he thinks of Kris; he saw her leave earlier and she said she was going home. Then he thinks of Cecil. He remembers seeing him behind the bar earlier and he immediately steps away from Minden toward the lights of the kitchen.

"He's working. Let's get him."

"No. Clarence and somebody else are behind the bar. I just walked past there and checked."

Herm murmurs to himself. "Cecil's off early. Kris! I've got to go get her."

Just then, a metallic crack comes over Minden's radio. "Wait a minute, Herm!"

"Base to Minden. Base to Minden. Come in."

"This is Minden. Go ahead."

"We've got a large bear located by Lupine Dormitory. It was just sighted across the street from the entrance. Howard, it sounds like bear 397."

Cecil hears their running footsteps disappear down the corridor toward the kitchen. He feels as if his heart will explode in his chest. Fear grips him, and he starts to shake. A chug of the whisky doesn't help, so he throws the bottle into the corner, breaking it. Run for it, he thinks. They will never catch me.

He opens the door, but he sees a waiter punching out at the time clock in front of him, and closes it quietly.

Yes, run. But if I'm going to run, I'm going to take Kris with me. If they're going to catch me, we'll die together first.

He lunges to the phone on Clarence's desk. He runs his finger down the list under the plate of glass, finds the Lupine Dorm number and punches the buttons, using his left hand to steady his trembling finger.

What can I tell her? Think! Think! I've got to get her out of there before the asshole gets there. I'm leaving! That's it! I'll tell her I just quit and I want to see her one more time before I take off. My tapes! That's it! She still has my tapes! I need my tapes. Please bring them at once. She'll use the foot path and miss Herm. Then I'll take her. She will love me.

"Hello."

"Yes, I need to speak to Kris Richards right away!"

"Just a second."

Each second that passes he slams his fist down on the desk harder and harder. "Come on! Come on!"

"Hello?"

"Kris, I need to see you right away. I. . . ."

"This is Salina. Cecil, is that you?"

"Yes! Damn it, Salina, I need to talk to Kris right now!"

"Cecil, you've got to help her! There's a bear headed over toward the boardwalk and Kris is out there somewhere walking around. I just tried to get a message to Herm, but he's not on his radio. I called the rangers and they're on their way over here but the bear's run off. You've got to get her! Get all the bellmen, or something."

"She's out walking around the boardwalk?"

"Yes, Cecil. She's wearing. . . ."

Cecil sets the receiver on the hook and smiles.

He walks to the stack of boxes of 151-proof rum, pulls down the top box and sets it on the floor. He rips open the top and hurls the first bottle against the floor, breaking it. Quickly, he unscrews the lid off the bottles in the case and sets it on its side, letting the volatile liquid run out onto the floor. With occasional bursts of profanity, he takes the half-empty bottles and slings the liquid contents at the stacks of cardboard boxes. He checks to see that no one is in the hall, then takes a second case and hurls it with raging might toward the ceiling, letting it crash to the floor, and crushing the bottles from the bottom.

"A good bartender should always carry a lighter. For lighting ladies' cigarettes," he sneers and flicks the lighter. "You're welcome. Ninety years without a good fire is much too long. Here's one for you, Herm."

Kris's face flashes in his mind. He puts the lighter to the closest reaches of the puddle and, immediately, a blue flame springs up and crosses the floor, then spreads quietly up the boxes. Cecil opens the door, sees that no one is around, pushes the lock in and steps out into the corridor. He squints at the florescent light of the kitchen as he pulls the door closed behind him.

He walks through the kitchen and dining room, and into the lobby. He stops at the fireplace and grabs one of the fire irons. He does not notice the inquisitive look on the faces of the guests sitting around the fireplace. Looking straight ahead, he passes through the red wrought iron doors and into the night.

9:16 p.m..

They take the short cut, speeding down the fire lane to Lupine Dormitory, Herm handling the controls of the search beam. When they pull up, Salina runs out of the crowd toward them.

"Salina, where's Kris?"

"Herm, I've been trying to get a hold of you. There's a bear running around. . . ."

"We know, Salina. Where's Kris?"

"She's out walking around in the geyser basin. Cecil just called and I told him to go out there and get her. . . ."

"You what?"

"Kris is out walking around the boardwalk! There's a bear headed over there! You've got to find her! Cecil. . . ."

"Stay inside the dorm!" Minden shouts to the crowd as the men both turn and run back to the ranger car.

"Good God!" Herm cries. "Hurry!"

Minden peels the sedan out of the gravel parking lot and speeds back toward the Inn. Halfway down the fire lane, the low wail of the fire siren becomes louder.

"No, it can't be," pleads Herm with a look of confused terror. They hear two short blasts. "The Inn!"

"Base to Minden. Base to Minden. Come in."

"Answer it!" Minden yells.

Herm picks up the radio. "This is Minden. Go ahead!"

"We've got a definite blaze coming from the Inn. Located in the liquor storage room. It's spreading behind the main kitchen toward the west wing. The Comm Center has been called. The fire chief has responded."

"Liquor storage room! We were standing right next to it. . . You don't suppose Dolen. . . . He was there at four. He must. . . ."

Just as the ranger's car screeches to a halt behind the Inn, the internal hotel alarm goes off.

"I hope to God that old Grinnell system is working," Minden says.

"Howard, I've got to get Kris." They hold each other's gaze for less than a second.

"Here, take my belt," says Minden, unstrapping and handing Herm the thick, black belt that holds the ranger's flashlight, night-stick, handcuffs and revolver. "The safety catch is off. The gun is loaded."

Herm buckles it as he runs through the lobby of the Inn, past scurrying guests, and out the front door toward the geyser basin.

Strong now. Night now. The hunter with a weapon. I am alive. Where is my little princess? A little dark, but soon I should have light to see by, shouldn't I? Her blond hair looks so nice by firelight. Strong now. Finally after a summer of being weak I am alive again. They cannot stop me now. Not when I'm like this. This is alive! No. A man. A hunter. Yes. Muscles. Did you come out here to get away from it all? Did you come out here to think? John, what a stupid name. You won't need to do much thinking when I get through with you. No. Just lie down, little cheerleader, and take what's coming to you. Take the man. A real man for once. Sleep with Herm? Sleep with a football player? Little boys. Too soft. Too proper. Sleep with the strong one now. Finally, after a summer of being weak, I am alive again. They cannot stop me now. Walk quietly. The hunter sneaks up on his prey. Take her.

Identification with my hair? How did they identify. . .? Ahhh! That's how we got a little of Cecil's hair, huh? Yea. A little deception of old Cecil. . . I'll brush your hair for you, if there's any left to brush.

Oh yes! Beautiful! Perfect. Walking right toward me! Don't shine the flashlight on the geyser. Shine it here. Shine it on me. Yes, keep coming.

"Cecil! What are you doing?"

Cecil takes three running steps toward Kris and lashes out with the fire iron. She ducks, but not in time. The metal rod catches the top of her head, knocking her off the boardwalk into a warm spring runoff.

"Brushing your hair, huh?"

Wide-eyed, she looks up to see Cecil raise the fire iron high above his head. He brings it down in a wide arc with the sharp tip aimed for her head, but Kris rolls on her side, the blow just missing her. As she rolls in the mud and water, she catches the inside of Cecil's leg, and he falls to his knees next to her. She scampers to her feet. As she takes one step away, Cecil grabs her ankle and she falls face forward, half onto the boardwalk. She lets out a loud scream, and rises again but he grabs the back of her jacket. As she follows through with a step, she kicks Cecil in the face, and he releases his grip. She staggers, then springs toward the trees, wiping blood and water out of her eyes. Cecil pursues her.

The scream galvanizes Herm, who is running down the boardwalk, and his legs move even faster. He passes Castle Geyser, bounds down the steps and over the bridge spanning the Firehole River. He sees Salina's flashlight, shining on fresh blood, and he whips out the flashlight and revolver from his belt.

"Kriiiiis!"

She runs as fast as she can but she can feel Cecil gaining on her. She runs at full speed off the boardwalk and toward the trees, then trips over a branch, falls skidding on her stomach, and Cecil is upon her. The momentum of Cecil landing on her turns her over and she strikes out wildly at him, scratching his face.

"Like it rough, huh? Yes? I'll show you rough! Now your time has come, you bitch. How about a cheer for old Cecil? Cheer!"

He hits her with his fist once, twice, three times. He takes her by the neck and bangs her head against the rocky ground. As he feels the resistance drain from her, he grabs her wrists and holds them away from her. Just as he is about to kiss the babbling, nearly unconscious girl, Herman Pangilnan's huge form crashes into him like a charging buffalo, rolling him off of her. They flail at each other and grovel like two starving wolves in a fight.

"You bastard!" Cecil shouts. Herm hits him across the side of his head with the metal flashlight, breaking the lens. He hits Cecil in the neck with the butt of the revolver, knocking him nearly unconscious.

Herm stands over Cecil, points the revolver three feet away from Cecil's face, and pulls back the hammer.

"Herm, don't!" Kris moans, rising to her elbows eight feet away. As Herm looks at Kris's bloodied face, he aims the revolver again.

"No, Herm. Don't shoot him!"

Cecil shakes his head and spits at Herm. "You fat pig, you don't have the guts!"

Herm kicks him in the crotch, choking off the words. Cecil coughs and collapses into a fetal position.

"Are you all right, Kris?"

"I'll be OK." She tries to stand but falls again. "I think I've hurt my knee."

The sirens and the alarms come into focus now. Herm looks across the geyser basin and sees the tiny figures of guests standing out in front of the hotel and a plume of smoke rising from behind the west wing.

"What is it?" Kris cries.

"Our friend here set a fire. OK, little friend. I'll handcuff you to this tree for now. Then, how would you like to go on a little ride back to Seattle?"

"Campus cop."

"Yes, that's right."

Cecil starts to rise, and Herm punches him in the face with his bare fist. Then he drags Cecil five feet over to a two-foot-thick lodgepole pine and cuffs his hands together around the tree.

"You can't leave me here. I've got rights. I didn't do nothing."

With Herm carrying Kris piggyback, they start back down the boardwalk.

"Campus cop! Bastard! I'll get loose. I'll get out. I'll come find you!"

It takes 15 minutes for Herm to carry Kris back to the Inn. He does not stop when blood pours from Kris's scalp into his eyes, mixing with his sweat. Just as they get to the end of the boardwalk, Minden pulls up in the patrol car and helps Herm get Kris into the back seat.

"She'll be OK," Herm says.

Herm answers the question in Minden's expression. "I didn't shoot him. He's out there by Grand Geyser handcuffed to a tree. He won't go anywhere. How's the fire?"

"We've got it under control. No one was hurt, thank God. The Grinnell system worked perfectly. The Teddy Bear did its job. Why don't you come with me to check on the west wing while Judy gets Kris some first aid. Dolen will be OK?"

Herm looks out across the geyser basin. "Yea."

Herm walks over to Kris and puts an arm on her shoulder. "You're all right now."

She smiles weakly at him and reaches out to touch his sweat-moistened cheek.

Herm and Minden walk through the lobby of the Inn and around back to where the brigade of firemen are still dousing smoke and a few flames. They don't see the grizzly, number 397, as it descends from the trees. They don't see the bear gather momentum as the man smell in its nostrils grows stronger. Only the guests standing in front of the Inn waiting to get back to their warm beds hear the terrifying screams coming from somewhere in the geyser basin, chilling them to the bone.

September 19. Outside Lupine Dorm.

Three days after getting beat up, Kris's face is starting to heal. As she stands in front of Lupine Dormitory waiting for the bus that will take her to the West Yellowstone Airport, Salina, Herm, Steve, Yvonne, Wilbur and Kitty congregate around her. Scattered about the gravel front yard are several other groups, saying their good-byes to each other.

"I still can't believe you were out there alone camping with the Green River murderer," Yvonne says. "And I went hotpotting with him!"

Salina watches her friend avert her eyes at the thought. She knows the bruises and scrapes will heal, but she wonders how Kris will handle the psychological wounds.

"Yea, and I was afraid of the bears!" She forces a sheepish smile through the wounds, and it is reflected in the faces of her friends.

"There's the bus," Steve says, pointing.

"Now you guys aren't going to change your minds, are you?" Kris asks Salina and Yvonne. "You're really going to stop by Tallahassee and see me?"

"Yup," Salina says. "Yvonne's going to take me to Vermont before she goes to Pittsburgh. We're going to do a six-week road trip. After California, we're going to see Alex and Walt in Texas, you in Tallahassee and, let's see, there was somebody else in South Carolina. . . or was that Maryland?"

"Virginia!" Steve interjects. "Lynchburg, Virginia. Don't you be getting lost now." He takes Salina's hand.

Kris steps aside with a limp as the bus driver charges past them with a leather mail pouch.

"Will you take us to a football game?" Yvonne asks.

"Yvonne, not football," Salina admonishes.

"Ooops! Sorry."

"It's OK," Kris says. "Maybe a symphony or something a little more soothing, huh?"

"Fall means cross country," says Steve, stretching in his warm-up suit.

"Fall means work for at least one of us," Herm adds.

Kitty moves to him and puts her hand on his arm. "But you're still going to Mexico with Wilbur and me for a couple of weeks, aren't you?"

"OK," the bus driver shouts, reappearing from the dorm. "Let's load 'em up." He slings open the long cargo door to the bus's undercarriage.

"I'll get them," says Wilbur. He picks up Kris's suitcase and travel bag and carries them to the bus.

Sadness overtakes Kris as she embraces each of her friends. When she gets to Salina and Herm, she can't hold back the tears any longer. "I'm really going to miss you guys."

"I'll see you in a month," Salina says.

Kris throws herself at Herm, giving him a big hug.

"Herm, you were there when I needed you most. You saved my life. If it wasn't for you. . . ."

"I'd do the same for any girl that I was in love with and rejected me for five months."

"Will you come back next year?" Kitty asks.

"No, I don't think so," she says, with a far-away look in her eyes. Then she injects brightness into her voice. "I'll graduate and probably have to get a job in the real world!"

"Time to go!" the bus driver shouts.

With an arm around Herm's shoulder, Kris limps to the bus. She turns one more time, shaking hands, hugging her friends until she is the last person to board. A loud rev of the diesel engine tells her she cannot put it off any longer.

"Bye, you guys."

"Bye, Kris."

"Good luck."

"Take care."

Herm helps her to her seat and sits down next to her.

"OK, Tallahassee, here we come," he bellows.

"I would like that, Herm. I could keep you in my room and turn you into a big teddy bear anytime someone came in."

He takes both of her hands in his. "I'm really going to miss you. Take care of yourself. And you promised me you'd write."

She hugs him and kisses him on the lips. "I love you, Herm."

"Herm, are you going or staying?" the bus driver booms.

"Bye," Herm says, weakly, wiping away tears of sadness. She watches him walk down the aisle and off the bus.

As Kris opens the window to wave good-bye, Linda Jennings, the resident assistant, runs out of the dormitory. "Wait! Isn't Kris Richards on this bus? Kris! I just got a letter for you."

As the bus starts to pull away, Kris reaches down and grabs it.

"It's from John!" Kris shouts over the roar of the diesel engine.

"Well, what does it say?" shouts Salina, running after the fuming bus.

Salina can see Kris but cannot make out her words, and the bus disappears around the bend and out of sight.

Dear Kris,   September 14.

I don't mean to bother you again. I guess this is my fifth letter, or is it sixth? It's just that it is so slow around here in the break between classes, and since I can't scrimmage with the team, I have a lot of spare time. Time I can't help but spend thinking of you. I thought we had it so good together. Anyway, I hear you'll be coming back next weekend. It will be hard, but I won't call you.

I suppose that since I suddenly stopped getting letters from you, I should have suspected but ever since Dori got that letter from you saying you had fallen in love with someone else, my attitude about football and class has not been all that great. I was surprised and hurt when she told me that you said you didn't want to see me when you got back, but I will respect your wishes. I guess after five months away from each other, that kind of thing was bound to happen. I still miss you very much.

Dori was nice to help me out at first, right after I broke my leg. She'd help get books and work from class, bring up my meals, even go to the post office for me, mail my car payments and your letters. But now, to be honest, she is getting on my nerves a little. One of my offensive linemen said he heard we were not only dating but would soon be engaged to be married! Dori! I haven't even so much as kissed her, but I have to admit, in these lonely times, I've become more and more dependent on her.

Campus is nice this time of year, but without being involved with football—and you—I guess I've been a little apathetic. I don't know.

Greg Hughes went 18 for 32 with three TDs against Virginia Tech last
week and is playing really well for a sophomore. I should get the cast
off next week, but at this point, I'm thinking about just going for
good grades.

Well, Kris, I am happy for you, that you've found somebody there
that you're really happy with. Maybe someday I will find that kind of
happiness again in someone else. Dori says you'll be moving out to
Montana as soon as you graduate next year. I've heard it's nice.
Perhaps if we run across each other on campus sometime, you can
tell me about it.

Take care,
John

Kris slams the letter into her lap. "Oooh!" she squeals loudly and
grimaces at the pressure on her stitched cut. Several faces turn to her.
"Are you OK, Kris?"
"Yea!" She reads the letter again. When she finishes it, she turns
suddenly and looks out the window, wanting to tell Salina or Herm
about it. She lets out an angry breath and clenches her fist. "Dori!"

October 4. Fairy Creek Trail.
God, at least they got that grizz. Eight hundred and twenty
pounds! How many times did I run up to Mallard this summer?
There must be some still out here, but I can't keep off these trails.
Why not? Maybe it's *because* they're out there that makes it so intense
here. Charges the air with energy. Breathe it in.
Easy stride, long stride here on the flat. . . The hell with the long
stride. Just let it feel good now. Yea, run with your heart. That's it.
Dolen. How many nights were Wilbur and I alone with him in the
office? Our backs to him while he counted his deposit. I never could
have guessed. Herm said they put his remains in a bag the size. . . .
Slow down. There's nothing to run from.
I'm going to miss this place. A summer I'll never forget. But sorry,
guys, the treasurer won't be back. Time to settle down now. This is
great but it ain't home. Ain't Virginia. How can Kitty travel around
like that constantly, never setting down any roots? Always coming
back here? Such a hard place.
Smitty ran a 28:22 to win the Norfolk 10k. Run a few steps for him
and Jim. I'll be back. I'll race. Run because I love it. Compete, yea,
because I love it. But hey, it's not everything anymore. Need energy
for the other things in my life.

Once more past Fairy Falls. Snow's coming. I can feel it.

Can't wait to get some good home cooking. Mom's fried chicken. Run a few steps for her. You too, dad. Let's go catch some fish as soon as I get back. Or take Bullet out and shoot a turkey.

October 13. Old Faithful Inn, dining room, 8:59 p.m..

At the year end survivor's party Erbine Kaplowitz and Barry Aardel serve the last of the 147 employees, Barry takes out a 12-by-12-inch baking pan from under the steam table and peels back the aluminum foil, revealing 22 steaming shrimp, sauteed in wine, garlic, and Barry's secret blend of spices and butter sauce.

At the long table at the far end of the dining room from Erbine and Barry, Faysal sits down across from Billie Mackey and Angel Ferguson and fills their glasses from wine bottles in each hand.

As everyone finishes their dinner, Faysal rises to start the employee-of-the-year awards.

As other departments are announced and awards presented, Imre becomes visibly more nervous, for two reasons: One, she hasn't had a cigarette in eight days and, two, she dreads talking in front of crowds. Holding Ross's hand helps. As the applause dies down after the maintenance-crew award is given, Faysal steps back up to the microphone. "Imre?"

She walks to the podium. Her voice starts out high and tense. "I have. . . a tie. I still never could decide whether to fire them or keep them around so they could annoy me at 6:30 in the morning. They almost lost their heads when they hid their dinner trays in the safe, but they are the best audit clerk-and-auditor combination I've ever had. The tie goes to Steve Mathewson and Wilbur Hardisty!"

Wilbur and Steve get a kiss from their dates and walk up to receive the check and the award. Wilbur whispers in Steve's ear. Wilbur takes the check on one side of Imre, hands it across the podium to Steve and they tear it in two parts. Each of them gives Imre a kiss on the side of the cheek, grabs a hand and pretends to pull her apart down the middle.

"Stop it, you two!" she yells, as her face turns crimson. Wilbur and Steve take bows and escort Imre back to her seat.

"Erbine?"

"This goes to my most consistent employee. He was always on time, worked the hardest and had the best attitude. He wants to be a waiter next year and he's got my recommendation. Jorge Riez!"

The cheers and the applause are the loudest yet as Jorge walks up to the podium. "When I come to the United. . . . When I *came* to the United States, I had heard many different things from people, telling me what to look for. And since I have worked in Yellowstone Park, I am sure I have seen every American at least one time. Someone at the table asked me what I think of America after one summer. I tell him it is a very nice country, but I have learned it is better to be nicer than to spend too much money. It is happy and helping and working together that is the best. Like one big family. Find me when you come to San Blas! *Muchas gracias. Debo regresso!*"

As the applause dies down, Faysal returns to the podium. "I think a lot of people did a great job here this summer. It just makes my job easier. I'm real glad to be a part of it. The survivors are the heartiest, and I'd like to see everyone here come back next year. The dance in the Pub will start in 20 minutes!"

George, the bartender, luminous with wine and cheer, leans over to talk to Clarence. "Kitty wants to buy four more bottles of Mouton Cadet, Clarence, and we don't have any more at the bar. Is there any in the back?"

Clarence takes a last bite of cake, rises and crosses to the bar. "Come with me, Kitty, we'll have to get it out of the back."

"Is that a problem, Clarence?"

"Nope, just follow me."

As they walk past the boarded-up old liquor-storage room to the dry-storage room now serving a dual purpose, Kitty asks, "So what did you decide to do this winter, Clarence?"

"I'm going to start up a theater group in Milwaukee. It's amazing how much money I saved once I stopped drinking. Wilbur told me you and he are going to Mexico. And you're going to take Mr. Security with you, I hear."

"Yes. He'll only be there for a couple of weeks. Then we're on our own."

"Sounds like you'll have a great time."

"I hope so."

As Kitty appears back at the table with four more bottles of wine, Wilbur slaps his palm on the table and tings his water glass with his fork three times.

"Hear ye, hear ye! A final meeting of the Mouton Cadet Sunset Society will now come to order. Place: the boardwalk seats facing Old Faithful. Time: now!"

"Herm ate earlier and he's playing poker in the lobby already," Salina says. "I don't know if he'll come."

Steve, Salina, Wilbur, Kitty and Shannon walk past the noisy tables toward the lobby, and one of Kitty's maids runs up and hugs her.

"You're the best boss I've ever had," she cries.

"Come back next year, Martina, and you can have that inspectress position."

"Nothing will stop me. Merry Christmas and all that. See ya next spring!"

White tablecloths cover all the lobby furniture except for the square table next to the fireplace and the seven chairs occupied by the poker players. Wilbur leads the group into the lobby where, at the sight of Howard Minden seated at the poker table, he stops and diverts himself and Kitty to a maid's cart.

"Wilbur, this is no time to want to clean rooms."

"Minden's over there. If he sees us with bottles of Mout. . . ."

"Good thinking," says Kitty. They put their backs to the poker players and wrap the four bottles in white towels. As they step to the table, three players have dropped out of a hand on the fifth card of a seven-card stud game, leaving Bob Tagore, Gust, Minden and Herm in.

"Are you coming with us, Herm?" Wilbur asks. "Last meeting?"

"Let me win this hand first," Herm chirps.

The group of five spreads around behind the table to watch the action. After the seventh card has been dealt, Gust opens with a quarter bet and Tagore folds on his left.

"Raise you a dollar," Minden says.

Herm reclines in his seat, scratching a two-day-old growth and glimpsing at his three hole cards. "One-and-a-quarter to me. Raise you two dollars."

Salina moves over behind Herm and pats him on the back. "Way to go, Herm! Herm, why is this ace tucked into your collar back here?"

"Funny, Salina."

Gust folds, and Minden raises Herm another dollar. Herm lets out a breath, looks at his friends and calls with his last chip.

"Full house, Herm. Tens over threes."

"Pair of kings."

The other men laugh. "What the hell were you doing in there with a lousy pair of kings?" Gust says. "I folded with two low pair."

"You had Herm's hand," says Minden.

"Wasn't much of a bluff, Herm," Slim says.

"He never was much of a bluffer," says Minden.

"What d' ya mean? I've won lots of money from you guys with not so much as a pair. I'm going to step outside to say good-bye to my friends. I'll be back in 10 minutes. Then I'll show you the art of bluffing."

"Here, Herm. Here's three of a kind to start you off," says Minden, handing Herm three folded squares of sticky paper.

As Herm and the other five start to walk away, Herm unfolds the wad in his hand, revealing three Mouton Cadet labels. He, Kitty and Wilbur stop and turn around. Ranger Minden gives them a wink and a broad smile before turning his attention back to the table.

"It's cold out here," Salina says.

"I can't believe he knew!" says Wilbur. "How long has he known?"

"I don't know," says Herm. "Next year I'm going to be good. I've got too many years invested in the company to blow it. I could be head of security for the whole park before too long."

"Who's got the corkscrew?"

"It's starting to snow," says Steve.

"You guys, this is it," Salina says. "We're never going to get to see each other again."

"Well, let's not get depressed about it," Shannon says.

"Let's drink the wine first and then be depressed," says Kitty.

"Here's the corkscrew."

"I love you guys," Salina insists, as everyone sits down on the bench facing a quiet Old Faithful geyser steam phase.

After a loud "pop," Kitty divides the contents of the bottle into six plastic glasses and passes them out.

"A toast!" says Steve, holding out his glass to Old Faithful. "May bad luck follow everyone here for the rest of their lives. . . and never catch up to anyone!"

There is a moment of silence as they sip.

"To the best friends I've ever had," says Salina. "And to the best summer I've ever had."

They sip again.

"To 10-Minute Geyser!" says Kitty. "That was *my* favorite."

"Remember Kitty's knoll?" Salina adds. "We were going to have weekly Mout meetings out there, and we never went back there once all summer."

Herm pours from another bottle and passes it to the right.

Kitty says, "We touched the buffalo, Salina. Remember that? That was the beginning of the Society and the beginning of summer."

"I wish it was spring again," Salina says.

"It's snowing harder," says Shannon. "I hope we'll be able to get out of here tomorrow. It's starting to settle."

"Maybe we should go back in," says Salina.

"We can't," says Shannon.

"We could drink the wine inside," says Salina, "by the fire."

"Why can't we go back inside, Shannon?" asks Wilbur, bending over and looking down the line at him.

"I've never seen Old Faithful go off."

"What?"

"You've been here all summer and you've never seen Old Faithful go off?" Salina asks. "Why not?"

"I must have unloaded 2,000 boxes of postcards with Old Faithful's picture on it this summer. I just didn't think I needed to see it. Now I feel like I'm going to miss it."

As if on cue, Old Faithful plays to 10 feet.

"We've got to stay," says Kitty. "Let me open another bottle of wine."

"I'll stay until everyone else wants to go," says Herm.

"What about the poker game, Herm?" asks Kitty.

"Gambling. I don't know. I've won and I've lost. I just don't think I should gamble anymore. You know, it doesn't look good for security. There must be better things to do with my spare time and money."

"Yea, like writing?" Wilbur asks, with a hint of sarcasm.

"That's right!" says Steve. "Did this third guy buy your story?"

"No. I just got the reject back two days ago. I don't think there are any more running mags that would consider it. When Kitty and I get back from Mexico, I'm trying to talk her into going someplace where I can take some writing courses."

"If it's warm and by the water, I'll do it," says Kitty.

"It's good that you keep trying," says Shannon.

"It's those standard reject letters that piss me off so bad. They inspire me to keep writing."

"Letter!" shouts Salina. "I almost forgot! I got a letter. . . . Here it is. . . from the Mouton Cadet estate. Written by the Baron Philipe de Rothschild himself. From France. He won't give us any free wine. He says they're represented by this corporation in the U.S."

She passes the letter with the flowing French script on a raised letterhead.

"Well, you can't get something for nothing, I guess," says Herm.

They sip in silence as the snowflakes fall and settle on their shoulders.

Herm breaks the silence. "There are a lot of good people up here," he says. "I'm glad things worked out for Kris."

"Yea." Salina says, "She wrote me that when she first got back to campus and got back with John, they were limping around with their arms around each other like they were in a three-legged sack race. She said John will be starting at quarterback again." She pauses. "I wish she was here."

They sip and think.

"Gosh, I could be back in Los Angeles right now. I'd be in school. . . . So many unfriendly faces. The. . . Kitty, why are you crying?"

"That's just it. What Herm said. There are a lot of good people up here.

"You people are my only friends and everyone is leaving again. Eight years ago, well, we had a circle of friends that worked here summer after summer, and we all thought that it would never end. All those friends are gone now. Their letters come less and less often until someday I think, 'Whatever happened to Donny or Karen,' whoever. It's the worst part about working here, to see people I love leave and not come back.

Wilbur puts his arm around Kitty and pulls her closely to him.

"The summer's over," Steve says, as if he is just realizing it for the first time. "But we're all going to write, OK? And everyone is invited to Virginia anytime."

"Or Philadelphia," says Shannon.

"Or wherever I am," says Salina.

"Wherever any of us are," says Kitty. "Of course."

"It's really starting to snow," Steve says. "We should get back, Sal. Yvonne's coming at seven to get you and I wanted to get an early start too, especially if the roads are going to be bad."

"We can't leave," says Shannon. "I haven't seen Old Faithful."

"Here," says Wilbur, standing. "Here's a cork for you, Shannon, one for Herm, one for Salina, and Steve, and here, I saved these from dinner, one for Kitty and one for me."

"Let me guess," says Herm. "We've got to find a buffalo and stick them up his butt."

"Nope. Come quickly. We haven't much time," Wilbur shouts, jumping off the boardwalk and running toward the geyser cone. He stops and turns around. "Well, come on! It's going to go off in a few seconds! The corks!"

Laughing in shrieks and squeals, the others jump off the board-walk and run with Wilbur to the slanted oblong opening.

"I never knew what Old Faithful looked like," says Kitty. "Nine years here and I always pictured it as a perfect circle."

A tremendous roar wells up from what seems to be the very center of the earth. The ground around them starts to shake. "Drop them in now!" Wilbur shouts.

They each toss their cork into the black opening, then scramble to the boardwalk just as the geyser erupts into steam and water 190 feet above them. Under great, natural pressures, the water is forced upward to meet with the dark, snowy heavens. "The Mouton Cadet Sunset Society!" shouts Wilbur, "for the enjoyment. . ."

"Of," says Steve.

"Life!" says Salina and Kitty.

"A whole lot better than post cards!" Shannon shouts.

October 18.

High above the Yellowstone Plateau, moisture is freezing into snow crystals, each one different, and the weight of gravity pulls them down to earth. They fall on the mountains reaching upward to 11,000 feet. They cover the lichen growing there. They pile up and cover the rocks and the short grasses and shrubs. They cover the winter homes of the marmots, the chipmunks, and the ground squirrels, as these mammals fall into the deep slumber of hibernation. The wind blows the snow into drifts and cornices on the ridges.

Lower on the mountain, between 7,800 and 9,200 feet, the grizzly bear now moves to its den, instinctively knowing this storm will cover its tracks, and hide its winter concealment. Though ovulation and conception occurred in June, it is only now that the sow is in her den that the tiny embryos will begin to develop. Six to eight weeks later they will be born sightless, hairless, and weighing only one pound, depending on the lactation of the sleeping mother to sustain them until spring. Her cousin, the black bear, has already been asleep for a month.

The snow accumulates on the lodgepole pine, alpine fir and spruce trees, weighing down their receptive branches, and with their shallow roots the trees that cannot bear the pressure will uproot and crash to earth. The small streams and lakes start to freeze from their shorelines inward; even the big Lake Yellowstone with its 130-mile shoreline begins to weave its winter blanket that will, by January, cover it like a cocoon.

The snows tumble into the Grand Canyon, sticking only where the gradient is kind enough to permit it, or on the top of the spires and pinnacles where it creates a layer of cold, white frosting. The runoff from hot springs supports its own ecosystem; the ephrydrid flies cannot venture far from the algae-laden waters of the hot streams or they will freeze. On the boardwalk railings the wind and steam form bizarre ice sculptures.

Some of the buffalo have been led by the herdmaster to the thermal areas, where forage is more easily available. In Pelican and Hayden valleys, other bison shovel the deep snow with their muzzles to locate frozen sedge or sage, as the unchecked wind blows against them.

The moose follow their local migratory instincts, staying close to their watery home, where they can still find aquatic plants, shrubs or willows to eat. Coyotes grow thick winter coats and search for animals that cannot survive the cold.

For five weeks, as the snow covers the boardwalks and roads, humans will be excluded, until the first snowmobilers with their whining two-stroke engines buzz around the packed Grand Loop Road like frenzied insects.

At Old Faithful the gas stations and the general stores are closed and boarded up. Inside it is dark and still, the racks and shelves like silent monuments of the past.

The visitor center is also closed, the sign which shows the next predicted eruption of Old Faithful says 5:15 on October 14th. It is now a gray noon on another day.

Outside of Old Faithful Lodge, a 'LODGING' sign swings on hooks and creaks as it blows in the wind. Across the way, snow is accumulating on the roof and eaves of the Inn. The lower windows are boarded up. But the lobby is not empty. Not totally empty. Jim Petersen is there, sitting in one of the red leather chairs he pulled from under the sheets. It is near dark inside; the gray light spills in from the unboarded windows above. He is there, alone, with his flashlight; the belt with his tools is on the floor beside him.

"Well, here we are again, " he says in the still coldness of the big lobby, and thinks, no, not 'we' this time. Me. There is no one in the trailer at lot 49 waiting for me to come back home now, waiting with something warm on the stove.

"It's just you and me now," he says quietly, to no one. He looks over to the spot where Adele fell, where her life came to an end. He puts his face in his hands, suppressing the urge to cry.

He sits back in the chair and lets the ghosts take over. He looks up at the balcony and sees people leaning over the railing. He sees the stories of the people he has known over the years, characters and events from his 31 years in the park.

He goes into the controller's office and lifts up the huge, old mechanical typewriter, carries it out, and puts it on the table. In Faysal's office, he finds paper beneath the copier. He finds three candles, lights them and puts them on the table.

Then, leaning back in the old chair, he focuses on the blank page staring back at him an inch above the ribbon.

He looks up at the ghosts. Where do I start?

He sits up and slowly starts typing.

In just three days. . .

❈❈❈